Julia's Daughters

Books by Colleen Faulkner

JUST LIKE OTHER DAUGHTERS

AS CLOSE AS SISTERS

JULIA'S DAUGHTERS

Published by Kensington Publishing Corporation

Julia's Daughters

COLLEEN FAULKNER

KENSINGTON BOOKS
www.kensingtonbooks.com

KENSINGTON BOOKS are published by

Kensington Publishing Corp.
119 West 40th Street
New York, NY 10018

All Kensington titles, imprints, and distributed lines are available at special quantity discounts for bulk purchases for sales promotion, premiums, fund-raising, educational, or institutional use.

Special book excerpts or customized printings can also be created to fit specific needs. For details, write or phone the office of the Kensington Sales Manager: Kensington Publishing Corp., 119 West 40th Street, New York, NY 10018. Attn. Sales Department. Phone: 1-800-221-2647.

Kensington and the K logo Reg. U.S. Pat. & TM Off.

eISBN-13: 978-1-61773-934-7
eISBN-10: 1-61773-934-0
First Kensington Electronic Edition: November 2015

ISBN-13: 978-1-61773-933-0
ISBN-10: 1-61773-933-2
First Kensington Trade Paperback Printing: November 2015

10 9 8 7 6 5 4 3 2 1

Printed in the United States of America

*For my mother, who taught me
the width and breadth of the word*

Chapter 1

Julia

47 days

I've always thought the worst thing that could happen to a mother would be the death of a child.

I was wrong.

I lie in the middle of my king-size bed, my eyes closed, listening to the sound of the ceiling fan spin overhead. I feel the firmness of the mattress beneath me and smell the fabric softener I used yesterday when I washed the sheets.

I've been lying here for hours. Since Izzy and Haley left for school at seven thirty this morning. It's my daily MO. Sometimes I'm still here when Izzy gets home at three forty-five. Ben takes them to school now since obviously Haley isn't allowed to drive Izzy anywhere. Which, when you think about it, is kind of ludicrous. Izzy is probably safer with Haley driving than Ben or me. What are the odds that a seventeen-year-old would kill *two* sisters in two *separate accidents?*

Tears fill my eyes. I don't wipe at them. They've become as much a part of me as my blond hair or the freckles across my nose that I hated when I was a teenager. I cry day and night. Sometimes for hours. I had no idea a person could cry so much for so long. I was never a crier, before.

Before Caitlin died.

It's been forty-seven days. Forty-seven days since the police called at 11:27 p.m. The girls wouldn't even have been home late. If they'd made it home.

It's interesting how many things you learn when something like this happens to you. For instance, I didn't know that when your child is dead at the scene of an automobile accident the police don't tell you that on the phone. They tell you your child has been in a serious accident and ask that you come to the hospital. Even though your child's heart has already stopped beating. Even though yours will soon feel like it's stopped beating . . . like it will never beat again.

Somehow it seems cruel to me to have parents rush to the hospital, praying the whole time that, worst-case scenario, they'll see their child alive one more time. Only to learn that there was no need at all to hurry. That the child of their body is already dead. Has been dead for almost an hour by the time you reach her.

Looking back, the intimation was there when the officer called. I should have known there was no reason for us to hurry. It was his tone of voice. I heard it in the receptionist's voice when I identified myself at the front desk of the ER, too. Then there was the little room. A nurse led us to a room without windows to wait for the doctor to talk to us. It was just Ben and I in the room. No one else was waiting to hear someone tell them that their sweet, smart, laughing daughter who'd plucked her eyebrows too heavily that morning was dead.

My tears run down my face; eventually they'll wet the clean duvet cover. If my ten-year-old daughter's ten-year-old cat hadn't puked Cat Chow all over it I wouldn't have washed it yesterday. Since Caitlin died, it's been hard for me to wash or put away things she might have touched. Ben had to pick up her dirty clothes off the bathroom floor two days after the funeral. He said it wasn't healthy, her running shorts and lavender T-shirt still there on the floor and her gone a week. He washed and put away her clothes; he put away her school backpack, her pink raincoat that had been hanging in the laundry room. Her new running sneakers. He put them somewhere where I wouldn't see them; I don't know where. But he didn't get everything.

There's still one of her empty juice bottles rolling around on the floor of my car. It's my little secret. A part of her I'm not ready to give up because in some crazy way, that glass bottle, the sound of it rolling around under the seat, comforts me. It has to go eventually of course. I know that . . . along with her other things.

I can't imagine right now, though, how I'll ever be able to go into her bedroom and pack up her clothes, her books, the ribbons she won cheering. I *do* go into her bedroom, but just to cry on *her* bed.

A change of scenery.

The house phone rings. I ignore it.

I wonder if Caitlin's toothbrush is still in the pink Disney princesses cup in the girls' bathroom. Did Ben toss it when he picked up her dirty clothes? Or is Izzy using it, which was something that used to really gross Caitlin out.

The day before she died, Caitlin came to me complaining about her little sister's use of her personal hygiene products in her bathroom: her comb, her toothbrush, her favorite organic lip balm. Caitlin was into organic products and foods. I told Izzy to stop using her sister's belongings without asking permission. I told Caitlin to stop whining. Had I known my middle daughter was going to die, I wouldn't have dismissed her complaint so easily. I'd have put down the basket of laundry I was carrying to the couch to fold. I'd have ignored the incoming text on my cell and I'd have asked Caitlin how it made her feel when her little sister used the last of her green apple shampoo. I'd have taken a moment from my busy day to be in the moment, one of my last one-on-one moments with my daughter, as it turned out.

The house phone stops ringing. I wipe my runny nose with the sleeve of Ben's sweatshirt I'm wearing. I'm not crying hard like I do sometimes. Sometimes I cry so hard that I make myself retch. It's fascinating how long you can cry and still have tears. You'd think that eventually you'd dehydrate, shrivel up, and die.

I wish.

My cell phone, plugged in on my side of the bed, starts to vibrate. Someone's calling. When a child dies, the phone rings constantly. Something else I learned. At first people call to tell you how sorry they are and to ask if they can do anything for you, then they call to see if you're okay.

I rarely answer the phone. What do I say? How the hell can I be *okay?* I can't even fathom how I can still be alive. In the first days after, my pain was so great that I thought it really *would* kill me. When it didn't, I thought about speeding it along. I thought about it so far as to consider stealing a bottle of my mother-in-law's sleeping pills when I spotted them in her handbag. I think the only thing that stopped me was the idea that I would have to *steal* the pills. How screwed up is that? I think it's okay to kill myself, leaving two girls without a mother, but I don't think it's okay to steal from my overmedicated mother-in-law?

The cell phone stops vibrating, leaving me with the sounds of the ceiling fan and my choked tears again.

Then it starts vibrating again. Again, I ignore it. I roll onto my side, my back to the phone and rest my hand on Ben's pillow. There was a time in my life when I might have taken a deep breath, hoping to catch a whiff of the smell of him. I used to think that he smelled so good, but I can't remember when the last time that thought crossed my mind. The truth is, a crack opened between us a long time ago; Caitlin's death just widened it to a chasm.

My cell phone starts to ring again and I roll over quickly, grabbing it. Three calls in a row is the family signal, the "pick up the damned phone" signal, Ben calls it.

I yank the phone hard enough to disconnect the power cord and stare at the screen; my eyes are blurry from all the crying. It's my best friend since college, Laney. "You okay?" I say into the phone. "Boys okay?"

"You're supposed to pick up the phone when I call," she says into my ear.

I roll onto my back. My heart's pounding. I'm so relieved Laney's okay. I never used to worry about people I love dying. Now I worry about it all the time. Last week I got the crazy idea that Izzy hadn't made it to class after Ben dropped her off. I actually got in my car, drove to her school, and insisted she be called to the office so I could see with my own eyes that she hadn't been kidnapped between her father's car and the school lobby. Kidnapped and murdered and thrown in a ditch.

"I didn't know it was you," I say to Laney.

"I don't want any excuses."

Laney never cuts me a break. It's one of the reasons I love her so much.

"You could have looked at your phone, Jules. Did you get out of bed yet?"

I sniff and wipe my nose on my sleeve again. "Yeah, I made Pop-Tarts for Izzy before school."

"But you got back in bed as soon as they left the house." It sounds a lot like an accusation.

I close my eyes. "I fed the cat, first. *Then* I got back in bed."

She doesn't laugh. "Julia, we talked about this. You can't lie in bed all day, every day. Did you call your boss to talk about going back to work?"

"I'm going to call him."

"He's going to fire you."

"He won't fire me. My daughter died in a car accident. You'd be amazed by all the perks."

Neither of us laughs this time, either. At least I've stopped crying.

"I'm going to book a flight," Laney says. "I can be there tomorrow."

"No, you're not," I say. "I'm fine."

"You're *not* fine," she argues, impatient with me now. "How can you possibly be *fine?*"

I exhale. "No, of course I'm not *fine*, but you know what I mean. I'm fine."

When she speaks again, her tone is kind and gentle, the same tone I imagine she uses with her third graders. "Jules, sweetie, it's been six weeks," she says. "I know we're not supposed to put time lines on grieving, but you can't keep lying in bed in the dark. You've got to get up and do something: Clean the house, go to the grocery store, take a walk. I think work would be good for you. It would give you—"

"Forty-seven days," I interrupt.

"What?"

"Forty-seven days," I repeat. "You said it had been six weeks since Caitlin died. It's been forty-seven days, so technically—"

"I'm getting on a plane."

"No, you're not. You're not." I try to sound firm. "You've got work and Garret's Scouts and Liam's surgery is coming up."

"It was two weeks ago, sweetie."

I open my eyes. "It was? Oh, Laney, I'm sorry. How is he? Oh, God, I'm so sorry."

"It's fine. He's fine. Still a little swollen, but he only missed two days of school. The oral surgeon said he was a champ."

"When Caitlin had her wisdom teeth out, she refused to stay home the next day. She said she didn't want to waste a sick day at home, feeling like crap. She made me promise to let her play hooky another day when she was feeling better." Tears fill my eyes as I remember and I make a little gasping sound. I close my eyes, feeling overwhelmed. Like I'm floating on top of water, but just barely. "Oh, Laney."

"I know, sweetie."

We sigh in unison.

"Listen, I hate to do this, but I have to go," she says then. "I need to go collect my little darlings from computer lab, but Jules, I'm serious. I'll take off and I'll come. We'll do something. Go for a drive. Clean out Caitlin's room. Whatever you want. If you can't get out of bed, I'll lie there with you."

"I don't want you to have to take off from work. Or leave your boys."

"Then come here. We're having a beautiful spring. Maybe you need a change of scenery. You always said you thought heaven would look like Maine."

Laney lives just outside of Portland. She's a schoolteacher

with two boys. A widow. Laney understands loss. The love of her life since the sixth grade, the father of her boys, Sean, was killed in Afghanistan three years ago.

"I can't be around people. Not yet," I tell her.

"Then come and stay in the cottage. You always loved the cabin." Her family's cottage is on Sebago Lake, west of Portland. When we were in college, where we met our freshman year, I stayed there two summers with Laney and her wacky, loving family. Theirs was the kind of family I dreamed of being born into, rather than mine. There was just me and my mom and my stepdad growing up and we were a quiet family, unlike Laney's, which is loud and boisterous. The thing that struck me the most when I met her parents and brothers and sister that first Thanksgiving that I went east with her was that they all *liked* each other so much. Her mother and father kissed in front of me. Her siblings hugged each other and talked about how much they missed each other. I never felt as if my parents liked each other . . . or me. Anyway, so for the last fifteen years I've been taking Ben and the girls to Maine every summer on vacation, although Ben skipped the last two summers. Work.

"Go get your students," I tell her. "Put them on their buses and go home to your boys."

She's quiet for a second. I can hear the sound of an authoritative female voice on the intercom: end-of-day announcements. They're serving pizza tomorrow for lunch. "I'm worried about you, Jules," Laney says softly.

I'm worried about me, too, I want to say. I think about the sleeping pills. Had they been my own instead of Linda's, would I have taken them? Would I really have tried to kill myself? Good girl Julia Renee Maxton who never liked to put anyone out? I think about telling Laney about the sleeping pills.

"Jules?"

"I'll call you this weekend," I tell her, knowing I won't tell her about the pills. You're supposed to be able to tell those you love anything. Anything at all. But I know I won't tell her because I *do* love her. She's already worried enough about me.

8   Colleen Faulkner

"Please call me."

"I will," I insist.

"You won't. You say you will, but you won't call, Julia. I'll call all weekend, but I'll either get the answering machine or Izzy, who will say you're asleep. The only way I'll get you is if I call three times in a damned row on your cell."

"You're not supposed to curse," I tell her. "You're a third grade teacher. And three calls in a row is only supposed to be for emergencies." I close my eyes again, resting the back of my free hand on my forehead. Then, "I'll call. I swear. When Ben and Izzy go to Sunday dinner at his mom's, I'll call."

"You better, or I'm getting on that plane," Laney threatens.

"I'll call," I say. And I mean it. I mean it now, at least. But by the time Sunday comes, I probably won't be able to bring myself to do it. "Give the boys my love."

"Call Sunday and do it yourself."

I disconnect and hold the phone to my chest. She's a good friend, my Laney. The best. All these years and all the miles between us, and somehow we've been able to maintain our relationship . . . which is amazing considering the fact that I haven't been able to do that with the man who sleeps beside me.

The night Caitlin died, Laney left her house to go to the airport at four in the morning. She called her mother-in-law, an angel, albeit a wacky one, to stay with her boys. Laney stood in lines at the airport in Portland, Maine, for hours until someone found her a flight to Las Vegas by way of New Orleans.

My cell phone rings again. I hit the green square on the screen without opening my eyes and lower the phone to my ear. "See, I told you I'd answer."

There's silence on the other end of the phone for a split second, then a man clears his throat. "May I speak with Mr. or Mrs. Maxton, please?"

I sit up, gripping the phone, my hand unsteady. That was what the police officer said when he called to tell us about the accident. Panic tightens my chest and for a second I can't find my voice. I feel light-headed. "This is, um, Mrs. Maxton."

"Mrs. Maxton, this is Dr. Carlisle, principal at Smythe Academy."

I manage to exhale a little gasp of air. "Yes?" My voice sounds high-pitched, not like my own raspy voice usually does.

"I'm sorry, Mrs. Maxton, but I'm going to have to ask you to come pick up Haley. She's been expelled."

Again, it takes me a moment to respond, but this time it's because I'm so relieved. Haley isn't dead. She isn't hurt. She's just expelled. "Oh," I manage. "All right." I swing my legs over the side of the bed. "What . . ." I'm struggling to focus now. "Why has she been expelled?"

"I need you to come get her, Mrs. Maxton. We can talk when you arrive. When should I expect you?"

I do the math. I probably need to ditch Ben's sweatshirt and put on a bra and a shirt of my own. Brush my teeth. Shoes. Fifteen-minute drive. "I can be there in half an hour, Dr. Carlisle."

Chapter 2

Haley

46 days, 13 hours

"Right there."

The school secretary points to one of the three chairs in the hallway that runs between the front office and principal's office. She doesn't look annoyed or even all that interested in my latest insubordination. She doesn't look at me like I'm a murderer, either, which is kind of nice. Of course she's not really looking at me at all. She's more interested in one of the charms that dangles from a gold bracelet on her left wrist. It looks like a potato. I wonder why anyone would wear a miniature potato on a bracelet, even if it was real gold.

"You know the drill, Haley. Don't get up unless the school's on fire or we've got a shooter, and then it better be a five alarm or automatic weapons," she deadpans.

I've decided I like that word. *Deadpan*. I added it to our list (mine and Caitlin's) yesterday. I like the action . . . or lack of action. I'm getting good these days at deadpanning. I keep thinking that if I don't show any emotion, maybe I won't feel it.

"You shouldn't kid about that kind of stuff," I say, looking at her. She's kind of cute in a weird Zooey Deschanel way, but she's wearing black patent-leather clogs and her roots need a touch-up. "You can screw up impressionable young women like me saying things about Columbine shit."

"Language." Her voice is still monotone. Nothing ever upsets her. She'd make a better principal than Dr. Hairball. My friends and I call him that because he's got this creepy goatee that looks like he coughed up a hairball onto his chin.

She starts for her desk out front; hers is the biggest because she's in charge of the other two ladies who work in the office. She has a glass jar of candy on it filled with mini chocolate candy bars, but in the almost four years I've been here, I've never seen her eat one or give one to someone. I can't figure out why they're on her desk. Maybe to try to make people think she's someone she's not? Like she's this person who gives students treats?

"Be sure your mom signs you out before you go," she tells me.

I drop my backpack on the floor beside the chair where I'm supposed to sit. I know from past experience that if you sit in that chair and lean to your right, you can watch kids go by on the other side of the glass. Wave, if you see a friend. "Even if my mom's coming in to talk to Dr. Carlisle and he's the one expelling me?" I ask.

"Even if the risen Christ expels you," Miss Charter says over her shoulder, "she still has to sign you out."

I can't tell if she's one of those crazy Christians or if she's being sarcastic and she's an atheist. I can't decide which would be worse.

"I'm going to be eighteen in a couple of weeks," I tell her. "Then I can sign myself out."

"You sure could." She stops and turns around; she has this stupid smirk on her face. "If you were still going to be here, which you're not."

I'm so surprised that she'd say that to me that I don't even have a snappy comeback. I'm surprised because it was kind of mean. Adults have been really careful about what they say to me since I killed Caitlin. Like they're afraid of me or something.

I've been getting away with mad shit since I came back to school. So much shit that I was genuinely surprised when Dr. Carlisle said he was expelling me.

Miss Charter disappears around the corner and maybe out of my life. I sit down in the chair closest to the front office. It's blue plastic, stolen from the cafeteria. Not stolen, I guess, if the principal told someone to bring it here. But it's definitely not an office chair; it's a cafeteria chair. The legs are uneven so it rocks unless you push back with your foot. It's probably missing the little disky-foot thing like my chair in my chemistry class.

I lean to my right; the hall outside the office is empty. Classes have already changed. I lean back in the chair and get my ball out of the front pocket of my backpack. The stupid uniform skirts we have to wear don't have pockets. We can wear long khaki pants like the guys, if we want, but they're even uglier than the skirts. I throw the pink ball against the wall in front of me, just an easy throw, to judge the distance and surface of the wall. The little glow-in-the-dark bouncy ball comes straight back. I've gotten good at bouncing it over the last few weeks.

It hits the wall and comes right back to my hand like magic. The magic of physics, Caitlin used to say when she bounced it. For every action, there is an equal and opposite reaction. Newton's Third Law of Motion.

I wonder if my mom will be mad at me for getting expelled. She used to get mad at me all the time. All she did was criticize me: Haley, why don't you get better grades?

Bounce. Catch.

Why don't you have nicer friends?

Bounce. Catch.

Why do you wear that black eyeliner?

Bounce. Catch.

What she always meant was *why don't you get good grades like Caitlin? Why don't you have nice friends like Caitlin does? Why don't you just wear pink lip gloss like Caitlin?*

I throw my ball too hard and I have to jump out of my seat to catch it.

My mom is such a bitch. The worst thing is, she pretends she isn't. Or at least she did before Caitlin died. Since then, Mom hasn't really acted like anything. She barely speaks to me and when she does it's in this quiet breathy voice that's worse than if she just yelled at me.

She thinks it's my fault Caitlin is dead. She just won't come out and say it.

Bounce. Catch.

The thing is, it *is* my fault. Completely my fault.

Bounce. Catch.

I hear the front office door open and lean to see my mom walk in. She's wearing jeans and flip-flops and an orange T-shirt she usually puts on to clean house. When she used to clean house. Now if anyone cleans anything, it's Izzy. Dad says we're going to have to get a maid if Mom doesn't stop lying in bed all day.

Mom walks up to the counter. She's not wearing any makeup and her hair, pulled back in a messy ponytail, looks like it hasn't been washed in days. I always wished I had blond hair like hers and Caitlin's. I've got ugly brown like my dad's. Or it was ugly brown before I started dyeing it black. Izzy's got red hair. I don't know where she came from. Caitlin and I used to tease her and tell her that she was adopted and that's why she doesn't look like us.

"Julia Maxton," my mom says. "I'm here to see Dr. Carlisle."

"You can go in," I hear Miss Charter say. I can't see her because she's around the corner. "You know the way."

Mom doesn't seem to get her little dig, but I do. What she's saying is that Mom knows the way to Dr. Hairball's office because she's been called in before about me: academic probation meetings, behavioral evaluations, suspensions. This is the first time I've been expelled from a school. Well, except for preschool, but I don't really think that counts. My biting was just my way of expressing my individuality and exercising my newfound freedom.

Mom turns toward the hall and sees me, but she doesn't really *see* me. It's like her eyes glaze over. She can't bear to look at me, which is okay because I can't stand looking at her, either.

I stare straight ahead. The wall is cinderblock, painted a pale green. As much as tuition is here, you'd think the building would be something other than cinderblock, but apparently they bought the building cheap. It used to be something else. I bounce the ball against the wall in front of me. Catch it.

She comes up to me and just stands there; she's not even carrying her purse, just her keys. "What have you done now?" she asks. She doesn't look like she really cares.

"Smoking," I say.

"Pot?" She says it like she's asking me if I had an apple for lunch.

I make a face. I bounce. I catch. "Marlboros. In the solarium."

"In the school," she says. Not quite deadpanning, but almost.

I shrug. "I didn't want to be late for physics class."

I wait for her reaction. If my friend Danielle said something like that to her mother, she'd get her face slapped. My mom doesn't slap me. She just presses her lips together really hard and looks like she's going to cry.

I never saw my mom cry until Caitlin. Now, most of the time she's either crying, getting ready to cry, or just wrapping up a good cry.

She walks in front of me as I catch the ball again. "Could you please put that away?" she asks me.

I draw my wrist back, adjust the sleeve of the T-shirt I wear under my uniform polo, and I toss the ball against the wall. It bounces right back into my hand. Physics. Magic. Depending on how you look at it.

My mom walks down the hall to Dr. Hairball's office. Third door on the left. It's open. She knocks on the doorframe.

"Mrs. Maxton, come in."

My mom says something in a teary voice, but I don't quite catch what it is. It doesn't matter. I don't listen to them. I just sit there and bounce my bouncy ball and wonder—if I died, would my mom cry more or less?

Chapter 3

Julia

Still 47 days

I walk out of the principal's office. My daughter is still sitting in the same chair, bouncing a kid's gumball-machine ball against the wall. She's dressed like the other girls I passed in the hallway, but the similarity doesn't go beyond the uniform embroidered with the school crest. (The black polo she's wearing is supposed to go with the red skirt, not the black one. And she's the only one wearing a long-sleeved black T-shirt under her polo. She always wears a long-sleeved black T these days.) Haley looks like she belongs more on a punk rock stage than at an exclusive high school. Her hair, an unnatural shade of shoe polish black, is cut ragged around her face like she hacked at it herself. Which she did. She's got multiple rings in her ears and her fingernails are painted black. Her face is pale, but her green eyes, my eyes, are rimmed in heavy, black liquid liner. She looks tired. Sad. And older than her seventeen years.

I walk up to her, my feet so heavy I can barely lift them. I stop. She continues to bounce the ball. She's been bouncing the same ball for weeks. I wonder if she knows how much the bouncing annoys me. Probably.

"You said you were expelled for smoking a cigarette, Haley," I

say. "Dr. Carlisle says he expelled you for possession of marijuana and what appears to be prescription painkillers he found in
your backpack." I hold up one of the two Baggies the principal
handed to me. "Where did you get Percocet?"

"Linda. Don't worry." She bounces the ball again. "She's still
got plenty."

I want to snatch the bouncy ball in midair and throw it. Hard.
Possibly bounce it off my daughter's head. Or maybe the snooty
secretary's . . . or the arrogant principal's. I take a breath. I have
to stay calm. Haley's been through so much. I can't "lose my
shit" as she would say. I take another breath. "Dr. Carlisle could
have called the police, Haley. You could have been arrested for
this." I shake the Baggies of pills and marijuana at her.

"Nah." She doesn't look at me. "They're trolling for new students for next year. He'd never want that kind of thing in the
newspaper." She tosses the ball against the wall again, a slow,
taunting motion. It bounces. She catches it.

The repetitive sound grates on my already strung-out nerves. I
feel light-headed. I can't remember when I last ate something.
Yesterday at lunch time, maybe? "We'll talk about this at home,"
I say. "With your dad."

She doesn't respond. She just bounces the ball again.

Tears well in my eyes and I glance away. I'm tired of crying. I
wish I could stop. "Come on," I say. "Let's go home."

Haley takes her time getting out of the chair, picking her
backpack up off the floor and slinging it over her shoulder. She's
the living-color epitome of the clichéd sullen teen, or in black-
and-white, in her case.

Haley walks into the main office and out the door.

"Please sign her out, Mrs. Maxton," the secretary tells me.

"She's not coming back. She's been expelled."

The woman offers a perfunctory smile from her desk. "Rules
are rules."

I sigh as I walk over to the counter and sign Haley out. It takes
less energy than arguing with the secretary.

I find Haley waiting at my car. It's new. Ben bought it for me in January for my forty-second birthday. I had wanted a sportier car, one less mom-like than my old minivan. I'd been so happy when he drove the little Toyota RAV4 into the driveway. It had everything I wanted: leather seats, GPS, sunroof.

I hit the unlock button on my keys. When I get in, I can still smell the scent of new leather. It's funny how something that had been such a big deal could so quickly become something furthest from your mind. I haven't thought about the car in weeks. Forty-seven days.

I throw the Baggies onto the console as Haley gets into the front passenger seat, taking her time. I wonder if I get stopped for speeding and a cop sees my weed and pills if he'll arrest me. I wonder if I'd put up an argument. A jail cell seems appealing right now. If I go to jail, Ben will have to deal with Haley. I'll have to deal with an orange jumpsuit. I almost smile. Caitlin had been a TV addict. One of her favorite shows had been a Netflix series about a woman in jail for a crime she'd committed years before. Caitlin had dressed last Halloween as the main character, Piper Chapman. The orange jumpsuit is still in the front hall closet.

It's funny the things that go through your mind. . . . She'd looked so cute, my daughter dressed as a convicted felon.

I start the car because it's warm inside, but I just sit there for a moment, my hands on the steering wheel. My thoughts drift from the Halloween costume on the floor of the closet to my daughter sitting beside me. Drugs? Now she's taking drugs? Or selling them? She didn't even attempt to offer a flimsy *they're not mine, they're a friend's*. I know I should say something, I just don't know what to say. Tears fill my eyes.

"Oh, Jesus," Haley mutters.

I lean forward, pressing my forehead to the steering wheel, covering my head with my hands. Haley makes no attempt to comfort me . . . or argue. I hear her digging around in her backpack. When I lift up my head and glance at her, she's got her earbuds in her ears and she's staring straight ahead. She rubs her left arm, another habit she's developed since the accident.

After a couple of minutes, I wipe my nose with the back of my hand and shift my little silver SUV into reverse. And drive home with my Percocet, my marijuana, and my daughter.

"What are we going to do, Jules?" Ben sits down on the edge of the bed. Our bedroom is dark, except for the light that comes from the bathroom.

It's after dinner, eight or so, I imagine. Ben brought pizza when he came home from work. I heard him and Izzy talking in the kitchen. Not what they were saying, just their voices. Then the sound of the TV. I'm sure they ate their pizza in front of the TV watching something on the Discovery Channel. The one interest he and our ten-year-old share. Haley went to her room when we got home from school, where she'll stay until everyone goes to bed. Only then will she get up and forage for food. Or maybe drugs from our medicine cabinets . . .

When I don't respond to Ben, he makes this sound in his throat that signals that he's frustrated with me. He's been doing it for weeks. He doesn't understand the devastation of my heart, my soul. I know Caitlin was his daughter, too, but he doesn't seem to feel the way I do. About anything. He missed two days of work after she died. He didn't miss bowling league with his brothers or a single weekly Kiwanis club meeting. He said it was easier for him to *carry on*. What does that even mean?

"We need to talk," he says.

"I know," I murmur. And I *do* know that we need to talk. About Haley, about Caitlin, about the state of our marriage, but I'm not ready. I'm just not.

"There's salad from Tony O's in the fridge," he tells me.

I'm lying on my back, my head on my pillow, my arm across my forehead. "Thanks. Maybe I'll get some later." Of course I have no intention of eating it. I was always a little on the chubby side, particularly after having my girls. A size twelve, sometimes a fourteen squeezing into size twelve jeans. For the first time in my life I'm not counting calories or trying to make *good choices*. I'm on the dead child diet; just the thought of food makes me queasy.

Ben sighs again, but he doesn't get up from the bed to go back to the TV. I get the idea he means business tonight. In the first weeks after *the accident*, he came into the bedroom two or three times each night to ask me a question or try to say something that might draw me back into the normalcy of the life we used to have. As the days passed and I didn't *snap out of it* (Linda's words, not his), he began to come in less frequently. This is the first time he's been in here when I was awake in days. Most nights, he stays out in the living room and sleeps in front of the TV in his recliner.

In made-for-TV movies, the kind Caitlin loved to watch, you always see couples clinging to each other after a tragedy. Sobbing together, the husband holding the wife against his chest, comforting her, but that's not real life. At least not in the Maxton household, though maybe it was a few years ago. I don't know.

I think we held onto each other after the ER doctor came into the little waiting room and told us they'd been unable to revive Caitlin, but that was instinctive. Like clinging to a life raft as the ship goes down. We held hands at the funeral, but that's been the limit of our physical contact. It's not that I don't think Ben is hurting. That's not it at all. Maybe it's the opposite. I know he's hurting so badly that I'm afraid to touch him, afraid his pain will rub off on me and it will be too much. I'll collapse under the weight of our combined pain. Or maybe I'll just disintegrate. I'll disappear in a wisp of smoke or a puddle of green plasma goo.

"Jules." Ben's voice penetrates my thoughts. He and Laney are the only people who ever call me Jules. The only people who know me intimately enough to call me Jules.

He turns on the light on my side of the bed and I squint. I have to make myself look at him. I fight tears on the verge. I know he's got to be sick of listening to me cry. I'm sick of listening to me cry.

"Drugs?" he says. "She's doing *drugs* now?"

"Marijuana," I say, meeting his gaze for just an instant. I sit up. His eyes are brown. Nice eyes. His eyes were the first things I noticed the night I met him at Cal State, Bakersfield, where we were both students. "It's practically legal." I consider reminding him that he's been known to take a hit from a joint with his brothers on Sunday afternoons in their mom's backyard, but I don't. It's never really been an issue between us. I don't smoke it; I don't have anything morally against it for adults, but a glass of wine or beer is my limit to mind-altering substances.

"What about the pills?" he asks. "Where did she get them? One of her friends, I bet. Cassie or . . . or that asshole Todd." He strokes his receding hairline. "I told you we should have forbidden her to see him after that run-in with the police at Christmas. Mom said we'd regret it if we didn't."

I exhale. "It wasn't a *run-in* with the police. They were in a *fender bender.* He wasn't even at fault." Ben's right, though. Todd *is* an asshole. Just not the responsible asshole, in this case. "Haley says she stole the Percocet from your mom's medicine cabinet."

He doesn't react. He rarely does when the conversation has anything to do with his mommy doing something or saying something she shouldn't. It's like he's totally blind to her flaws.

"Was Haley taking the pills?" he asks. "You said it was a whole bagful. Was she taking them or selling them?"

I close my eyes for a moment. "Probably both."

He pinches his temples between his thumb and forefinger as if he can squeeze the truth out of his head, or just the knowledge of it.

I note he's not interested in discussing the fact that his mother is making drugs available to our daughter. There had to have been forty in the sandwich bag. I wonder how Linda didn't notice that she was missing *forty* Percocet.

"I can't believe she's been expelled." He throws up his hand. "How the hell is she going to graduate now? She can't even go to community college without a high school degree. I guess we could send her away for a semester or two." His gaze darts to mine for just an instant and then he looks at his shoes.

I frown. "Send her away?"

"Mom thinks we should consider a boarding prep school. St. Andrews won't take her, of course, but maybe even outside the

US . . . France, maybe." He's talking too fast for these to be his own words. He and his brothers all attended St. Andrews boarding school from the sixth grade through the twelfth. Linda couldn't be bothered to parent through the *difficult* years. "Haley wanted to go on that trip last Easter to France. Kids do it all the time. She could finish her high school degree and then maybe take some college classes. It might be the best thing for her. A little tough love."

"Send her away?" I say it again, unable to believe he would even suggest such a thing. I lose one daughter and my husband wants to send another away? The idea is so absurd that I don't know if I want to laugh or hit him with something. If I were the kind of person who hit people, I definitely would have. I wonder if I'm becoming a person with violent tendencies. Earlier in the day I had the impulse to throw a ball at Haley. "We don't have money for that sort of thing. Do you know what it costs for boarding school in *France?*"

He hesitates and I know what he's thinking before he says it. "You have your money. The money your mom left you."

I exhale. I can't meet his gaze. The money's been sitting for years in an investment account. *Dirty* money. Money my mother left me when she died of cirrhosis of the liver. My stepfather left it to *her* when he died. Money he won in a lawsuit I never thought he should have won. If I were ever going to spend the money, I'd certainly spend it on my children, but not like this. "We're not sending Haley away," I say quietly.

"Well, we've got to do something. She's out of control. The crazy black makeup, the lying, the constantly late on curfew. And now we can add drugs to the list. I've got enough problems at work, Jules. I don't need this. I told you she looked zonked on something the other day."

He gets up and goes to the laundry hamper near the bathroom door. He begins to pull dirty clothes out and drop them on the floor, dividing them between lights and darks the way I taught him when we were first married. His mother had always done his laundry for him, even when he was in college, before I introduced him to the washing machine. If I'd let her, she'd still be doing his laundry.

"Maybe getting out of here, out of this house, out of the state would be good for her. New friends. A fresh start."

"Out of sight, out of mind?" I ask.

He doesn't refute the accusation. We both know that's one of his best coping mechanisms. Sweeping things out the door or at least under the rug. Always has been. His whole family deals with problems that way.

We're both quiet for a minute. I feel so alone. So isolated. So sad and lost. I know at least part of this is of my own making. I've allowed our marriage to fall apart, but that doesn't make it any less painful. I think about the fact that if Caitlin were here, she'd have an opinion on what we should do about Haley. She was always better at handling her sister than we were. *If Caitlin were here. If Haley hadn't—*

I feel myself teetering on the edge of the precipice I've become too familiar with in the last forty-seven days. I know I shouldn't be angry with Haley. It was an accident. Just an accident. A terrible mistake. She had not been drinking alcohol that night, not taking Percocet or even smoking a joint. Her tox screen had come back negative for any illegal substances. She really just made a mistake and didn't see the stop sign. Didn't see the big pickup truck coming from her right.

Ben picks up an armful of dark clothes and heads for the door.

I guess our talk is over.

Chapter 4

Izzy

3 years, 8 months

I close my eyes. Open them. Close them. Open them again. Fast.
It's so dark under my bed that it doesn't make a difference.

The box springs feel closer to my nose tonight. I wonder if I'm
having another growth spurt. No boobs yet. I slide my hand across
my chest to make sure they haven't popped out since I checked
this morning. I don't feel anything. Flat as a board, that's what She
Who Shall Not Be Named says. She says I'll never grow boobs.
She says I'll be a freak and she can sell me to a freak show.

Amanda Durum, in my class, is getting boobs even though
she's the same age as the rest of us in the fifth grade. Her mom
bought her some real bras at Target, like the kind you hook in the
back. Not the stretchy sports bras my friends and I wear.

My mom has medium boobs, but my sister Caitlin, hers were
big. Like Nana's. If I grow big ones like Caitlin's, and I really do
think they will grow because She Who Shall Not Be Named is a
liar, I wonder if I'll be able to fit under my bed still. If Caitlin
were here, would she be able to fit under here? It's an interesting
thought. One I should *contemplate*. (One of my vocabulary words
this week at school.)

I'm getting sleepy. I should probably crawl out from under my bed and get in it. Mom will worry about me if she finds me under here. She'll ask if I'm okay, even though she knows what the answer is. Of course I'm not *okay*. Caitlin kicked the bucket.

I close my eyes and think about the white coffin we put Caitlin in. Is this what it feels like to be in a coffin? The lid has to come pretty close to your nose. Did she need a tall one to fit her boobs? Did we pay extra for it?

I hear someone in the hall and I wonder if it's my mom coming to check on me. Sometimes she checks on me. She used to come all the time *before;* now not as often. Mostly she just lies on her bed in the dark and cries. A lot. If it's Dad and not Mom who comes into my room, he'll pretend I'm not under here. He'll stand in the doorway and say "sweet dreams" or something dumb like that. Who says that to their eleven-year-old daughter? (Well, I will be eleven soon. In a few months. Six.) I mean, aren't there books out there that teach parents what you're supposed to say to your kids after their favorite daughter, the best sister in the whole world, dies? Or at least what the H *not* to say? Because "sweet dreams" has got to be one of the dumbest things he could say. I don't have "sweet dreams." I dream about a big, black truck slamming into our Kia Soul. I dream about Caitlin splattered all over the road. Sometimes I dream about me splattered all over the road.

I hear Mr. Cat meow and I stick my hand out from under my bed and wiggle my fingers. "Kitty, kitty, kitty," I call. I have to say it kind of loud because the vet says he's losing his hearing.

I hear him purring. Then I feel him bat at my fingers with his paw. I tease him with my finger. I don't hear anyone out in the hall now. Maybe it was just my imagination. I have a pretty good imagination. Once I thought I really heard Santa's reindeer on the roof. I mean, I *really* thought I heard the prancing and pawing of each tiny hoof. That was when I believed Santa was real and that life was good and bad things happened to bad people and stupid stuff like that. And right after Caitlin bought it, I woke up in my bed thinking I could smell her in my room. She always smelled good even when she didn't use spray stuff from Victoria's Secret. She had a special smell. *Her* smell.

I pet Mr. Cat on the head and he meows. He's been hiding tonight. Like me. She Who Shall Not Be Named got in some kind of big trouble today. She was already home when I got home from school. In her room.

I wanted to ask Dad what happened, but I didn't. Nobody tells me anything around here anymore. Then my friend Ann texted me and asked what she did to get expelled. Her sister goes to Smythe, too. Instead of texting her name, which is not permitted in my presence, she made a line of asterisks and pound signs and stuff so it looked like a curse word. Which was funny. If I ever have to write her name, which I never intend to do, I'll have to remember that. I just told Ann I didn't know what she did. So now I know why she was home early and I'll know why when she doesn't go to school tomorrow, and I didn't have to ask anyone. I don't know why she got expelled, but I'm sure I'll know in a day or two. Ann's sister will tell her and Ann will tell me.

Mr. Cat jumps up on my bed. It springs down a little bit and I can feel his weight over me. He meows again. He wants me to come up and lie down with him. "All right, all right," I tell him, and I slide out from under the bed. "I just have to pee." I pet his head. "I'll be right back."

He meows like he understands me, which is interesting because how can he understand me if he can't hear me? I wonder if the vet lied. People lie to me all the time. Adults, mostly. What I can't figure out is why would she lie to me about something dumb like a cat's hearing?

I slip out of my bedroom into the dark hall. I can see shadows dancing from the living room and hear the muffled sound of gunfire. My dad's asleep out there. The TV is on; he was probably watching something about World War II. He likes Nazis. Well, he doesn't *like* them. Who likes Nazis? He just likes to watch stuff about Nazis and Hitler. A few days ago he and I watched a show about German concentration camps and I got to see pictures of the ovens they put people in. I think I'd like to go see those ovens someday.

I walk down the hall in the dark to the bathroom. The door's open. I don't turn on the light. I'm not afraid of the dark. I think people are afraid of the dark because they're afraid of what bad things might happen in the dark. I don't worry about it. Bad things happen with the lights on, too.

I pee, but I don't wash my hands. I only do that when I'm with my friends because everyone washes their hands after they use the bathroom when they're with other people. I don't really know why people expect you to wash your hands. I don't pee on my hand.

Instead of going back to my room I hang a left and head for the kitchen to get a drink. On my way back to my room, I'll shut the TV off. But I won't wake my dad and tell him to go to bed like I used to before Caitlin checked out. I don't think my dad sleeps with my mom anymore. I don't think she cares where he sleeps.

It's not until I grab the orange juice container from the fridge that I realize someone is in the kitchen, sitting at the breakfast table under the window. I turn around as I unscrew the cap. She Who Shall Not Be Named is sitting in the dark, eating cereal dry out of a box. Apple Jacks. I don't say anything. I can feel her watching me.

I don't talk to her anymore. She killed Caitlin and I loved Caitlin. She's been trying to be nice to me since she ran through that stop sign and let Caitlin splatter all over the road. I don't want her to be nice to me. I don't want her to talk to me or look at me. I wish she'd bought the farm instead of Caitlin. I know I'm not supposed to feel that way, but I do. And if Caitlin did have to croak because of some crazy thing in the cosmos, I wish She Who Shall Not Be Named were pushing up daisies, too.

"Hey, pipsqueak."

I act like I don't see her. Don't hear her. I tip the juice bottle and chug. It's the wrong kind of juice. I like the kind without pulp. But Dad's been doing the grocery shopping since Caitlin died so I'm lucky he remembered juice at all.

"You can't ignore me forever," she says, crunching the cereal. The kitchen smells like pizza, Apple Jacks, and cigarette smoke. She smokes sometimes, which I think is disgusting. Last year, in fourth grade, I wrote a report about the dangers of smoking, about all the kinds of gross cancers you can get like lip cancer and throat cancer where you have to talk out of a box. (With color photos and everything.) I got an A. I gave it to She Who Shall Not Be Named. That was when I still called her Haley and still talked to her, or at least tried. I don't know if she ever read it. Probably not.

I take a breath and then one more drink of OJ. She munches on her cereal.

I screw the cap on slowly and take my time putting the bottle back in the almost empty refrigerator, even though I want to run back into my room and get under my bed with Mr. Cat.

I close the refrigerator and I can't see her anymore without the light. It's like she just disappears, which is what I want to happen. I want her to just vanish.

Chapter 5

Julia

48 days

I lie on my bed staring at the ceiling, watching the fan spin. My favorite pastime. My only pastime. Light spills from the bathroom into the bedroom. It's gotten dark out. Ben texted me to say he was going out for a beer with his brothers so it's just the girls and me. Earlier, I had Izzy order pizza delivery. She brought me two breadsticks and marinara sauce, which I ate, not because I was hungry, but because I could tell she really wanted me to eat it.

I can hear the TV out in the living room. Izzy. She loves the Discovery Channel and the History Channel. Parents aren't supposed to rank their children and I try not to, but Izzy is probably the smartest of my three girls. Caitlin and Haley are bright, but Izzy, she's scary smart.

Caitlin *was* bright . . . I can't get the hang of speaking of her . . . *thinking* of her in the past tense. It's just too much to wrap my head around.

I wonder what Haley's doing. I haven't seen her since I picked her up from school yesterday. I know she's in the house. I heard the toilet in the girls' bathroom down the hall flush today while Izzy was at school. I saw an empty Coke can in the trash, which I moved to the recycling; Izzy doesn't drink Coke. She watched something on TV about corn syrup and is boycotting any food or drink that contains corn syrup. She and Caitlin were doing it together. It took forever at the market with the two of them because they insisted on reading every label.

I hear the sounds of an explosion coming from the TV in the living room. I wonder what Izzy's watching. I should go see. See how she is. I can't remember when we last talked about anything other than takeout or lunch money for school. She hasn't even asked me to sign anything for school; I guess Ben signs her homework now.

I roll onto my side. It takes a lot of energy to get out of bed. But I know I should. I know I need to. Ben is right. Laney's right. Even my mother-in-law is right. It's just that my heart is so broken that I—

I stop that thought right there because I know that if I don't . . . I know that if I let that thought unravel, I'll just lie here and cry some more.

I exhale and sit up. I perch on the edge of the bed until the dizziness passes. I probably need to eat something more than two breadsticks. Drink something. Maybe some peppermint tea. Caitlin was my tea drinker. Sometimes, on Saturday mornings, before anyone else got up, she and I would sit at the breakfast table in our PJs and drink tea and have rye toast.

I close my eyes as tears trickle down my cheeks. I'll never have tea with Caitlin again. We'll never fight over the heel from the loaf of rye bread from the German bakery we both like. Not ever again.

There are more explosions coming from the living room, followed by the sound of Izzy's voice. I wonder whom she's talking to. I didn't hear Ben come in. Maybe she's decided to speak to Haley again. To my knowledge, she hasn't spoken to her in . . . well, forty-eight days.

I make myself stand up. I wipe my face with the sleeve of my T-shirt, slip my feet into my flip-flops, and shuffle out into the hall. The house is mostly dark, though I see light coming out from under Haley's door at the end of the hall. Caitlin's door is closed and the light is out. *Forever extinguished.* I turn the other direction and follow the sounds coming from the TV.

I find Izzy sitting on the couch, an open book beside her. There's no one else there.

"Who were you talking to?" I ask, sitting down beside her.

She stares straight ahead and bites down on her lower lip. It's her guilty look. "No one."

"Oh. I thought I heard you talking." I lean over. "Isobel," I murmur. I kiss the top of her head, taking notice that she could use a shower.

"Mom." She rests her cheek on my arm.

I take a shuddering breath and put my arm around her. You would think it would be comforting at a time like this to feel your child in your arms. When you'll never wrap your arms around another child again. But it's the complete opposite. Izzy's warmth, her touch, only makes me ache for Caitlin more. I hang on to her anyway.

"What are you watching?" I ask, staring at the TV.

"A show about works of art that were lost during World War II." She looks at me. "Did you know that Hitler stole all this artwork from Jewish people? Real art like van Goghs and Degases and Klimts."

"Klimt?" I ask. I had no idea Izzy knew who Degas and van Gogh were.

We watch the screen. There are men in a World War II army jeep careening along a mountain pass.

"He was an Austrian painter. He painted portraits and stuff," she explains. "This guy named Bloch-Bauer hired Klimt to do a portrait of his wife. It had gold in the paint. Real gold. Then, during the war, the Nazis took the painting. Then it ended up in a museum somewhere. The guy's family didn't get it back until 2006. Can you believe that?"

I look at her and almost smile. Almost. "How do you know all this, Miss Smarty Pants?"

She points at the TV. "History Channel. And I think there was a movie about it."

An advertisement comes on for antacid and both of us sit there and watch it. The next commercial is for cat food.

I feel like I should say something, start a conversation with my daughter, but I weirdly don't know what to say. Too much time alone with the ceiling fan maybe. "How's Mr. Cat?" I ask, grasping. The orange cat on the screen looks nothing like Mr. Cat.

"Pretty good. Not puking too much." She's still nestled against me.

"That's good." We're quiet for a minute. Two more commercials: deodorant and fast food. "Have you seen your sister?" I ask.

"You mean like her ghost?"

When I realize she's making a joke about her dead sister, I'm so totally taken aback that it takes me a moment to answer. This would be the perfect opportunity to talk to Izzy about Caitlin's death. We haven't really talked about it beyond the barest facts. But I can't do it right now. I just can't. Not yet. "Have you seen Haley?"

She looks at me, then the TV again. I can feel her shoulders droop. "In her room, I guess."

I look down at my sweet daughter. I know she's angry with Haley. I understand why. She blames Haley for Caitlin's death. Of course she does. She's at that age where she just can't accept an accident as an accident. She has to hold someone responsible. I need to talk about it with her. Soon.

We watch a segment of the episode about finding the stolen paintings at the end of the war. Izzy provides additional narrative to accompany the voice-over. I'm not really listening to either of them. I was thinking that Izzy needed a shower, but now I suspect it might be myself I smell. I can't remember what day I last showered. Tuesday? Monday?

They go to commercial again. Izzy is telling me about a salt mine in Austria where paintings were found. I hear a door open and I glance in the direction of the hall. I wonder if it's Haley or Caitlin, but then I know. I remember.

I'm surprised that I could have forgotten for a whole split second that my light, my sunshine is gone.

Darkness comes to stand at the end of the couch. We all watch a preview for a show that promises to reveal the secrets of the real Jesus.

"*Jeezus,*" Haley swears under her breath.

I look up at her. Izzy picks up her book and starts to read. Or pretends to be reading. I notice that Haley is wearing her usual uniform: black jeans, long-sleeve black shirt under her black leather jacket. I feel the lines on my forehead crease. "Where do you think you're going?"

"Out." She's got enough eyeliner rimming her eyes to make her look like an exotic half-girl, half-raccoon Japanese anime character.

"No you're not." I keep my voice even. I don't shout. If Ben were here, he'd bellow. I was never a yeller like him, although I've certainly been known to raise my voice with my daughters. Mostly out of frustration more so than anger. I haven't, however, raised my voice to Haley since Caitlin died. What kind of mother would I be if I did, after what she's been through?

"You can't go out because you're grounded," I point out, calmly.

"You never told me I was grounded." Her words are vicious.

I glance at Izzy, who's still reading, even though her show is back on. I rub my forehead. "Of course you're grounded. You were expelled from school for drug possession."

"Not *drugs*. It was weed, and a couple of Percs," she scoffs. She doesn't make eye contact with me. She stares off into space.

I glance at Izzy again. I didn't tell her why Haley had been expelled. She hasn't asked. I don't want her to think her sister is a druggy. Izzy doesn't understand how hard things are for Haley right now. She can't see Haley's pain for her own.

I decide not to get into an argument with my daughter right now over what constitutes drugs. I still have Linda's Percocet. In my underwear drawer, along with the marijuana. I'm not sure why. "You're not going anywhere," I say, still sounding calm even though a part of me wants to grab her and shake her. Or hold her down and scrub the black eye makeup off with a washcloth and some old-fashioned cold cream. Haley used to be such a pretty girl. Before she started wearing black clothes and black makeup and black nail polish last year. Before she invested in half a dozen black eye pencils.

"I was going to take your car. Just for a while." Now she's looking at her clunky black shoes. Doc Martens. I'd bought them for her last fall.

Izzy picks up the remote and turns the TV off, leaving us in semidarkness. "I'm going to bed," she tells me. She kisses my cheek, gets up, and leaves the living room without glancing in her sister's direction.

Haley just stands there. Long enough for me to feel like I have to reiterate my point. "You're not going anywhere, Haley. Not for a while. Not until . . ." I waver because I haven't really thought about what we're going to do about her. I'm too busy thinking about my other daughter turned to ashes, sitting in an urn. I don't know how to deal with Haley's expulsion. "Your father and I . . . need to talk."

She glances at me for the first time since she's come into the living room. The look on her face, angry, defiant, makes me wonder what I'll do if she grabs my keys from the hook by the back door and takes my car. Will I call the police? Call Ben? Or go back to my room and hope she comes back before Ben finds out she took my car?

"I just want to go out for a couple of hours." She tugs on a lock of black hair. "I miss my friends," she says, but without emotion.

It's on the tip of my tongue to ask her if she misses Caitlin. I feel the sudden urge to get up from the couch and throw my arms around her and hug her tight. Tell her it's okay to cry. I can't even remember seeing her cry since the hospital, the night of the accident. She's like her father. Keeps everything bottled up inside. Ben's taken Caitlin's death the same way, few tears. He doesn't talk about how he feels, about anything, something I already knew from living with him all these years. He just plods on.

I get up from the couch. "You're not leaving this house," I say softly, a slight edge to my voice.

We both just stand there for a minute, staring at each other. It's the first good look I've gotten of her in . . . weeks. She looks terrible: too thin, skin that's patchy with breakouts, eyes that look sunken in.

Haley stands there for another second, then walks away, thankfully, in the direction of her room. I go into the kitchen and turn off the lights, leaving the laundry room light on for Ben. I get into bed without taking off my clothes and bury my face in my pillow for a good cry.

The sound of the vibration of my cell phone on the nightstand wakes me and I roll over, groggy, reaching for it. Did Ben not come home? Is it Ben? I squint to read the screen; I'm getting to the point where I'm soon going to need reading glasses. It's not Ben. It's Haley. Why would Haley be calling me from her bedroom?

I drop back onto my pillow, bringing the phone to my ear.

"Mom." Her voice is so hushed that for a minute she sounds like Caitlin.

"Haley?" I say into the phone, wishing I could stay in the moment for just a couple more seconds. The moment when it's Caitlin calling me.

"Mom, I need you to come get me," she whispers, talking fast and breathy. I can hear pounding in the background, like someone banging on a door.

"Ha—"

"I need you to not ask any questions right now," she interrupts. "I just need you to come get me."

I sit up, throwing my legs over the side of the bed. I brush my hair out of my face. "Are you okay?"

A man hollers something indistinguishable in the background.

"Mom, please," my daughter begs. Then she shouts, obviously not to me, "Out in a minute! Jeeze." Then softer again, "Please come get me." She sounds like a little girl.

I stand up, feeling for my flip-flops with my bare feet. I'm still dressed in sweatpants and T-shirt from the day before. I slip one foot into the first flip-flop. I want to ask Haley why she isn't in her room where she was when I went to bed, but I'm now awake enough to know this isn't the time to ask. Hairs prickle on the back of my neck; my baby's in trouble. Suddenly, I'm wide awake. "Tell me where you are."

"I'll text you the address."

I slide my other foot into a flip-flop. "O . . . okay. You're at someone's house?" I head for the bedroom door.

Again, I hear the male voice and the pounding. I hurry through the living room. Ben's asleep on the couch, a knitted afghan thrown over him. His mouth is open; he's snoring. "Haley, what's going on?" I whisper into the phone. I don't want to wake Ben. He was asleep the night the police called about Caitlin. I can't do that to him again. Haley's okay; she just needs a ride.

"Mom, my phone's about to die. Just come. I—" Haley's voice breaks. "I'll be okay until you get here."

Then I hear that dead sound on the other end of the phone. She's gone. "Haley? Haley?" I whisper into the phone. She hung up. Or the call failed. I consider calling back, but if the battery in her phone is about to die, I don't want to risk it. What if I can't find her? What if I have to call her back? I run through the kitchen to the laundry room, grab my keys from the key hook, and go out the back door.

For some reason, Ben's parked directly behind me. Maybe because I never go anywhere anymore? I race back inside, grab his keys, and drop mine on top of the clothes dryer.

My phone dings as I get into Ben's pickup. A text message. I start the engine with one hand and hold up my phone with the other. My heart is pounding now.

Haley's sent me the address. A not-so-nice part of town.

Ben's truck smells of fast food; it makes me slightly nauseated.

I back down the driveway onto the road and pull away too fast. The tires grab and the pickup leaps. I'm not used to driving something with a big engine. The trash on the floor of the passenger side shifts and I hear the rustle of heavier objects colliding with paper wrappers and bags. It's no wonder Ben's getting chubby. I seemed to have lost my appetite since Caitlin died. From the look of the trash in his truck, he's found his.

I barely come to a stop at the end of our street. Speeding, it takes me thirteen minutes to reach the address Haley texted me. I only make one wrong turn and have to go around the block. It's an area I've warned my teenage girls not to drive in. I pull to the curb. I'm not used to driving such a big vehicle so my parking isn't so great. I shift into park and text Haley:

I'm outside.

I wait for her to text back. I study the dilapidated stucco bungalow I'm parked in front of. There are lights on and music coming from inside. There's a chain-link fence. It looks like someone hit it with a car. Or possibly a bulldozer. I hear a dog bark behind the house. A big dog.

I check the time on the dash. 2:57 a.m.

I wait another three minutes and text again.

Where are you? I'm out front.

Three more minutes pass.

Haley? I text.

Still nothing. A police car rolls by slowly in the opposite direction. I wonder if I should flag him down. Tell him my underage daughter's inside. Then I think about the drugs found in her locker. About what's probably going on inside the house. I can't let Haley get arrested. We've got to figure out how she's going to graduate now. And I know she's not keen on college, but she's young. I think she'll go to college one day. She'll find her way. She really does have a future, even if she can't see it right now. It's my job as her mother to protect that future.

I look at the house and the clock on the dashboard again. I've been here nine minutes. It took me thirteen minutes to drive over. Haley has to know I'm out here by now, even if her phone has died.

I see the silhouette of two guys, hoods up on their sweatshirts, walking on the opposite side of the road from me. Two young guys who scare me. What could they possibly be doing on the street at this time of night? They have to be up to no good. Who am I kidding? What could my daughter be doing here this time of night except something she shouldn't be?

I grab the door handle, clutching my phone in the other hand. I open the door, then remember the car keys. I pull them from the ignition and get out. The light from the interior of the trunk blinds me temporarily. I close the door quickly and look around. The two guys I saw keep walking, but one is watching me over his shoulder.

I'm scared. I wonder if I should get back in the trunk and call Ben.

But Haley's inside. She wouldn't call me if she didn't need me. *Really* need me. I walk slowly to the gate, hanging off its hinges, and follow old cement stepping-stones to the door. I take a breath and knock. My heart's thumping again. I feel a little dizzy. I wish now that I'd had another breadstick.

No one answers. The music, pounding, angry music, is too loud. No one inside could possibly hear me. I knock again, this time with my fist. I check my phone, hoping, praying Haley's texted me back.

The door swings open and the light from inside is bright in my eyes. The music offends my ears. It's more screaming than music. It's a man who answers the door. It's hard to tell how old he is. Twenty-five, maybe thirty. His hair's long and dirty. Dirtier than mine or Izzy's. He's got a sleeve of bad tattoos.

"I . . . I'm looking for my daughter," I say. "Haley." My voice quivers.

He leans closer to hear me. The house is smoky behind him. I smell stale cigarette smoke and fresh marijuana.

"Haley Maxton," I say louder. I dial her number on my phone with my thumb.

He stares at me for a minute through heavy-framed black glasses. I hear my phone in my hand ringing. I can't tell if his black hair is natural or dyed like my daughter's.

"Who?"

"Haley. Five-five. Black hair."

The guy starts to close the door as Haley's voice message comes on: "Leave a message, don't leave a message, whatever," she says in a bored-sounding voice.

I hang up. "She's seventeen years old," I shout above a blast of music as a new song begins. It's rap music. The kind I hate, the kind that talks about shooting cops and abusing women. The kind I've told my girls I don't want them listening to. When I move to the left to keep him in my view, I see two guys and a girl sitting on a couch passing a little pipe back and forth, lighting it with a lighter. Whatever they're smoking, it's not marijuana. I put my hand on the door. The phrase *crack house* comes to mind. Is this what they're talking about in the papers when they say crack house?

"Please," I say. "I just want my daughter." I look up at him. Make eye contact.

"I said, she ain't here." His tone is more forceful this time. He's scaring me. But I'm not leaving without Haley. I'm not leaving without my daughter. I know she's here. I can *feel* her.

"You hear me, lady? Take a hike," he tells me with a hatred that can't possibly be directed just at me. It's a hatred meant for the whole world.

I don't know what makes me do it. I'm not naturally a bold person, but I put both hands on his chest and push him out of my way. I push right into the house. "Haley!" I shout. "Haley!" I'm almost screaming now. The house is full of people. Scary people. Most of them dressed in black like Haley, but with more piercings. Tattoos. "Haley, where are you?"

Chapter 6

Haley

48 days, 4 hours

I'm sitting on the lid of the toilet, bouncing my ball, when I hear my mom call me. Her voice is so out of place that it startles me; like hearing a bear in my calculus class. I stand up. "Mom?" I say coming off the toilet, which is stupid because obviously she's not in the bathroom. No one's here but me. I wouldn't let Dodge in. He's being a complete asswipe. He hit me because I told him I wasn't going with him to go get his stupid money some junkie owes him. Then I ran in the bathroom and locked the door. That was when I called Mom. I caught a ride here with a girl I know, but she left with some guy hours ago. It was probably stupid to call Mom. She'll blow this all out of proportion. I just didn't know who else to call. I got scared when Dodge wouldn't stop pounding on the bathroom door. If he got in, I knew he'd pound on me with those fists.

"Haley!" I hear my mom holler.

I didn't figure she could get here this quick. She drives like an old lady.

I start to pace in the confines of the little bathroom as I push the ball into my pocket. This is bad. Mom in Dodge's house. Really bad. I stop and unlock the bathroom door. "Mom?"

"Haley!"

First I see her at the end of the hallway, then I see Dodge, sitting on the floor next to the bathroom door. He jumps up as I hurry toward my mother. "Mom, what are you doing?" I ask. I'm mortified. Obviously I don't want her in here. She's liable to call the cops or something. I can't believe she'd come inside.

"Are you okay?" she asks me. Her face changes and she reaches out to try to touch my face. "Oh my God. Haley, what happened?"

I pull back because I don't want her touching me. The side of my face hurts. Dodge's ring caught on my cheekbone and it bled a little. But it's not a big deal. He didn't mean to hurt me.

Dodge grabs my arm from behind me. "You called your mom, you little c—"

"Let's go," I tell my mom, giving her a push. Not a hard one, just enough to make her understand she can't be here. As I try to follow her, Dodge tries to stop me.

"Let her go!" my mother hollers. I think she's hollering because "Get Bread" is blasting from the speakers in the living room. It's Trick-Trick. I like Trick-Trick. Sort of. Caitlin hated rap music. She liked hippie stuff like Ben Harper. We used to talk about going to the music festival Bonnaroo. We were going to camp out and wear homemade tie-dye shirts and stuff.

I spin around and shove Dodge. He's a big guy, a lot bigger than me, but he's not expecting me to fight back, I guess. He lets go of me, but he's pissed. *Really* pissed.

I turn back to Mom and say, "Let's go," in her ear as I push her into the living room. She's wearing a T-shirt and sweatpants. Her hair's all messed up. She looks so bad she almost looks like one of Dodge's junkies who come to his door.

Everybody in the living room is looking at us. My friends. Well, they're sort of my friends. Not really. They looked pissed now too. We're almost out the door when this dude I don't know grabs my arm. His fingers sink into me until it hurts.

"You goin' somewhere?" he asks me. "Hey, Dodge! She goin' somewhere?"

My mom's almost out the door, but she turns around. "You better take your hands off her," she tells the dude, like she's going to do something about it if he doesn't let go of me.

I can't believe this is my mom. I've never seen her act like this before. Pretty badass.

I jerk my arm from the guy's and start for the door again.

"Want me to stop her?" he asks Dodge.

"Nah. Let her go," Dodge says. "Bitch," he calls after me.

I flip him the bird with one hand while I push my mom out the door with the other. Dodge's pit bull is mad barking in his kennel in the back. "Come on. Hurry," I say under my breath. I wouldn't put it past Dodge to sic his dog on us. I've seen him do it before to deadbeats who owe him money and people he just doesn't like.

"What are you doing here in the middle of the night?" my mom asks. Now she's started to sound like herself again. Criticizing me. "I told you you were grounded."

"Let's get in the car," I tell her.

"Haley, do I have to tell you how dangerous a place like this is? These people? How did you get here? Did that man pick you up from our house?" She throws a look over her shoulder that's straight out of one of Caitlin's made-for-TV movies. The face moms always make when they're disappointed in their children's "choices." "How old is that man? He's got to be thirty. Please tell me that's not your boyfriend."

I hurry to the passenger side of Dad's truck. I have no idea why she brought the truck. Some people follow us out. I hear Dodge yelling inside and breaking shit. I don't care. I'm so done with him. But the dude from the house is coming our way and he scares me. "Get in the effing, car, Mom!"

She gives me another one of her looks, but she unlocks the door with the remote thingy. I jump inside.

She gets in.

I lock all the doors with the button on my door. I realize that my heart's pounding. I don't like how it feels. I don't like being scared like this. But the weird thing is, it doesn't feel much worse than I normally feel. I'm always scared since Caitlin left me. "Let's go, let's go." I sit back and yank my hoodie up. I left my leather jacket inside somewhere, which pisses me off because one of Dodge's crack hoes will get it, but I'm sure not going back for it.

Mom starts the engine, but she's taking too long. She's messing with her seat belt. The joker who tried to stop me from leaving is almost to the truck.

"Today, Mom," I say, slumping down in the seat.

The guy hits the tailgate with his fist or something.

Mom throws the truck into gear, hits the gas, and surprises me again. She pulls away so fast that she burns rubber.

Chapter 7

Izzy

3 years, 8 months

"Are you there?"

I wait and then I whisper, "I can't sleep. I don't know where Mom went." I roll onto my side in my bed, hugging the stuffed bunny that was mine when I was a baby. It's kind of ratty looking; he's missing part of his left ear and he's got nail polish on his back. I've been told he stinks, but I don't think so. He just smells like . . . an old stuffed bunny.

"She's been gone almost an hour," I say, glancing at the digital clock next to my bed. I wait for her to answer.

When Caitlin talks to me, it feels like her voice is coming out of the dark, but from no one place in particular. I only hear her when it's dark. I know she's probably not in the room, or if she is, she's invisible. Maybe she just talks in my head. I don't really care how she talks to me. What matters is that she does.

"I don't know if I should do something. Should I wake up Dad?" I ask. It occurs to me that it's pretty crappy that the only person I have to talk to is my dead sister, but I've already got enough things to be upset about right now. "Should I tell him that She Who Shall Not Be Named went out her D window, then Mom's phone rang and now she's gone too?" I wait. There's always a long second of silence between when I speak and Caitlin answers, like we're talking over short-wave radios or something. I learned about short-wave radios on the Discovery Channel.

"Who called Mom?"

She finally speaks and I smile, even though I sure don't have anything to smile about.

"I don't know. Maybe the police. They called Mom when you flatlined. Maybe She Who Shall Not Be Named got in another car accident and she bit the bullet too." The minute I say it, I realize it wasn't very nice. I mean . . . I know Caitlin knows she's as dead as a doornail, but it's not exactly a nice thing to bring up. "Sorry," I say in a little voice. "I didn't mean to remind you that . . . you know, that we cremated you and stuff."

Caitlin laughs.

There's no time delay this time. She just laughs. I love it when I make her laugh because I hear her laughter not just in my ears, but in my chest. As crazy as it sounds (and I know crazy is already a possibility because a dead person talks to me like in that old Bruce Willis movie), I feel like I hear her in my heart.

"It's okay, Sizzy Izzy," she tells me. *"No worries."*

She used to call me that all the time. Sizzy Izzy. It's a play on Sissy Izzy. I know I'm too old for silly baby names (and stuffed animals), but I like it. I miss it. I miss Caitlin calling me Sizzy Izzy, even though when she was alive, I didn't like it. It's one of the things I wish I could take back now that she's dead. I think about telling her that, but I don't. I think she knows.

"What if Mom got in an accident?" I whisper, afraid again.

"It's going to be all right."

"It's not," I say kind of loud and mean. "It's *not* going to be okay. Not ever again. That's just something adults say because they think they're supposed to. Like kids are stupid and are going to buy it. Things aren't going to be *okay*, Caitlin. If anyone knows that, you of all people should." I don't want to cry. I don't want to be a crybaby like Mom, but I can't help it. My eyes fill up with tears and I squeeze my bunny tighter. I rub his front paw against my cheek like I used to when I was little. I sniff so snot doesn't run out of my nose. Bunny's too old to get snotted on.

I wipe my face on my pillow. "How'd things work out for you?" I ask Caitlin. "Things work out *okay* for you?"

She doesn't answer and I feel bad that I said that. I sound like She Who Shall Not Be Named when I say mean things like that. And I don't want to be her. Not ever. I want to be like Caitlin. I want to be smart and funny. I want to be pretty like her, too, but I'm smart enough to know that's never going to happen.

"Caitlin? Are you still there?" I whisper. I'm afraid she's gone. Please *don't be gone*, I think. Every time she leaves, I'm afraid she won't come back. Or I'm afraid I'll convince myself she can't really be here. Because she's de facto deceased. And then I'll never talk to her again.

"Caitlin?" I say again.

My room is quiet except for the sound of the air coming through the vent. I can hear my dad snoring in the living room. That's how loud he snores. He's supposed to put a mask on his face, connected to a machine, to help him breathe at night and make him stop snoring. He says it doesn't work and he keeps it in the closet. It's called a pap something. Not a pap smear. I know what that is and that's not for guys.

"*Shhhhh,*" Caitlin soothes. Her voice is right in my ear and it's so soft and so pretty that I close my eyes. She seems so close that I think if I reached up, I could touch her. Like she's leaning right over my bed. I'm pretty sure I can smell the perfume that she gets from Victoria's Secret. But I don't reach up because what if she's not there?

"I'm worried about Mom," I tell her. I'm starting to feel sleepy, which is another hint that I might be crazy. How could a person fall asleep under these circumstances? How could I have slept at all since February 17th? "What if she bit it too?" I ask Caitlin. "What if She Who Shall Not Be Named killed her, too?"

Again, silence. The whistle of the cool air in the vents, my dad's snoring.

"It wasn't Haley's fault, Izzy," my pretty, smart, dead sister tells me.

"It *was* her fault," I answer stubbornly. "*She* didn't stop her car at the stop sign. *She* went through the intersection and *she* let that truck hit you. *She* made you go through the windshield and *she* splattered your brains all over the road!"

I'm crying again. Not loud crying like the way Mom cried the first week after Caitlin died. Quiet crying, like the way you cry when you don't really want to bother anyone. Like the way Mom cries most of the time, now.

"It was an accident," Caitlin murmurs. I can almost feel her touch my hair, smoothing it with her fingers. *"She didn't mean for it to happen."*

"If she didn't mean for it to happen, she should have stopped at the stop sign. I'm ten, I don't have a driver's license, and I know you have to stop at stop signs or cars will hit you and kill people."

"It was an accident. And if it was anyone's fault," she whispers, *"it was mine."*

I rub Bunny's paw against my cheek. I don't want to fall asleep. I want to stay awake and see if the police call to tell us someone else is dead, but I can't help it. I can't stay awake. "That's ridiculous," I tell Caitlin. "It can't be your fault."

"Sure it can. If I had been wearing my seat belt, I wouldn't be dead right now."

Chapter 8

Haley

48 days, 13 hours

I hear my cell phone vibrating on my nightstand. It's the second or third time it's gone off. I groan and roll over and pick it up. WTF? I look at the screen. It's Marissa. My best friend. Well, my best friend now. Since the other one is in the cemetery in a jar. I slide the thingy on the screen. "Hey," I say, flopping back on my pillow.

"Hey. I've been calling you. Why didn't you pick up?"

I close my eyes. "I thought you were supposed to go shopping with your grandmother or something today."

"I am," she says. "I'm in the dressing room at Forever 21. She said she'll buy me whatever I want. I've got a whole pile of stuff. You should come here."

I squeeze my eyes shut and open them again. My curtains are closed on my window, but there's light around the edges. I feel hung over even though I didn't drink that much last night. "I probably can't. I'm in deep shit."

"Get caught sneaking out? I told you it wasn't a good idea. Do you think I can wear yellow? I think it makes my skin look yellow."

I tuck my phone between my shoulder and my ear and rub the

little bumps on my forearm under my T-shirt. I can feel the need bubbling up. I try to ignore it. "Don't buy anything yellow."

"But I like yellow," Marissa whines.

"You look shitty in yellow. Everybody does." I exhale, remembering the nightmare of a night. "I had to call my mom last night to come get me at Dodge's."

"You're kidding. Holy shiite."

I close my eyes and wince. One of the bumps on my forearm really hurts. I should probably put Neosporin on it. "He wanted me to do something I didn't want to do."

"Like kinky sex stuff?"

"It doesn't matter."

"I can't believe you called your mom to come get you. Did she even know about Dodge?"

"She knows now." I rub the bump that hurts. "I didn't know who else to call. Your car's in the shop and you're not allowed to drive your mom's. Cassie wouldn't answer her phone. I got scared."

"You? You never get scared." Marissa groaned. "God, I have got to stop eating. My butt is getting bigger by the day. Do they have this in a six?" she hollers to someone. Probably her grandmother. She talks to her grandmother that way. Like they're friends. I don't have a friend kind of grandmother. My mom's mom is dead and my dad's mom . . . I can't stand that bitch. She's so judgmental, such a hypocrite. I don't even feel bad about stealing her drugs.

"What'd your mom say when she picked you up last night?" Marissa asks. She's grunting and groaning, trying to fit her size six butt into a pair of size four jeans, probably.

"She came inside Dodge's house," I say.

"What?"

"I locked myself in the bathroom after he hit me. She walked right in the house."

"Holy crap."

"Yeah," I agreed. "These people were smoking crack right on the couch."

"You're in sooo much trouble, Haley."

I sigh and rub harder. My shirt is wet under my fingertips. Blood. "I doubt it. Mom's afraid to say anything to me. She's afraid I'll go stark raving mad or something. And you know how Dad is. He checked out months ago."

"Because of Caitlin?"

"I guess. I don't know. It's been worse since then for sure. He's not really into being a dad or a husband. He's already got his mommy and his brothers and his business."

"But you said you heard him telling your mom they should send you away to boarding school. You think he will?"

"I doubt it." I press my lips together. My arm's really starting to bleed. I can smell the blood now. It smells like Caitlin's blood that night. It's weird, but the blood makes me feel better. "Whatever," I add.

"I don't think your mom will send you away. I don't think Julia's got it in her. You're still her daughter, no matter what you did."

"Yeah, but she's still got another one. Izzy's smart and she always does the right thing."

"I got news for you; your little sister is weird. All those weird facts she's always telling us. And getting under her bed all the time. Certifiable."

I smile. "She is, isn't she? A little weirdo."

"Almost done," Marissa says loudly. "I gotta go. G-mom's hungry. Low blood sugar. You sure you don't want to come to the mall? We're going to Chipotle for lunch."

"I better stay here," I say, slowly pushing up my sleeve. I feel like I'm stretched tight like a rubber band, like something bad's going to happen if I don't relieve the tension. Something really bad. I open the drawer in my nightstand and dig around. "Just in case Mom wants to come in here and lose her shit on me."

Chapter 9

Julia

49 days

"You called me!" Laney exclaims into the phone, clearly tickled. "Jules, I can't believe you actually called me."

"And a day early," I point out. "And I'm not in bed."

"Good for you. How about a shower?"

This is so like Laney. You give her an inch, she wants a mile.

"I even shaved my pits."

"I'm proud of you."

I'm standing in front of the mirror in my bathroom, just out of the shower. It's noon. I haven't talked to Haley yet; she's still in bed. I've been trying to figure out what I'm going to say. What I *need* to say. I think that's why I picked up the phone and called Laney. Not because I told her I would call her. Not because I'm hoping for answers from her (though I'm sure she'll have an opinion; Laney has an opinion on everything), I just think I need her strength. Because I *have to* say something to Haley. I have to *do* something.

My towel slips and I stare at my naked reflection in the mirror. I don't recognize my body anymore. I can't remember the last time I've seen my hip bones when standing. Pre-puberty? I like this new thinness-without-even-trying, but I don't like what it's done to my face. I look like I've aged ten years in the last seven weeks. There are fine lines around my mouth and eyes, lines I didn't have two months ago.

"I'm serious," Laney says gently. "I know how hard it is to get out of bed. You *know* I know."

I do. After Laney's husband died, after she got through the funeral and all, she took to her bed too. But she was only there weeks, not months like me. Maybe it was because she had little kids that she found her way out sooner. That's what she attributes it to. I attribute it to her strong character, her perfectness. Laney is the woman I'll always wish I could be, but know I never will be. Things are so simple for her, they're black and white. Her actions, her thoughts, her emotions have none of the messiness of mine.

I put Laney on speaker and set my phone on the sink. I rewrap the towel, lean closer to the mirror, and wipe at the steamy glass. My green eyes are still pretty, but I can't say that I'm pretty any longer. Is that why Ben isn't interested in having sex with me anymore?

I don't think sex has even crossed his mind since the funeral. It certainly hasn't crossed mine. I don't want to have sex with my husband or anyone else. My child is dead. I want to cover myself in ashes, hack off my hair with a kitchen knife, and throw myself on the ground in the cemetery where what's left of her rests in a little marble alcove in a wall of urns.

But before that. Why didn't he want to touch me? What happened between us? Ben and I always had a great sex life, even after having three children. And it had been a mutual thing, unlike with a lot of women my age; I enjoyed our relationship in bed as much as he did. Only three or four years ago, we were the envy of our friends/acquaintances. Those who weren't getting divorced were moving into separate bedrooms because the men snored. My now ex-sister-in-law had called us The Love Birds. People used to tease us because we held hands and kissed each other hello and good-bye with something more than a peck on the cheek. Where did that couple go? Thinking back, there was no specific event that threw cold water on our physical relationship. It just kind of . . . faded away.

And I've missed it. I've kept myself busy with my life with my girls and I've made excuses for Ben and for myself, but when I think about it, I have to admit that I've missed that intimacy. The emotional and the physical. Ben was once my best friend; he rivaled Laney. And now he's the guy who sleeps in a recliner in my living room and asks me to pick up a pack of boxer briefs for him at Target.

I exhale and focus on my image in the mirror. I can hear the exhaust fan rattling overhead; it needs to be repaired like a lot of things around the house. "I've got serious roots," I tell Laney, pulling at my wet hair. I wear my natural blond hair that's not so natural anymore in a long bob. When it's cut at the salon, it falls just above my shoulders. I haven't had it cut or colored in two months and it looks it.

"So go get it colored. Get a cut. Get a mani and a pedi while you're there."

"Maybe I should." I lean closer to look at the red spot on my chin. Maybe I should make an appointment at the salon. I always enjoy getting my hair cut, my nails done. It's a guilty pleasure.

I meet my gaze in the mirror, horrified by that thought. What kind of mother am I? What kind of monster? What kind of mother monster? A monster of all mothers. My child is dead and I'm thinking about how nice it would be to go to the *salon* and get my *toenails* painted.

Caitlin loved getting her nails done. She used to get crazy colors: blue, green, purple. I remember the last time we went, just a week before she died. She got her toenails painted purple. At the memorial service, when she lay in that closed white coffin, before she was cremated, her toenails must have still been painted purple.

I close my eyes against the pain that's so overwhelming that I'm afraid it will crash over me and take me under, take me out. A tidal wave of black sorrow.

"Jules? You still there?" Laney's voice pushes against the void, drawing me back toward her.

"Yeah," I say. I close my eyes and open them again. "Can't get my hair done. I have to do something with my daughter."

"Which one?"

"Which one do you *think?* Haley."

"What's she done now?"

"Let's see." I turn around and lean against the sink, picking up the phone again. "You want to hear about her getting expelled from school or the drug house where I picked her up in the middle of the night last night? How about the bruise on her face from where some guy hit her?"

Laney makes a sound of disbelief.

"She called me scared to death of some maniac trying to break into the bathroom where she was hiding. It was the middle of the night. I thought she was in bed, Laney," I go on. "When she called, she woke me up. I couldn't figure out why she was calling me from her bed."

"Shit. *Expelled too?*"

"Sure thing. Not suspended, like last month. Expelled. Smoking cigarettes on campus, with marijuana and pills she stole from Linda in her bag."

"She stole weed from her grandmother?"

I sort of laugh, but only to keep from starting to cry. "I don't know where she got the weed. Probably one of her uncles." I'm being facetious now. Ben's brothers would never give my daughters weed. I don't think . . . "I'm more worried about the Percocet, Laney," I say, thinking out loud. "It was a *lot* of Percocet."

"She's taking it?"

"I don't know," I sigh. I honestly don't think I've seen her high, or zonked out or whatever, but how much time have I spent with her in the last two months? I've been too busy drowning in my tears in my bed. "I'd be a fool to think she isn't taking them. Wouldn't I?"

"Well, does she act like she's on drugs? Like she's sedated? That's what Percocet would do."

When I don't respond, she exhales. "Right," she says, and I know she's remembering what this was like. "I know. You all look like you're sedated. You all feel like it. So, this all happened yesterday?"

"She was expelled Thursday. I rescued her from the bathroom on Drug Street last night."

"Wait a minute."

I can almost see her doing a double take.

"She got expelled *Thursday* and you haven't asked her about the Percocet yet?" Laney asks, her tone incredulous. "What the hell, Jules?"

Laney would never let two days pass without getting to the bottom of drug possession by one of her kids. Of course one of *her* kids would never have drugs in a Ziploc in her Lucky Brand backpack to begin with. They're all perfect boys; good grades, good behavior, adoration of their mother. And they're boys. An entirely different species. And one of her kids didn't kill one of her other kids. She can't possibly know what this is like for Haley.

"Why haven't you talked to her about it?" She didn't give me a chance to answer before she went on. "And what was she doing at a drug house in the middle of the night? I'm not even sure I know what a *drug house* is."

"Just what you would think. I saw, firsthand, what I realize now was a crack pipe." I hold the phone with one hand and rub my temple with the other. The towel is slipping again. "I can't imagine what she's going through, Laney. She and Caitlin, they were best friends, they—" I feel the tears coming. "I can't imagine," I repeat. I can, of course. I understand the devastating, debilitating loss, but there's no way I can know what it feels like to be Haley. Not really. My daughter died, but Haley was the one responsible for her sister's death.

"You can't just let it ride, Jules. I know she's been through a lot, but you can't let this go."

"I know," I say.

"She's your daughter and you're responsible for her, for her choices, for her life," she says passionately.

"I know. I know." I sniffle. "But I don't know what to do," I whisper. Suddenly I'm shaking, not with cold, but with fear. "I can't lose her, too," I murmur as much to myself as to Laney as I realize the threat might be real.

"So get her out of there. Change of scenery. Get her away from the people and places that are negatively influencing her."

"No." I reach for a tissue from the box on the sink. Empty. I lean over and pull a length of toilet paper from the roll. "No," I repeat firmly. "Absolutely not. I'm not sending her to boarding school. That's what Ben wants to do. She's not a boarding school kind of girl. I send her to school in another state and she'll end up a runaway or worse, Laney. I know she will," I whisper desperately.

"So send her to me. I'll put her in school here."

I smile sadly. Not only does Laney always have a plan, but she's willing to throw herself off a cliff to see it executed.

"I can't push her off on you. It wouldn't be fair to you or your boys." I dab at my nose with the toilet paper. Ben's bought the wrong kind again. It's like wiping my nose with a piece of newspaper. I would never complain though. I haven't been inside a grocery store in, well, at least forty-nine days. "She's my daughter," I say. "I'll figure it out."

"I know you will because if you don't, if you don't do something sooner rather than later, Jules, she's going to end up in jail or in drug rehab."

Or worse. I think it, but I don't say it. I can't bear to say it. I think about the pills, about Haley's dangerous behavior since Caitlin's death. It's about Caitlin; I know that. While I may have been in a fog for the last two months, my visibility hasn't been *that* reduced. I'd have to be blind and an idiot not to see it. Before Caitlin died, Haley was certainly no angel. But it had been typical rebellious teenager stuff: being late for curfew, not turning in homework, saying she was one place when she was actually at another. But nothing serious. Nothing like stealing drugs and sneaking out in the middle of the night to go to a crack house.

"I know I have to do something," I say into the phone when I find my voice again. "I just don't know what."

"So Ben says send her to boarding school. Is that his only idea?" Laney asks.

She's being pushy. *Really* pushy. I'm beginning to wish I hadn't called her. I can't do this right now with her. I don't have it in me to defend my family or myself.

"What's Ben saying?" Laney asks when I don't answer.

She's like a dog with the proverbial bone. I know her too well. I know she's not going to let go of it.

"Julia?" Ben calls from the bedroom. "You in there?"

"Can I call you back?" I ask Laney, thankful for the reprieve. I don't want to talk to Ben, either, but I'd rather talk to him right now than to Laney. "In the bathroom," I call. Then into the phone: "Ben's looking for me. I should go."

"You two need to sit down and talk about Haley," Laney tells me. "You're her parents. You owe it to her. You owe it to Caitlin," she says fervently.

I dab at my eyes with the toilet paper. I hear Ben's hand on the bathroom doorknob. "Call you later," I say, trying to grip the phone and my towel.

Ben opens the door without knocking, which irritates me. I've always liked my privacy in the bathroom. If the door is shut, in my book, that means you're not welcome, unless invited. It's not that way with Ben's family, though. They think nothing of brushing their teeth while a spouse sits on the john. I don't want to see Ben clip his nose hairs or have him watch me remove my tampon. Some things should remain private, shouldn't they? Isn't that a way to keep up the romance in a marriage?

Of course, obviously we're not doing so hot with that. *That* writing was on the wall even before Caitlin died.

"There you are," he says. He's dressed in jeans and a red polo with his family's lawn care company logo on it. The shirt looks too small; it's pulling across his belly.

"I was talking to Laney." My towel begins to slip and for some reason I feel a sense of panic. I don't want him to see me naked.

Why don't I want him to see me naked? He's been seeing me naked since I was twenty years old. I set the phone on the edge of the sink and cover my exposed left breast. I don't know if he doesn't see it or he just doesn't care. Even a year or so ago, Ben's face lit up at the sight of a bare breast, even one he knew well. The look on his face, or the lack of response in this case, makes me so sad and I don't know why. This isn't solely his fault, the state of our marriage. I know that.

"I . . . we need to talk," I say, fussing with the towel.

"You're telling me." Ben's not usually a cynical guy, but his words are dripping with sarcasm.

He turns around and grabs my white terry robe off a hook on the back of the door. He opens it for me. I hesitate, then turn my back to him and let the towel slide to the floor. I'm relieved to feel the robe around me. I tie it tightly before I face him.

"About Haley," I say, not sure what he means.

He exhales. "Izzy told me."

"Izzy told you what?" I walk out of the bathroom. I feel exposed. I need to get dressed. "What does Izzy know?"

"Izzy said you went out in the middle of the night and brought Haley home. Where the hell was she?" he asks, raising his voice.

I walk to my dresser. He stands near the bathroom door, watching me. I pull on panties and slip out of my robe, my back to him. I grab a sports bra and pull it over my head. I don't turn to face him until I'm wearing yoga pants and a T-shirt from some camp one of the girls attended.

He's just standing there, looking at me. Even heavier than he's ever been, he's still a good-looking man: short, dark hair, a day-old beard that's sexy on him rather than making him look unkempt. He's a big guy. Six foot two, stocky, though he's never been heavy, until now. I always had a thing for big guys.

"Where was she?" Ben asks, clearly ticked off. I can't tell if the anger is directed at me or Haley. Probably both of us.

"She was at someone's house. On Third."

"In that neighborhood? At three o'clock in the morning? I

thought she was grounded. Why the hell was she even out of the house?"

"My guess is that she went out her window again." She'd done the same thing a couple of weeks ago and strolled back in the back door around noon the following day.

"And exactly why did she sneak out the window, then call you to come get her? Why didn't you wake me up?"

I want to say *I didn't wake you up because it's pretty obvious you're more interested in what fertilizer you're spreading on lawns this week than your family,* but I don't. I walk over to the bed and sit down. "She went to this house where there was sort of a party and I think things got out of hand." I look up at him. "I'm just glad she had the sense to call me. That's good that she still feels like she can call us if she gets into trouble, right?"

He shakes his head. "I have no idea what you're talking about. We're going to have to get into this later. I have to meet with a client. Are you coming to dinner tonight? Mom's birthday. She's expecting us all there."

I close my eyes.

"I already told her the girls were coming. She needs a count. She's making beef bourguignonne."

I don't want to go, of course, but I know I should. It's time for us to start acting like a family again. Haley and Izzy need that. I know they do. I just don't know if I can do it.

My eyes are still closed. "She's cooking for her own birthday? Why aren't we just going out?" Having to sit with his family and have dinner in a restaurant is torture enough. Being in that house, with them, just seems . . . impossible.

"You know Mom. She doesn't like to eat out. She likes to eat at home. It's her birthday, Julia." His tone is now hostile. "If she wants to cook for us for her birthday, we can let her cook. It won't kill you to come."

We're both silent for a moment and the silence almost hurts more than his stinging tone.

"It might be good for you," he says more gently. "You know, to get out and do something normal?"

Tears immediately spring in my eyes. "What's normal now, Ben?"

"You know what I mean." The anger is gone from his voice now. Now I hear his pain. "We have to find a way to move on. I know things can't be the same. Be the way they were before. But we have to think about Haley and Izzy. About what they need."

He's right. I know he's right. "Fine. I'll come," I say, opening my eyes. Right now I can't imagine going to Linda's for dinner, listening to Ben and his brothers laugh and talk and carry on the way they do. Theirs has always been a loud family, something I've never been quite comfortable with. I can't imagine going, I can't imagine putting a fork of Linda's beef bourguignonne into my mouth. I can't imagine making small talk with my sisters-in-law or Jeremy's new girlfriend. "I'll be there," I say.

He walks to the bedroom door. "Six o'clock. I'll just meet you and the girls there. I've got work to do."

I look up. "I thought we were going to talk about Haley."

"I told you I have to meet a client." He stands there for a minute. "You want me to go talk to her? To get to the bottom of this?"

You know what's at the bottom of this, I want to holler. Your dead daughter is *at the bottom of this!* But I don't raise my voice. I don't say those things. Instead, I just say, "Go meet your client. I'll try to talk to Haley, but you and I need to sit down and discuss this, Ben. We need to have some kind of plan. And you need to talk to your mother. Obviously Haley shouldn't have stolen Percocet from her, but where is she keeping it in her house that it's so accessible?"

He holds up a hand. "I'm not doing this with you right now," he says. His voice isn't hostile anymore, or angry. He just sounds so sad.

I stare at the floor. "We'll see you at six."

Chapter 10

Izzy

3 years, 8 months

"Izzy! Give Nana a hug." My grandmother is loud and kind of fakey-sounding. She opens her arms, her gin and tonic in one hand.

I just stand there in the doorway between the mudroom and the kitchen of the house where my dad grew up, causing a backup. She Who Shall Not Be Named and Mom are behind me. We came in Mom's car because Dad was already here. Dad's always here. I got to ride shotgun though, and She Who Shall Not Be Named had to ride in the back. She's lucky Mom didn't make her run behind the car.

I look over my shoulder, past you-know-who to look at Mom. *I told you Nana would want to hug me with her drink in her hand*, I say inside my head, hoping the message will reach her telepathically. I know that sounds stupid, but there are a lot of people who think telepathy is real; I saw a whole show about it.

I can't hear what my mom is thinking, but I'm pretty sure she's telling me to suck it up and hug Nana. My only other choice is to say no and then Uncle Jeremy and Uncle Bruce and Dad will all gang up on me. They'll probably pin me to the wall so Nana can force-hug me.

I feel She Who Shall Not Be Named poking me in the back.

"This is Maxton Airlines, flight double-zero. Please remain in your seats and do not block the aisle," she says.

If Caitlin had said it, I probably would have laughed. I turn back to Nana and walk all stiff, like I'm going to the electric chair. I keep my arms at my sides. She hugs me and gives me a big kiss on the cheek. I can smell the gin on her breath. It smells mediciney and gross. "How are you doing, Bug?" she whispers.

Bug. I don't know why she calls me that. Like I'm some kind of insect. Something she wants to crush under her orange patent-leather flip-flop. She's asking how I am, but I know she doesn't really care. She doesn't care about anyone but *her boys.* I wonder if I'd been a boy if she would have cared about me. I guess the Maxton boys don't have any male sperms though. Just the kind that make girls. Uncle Bruce, he's the oldest, he has four girls, two with wife number one, two with the second wife. Then comes Dad with the three girls minus one, and Uncle Jeremy, who just got divorced again, with two girls.

"How you holding up?" Nana asks me, breathing her gin breath on me.

"Fine." I duck under her arm to get away.

She Who Shall Not Be Named holds up her hands, palms toward Nana. "Don't even try it, Linda," she says. She's wearing fingerless black gloves and fresh black nail polish on her stubby fingernails. Her eyes are extra black. It's like she turns up the Goth-girl thing when she comes here.

Nana stiffens when her gaze moves to my mom. Like, you can actually *see* it. She takes a sip from her glass. "I'm so glad you came, Julia," she says, not sounding like she's all that glad. Nana doesn't like Mom. I don't think she ever did. She sees Mom as the competition. She sees all of us Maxton girls that way. Like every second of Dad's life that he gives to us, takes away a second from Nana. I think she was actually pissed at Caitlin when she got killed. Because Caitlin sucked up all that attention.

"Happy Birthday, Linda," Mom says. She leans in to kiss her

even though you can tell she doesn't want to. But she doesn't say anything mean. My mom's classy like that.

"Hey, kiddo!" Uncle Bruce pulls me into a bear hug all rough and kisses me. His red beard that's the same color as my hair is scratchy on my cheek.

"Hey, Uncle Bruce," I say. He always embarrasses me, hugging me like this. Dad's not all huggy like Uncle Bruce and Uncle Jeremy. I mean he *does* hug me, kind of that side-arm thing. And I know he loves me, but we're not huggy in our house. Not like here. Maybe because we get enough hugs here.

Uncle Bruce spins me around and almost throws me to Uncle Jeremy. "Kiddo," Uncle Jeremy says, kissing me on top of my head. "You remember Tabitha?"

She's Uncle Jeremy's new girlfriend. She'll probably be wife number three. He started dating her before he moved out of Aunt Pat's bed. That's what I heard Aunt Maria whisper to my mom when we were introduced at the funeral. Aunt Maria is Uncle Bruce's second wife. I wonder if Tabitha realizes that eventually Uncle Jeremy will cheat on her too when she's his next wife.

"Casey here?" I ask Uncle Jeremy. Casey's a year older than me, but we get along really well. She's always been nice to me. Even before my sister died. She never thinks I'm weird, even when I talk about something cool I learned on the History Channel or in a book. Or if she does she doesn't tell me I'm weird to my face.

Uncle Jeremy frowns. "Sorry. Her mom's weekend."

"But Alice and Maddie are here," Uncle Bruce tells me. "In the den."

"Okay." I walk over to say hi to Aunt Maria, who's taking rolls out of a bakery bag to put in a bread basket. Uncle Jeremy's new girlfriend is standing there with a glass of wine in her hand. She has a lot of makeup on for a family dinner at somebody's house. Especially for dinner with a family who's still in mourning. I've been reading a lot about mourning rituals. According to the Victorians, we're still in *deep* mourning. Technically, Mom and Dad have to wait nine months before they can go into half-mourning. "Hi, Aunt Maria," I say.

She smiles kind of sad. "Hey, Izzy." I've always liked Aunt Maria, but I like her even better since Caitlin bit the dust. She doesn't try to cheer me up and she doesn't constantly ask me how I'm doing. It's like she knows how bad it is to be me right now.

I turn to Tabitha, who is younger than Aunt Pat, who was younger than Casey's mom. She's prettier than either of them, though. "Hi."

She says something, but I'm already walking away. I'm not sure I can invest myself in another one of Uncle Jeremy's wives. I really liked Aunt Pat; she was funny and she used to talk to me like I was a friend instead of just a stupid kid.

I guess I'll go find Alice. She's the same age as me. Fifth grade. I like her fine, but she paints her fingernails with sparkly pink nail polish and she watches Nickelodeon so we don't have a lot in common.

I hear Mom's voice and I stop and turn around to observe the crazy phenomenon called family. It's not like I'm in a big hurry to catch a rerun of *Sam & Cat*.

The kitchen is big, the kind you see in TV shows that want to depict a big-happy-family kind of kitchen. The floor is Spanish tile; there are big granite countertops and a place to sit at to watch Nana whip up smoked salmon pâté and fruit on toothpicks. And of course there's a wet bar. Mom says that Nana had it put in after Dad's dad died. That was when I was a baby, so I never knew him, and I never knew Nana when she didn't have a gin and tonic in her hand or wasn't talking about the next one. I guess, technically, she might be an alcoholic, even though she never seems drunk. Not the way Uncle Jeremy gets sometimes where he laughs a lot and throws beer bottles at Dad and Uncle Bruce and says funny things about people.

I check out everyone in the room, kind of making a picture in my head so I can analyze everything later. She Who Shall Not Be Named is in Nana's refrigerator digging around, looking for a Coke, probably. Everyone is ignoring her; she's ignoring them.

Nana is *freshening up* her drink at the wet bar. Mom's talking to Aunt Maria, but they're being so quiet I can't hear what they're saying. Tabitha is kind of standing there, looking like she doesn't belong here. Which she doesn't. Dad and his brothers all have beers in their hands and they're talking together. Dad looks happy, which makes me sad because he never looks happy at our house. I mean, I know he's sad about Caitlin, but he was sad before that.

"Oh, Julia," I hear Aunt Maria say, and I wonder what she and my mom are talking about. Well, that's not true. I know what they're talking about. The same thing everyone is always talking about. Either Caitlin or She Who Shall Not Be Named. My guess is the live one.

The kitchen smells good. Nana's a good cook. We used to come here almost every Sunday for dinner. Even Mom. Before Caitlin made her smashing exit.

I smile to myself. That's a good one. *Smashing exit.*

Then I accidentally meet She Who Shall Not Be Named's gaze and for a second, I can't look away. She's standing in front of the refrigerator that's covered with photos, mostly of the Maxton boys, but there are a few pictures of us granddaughters. There's a big one of Caitlin laughing. It was the one they put on the cover of the memorial-service-paper thingy. When I look at Caitlin's face and then the other one's face, I see how much they look alike. It's just that Caitlin seems like she's surrounded by light. Maybe it's her beautiful blond hair, or the backlight or some kind of magic that happens when you go to the angels. She Who Shall Not Be Named looks like she's in darkness: black hair, black eye-pencil eyes and eyebrows. But there's a cloud around her, too. A cloud that scares me and makes me feel bad for her at the same time.

Since the accident, I've pretended not to see her, but she's caught me. She knows I see her and I suddenly feel shaky and my eyes get watery. The crazy thing is, her eyes look wet, too. The eyeliner probably. She just keeps looking at me. It's like she wants something from me. But I don't know what it is. And I don't know if I could give it to her, even if I wanted to.

I turn around and walk into the hall. I hear the TV. Nickelodeon. I wipe at my eyes so I don't look stupid and I call Alice's name.

Chapter 11

Julia

49 days

I stare at the powder room door. I've been in here at least ten minutes. I'm surprised no one has come looking for me.

Not really.

Who would come looking for me? Izzy? Possibly. Certainly not Haley. She hates me. Not my husband. Ben's thoughts are a thousand miles away from me right now; he's in the bosom of his family.

I groan to myself. How is it that after all these years, I still haven't outgrown, outsmarted, out-*somethinged* these petty jealousies?

I have no right to be covetous. I know that.

I knew what I was getting myself into when I married Ben almost twenty years ago. I was an adult woman, making adult choices. I knew what his family was like. How they could be overwhelming and all encompassing. And it's not like we didn't talk about it. Ben warned me when we started discussing the possibility of marriage, our senior year at Cal. He flat out told me that he was a mama's boy. He told me his brothers were his best friends.

But I wasn't really listening. Looking back, I see that now. Ben was so much fun and I was so in love. I was too busy thinking about a house with a finely manicured lawn, thanks to Maxton and Sons, and a baby in my arms. I didn't read between the lines. The truth is, I was young and dumb. And I didn't want to listen to my mother. I didn't want her to be right. About me or Ben. About anything.

But she was right. She'd been wrong about a lot of things, but this one thing, she'd been right about. What Ben had been trying to tell me was that I would never be the most important woman in his life. That I would never be his best friend.

That was exactly what my mother told me. Damn her.

So I have no right to ask to change the rules now. Not after all of these years. Not after having three children. Certainly not after burying one.

And then here I am again, back to Caitlin. It's like that silly movie Caitlin loved, *Groundhog Day* with Bill Murray. He keeps living the same day, over and over again.

I lean back on the toilet. The lid's down; it's actually not an uncomfortable seat. And it smells good in here. Linda always has Yankee candles burning all over her house. The one burning on the sink smells like vanilla. It's nice. I used to burn candles in our house too. Before we draped the mirrors with black crepe and piled ashes on the furniture.

I came into the bathroom to pee . . . going on fourteen minutes ago, I see from my cell sitting on the edge of the sink. But then I realized I needed a minute. A minute to what, I'm not sure. Not necessarily to cry. Although this is probably the longest I've gone without crying in forty-nine days.

I think I just needed to catch my breath.

Tonight's been hard. Harder even than I thought it would be. So hard that more than once I seriously considered getting up and walking out.

But I didn't leave. I just hid in the bathroom. That's progress, isn't it?

I close my eyes.

I should cut myself a break. This is my first real foray into some sort of normal outing. A birthday dinner at my mother-in-law's. A protected environment where someone who doesn't know won't ask how Caitlin is doing in her cheering competitions. Which is what happened to me last time I tried to go to the market. I ended up leaving my half-filled cart near the dairy case. Frozen fries and all.

So, tonight. Relatively safe, but still hard. It hasn't been easy to listen to the conversations at the table. Even without anyone expecting me to say anything. It hasn't been easy to sit there watching other people's lives go on.

I gave up pretty quickly trying to follow any of the multiple conversations running at the same time at the big dining room table. Ben's family's always been like this; they're loud and they'll talk over you if you don't fight to get in a few words. Tonight I didn't even mind because I didn't have anything to say. I don't care what kind of grass seed Jeremy thinks they should try to combat the summer drought issue. I don't care how outraged Tabitha is about the price of permanent makeup. I'm not even sure I know what permanent makeup is, although, checking out Tabitha across the table, I wondered if that's what's wrong with her face. And here I thought it was an overdose of Botox.

I doubt anyone at the table noticed I wasn't talking. That I was just sitting there sipping my wine, pushing my food around my plate.

Haley was doing the same thing: making no attempt to join in, moving her food around with her fork so it sort of looked like she was eating. But she wasn't eating.

That thought suddenly worries me. When was the last time I saw her eat anything? Is that why she looks so pale? She has to be eating, doesn't she? I haven't been present for a family meal since Caitlin died. There haven't *been* any family meals since Caitlin died.

I need to talk to Haley. I can't put it off any longer. I know that. I fully intended to do it this afternoon. I was just trying to come up with a plan of attack. Instead, I took a nap.

I lower my head to my hand. I need to pull myself together. I just—

A knock on the bathroom door startles me. I instinctively come up off the lid.

"Julia! It's Linda."

"Just a minute," I call, reaching back to flush so she won't know I'm just hiding in here.

The door opens and in she comes. Of course she does.

I want to take a step back and get her out of my personal space, but there's not really anywhere for me to go. I can't believe I forgot to lock the door.

"You okay?" Linda asks, closing the door behind her.

Now she's *really* in my space, which I find profoundly intrusive. Far more intrusive than I would have a few months ago. A few months ago, I might have thought *oh, this is just Linda being Linda. She gets in people's space all the time.* But now she's not just intruding into my personal space, she's intruding on my grief. The deepest part of me.

"Um." I sidestep to get to the sink and I turn on the faucet. "I'm okay."

"I want to talk to you about Haley."

I glance at myself in the mirror. I look like a hag. A hag with gray roots.

"Ben told me about her getting expelled. About the drugs."

I pump soap into my hand; it smells like a shower gel Caitlin used to use. I savor the scent for a moment, then glance at Linda in the reflection in the mirror. "Did Ben tell you where she said she got the Percocet?"

"That she stole them from me? He did. Which means she's a drug addict *and* a thief?"

I take my time rinsing the soap off my hands. I rarely argue with Linda. I certainly never confront her. I've always told myself I don't disagree with her openly in order to keep the peace in Ben's family. But *my* family is shattered and honestly, tonight, I just don't give a crap about Linda's. "Why do you have that much Percocet lying around? It's a controlled substance."

She folds her arms over her chest. She's a petite woman. Pretty, but the drinking and the pills are beginning to show on her face. She looks pinched and there are bags under her eyes. Not bags as big as mine, but she's definitely looking rough.

"I have a prescription, if it's any of your business," she says, getting snotty with me the way she does when anyone challenges her. "My back. Remember, I had that car accident. But that's neither here nor there. You're not going to redirect this conversation, Julia. I'm very concerned about Haley. We all are."

I turn around and park my skinny butt on the edge of the sink. I can smell Linda's perfume. It's an Estée Lauder scent. I pull the white hand towel with an embroidered sailboat on it off the rack and dry my hands. "Ben says you think we should send her away to boarding school."

She still has her arms crossed. Between the candle and her perfume, I can barely smell the gin on her breath. Just barely. But she doesn't seem drunk. Of course, she never does. If I had as many gin and tonics as I saw her down tonight, I'd be unconscious under the dining room table.

"I think it would be good for her." Linda's dark eyes bore into me. Ben's eyes. "I'm willing to pay for it. There are some good schools in Oregon. Schools that would—"

I cut her off. "It's not about the money, Linda. I'm not sending my daughter away." I sound stronger than I feel. "How do you think I could send her away after what happened—" My voice cracks. I can't say *to Caitlin.*

"Just for a semester." Linda softens her tone. "Two. It would give her some time to think, somewhere where she'll be safe. We can send her somewhere where she'll be closely monitored day and night. No drugs. No negative influences. Just academics and structure. And having her out of the house will give you and Ben some time," she goes on. "To work on your marriage."

"My marriage?"

"Well, let's be honest, it could use it right now, couldn't it?"

I lift my gaze. "What's that supposed to mean?"

"Come on, Julia, this is me you're talking to. I'm Ben's mother.

You think I don't know how unhappy he's been? You think I didn't know your marriage was a mess before we lost Caitlin?"

I glance at the door, considering just walking out, but she's pretty much blocking my way. I'd have to knock her down to escape. Possibly knock her out.

Linda sighs, trying to sound sympathetic, but I know her better than that. Doesn't she *know* I know her better than that after all these years?

"You know, Peter had an affair. Did Ben tell you that?" It's rhetorical. She goes on. "We were about the same age you and Ben are now. It's the age couples are when there are affairs."

"No one had an affair, Linda." I stare at her, what she's saying slowly sinking in. I feel my forehead crease. "Wait a minute. Are you telling me Ben's been cheating on me?"

"I don't know anything about that. My point is that we got through it. We went to counseling, we promised to be better to each other." She shrugs. "We both agreed that one little sexual indiscretion wasn't worth ending our marriage, our business partnership, our life together. We put it aside and we went on. Which is what you and Ben have to do. You have to get past Caitlin's death."

I'm still stuck on the part where Linda insinuated that Ben was having an affair. Granted, things haven't been good with us lately, but I just can't imagine him cheating on me. But now I'm starting to imagine. Is that what was going on in the months before Caitlin died? Was that why he was working such long hours? I meet Linda's gaze. "This—conversation—is—over—Linda." I emphasize each word, imagining myself returning to Montgomery's funeral home to pick out a coffin for my husband. After I kill him.

She just stands there, arms crossed over her chest. "You know, when Ben came to me to tell me he'd asked you to marry him, I begged him to reconsider."

Tears suddenly well in my eyes. I *didn't* know that. Ben never told. And suddenly I feel a tenderness for my husband that I haven't felt in a very long time. Which seems completely crazy because a second ago I was thinking he'd cheated on me.

"I told him that while I thought you were a nice enough girl, I didn't think you two were well suited for each other. I warned him that with the kind of people you come from—"

"Linda," I interrupt.

She keeps talking right over me. "You'd never understand what it meant to be a part of a real family. You'd never—"

"Linda," I repeat, holding up my hand. "Linda, this is neither the time nor *the place* to have this discussion. In fact, I can't imagine when would be a good time for you to tell me this. Ben and I have been married nineteen years." I reach around her to grab the doorknob. "I'm not going anywhere. We're not getting a divorce."

As I turn the door handle, she lays her hand on mine. "You have to do something about Haley."

"I know." I yank open the bathroom door.

"Before it's too late," she calls after me as I push past her.

"Girls?" I call, my tone bordering on shrill. "You ready to go?"

Chapter 12

Izzy

3 years, 8 months

I'm lying in my bed listening to She Who Shall Not Be Named bounce that stupid ball against the wall in her room while I consider what outfit I would want to wear for my own funeral. It was a big question when Caitlin went for the big sleep. Dad wanted her to wear this blue dress she'd had since eighth grade graduation. It looked like something a girl my age would wear to have tea with the queen of England. It didn't have ruffles, but it could have. I'm sure it was something Nana bought her that Mom made her wear. I don't even know why Caitlin still had it. So Dad wanted the little girl dress. Mom wanted to send Caitlin's favorite jeans and T-shirt to the funeral home.

I didn't get a vote. Neither did the one who killed her.

Mom and Dad didn't exactly argue about which outfit the people at the funeral home should put on Caitlin. They don't argue much; at least I don't see it. But that day, I could hear them talking in her bedroom after they went into her closet. Each one just kept repeating what they wanted and why. Mom cried a lot, of course. I don't know why they cared. No one got to see what she was wearing. There was no viewing. I didn't get to see her dead even though I begged Mom to let me. (She said it wasn't *healthy,* whatever that meant.) I think Caitlin's head was pretty messed up from where she hit the road when she went through the windshield. The funeral home incinerated her. That's what they do when you're cremated. I looked it up. They cook you at fourteen hundred degrees Fahrenheit. It takes two to three hours. There's a YouTube video showing how they do it. I watch it sometimes when I can't sleep.

I wonder if Caitlin ever thought about what she wanted to be cooked in, if she died. I doubt it. She wasn't weird like me. She didn't think about things like that. She was what people call happy-go-lucky. Who wouldn't be if they were tall and blond and pretty and smart? We never talked about dying, although I once had a goldfish that went belly-up in its fishbowl and she helped me bury it near the blue rhododendron in the backyard. She read a poem by Robert Frost. I remember it because one of the sentences was "Nothing gold can stay." The same poem is quoted in this book I like called *The Outsiders*. But as far as the possibility of people dying, we never talked about it in the Maxton house. Not Caitlin and me. Not Mom and Dad and me. I never even knew a dead person until Caitlin bought it in that intersection.

Mr. Cat, who's been sitting on the end of the bed, climbs up on me and lies down on my chest. I pet him and he purrs. "You missed birthday dinner at Nana's," I tell him. "Uncle Bruce got drunk. Uncle Jeremy's new girlfriend gave Nana a really ugly wreath for her front door and everyone ignored Mom like she wasn't there. I guess because she hasn't been coming for family dinners and they're mad at her. We had chocolate cheesecake for dessert."

Mr. Cat doesn't say anything. He just keeps purring. I'm not saying I'm expecting him to say anything. I know cats don't talk. But there's still a little tiny bit of a question in the back of my head because dead sisters aren't supposed to talk either.

I close my eyes for a minute, wondering if maybe Caitlin is there in the dark with me. I can't feel her. I think about calling her name, just in case, but I don't really need her right now, so I don't. I'm a little worried that maybe she can only come talk to me a certain number of times before she can't come anymore. Like a genie in a lamp granting wishes. Before her soul goes away, or whatever. I don't want to take the chance of wasting time with her. So I don't call her.

"Oh," I tell Mr. Cat. "And I think Mom and Nana got into an argument in the powder room." I kiss his head and his ear tickles my lips. "I have no idea why they were both in the bathroom with the door closed. I was just—"

There's a soft tap at my door and me and Mr. Cat look that way. We both stare at the door. My first thought is that it's Caitlin, but that doesn't make any sense because I think she just comes through doors and walls and stuff.

I hear it again. It's definitely a live person, not a dead one.

The door opens a little bit. "Izzy? You still awake?"

It's my mom and I'm so happy. She never comes in my room anymore. "I'm awake," I whisper loudly, sitting up and pushing Mr. Cat off me.

She comes in and closes the door. It's dark in my room, but I can still see her because there's a big security light outside my window and even with the blinds closed, a little bit of light leaks around. She's wearing a T-shirt and sweatpants. Her pajamas. She just stands there over my bed for a second looking down at me. I can't see her face. Then she surprises me by sitting down and then sliding into bed with me, putting her head on my pillow.

"I was wondering how you were doing," she says softly. She rolls onto her side to face me and puts one arm around me.

Mom's arm feels so good around me that I feel like I might cry.

Mr. Cat tries to climb on top of me again, but I push him down. He meows, but he doesn't get off the bed. "I'm okay." I whisper too, but not because Mom's whispering. I whisper because I'm afraid if I talk out loud, she'll disappear the same way Caitlin disappears.

Mom brushes some hair out of my face and then keeps touching my hair. Kind of like petting me. But I don't mind. In fact, I like it. I close my eyes and breathe deep. She must have taken a shower this morning because I smell her shampoo. She hasn't been showering much, so I notice it right away. But past that fruity smell is something I can't describe. It's just . . . my mom's smell. A smell that makes me feel warm and not so afraid.

"Really, Izzy?" she asks me, kissing my temple. "You're okay? You'd tell me if you weren't?"

I don't know exactly what she's asking. How I'm coping with Caitlin pushing up daisies, I guess. But maybe she's asking about school. Or my friends. I don't really care; it only matters that *she* cares. I nod because I don't want to break the magic spell and for Mom to poof away, into thin air.

"How was dinner tonight? Was it okay?" She's still petting me and I close my eyes.

I nod again. "Was it okay for you?" I whisper.

When she doesn't answer right away, I say, "You didn't look like it was okay." I'm quiet for a second and then I say, "What did Nana say to you in the bathroom? I heard you arguing."

"We weren't exactly arguing."

I don't say anything.

"Did anyone else hear us?" Mom asks.

I shake my head. "Just me, I think. I wasn't sneaking around being nosy or anything. I went into the kitchen to get more pom juice and I heard you." The powder room is in the hall between the kitchen and the family room.

It takes her a long time to say anything. Mr. Cat stretches out beside me on the edge of the bed. It seems like he's purring really loud.

"I'm sorry you had to hear that," Mom finally says.

"I didn't hear what you guys were saying," I tell her quickly. "I just . . . I could hear your voices. Like Nana was telling you something you should be doing. Nana does that a lot," I add. "She thinks I should cut my hair short. I told her I'd look like a dork, but every time I see her, she pulls my hair back kind of tight and says it looks good on my round face. She thinks I'm fat and I have a fat face."

"You don't have a fat face," Mom whispers. "You have a beautiful face, Isobel of mine." She kisses me again.

I feel the tears coming back and I swallow. I think about telling her how glad I am she came into my bedroom. I think about telling her how much I've missed her since Caitlin flatlined. It's almost like Mom's been dead too. But I don't want her to feel bad. She already feels bad; you can just look at her face and see it. Sometimes I think she looks so bad that she might die too. I don't know if that's a real thing, but I've heard of it. Dying of a broken heart. And I know Mom's heart is broken. Caitlin was her favorite. She was the prettiest. She was the smartest. She wasn't weird.

Haley and I used to tease Caitlin about how she was Mom and Dad's favorite. The princess in pink, Haley called her. It was kind of fun because Caitlin and Haley were best friends, but when we started ragging on Caitlin, it was like Haley and me were a team. I never minded that Caitlin was Mom and Dad's favorite and I don't think Haley did either, because in a way, it took the pressure off us. I never worried about not being pretty because Caitlin was pretty for all of us. And it was okay for me to be weird because I wasn't the princess in pink. In a way, it was freeing. I don't think Haley would have felt like she could wear all that black eye pencil or be in the drama club if it had been her responsibility to be the family princess.

"And as for what your grandmother and I were talking about," Mom goes on. "We were discussing . . ."

"*Her*," I say, exhaling the word with contempt. *Contempt.* Another vocab word at school.

"Haley," she says.

"Because she got kicked out of school?" I ask. "And because she's crazy?"

"Your sister's not crazy."

"She's batshit crazy," I say before I can stop myself. I look at her, afraid I'm going to get in trouble for saying *shit*. I'm not supposed to say *shit*. Usually I just say "S."

But Mom doesn't say anything about my bad word. She doesn't say anything for a minute and when she does speak, she sounds like she's talking to herself more than to me. "Haley's not crazy. She's just . . . really hurting."

I think for a minute. "Well, we could send her to school in Switzerland," I suggest hopefully. I saw a documentary about the Alps. This guy called Hannibal tried to cross the mountains with a bunch of elephants. It didn't work out too well. "She might like it there and we could go visit and go skiing in the Alps."

Mom sort of laughs, which makes me smile and wish I could think of something else funny to say to make her laugh again. I love how she laughs. She sounds like Caitlin. Or I guess, technically, Caitlin sounded like her.

"I'm not sending her to Switzerland. I'm not sending your sister anywhere, Izzy. She belongs with us. Now, more than ever," she adds, so softly that I have to listen hard to hear her.

Luckily, I'm smart enough to keep my mouth shut. Mom doesn't say anything, either, and after a while, I start to feel sleepy. Mom's so warm and she smells so good and Mr. Cat keeps purring.

A part of me doesn't want to fall asleep and have the time with her over, but finally I let myself go, thinking that if I happen to croak in my sleep tonight, this is the perfect memory I'll die with.

Chapter 13

Julia

49 days

I close Izzy's door quietly behind me and lean against it. I stayed until she fell asleep. She felt so good in my arms, warm and soft. It reminded me of when she was a baby, snuggled, asleep in my arms. Izzy is the baby I remember the most, not because she was the most important to me, but because I had known she would be my last. I had my tubes tied after she was born, so I was more aware of her milestones, more aware of my *last times:* the last time I would hold my own newborn, the last time I would breast-feed, the last time I would watch my baby walk for the first time.

Izzy had been so happy to see me tonight, happy to have me climb into bed with her. Standing here in the dark hallway, I realize how much I've missed my Isobel. Obviously she's missed me.

Guilt washes over me. I've been so lost in my own pain, I realize, that I haven't been giving much attention to my youngest. It's funny how the thought comes to me so suddenly. I don't think I've gotten into bed with Izzy or invited her to get in bed with me since Caitlin died almost two months ago. How have I not seen her needing me?

The obvious answer is that I've been in too much pain to see

Izzy. That makes me feel terrible. I've always prided myself on the fact that I'm a good mother. What kind of mother emotionally abandons her little girl in the middle of such a tragedy? Caitlin was my daughter, but she was also Izzy's sister.

I walk down the hall and stop at Haley's door and listen. Sometimes I hear her on her cell talking to friends this late, but not tonight. It's quiet. Too quiet? I feel a sudden sense of panic. Is she in there or has she taken off again? Should I have had bars installed on her window? I open her door without knocking. It's dark. No light filtering in around the blinds like in Izzy's room. Haley's added heavy drapes to her windows. I walk over to her bed and as my eyes adjust, I begin to make out the shape of her form. She's asleep on her side, her arms wrapped around a throw pillow. I listen to her soft, steady breathing and I remember her as a baby in my arms. She was my screamer. She didn't eat. She didn't sleep. She was my problem child from the minute she was born. I had the episiotomy to prove it.

But she was such a beautiful baby when she wasn't screaming. So inquisitive and full of life. I smile sadly and back out of Haley's room, closing the door behind me. I need to sit down with her and have that talk. I need to figure out where we need to go from here. But not tonight. I won't do that to her. I won't steal her away from the peace only sleep brings.

In the hall, I hear the sound of the TV. I see the flash of light in the dark, coming from the living room. Ben arrived home from his mom's house about an hour after we did and went straight to his recliner, taking two beers with him.

I stand in the hallway in indecision. Do I go to bed? Or confront my husband and ask him if he's been having sex with someone else? It's quite a dilemma. My bed is calling me. I haven't cried in hours. And do I really want to know if he's screwing someone else? Because honestly, there really is a certain bliss in ignorance. And if I find out he is, then what? I'm pretty certain I can handle only one catastrophe in my life at a time.

The hardwood floor is cool beneath my bare feet. I gaze in the direction of the living room. I really do just want to climb into bed and hide. Possibly pull the blanket over my head and deny everything that's going on in the other rooms of this house right now. I've lost a child. I shouldn't have to deal with anything else ever again, should I? No family problems. No boss that keeps e-mailing me and leaving me voice messages. In all fairness, I should never have to stand in a line again. Or pay for my sushi.

I force myself to put one foot in front of the other and walk toward the dancing light of the television.

In the living room, I stand behind the couch. Ben's watching something on how dams are built. The narrator is talking about the San Roque Dam in the Philippines. Images of its gated spillway flash across the screen.

I glance at Ben. He's awake. I take a deep breath and walk around the couch. I'm not sure if I have the emotional fortitude to do this right now, but I can't let it go. I can't go to bed without asking him about what his mom said. Or didn't say. "Hey," I say softly.

He looks over at me, almost seeming surprised to see me there. Like it's not my living room. Which I guess, in a way, it hasn't been in a while.

"Hey," he answers, sitting up a little straighter in his chair.

"I need to ask you something."

"Okay . . ." Right away he has a guilty look on his face. I know that look; it's his "what have I done now?" look. But all men have that in their repertoire, don't they?

I sit down on the edge of the couch next to him. It's funny, at a time like this, you would think I'd be loud. Accusatory. I'm neither. When I speak, I sound very calm. "Your mom cornered me in the bathroom. In the *bathroom*, Ben. She walked right in on me."

He groans. "I'm sorry. I know she's not always good with boundaries. She means well. It's just that she's worried to death about Haley."

I don't think Linda does mean well, but I don't say so. I learned a long time ago to pick my fights and that isn't my fight tonight.

"She just wants what's best for Haley," Ben goes on. "Anything she says, she says—"

"She said you were having an affair," I blurt.

"What?" He grabs the remote off the end table between us, knocking over an empty beer bottle.

I pick up the beer bottle. He hits the mute button. An enormous dam fills the TV screen, making it brighter in the living room.

"I am not having an affair, Jules." He grabs my hand, which surprises me.

I look into his face, wanting to believe him. The extra pounds aren't doing anything for his rugged good looks, but when I look into his eyes, I still see the man I fell in love with all those years ago.

"I swear to God I'm not," Ben tells me. "What the hell would make her say such a thing?"

My fingers curl around his. My first impulse is to believe him. Ben has his faults, but he's not a liar. And he's not good at lying. Early in our marriage, when he tried to get away with a few things, petty things, we both learned quickly that dishonesty wasn't going to work for him.

I exhale. So I believe him, but I don't want to be stupid about this. There are plenty of wives who see only what they want to see. I don't want to be that woman. I won't be. "Why would she say such a thing if there's no truth to it?" I ask, looking at him.

I hear him swear under his breath. "She actually *told* you I was cheating on you?"

I think about what was said in the bathroom tonight. "No," I confess. "But she wanted me to think she was saying you were cheating on me, *had* cheated on me. Something like that. You know your mother. You know that thing she does, insinuating without actually coming out and saying it."

"I'm not, Jules." He holds my gaze. "I've never cheated on you. Not in twenty years. I swear." He frowns. "She was drunk. You know she was drunk." Now a scowl. "What the hell were you talking about that such a thing even came up?"

I'm too tired to look away. I want to, though. I don't want to say it to his face. Admit it to him . . . because then I'll be admitting it to myself. "The poor state of our marriage. I think it was her idea of a pep talk. She was telling me how your dad cheated on her and they were able to get through it and make the marriage work."

"Maybe she just meant we could get through this, you know, losing Caitlin."

"Maybe." I glance at the TV. We both do.

There's a commercial with a woman and a man in a convertible looking romantically into each other's eyes. I wonder why the erectile dysfunction advertisements always feature young women and older men.

"But why would she even insinuate such a thing, if there was no truth to it?" I ask him.

He shakes his head. "I don't know, Jules."

"Have you been flirting with someone? At work? A client? Maybe someone flirting with you?"

He's still shaking his head. "Nothing like that. Me, cheating on you? That's the most ridiculous thing I've ever heard. I would never do that. You know me, Jules." He sounds hurt now. "You know I would never do something like that."

"It was a lot of information crammed into one bathroom," I tell him. "She also said that she told you not to marry me. That she warned you our marriage would never last."

He groans, closes his eyes, and runs his hand over his face. But he's still holding on to my hand. And I feel a tiny glimmer of hope. I've felt so far removed from Ben, from our marriage, for so long. I'd forgotten what the intimacy of talking together in a dark room could be like. It's actually kind of funny that the accusation that he's been cheating on me is what brings this about.

He lowers his hand. "I'm sorry. I don't know what else to say. It was her birthday. She had too much to drink. You know she has a mean streak when she has too much to drink."

I look at him. We've been married long enough for him to know what I'm thinking. We've had this discussion about his mother's drinking before. Many times before. Either he denies she has a drinking problem or he says there's nothing anyone can do about it until she's ready to admit she has a problem. Either way, it's a dead subject between us.

"That was mean of her to tell me that." I press my lips together. "I don't know why she wants to hurt me, Ben." My voice catches. "Doesn't she know how much I'm already hurting?" Tears fill my eyes, but, thankfully, they don't spill over. I don't want to cry. I'm tired of crying. I'm tired of feeling the way I feel.

"Come here," Ben whispers, pulling on my hand.

I sort of climb into his lap and lay my head on his shoulder. He wraps his arms around me and just holds me. We used to do this all the time; I can't remember when the last time was.

"You didn't have sex with another woman?" I whisper.

"Think about it logically for a second. With whom? When? You know what kind of hours I work. I know. With Margie," he teases.

Margie is one of the women who work in the front office at the Maxton lawn-care business. She's pushing seventy-five and has a mouth like a dockworker. I can't bring myself to laugh, but I smile. "Oh, Ben."

He kisses my temple. Not exactly a romantic overture, but it's the most physical we've been in a while and it feels good. It makes me feel like I'm still alive. Like I want to be.

"You've lost weight," he whispers, curling his hand around my hip and down over my butt. "You need to start eating. Keep up your strength."

"It's not like I couldn't stand to lose a few pounds," I murmur.

He sighs and strokes my back. I close my eyes.

"We still haven't talked about Haley," Ben says after a few moments of silence. "We need to figure out what we're going to do with her."

I lie there with my eyes closed, curled up in a ball on his lap. "I know. I just can't—I don't—" I take a deep breath. "Whether it's the best thing for Haley or not, Ben, I . . . I can't let her go. I can't send her to Switzerland to school."

"Switzerland? What the hell are you talking about?"

I open my eyes to see him looking down at me. "Izzy's idea. She wants to go skiing in the Alps."

"I still have no idea what we're talking about."

I sigh and close my eyes again, resting my head on his shoulder. I can smell the beer on his breath, but I don't mind. "I'm not sending Haley to boarding school. There's no way I can do that, but Linda might be right in suggesting that Haley needs a change of scenery."

"What? A vacation?" He sounds ticked. Just like that and the gentleness in his voice is gone. "She gets kicked out of school for drug possession and we're going to go on a European vacation? I can't get away from work, Jules. You know this time of year is bad. It's spring and—"

"Ben," I interrupt. "I wasn't thinking about taking Haley on a *vacation*." I sit up. Now *I'm* a little ticked. We're never on the same page anymore. Why are we never on the same page? What would make him think I think a vacation is a solution? Does he not know me any better than that? And why does the conversation move so quickly from the serious problem with our daughter to his work and what he can't do?

I give myself a second because I know that getting angry with Ben isn't going to help us come up with a plan on how to help Haley. "I was talking to Laney and . . . she suggested sending Haley to stay with her. I can't do that. I wouldn't do that to Laney, but maybe . . ." I'm thinking out loud now. "Maybe Haley and I should . . . I don't know. Go see Laney."

"What? Fly out for a weekend or something?"

"I guess. Maybe. I don't know." His arms aren't around me anymore and I feel awkward. I climb clumsily out of his lap and turn to face him. "Probably longer than that. Or . . . we could drive."

He looks at me like I'm an idiot. "Drive three thousand miles to Maine?"

"It's twenty-eight hundred," I say. "I checked on Google Maps."

"You've never made a cross-country trip like that. No. I

wouldn't be comfortable with that." He shakes his head. "It doesn't sound like a good idea, Jules." He thinks for a minute. "And what about Izzy? It would take you at least a week to drive cross-country. What would you do with Izzy?"

"I wouldn't *do* anything with Izzy. She'd just stay here with you. Go to school like she does every day."

"I can't be taking her to her tae kwon do lessons and stuff like that. That's why we agreed you'd only work part-time. So you can do that kind of stuff."

I rest my hands on my hips. "It's not like I've done anything for the last two months."

He just sits there, looking at me.

"If we did this, Izzy could just skip her lessons. Or get a ride with Ann's mom. Your mom could help out." I warn him with a finger. "As long as she lays off the afternoon cocktail."

He looks at me, shaking his head. "I don't know, Jules. When I said we needed to talk about Haley, I was thinking more along the lines of . . . does she need to go to drug rehab? Do we put her right back in school? Get a tutor? What?"

I exhale. Stare at the floor. He's in his stocking feet. He's left his boots in the laundry room, the way he usually does. There's a hole in his sock. A big one. Big enough so that his toe is sticking out. "I don't think she has a drug problem, Ben. She might be doing some drugs, but I don't think that's her problem."

"Based on what?"

I shrug. "I don't know. My gut instinct? My . . . mom instinct?"

The look on his face tells me he's not buying it.

"I was just thinking that maybe if we spent some time together, away from her friends, away from school, we could . . . talk." I push my hair back, looking past him. "Maybe it would be good for me, too, Ben. To get away. Because we both know"—I force myself to look at my husband—"we know I can't go on this way. Our lives can't go on this way."

"And you think driving alone in a car with Haley will help you do what? Deal with Caitlin's death?"

I fight the tears. The pain that threatens to swallow me up. "Maybe," I whisper. "Maybe it will help us . . . maybe we can find our way back."

"Find your way back to where?"

The way he says it makes me feel foolish. Naïve. He's right. It's a bad idea. What makes me think Haley would get in a car and ride across the country with me, anyway? It's all I can do to get her to ride to her grandmother's. "It's just something to think about," I say, feeling a little defeated. "A possibility."

I stand there for a minute, looking at him. Him looking at me. The closeness I felt with him a few minutes ago is gone. Or maybe it was never there.

"I think I'm going to go to bed." I motion in the direction of our bedroom. "You coming?"

"Maybe in a little while." He picks up the remote. "I'm not tired yet. But you go on." He points the remote toward the TV and the volume begins to come up.

I stand there for a second, considering begging him to come to bed with me. Not to have sex. Just so I don't have to be alone. Just to curl up against each other. Hold each other. But if he doesn't want to hold me, doesn't want to be with me, that kind of makes me a little pathetic, doesn't it? To still want him?

I walk out of the living room, fighting my tears that seem like a different kind tonight.

Chapter 14

Haley

49 days, 13 hours

I shuffle into the kitchen Sunday morning . . . Sunday afternoon, technically. It's almost one o'clock. The house is quiet. Dad's already gone to work; he catches up on paperwork at the office on Sundays, supposedly. I think he just says that so he doesn't have to hang out with us. Mom's probably lying in her bed crying because her favorite daughter is gone. I don't know where the sister brat/girl genius is. Maybe at Mass. She goes with her friend sometimes, which is kind of funny because we're not Catholic. We're not anything. Mom's stepdad was some kind of Holy Roller. After Mom left home, she never went to church again. She never took us to church.

Which suits me fine.

I go to the fridge. There's not much in it, but there's milk. In the pantry, I find a box of cereal and grab a bowl and a spoon. I carry it all to the breakfast table under the window. There's a bird in the bush outside looking right at me. It hops from branch to branch, watching me. I wonder what kind of bird it is. If Caitlin was here, she'd google *gray bird with pale yellow belly in eastern Mojave Desert*. She did silly stuff like that all the time. If she were here right now, she'd figure out what kind of bird it is and then she'd read the Wikipedia description to me while we ate our cereal.

I actually consider going to her room and getting her iPad and trying to figure out what it is. Then I realize that's stupid. If Caitlin were here, it would be fun because it would be my little sister Caitlin and she made everything fun. But me sitting here alone? That's just stupid.

I'm halfway through my bowl of slightly stale Golden Grahams when Izzy comes into the kitchen. My chubby youngest sister is wearing running shorts, a T-shirt, and her gym sneakers and she's got her frizzy red hair in a high ponytail. Too high. I've never seen her dressed like this before. It's not like she's athletic or anything. She does take tae kwon do lessons, but I think that's because she's still at an age when our parents can force her to do things like play a sport because it's healthy for preteens. It's a bunch of bull. Playing a sport when you're not athletically inclined doesn't make you healthier; it makes you feel like a bigger loser than you already are. Caitlin was the athlete in the family. I haven't played a sport or taken a lesson since the seventh grade when I quit club softball because I sucked so bad.

I think about asking Izzy what she's doing in the getup, but I decide not to waste my breath. She won't answer me. She hasn't spoken to me since Caitlin died. I know she thinks the accident was my fault. Which it totally was. And she thinks that if I hadn't been driving, Caitlin wouldn't be dead right now. Which is also probably true. But she doesn't know the whole story. I wish I could tell her. I wish I could tell *someone.* Then maybe everyone wouldn't hate me quite so much. But what would be the point? Caitlin would still be dead. So I might as well let everyone go on thinking she was perfect.

I stir my cereal with my spoon and watch the little bird outside the window. It's still flitting around from branch to branch, looking at me. I wonder if it can see through the glass. Or is there a reflection and it's really interested in itself and not me?

I can hear Izzy at the refrigerator. She's getting her orange juice. Dad bought the wrong kind again. When I make the grocery list, I'll have to write in bold or maybe circle "no pulp" so he won't screw it up again. Izzy never asks for anything from anyone. He could at least get the right damned juice for her.

"There's a bird out here looking at me," I say. I move my spoon in front of the window, but the bird doesn't react. It must not be able to see through the glass or it would have flown away. Or it's a crazy bird and it's about to fly into the glass and commit hara-kiri. "See it? It's kind of pretty."

I hear Izzy chugging the juice. Guess she doesn't hate it with pulp too much or she wouldn't be guzzling it, would she?

"It's gray with a little bit of green on its back. And its belly is a really pale yellow." I don't look at Izzy because I know if I do, she'll probably walk away. I don't want her to go. Even if she won't talk to me, I just want to hang out in the kitchen with her for a few minutes. I feel like people are always leaving the room I'm in. I mean, who wants to hang out with a sister-killer?

"I was just thinking," I say, my voice sounding weird in my ears, "that if Caitlin were here, she'd google what kind of bird it is." I kind of laugh a little. "You remember how she was always googling weird stuff? Like . . . *can you eat an armadillo*. Or *how many M&Ms are the in a one pound bag of peanut butter M&Ms*." I finally glance at Izzy because I'm beginning to feel pretty dumb talking to the room. She's writing something on a notepad on the counter.

I watch her put the pen down and take the jug of juice back to the refrigerator. She goes into the laundry room and out the back door without once looking in my direction.

So we sit there, the bird and me. I finish my cereal. I'm just getting up from the table when Mom comes into the kitchen. She looks like she just woke up too.

"Good morning," she says. Her hair is sticking out all crazy. She looks like she's already been crying.

"Morning," I answer, walking away from the table. I don't know what I'm going to do today. No homework. Which is a good thing about getting expelled from school, I guess. But now what do I do? I usually do homework on Sundays. Or hang out with my friends. I'm pretty sure I'm grounded. I could go out the window again, I guess, but I'm kind of lying low. Dodge has been calling me and texting me so I blocked him on my phone. Luckily, I never told him where I lived. *Who's the smart one now, Caitlin?*

I take the ball out of the little pocket of my sleep boxers. I bounce it gently, just hard enough so that it pops back into my hand. I'm getting good at it. I know just how much pressure to exert on a particular surface to make it come right back into my hand.

Mom leans on the counter, a coffee mug in her hand, and reads the note. "Izzy went running?" She glances at the clock on the microwave. "She just left? Since when does she run?"

She must have put the time on her note. She's such a geek.

"She just left," I confirm.

Mom looks at me, frowning. "To go *running?*"

"If that's what the note says." I bounce the ball. Catch it. "I guess that's what she was doing. She didn't say anything to me." *Bounce. Catch.* "Of course, she never says anything to me."

Mom sighs and turns to the coffeepot Dad turned on before he left this morning. He leaves coffee for Mom every morning, even though she rarely drinks it anymore. "You have to give her some time."

"Time." *Bounce. Catch.* "Right," I intone. Another word for our list.

Mom turns around suddenly, leaving the mug on the counter. There are little lines across her forehead; I don't remember Mom having wrinkles before. She's always been so beautiful. Maybe even more beautiful than Caitlin.

"Haley . . . where did that ball come from?"

I bounce it.

"It was Caitlin's, wasn't it?" She closes her eyes for a second. Then opens them. "I remember her bouncing that pink ball." She points at me, clearly trying to bring up a memory. "Not that day. A couple days earlier. We'd gone out for pizza. I asked her to put the ball and her cell phone away."

I don't say anything. Mostly because I'm afraid I'll cry. And

I'm not willing to do that. That next morning Caitlin had looked everywhere for her pink ball. I head out of the kitchen, bouncing the ball.

"Clean up the table, please," Mom says just before I make my escape. "And put the milk away."

I take my time going back to the breakfast table, *bouncing . . . bouncing*. Mom pours her coffee. I tuck my ball back into my pocket and carry the milk to the refrigerator. I put the bowl and spoon in the sink.

Mom heads out of the kitchen. "Rinse it off and put it in the dishwasher," she calls as she goes.

I flip on the kitchen faucet, annoyed and I don't even know why. I mean *logically*, I get that I shouldn't leave my bowl with milk and cereal on the table or in the sink to get all scuzzy, but I . . . I guess I hate being told what to do. As I reach for the bowl, I get my sleeve wet. I'm such an idiot. I yank up both sleeves, wondering why I got the stupid genes. Caitlin was so smart and Izzy . . . Izzy, she's scary smart. So why—

"I meant to ask you," Mom says, stepping back into the kitchen. "Are you going—"

She stops midsentence, just like they do in movies. And I kind of feel like I'm *in* a movie, all of a sudden. It's as if the world has slowed down. I'm thinking fast, *really* fast, but I'm *moving* too slowly. It's as if my body isn't getting the signal from my brain quick enough. That brain signal that's yelling "Sleeve! Sleeve! You moron." I reach with my right hand to pull down the sleeve on my left arm, but it seems like it takes forever.

Mom stands there in the doorway to the kitchen, her coffee mug in her hand, staring. She's wearing one of Caitlin's cheer shirts and no bra and I realize in a split second that she's gotten really skinny. When did Mom get skinny? I mean, she was never fat, but I've never seen her collarbone like that before.

"Haley." She says it in a half whisper, a half cry and I feel so bad. So bad because the look in her eyes, it just . . . it hurts so much that I feel dizzy. Like I'm going to faint. I know what it feels like because I fainted the night Caitlin died. Right there in the middle of the road. When I woke up, I was on a stretcher and the paramedics were talking to me slowly, like I was a two-year-old or had brain damage.

"Haley, what have you done?" She comes toward me, putting her mug down on the edge of the counter. I still feel like everything is in slow motion. Except for the running water. It just keeps pouring out of the faucet. Gushing.

Mom catches my left hand. I try to pull away, but she's strong. Way stronger than I would have thought. She holds my hand and pushes up my sleeve.

Both of us look down at my arm and I have the weirdest reaction, as if . . . as if it's not my arm. Like it's someone else's. Because this forearm, it doesn't look like mine. It's got ugly, raised welts. Scars. And red marks that are oozing. And white gauze taped on with packing tape because I couldn't find any of the white stuff under the bathroom sink where it's supposed to be. It's so weird because I remember pulling off pieces of packing tape, but I don't remember my arm looking like this.

"Oh, Haley, sweetie," Mom whispers, looking up at me, looking into my eyes. Her eyes are full of tears. "What have you done to yourself?"

"I don't know," I hear myself say, in the same soft voice.

Because, honestly . . . I don't know.

Chapter 15

Julia

50 days

I stand there for a second, holding Haley by the wrist, staring at her forearm that's scarred with bright red horizontal welts. I feel like I'm slogging through mud, trying to get my brain to register what it is I'm seeing. I *think* I know what I'm seeing. My mothering instinct, born the moment that Haley took her first breath, tells me what I'm seeing. But I don't want to believe it. I want to believe that it's a mistake. A misunderstanding.

My bright, obstinate, stronger-than-I'll-ever-be daughter could not be self-mutilating.

I fight my tears. Choke them back. Haley is trying to get away from me, but I won't let her go. I won't *ever* let her go again. "Did you do this to yourself?" I ask. Why am I even saying this? I already know the answer. "Haley, why have you done this?"

Her eyes are full of tears. There's black eye makeup running down her cheeks. "I'm sorry. I'm sorry, Mom," she keeps repeating, almost like a mantra.

I touch my finger very lightly to a smear of dried blood on her arm. I have no idea why. To be sure it's real?

It's real.

A part of me wants to tear off the wad of white gauze—taped

down with what looks like the packing tape. *Packing tape?*—but I'm afraid to do it. "Haley," I whisper again.

"Let me go." She fights me, trying to break free. The way she did when she was a toddler. Haley was always a disobedient little girl. *Spirited*, I used to say. I remember, as a young mother, laughing about her defiance. I used to make jokes about how it would come in handy someday, a rebellious woman in what is still a man's world.

What I would give now for a little submission.

I grasp her wrist with one hand and her arm at the elbow with the other. "Stop, Haley. You're going to hurt yourself or me. Stop!" I say it so loudly that my voice echoes inside my head.

But she stops.

"You're *cutting* yourself?" I search her black-tear-stained face. I can barely breathe. But I have to breathe, for Haley. For the beloved, insolent child of my body, of my heart. Because at this moment, I realize that no matter what she's done, she's still my child of my body and my heart. Worth no less than my Caitlin. Loved no less than my Caitlin, who I'll never hold in my arms again, the way I'm holding Haley now.

"Why didn't you tell me?" I press. "Why didn't you *come* to me?"

She turns her face away as if she can't stand to look at mine. "And say what?" She presses her lips together, lips devoid of any color.

She's so thin. So pale. When did this happen. How?

"You wouldn't have heard me anyway. No one hears me anymore." She whispers the last words.

I let go of her arm just long enough to throw my arms around her shoulders. "I'm sorry," I tell her, hugging her skinny body to my own. Bare bones to bare bones. "I'm *so* sorry."

"Let go of me!"

She pushes against me, thrashing to get away again. She fights me so hard that I lose my balance. I go down sideways on one knee to keep from falling, but I pull her down with me. I won't let her go.

I guess the sensation of hitting the tile floor startles her badly because she stops fighting me. Sitting down hard on my butt, I shift so I can lean my back against the island, my daughter still in my arms. "It's okay," I murmur, smoothing her hair with my free hand, still holding on to her with the other. "How long has this been going on? How long have you been doing this, Haley?" My voice is shaky, but I'm not falling apart. I *won't* fall apart.

I won't fall apart because I know deep inside that to fall apart would mean losing my child. A second child. And I'm not going to do it. I'm not, *damn it*. I'm going to pick up the pieces. I'm going to gather the broken shards of who I was and . . . and put them back together. I know I won't be the same person I was before Caitlin died; I can't possibly be. *That* Julia is gone and turned to ashes with my daughter's body. But something deep inside me tells me I can be *someone* again. I don't know who . . . but definitely a mother. Haley's mother. Izzy's mother.

I rock side to side and Haley lowers her head to my shoulder. "It's going to be okay," I murmur.

A sob escapes from her quivering mouth. "It's not. It never will be. She's dead, Mom. Caitlin's dead."

I keep rocking her, the way I did when she was a little girl. Haley was always falling, bumping herself. I must have bought a box of Band-Aids a week for her when she was a toddler. She was the one who broke her arm when she was six, trying to fly off the bunk beds she and Caitlin shared in our old house. She was the one who had to get three stitches under her chin when she fell off the slide at the park.

I look down at her and I can see the faint line of the scar from that tumble when she was eight. I kiss her dark head. I rock her. I make the little sounds a mother makes that only a child can understand.

I don't know how long we sit there on the kitchen floor, me rocking my seventeen-year-old daughter in my arms as if she's a baby. Long enough to begin to feel stiff. Long enough for Izzy to come home from her run.

My youngest walks into the house, slamming the door behind her. She slams it so hard that I want to holler, "Don't slam the damned door!" How many times have I asked Izzy not to slam the door?

But I know it couldn't possibly be as loud as it sounds. I've heard that door slam thousands of times, millions of times, in the eleven years we've lived in this house. For some reason, my senses seem more acute. Sounds seem louder: my breath, Haley's, the trickle of water filling the icemaker in the refrigerator. My sense of touch is heightened; I'm more aware of the weight of Haley's thin frame in my arms and the sensation of her hair against my cheek. I can smell the scent of her shampoo, the Downy fresh-ness of her clothes, and even the lemon fragrance of the polish I've always used on the kitchen cabinets.

"Mom? What's going on?"

I look up to see Izzy standing over us. Her face is flushed and beaded with perspiration. She's breathing hard. She's wearing a pair of shiny green running shorts hiked up way too high. "Mom?" Her pre-puberty-pitched voice is one beat shy of panic. "What's wrong with her?"

Instinctively, I push Haley's sleeve down. "Go to your room. Please, Izzy."

She stares down at us. I still have Haley wrapped in my arms. Haley's eyes are shut.

"Izzy," I repeat, sharper this time. "I need you to go to your room."

"What's wrong with her?" Izzy sounds angry. "What did she do now?"

"Isobel Mae. Go to your room and stay in there until I come for you." I don't give her a chance to talk back. "Now."

Izzy gives a huff, but thankfully, stomps off.

I take a moment to catch my breath. Haley's loose in my arms. So relaxed that I wonder if she's asleep. Or dead and broken. A sob rises in my throat and I choke it back. I brush a wisp of blue-black hair off her cheek and kiss the top of her head. I can hear her breathing. She's not dead. *Not dead.* I kiss her temple. It's damp from the effort of fighting me.

At least she didn't cut her face.

I wonder where such a thought could have come from.

I have images in my head from somewhere. The Internet, most likely. Photos I stumbled on accidentally while googling *self-motivation* or something like that. Photos of cuts very similar in appearance to the ones on Haley's arm, across a teenage girl's forehead. On another girl's cheek. Permanent scars. Scars they'll carry for a lifetime, even if the girls manage to heal inside.

"Haley," I breathe. "You need to tell me why you're doing this, so I can help you." "Haley," I repeat when she doesn't answer.

"No one can help me," she says, her eyes still closed.

"We can call Dr. Pullman. We can—"

"No doctor! No doctor!" She shudders in my arms. "They make me think of that night in the ER. About lying there in that bed, knowing Caitlin was still lying in the road."

Tears well in my eyes. I want to tell her that no one left Caitlin's body in the street. That by the time she reached the hospital, Caitlin was there, too. Her body, at least. But my instinct warns me that telling her that won't help. Not right now, at least.

"Haley, we have to find someone to help you. This . . . what you're doing to yourself . . . You could get an infection. You could—" *Kill yourself,* I want to say, only I can't say it because what if that's what she's trying to do?

"I'll be all right." She stiffens and then pulls away from me.

I let go of her. I hate to do it. But I do. Because the moment, whatever it was, has passed. And when I look into my daughter's eyes again, I see the sulky teenager I know, not the broken child that was in my arms a minute ago.

She gets to her feet, tugging down both her sleeves, but not before I see that her right arm is, thank goodness, unmarked.

"Where are you going?" I ask, getting up off the floor. One knee hurts, as does my butt. From where I went down so hard on the tile, I suppose.

"My room." Haley wipes at her eyes with her sleeve, smearing the black eye makeup even further. "I'm just going to my room," she flings.

I don't know why she's so angry with me. Because I saw that vulnerable part of her that she's kept so well hidden? Or is she not angry with me at all? Just with herself?

I don't stop her. I watch her walk out of the kitchen and I reach for my cup of coffee. I take a sip. It's cooled. I leave it on the counter and go to my room. I stand in the doorway of the bedroom, looking down the hall as I dial Ben's cell. Izzy's door is closed. Haley's door is closed. Caitlin's, too. I need to go into Caitlin's room and start cleaning it out, I think absently.

Ben's cell rings four times and is about to go to voice mail when he finally picks up.

"I need you to come home," I say without preamble.

"Why? I'm right in the middle of something. What's wrong, Jules?"

"We'll talk about it when you get here." I'm surprised by the strength in my voice. I don't feel strong. "I need you to come home. Now. I don't care what you're doing. It has to be now."

He's quiet on the other end of the phone. Quiet just long enough for me to wonder if he doesn't come, what will I do? Will I go get him? Or will I just say screw it and tackle this on my own?

For a moment, I'm not sure if I want him to come home now or not.

"I'll see you in a few minutes."

I exhale with relief and hang up.

Now what? I wonder. What do I do now? Do I go to Haley? Do I leave her alone for a little while? And what am I going to do long-term? How am I going to fix this?

I walk down the hall and listen at Haley's closed door. I hear her talking. On her cell. That's good. She's talking to a friend. I put my hand on the doorknob, then let go. If I were Haley, I wouldn't want me in my room right now. Too much.

I walk to Izzy's room, tap on the door, and walk in.

Chapter 16

Julia

50 days

"And you're sure she's doing it on purpose?" Ben's standing in the front of the door I made him close so the girls can't hear us. I wouldn't put it past Izzy to try to listen in. When I went into her room, I didn't tell her what Haley had done, only that her sister was having a particularly hard time dealing with Caitlin's death. Izzy hadn't seemed all that sympathetic.

I resist the temptation to say something inappropriate to my husband like, *Are you an idiot? Of course she's doing it on purpose. That's the definition of* self-*mutilation.* Saying something like that isn't going to help . . . and it's just plain mean. I don't want to be mean to Ben. Well . . . maybe a tiny part of me, a part I'm ashamed of, wants to be mean, but that's not something I can deal with right now. I just say, "She's doing it on purpose."

"Why?" He gestures with one hand.

It's clear he doesn't want to be here, in this house, in the middle of this mess that has become our lives, but like Izzy, I'm not feeling all that sympathetic right now.

"How is she doing it?"

"We didn't talk about that." I sit down on the edge of my unmade bed. "When I saw it, she was . . . it was pretty overwhelming."

"Well, I guess so." He's louder than he needs to be. But then he meets my gaze and takes it down a notch. "Do you think she tried to kill herself?"

I shake my head no. "If she wanted to do that, Ben, she's a bright girl." I glance away, trying to come to terms with even the *possibility* that she would attempt suicide. But I know my girl. I'm beginning to realize I may even know some of her demons because they were once mine. "If she'd wanted to kill herself, she'd have succeeded."

"I don't understand, then." He begins to pace. "Why would she be . . . hurting herself? It had to hurt like hell." He's thinking out loud. "To scar like that. It had to hurt when she was doing it, didn't it?"

I wrap my arms around myself. "I did a little research on the Internet while I was waiting for you. Cutting is a coping mechanism. More common than you would think, particularly with teenagers."

"Coping mechanism?" he repeats.

"The signs have all been there for weeks, Ben. We just didn't see it because . . ." I don't finish my sentence. I don't want him to think I think this is his fault because, honestly, it's more my fault than his. I'm her *mother*. I'm her mother and I should have seen past my own pain. I should have seen hers. "The problems at school—"

"The drugs," he injects.

"The other self-destructive behavior. We should have seen it for what it was—symptoms of her . . . attempt to deal with Caitlin's death."

He's still pacing. He reaches the bathroom door, turns, and walks back toward me. "I guess we need to find a psychologist, psychiatrist, something for her? I know the bereavement counselor was a disaster, but maybe . . . I don't know. Someone else? There's got to be other people who deal with this sort of thing. Professionals."

I exhale, trying to organize my thoughts that are flying in so many directions at the same time. I know the logical answer is to get her professional help immediately, but . . . but I'm not sure that's the right answer here.

I understand Haley's resistance to a doctor . . . or counseling. Her association with the accident makes sense. It's not enough reason in itself, but I have my own personal experience with counseling when I was a teen. I saw a psychologist, at my stepfather's insistence, when I was Haley's age. My stepfather thought there was something wrong with me: I was moody, I resisted his authority, I resented my mother for listening to him, for marrying him. The counseling hadn't been helpful, in fact it had made me angrier and driven a wedge deeper between my mother and me.

My instincts, at this moment, tell me that dragging Haley to a counselor she doesn't know tomorrow morning isn't going to help her. I'm not opposed to having her see someone, my instincts just tell me that's not the right thing to do right this minute.

But what do I do? I have to do something.

Those couple of minutes I sat on the kitchen floor holding Haley, I felt connected to her. At least to her pain. I need to figure out how to do that again, on a level where we can talk. Where I can help her work through the emotions I know must be overwhelming her. Hell, I'm forty-two and they're obviously overwhelming me. I've been lying in bed for two months staring at a ceiling fan.

I look up at Ben, who's come to stand in front of me. He's obviously upset, but I feel like he's angry, too. Angry with me for calling him home from work. Or maybe angry with Haley for causing all of this commotion on a Sunday afternoon. I don't know which. I don't know if I care right now.

"She needs to get away from here," I hear myself say. As I speak the words, my conviction becomes stronger. I stand and look up at him, forcing him to make eye contact with me. We rarely make eye contact anymore. "I'm going to take her to Maine to see Laney. We're going to drive to Maine."

"Is this about you thinking I'm having an affair, Jules? Because if it is—"

"It's not about that. I believe you." And I really do. "This is about Haley. And I think the trip would do her good."

He turns away from me, shaking his head. "It's a bad idea."

"Why? Why is it a bad idea? You've been worried about the influence her friends are having on her. Obviously we don't want her near that dope dealer. This would be a good way to get her away from them. And maybe she needs a break from this house, from . . . I don't know . . . Caitlin."

Ben scowls. "So you're just going to get in the car and drive to Maine? And leave Izzy here?"

"I can't take Izzy with me. She has school. And . . ." Now *I'm* pacing and he's watching me. "Maybe if we're alone, Haley and I can use the time in the car to talk."

"Talk?" He practically scoffs at me. "When has Haley ever listened to anything we've had to say?"

"I don't care." I shake my head. "It doesn't matter. I have to try."

"So you're going to drive across the country?"

I don't answer. I just said that.

He gazes off into space for a minute and then he looks at me again. "And how are you going to convince *her* this is a good idea if you can't convince me?"

"I'm not giving her a choice." I go to my closet because I feel like I need to do something with my hands. I pull a duffel bag out of the back, unzip it, and toss it on the bed. I go to my dresser.

He's watching me, looking at me like I've lost my mind. And maybe I have a little bit. I'm not exactly a spontaneous person. I plan family vacations for six months. I always make a grocery list. I plan my errand trips so I don't have to backtrack. But I used to be spontaneous, a long time ago, before I became a parent and thought there was no place for impulsiveness as a wife and mother.

"I think we should call Dr. Pullman," Ben says. "I don't think you should go anywhere until you talk to him. He can have a look at her, you know, her arm."

"Her pediatrician? The cuts aren't infected. It's not the cuts I'm worried about, Ben. They'll heal. I'm worried about her—" My voice catches in my throat. I'm worried about what? Her heart? Her soul?

"Yeah, but Dr. Pullman can tell us who she should see. Who we can take her to."

I don't know how to explain this to Ben, maybe because I don't understand it myself, but I know, on some fundamental level, that I need to take this trip with Haley. I know I need to get her in my car, far from her home and her friends. Then she'll have to talk to me, won't she?

I grab a handful of underwear and two bras from the top drawer and walk across the bedroom to throw them in the bag. I go back to the dresser and open the next drawer. A couple of T-shirts, long-sleeve and short. All neatly folded. I don't even look to see which ones they are. I wear the same thing most days: a cotton V-neck shirt in green or blue, jeans, loafers this time of year. By May, I'll be in shorts and flip-flops. Same T-shirts. My *uniform*, Caitlin used to call it.

"I can't believe you're doing this, Jules. This is . . . it's—"

"It's what?" I drop the shirts in the bag and go to the third drawer. Jeans this time of year for the East. It will still be cold in Maine. Especially at night. I pull out a pair. In the bottom drawer, I grab a green sweater that was once Ben's favorite. I've had it for years. He liked it because it was the same color as my eyes.

"It's *insane*, Jules, that's what it is. And . . ." He brushes at the hair that's fallen across his forehead. "And foolish. Dangerous."

I hold the sweater to my chest. "Dangerous? How so?"

"A woman and a teenage girl alone in a car? What if . . . if you break down?"

Now he's just being ridiculous. Does he really think I'm incapable of driving twenty-eight hundred miles? "I'll call triple A," I say.

"And where are you going to stay?"

I struggle not to be a smart-ass. I can't make this about stuff between the two of us. It has to be about Haley. About our daughter. "At hotels, of course." I walk around him to add the sweater to the growing pile in the duffel bag.

He's just standing there shaking his head.

"I've made up my mind, Ben. I think it would be good for Haley. And it can't make things worse, can it?"

He's frowning. "What if she tries to take off? Because I can tell you, she's really, *really* not going to like the idea of this."

"I don't care what she wants. She's going. We're going to Maine."

"And then what?"

I sit on the bed and throw up my hands. "I don't know. We'll hang out with Laney for a couple of days. We'll . . . go to that pizza place Haley likes in Portland. Go canoeing. Take walks. Whatever she wants to do. She likes Maine."

"And after your *vacation* you'll just come home and we'll go back to our life?"

I fall back on the bed, my feet still on the floor, and stare at the ceiling fan for a minute. "I don't know. I guess." My throat and eyes get scratchy, but I don't cry. Have my tears finally dried up?

He surprises me by sitting down next to me on the bed. I close my eyes for a second and then I sit up. "When Haley and Caitlin were toddlers, we used to talk about moving to Maine and opening a sandwich shop. Remember?" I rest my cheek on his shoulder.

Ben makes this amazing gooey sandwich that's a combination grilled cheese and cheeseburger. The girls call it the Ben Burger. It's morphed over the years as Ben refined his recipe and Caitlin became interested in healthy eating and insisted on using grass-fed beef and organic bread and cheese, but it's still our favorite family meal.

"You could sell your share of the lawn business and we could move to Maine," I say wistfully.

He doesn't even hesitate. "That was talk. Dreaming. It's not the real world, Jules."

I sigh. "I know," I say. I press my hands to the tops of my skinny thighs. "So we'll leave in the morning."

"You're really going to do this?" He gets to his feet, leaving me on the bed.

I think for a second, and then nod. "I'm really going to do it. I'm going to pack a few things, I'm going to call Laney, I'm going to write a letter of resignation."

"You're resigning from your job? You're not going back?"

"The only reason Robert hasn't fired me is because that would be in bad taste, firing a woman who took too much time to grieve for her dead daughter. I didn't really like it anyway. I guess I'll find a new job when I get back. It's not like we really need the money."

"I thought you loved your job. You've been there almost three years."

Does anyone love doing accounting for a florist? "I never said I *loved* my job," I tell him. He's at the door now. On his way out. My guess is that he won't stay here and help me break the news to Haley. I give him five minutes to be out the door. "I liked getting out of the house, Ben. I liked not spending my day cleaning the humidifier, organizing the hall closet, and waiting to pick up someone after school to take them to the orthodontist."

He rests his hand on the doorknob. "I never knew you didn't like it."

"Not your fault. Mine."

He just stands there looking at me.

"You going?" I finally ask, getting up and walking back to my dresser.

"Um, yeah. I'll be home after dinner at Mom's."

"You . . . don't think maybe you should come home?"

"I already told Mom I'd be there. Izzy said she wasn't going. Too much Nana for one weekend."

I don't know which one of us turns away first.

Chapter 17

Haley

49 days, 19 hours

It's after six o'clock when Mom taps on my door. I've been wait-ing for it, that knock that I know will be tentative. She won't bang on my door, just like she won't yell at me, because she feels sorry for me. Pities me.

I wish she *would* bang on my door. I wish she'd kick it in.

I've been sitting on the edge of my bed staring at my arm for a long time. I took the gauze pads off and it started bleeding be-cause I pulled some of the scabs off with it. And now there are red welts where the tape was. The packing tape was probably a stupid idea. But it's just one stupid thing I've done in a whole lifetime of stupid things.

I haven't been able to stop looking at my arm.

I keep thinking, what the hell is wrong with me? Why would I do this to myself? Why would I *keep* doing it?

I'm afraid I'm going crazy, that I'm becoming schizophrenic or something. We learned about schizophrenia in my psychology class last semester. It doesn't usually hit people until their teenage or young adult years; I'm the right age to go skitzo. Of course, cutting's not really a skitzo thing. Cutting's about control when things are out of control. I googled it, in honor of Caitlin. According to WebMD or some other bullshit site, I'm cutting myself because I'm in so much pain. Which sounds counterproductive, even to me, and I'm the one doing it.

I first started it in the ER after Caitlin died. Not the cutting. That came later. But that night, I kept pinching myself: my arm, my thigh. I was trying to wake myself up because, in those first few hours, I just knew it wasn't real. I *knew* what was happening was a nightmare.

If someone was going to die in that crash, it should have been me. For a hundred reasons. I remember that at one point while I was lying on a hospital gurney waiting for an X-ray that it actually crossed my mind that maybe *I* was the dead one and that the feeling that my heart was tearing into bits was part of some kind of purgatory or something. Not that I believe in that sort of crap, but I was definitely a little crazy in those first few hours, so nothing I thought surprises me.

When pinching myself didn't wake me up from the dream, I scratched myself with my fingernails. That was the day after she died. Or maybe the day after that. It didn't work; I still didn't wake up. And other people started bumping into my nightmare, forcing me to realize it wasn't a dream, it was reality: Mom crying, funeral arrangements, Mom crying. People calling and coming to the house, all crying. Mom crying.

Sometime that first week when I didn't have Caitlin anymore, I realized that if I pinched myself or scratched myself *really* hard I felt . . . I don't know. Better. The cutting kind of came out of that. Pinching and scratching made me feel better. Cutting made me feel even better. I stole a couple of Dad's razor blades from the little cardboard pack in his bathroom. He uses an old-fashioned razor and a brush and soap. The razor blade makes a sharp, sweet pain and then the blood bubbles up. Somehow, somewhere in that burning sting, I can breathe again.

I'm definitely crazy.

Mom taps on the door again. It's a sound that reminds me of a rodent scratching in the wall, somewhere.

"Come in already!" I say loud and meaner.

The door swings open. I don't pull my sleeve down. What's the point? She's already seen it.

"Hey," she says.

I sigh loudly.

She comes over and sits beside me, not touching me, but so close I can smell her mom smell. It makes me feel better, which makes me angry and I don't even know why. Now I feel like I'm going to cry, which in turn makes me even angrier.

"Your dad and I have been talking," she says. Her voice is gentle and controlled. I don't know how she's so calm. If I were my kid, I'd be losing my shit about now.

I don't say anything. I just sit there anticipating the whole counseling conversation: psychologist, psychiatrist. I'm so batshit crazy, maybe they want to hire both. In another state, if Dad has his way.

He and Linda were whispering last night; only she was so drunk that her whispering was louder than Mom's version of hollering. Linda wants Dad to send me to boarding school somewhere. She even had brochures for him that she left on his desk at work. She said she'd pay. I think she'd pay a lot to get rid of me. I wouldn't even put it past her to hire a hit man to kill me, I'm making such a mess of her family.

Mom looks at my arm and a sadness passes over her face that makes me sad. It makes me wish I wasn't being such a jerk and had pulled my sleeve over my ugliness.

"We've been talking," she says, "and—"

"You said that," I interrupt.

She looks down at her bare feet, then at me. "And I think you need to get away from here."

"I'm not going to any *freakin'* boarding school." I spring off my bed.

I was talking to my old boyfriend, Todd, earlier. After the

kitchen fiasco. He's a total dickhead, but we kind of hooked up again after Caitlin died. Not because I like him any better, but just because he doesn't act any different around me now than he did pre-dead sister. And he knows I cut myself so I don't have to hide it the way I have to with Marissa or Cassie. He's been telling me for weeks that we ought to take off, him and me and leave this shit show called our lives behind. He has a brother who works on the Alaska pipeline. He said we could probably stay with him for a few weeks. Todd was thinking about going anyway. He said he wasn't feeling the whole community-college thing. We actually talked about opening a coffee shop in Alaska. We've talked about it before. But Todd doesn't know exactly where his brother lives so I don't know how feasible that plan would be. Especially since Todd is probably the laziest person I've ever known in my life.

But if Mom and Dad are sending me to boarding school, Todd and I are hitting the road for sure.

"I'm not talking about boarding school, Haley." Mom looks at me like she's afraid to say what she's going to say. "We've decided that you and I are going to take a trip. A road trip."

I look at her like she's lost her mind, mostly because I think maybe she has. But also because that's kind of what's expected of me, the crazy girl who cuts herself. A girl like me, angry, defiant.

"We're going to drive to Maine," Mom says.

"I'm not going to *Maine* in a car with you." I shove down the sleeve of my T-shirt. "No way."

She gets up off my bed. "Actually, you *are* going, Haley. Your father and I decided."

I make a face of disdain. (*Disdain* is a word Caitlin would have liked.) "*Dad* decided? I didn't know Dad decided anything except for whose lawn gets mowed when."

Mom walks toward the door. "I'm not going to argue with you, Haley. You need to get out of here for a little while and I think I do too. So we're doing it together. It's not up for discussion."

I rub the bumps on my arm. It hurts, but I *need* the pain. I'm not going with her. There's no way I'm going to get locked up in a car with my mother for days. I can't stand listening to her cry for five minutes. A couple of days and I'll be wanting to throw myself out of the moving car.

"I'm not going, Mom." I rub the cuts hard enough to make them hurt. I feel warm blood under my thumb. "You can't make me go." I take a step back from her, feeling panicky.

"Actually, I *can* make you go." She surprises me with the firmness in her voice. I keep expecting her to burst into tears, but so far, she hasn't. So far, I've been the one crying today.

"I'm your parent and you're not eighteen years old yet," she tells me. "So I *can* make you go."

"I don't understand." I'm getting loud now. I'm still holding my arm. "We're going to drive to Maine? That's how you're going to fix me? We're going to take a *road trip?*"

"You like Maine. Every summer you're the one who says we should stay in Maine. Move there."

"Caitlin wanted to move to Maine. Not me."

"No," she says quietly. "*Both* of you wanted to move there. Don't you remember last summer when you two asked me if you could stay with Laney for your senior year?"

"Now you're just making shit up." I walk away from her, wishing I could get farther away than the other side of my bed.

This is it, I tell myself. As soon as she leaves, I'm calling Todd. I'm telling him let's do this. Let's move to Somewhere, Alaska, and open a coffee shop or maybe go with his idea of a pot truck, kind of like a food truck. Of course I know I won't have to call Todd and tell him I want to run away to Alaska with him even though he's a dickhead, because Mom will back down. She hasn't got it in her to make me go.

"Pack a bag." Mom reaches for the doorknob. "We're leaving in the morning."

I feel that panic again in my chest. A little bit like I can't breathe. "I'm not going," I tell her as she opens the door.

"You are."

"I'm not." I cross my arms across my stomach. We're having a stare-down now. "What are you going to do? Carry me to the car? Tie me in?"

She looks away from me and I know I've won. I know we're not going to Maine. We're not going anywhere.

She looks back at me. "So here are your choices," she says, her voice still calm. Except now it's creepy calm. Like she's crazy, too. "Either you get in the car tomorrow morning with me or I'm having you committed."

For a second I don't know what she's talking about. Committed? Committed to what?

Then it dawns on me. She's talking about the fifth floor of the hospital. The loony bin.

A girl in my physics class was committed for a psych evaluation last fall. On a suicide watch. She and her boyfriend broke up and she slit her wrists. Sort of. She didn't do it right, obviously, because it didn't kill her. My theory? She didn't really want to die.

"You understand what I'm saying, Haley? I'm your legal guardian," Mom says. "If I call nine-one-one and say I'm afraid you're going to kill yourself, once the paramedics see your arm, no one will argue with me."

The look on her face amazes me. She's totally serious and I'm caught between being so furious with her that I could throw something at her and being completely fascinated. I had no idea Julia Maxton had this in her. She's always been so easygoing, so . . . weak.

"*Mom.*" I say her name like I'm trying to get her attention. "You'd have your daughter put in a *psych* ward?" I manage. "You wouldn't really do that, would you?"

She just stands there looking at me and I recognize the look on her face. It's a Caitlin look. Caitlin's stubborn look. I don't ever remember seeing it on Mom's face before, but Caitlin had to have gotten it from somewhere, didn't she? And since Caitlin's genes were Mom's genes . . .

It's such a weird thought that it sidetracks me for a minute. Then I remember I'm standing in my bedroom discussing my possible commitment to the psych ward with my mother. My mother who's supposed to be on my side.

"Pack a bag," she says. "We'll leave in the morning when Izzy goes to school."

And then she just walks out of the room, leaving my door wide open. And I almost laugh.

Chapter 18

Izzy

3 years, 8 months

I'm not expecting Mom to come out of the bedroom so fast. I'm expecting the *evil one* to scream and cuss some more. I assume I'll have more time to get back to my bedroom and close my door so Mom won't know what an eavesdropper I am. *Eavesdrop* was a vocab word at school last week. Or maybe the week before.

I make it all the way to my door, but when Mom backs into the hall, I'm caught. I think about pretending I'm on my way to the kitchen or something, but I'm on the wrong side of my door. She's not stupid.

I look in her eyes and she looks in mine and I know she knows I was listening. Or at least trying to. I press my palms against the cool wall in the hallway.

I don't know exactly what She Who Shall Not Be Named has done. I could only hear part of what they were saying. But I know it's bad. Bad enough for Mom to tell her that either she's going to Maine with her or she's locking her up in the booby hatch at the hospital.

"You're not leaving me here?" I whisper.

She doesn't say anything. She just stands there. She looks really skinny, skinnier than I've ever seen her. And sad. But I see something else, too, something on her face that I haven't seen since Caitlin bit the dust. She looks . . . determined.

"Mom." I say her name like she's my true love the way people say their boyfriend or girlfriend's name in the movies Caitlin used to watch. "You wouldn't leave me. You wouldn't take *her* and leave *me* . . . would you?" I'm afraid I'm going to cry and I don't want to. I have to be strong for Mom. Caitlin wants me to be strong. She says I'm the only one in the house who's got his or her S together.

"Izzy." Mom sighs my name like she's really tired. Tired of the other one, I'd say.

But the way she says my name makes me think she really is going to leave me and for a second I feel like I can't catch my breath. I can't let her do it. If she leaves me, I don't know if I can stand it. I don't know if I can survive. I love Dad. I do. And I think he loves me, too. We're buddies. We both like the History Channel and black-and-white shakes. But how I feel about him is different from the way I feel about Mom. I don't know how or why, it just is.

"Izzy, your sister—" Mom looks back down the hall.

She Who Shall Not Be Named's door is slowly closing. Like magically, except that Mom and I both know who's on the other side of the door closing it.

"Leave it open!" Mom shouts, her voice so sharp it startles me. Like when you drop a glass on the kitchen floor in the middle of the night and it shatters. Or like the crack of a whip. Except I've never heard the crack of a whip in person, only on TV.

She Who Shall Not Be Named doesn't say anything, but the door stops moving.

Mom waits a second. We both stare at the door at the end of the hall. She turns back to me. "Izzy, I need to do this."

I shake my head. I keep shaking it. I'm fighting not to cry. "Let me go with you. I won't say anything. I won't say a word between here and the Maine state line." I make a motion like I'm zipping my mouth shut. "I swear I won't. You won't even know I'm in the car, Mom. You don't have to feed me or anything."

"I can't take you with us." She says it quietly, I know, so the killer down the hall won't hear her.

"I won't be mean to her," I say quickly, trying to up the ante. Usually you use the word *ante* when you're playing cards, but the term is appropriate here. I know I'm using it right. "I can't promise you I'll be nice to her because she killed my sister," I go on. "But, but I won't be mean. I'll ride in the backseat and I won't barf. She can ride shotgun all the way to Maine and I'll ride in the back and then she won't have to smell my stench."

Haley used to say that when she wanted me to scram. She'd say, "Beat it, Izzy. I can smell your stench."

I don't think I really stink. My armpits smell a little sour sometimes, but they don't smell like they smell after you reach puberty. We talked about that in health class. How hormones make your armpits sweat and sometimes even your lady parts. That's where good hygiene comes in handy. Or so Mrs. Wooters told us. I'm not all that excited about smelling, but I really want boobs so you have to take the bad with the good, I guess.

Mom's still standing there in front of me, but she keeps looking toward the bedroom door that was closing of its own accord a second ago. "I hear that window open and I swear by all that's holy, Haley Grace, I'll zip-tie your wrist to mine," she shouts down the hallway.

Mom sounds so loud, so scary, that I try to make myself smaller against the wall. I've never heard her talk to one of us this way. She's usually all calm and . . . reasonable. That tone in her voice doesn't sound reasonable and it scares me. What if she's the one who needs to go to the psychiatric ward?

Mom slowly turns her attention back to me. "I want you to stay here and go to school and take care of Mr. Cat." She smiles down at me, her sad smile, but not her pitiful smile, that smile of hers that makes me feel so bad for her. "We won't be gone too long, Izzy."

"It's not fair." My voice is shaky. I can't stay here with Dad. I can't do it. I'm scared. Not of Dad. Just of not having Mom. A mom who lies in her bed and cries all day is better than no mom.

She just stands there and looks at me.

"How long?" I ask.

"I don't know. It should take us five or six days to drive there, but after that, I don't know how long we'll—"

"A *week* to drive?" I just stare at her. "A *week* to drive? You stay a week, maybe ten days. A week back. That's a month. You're going to leave me here by myself for a month?"

"Izzy, you won't be alone. Dad will be here. And I won't be gone a month," she tells me. But I can tell in her voice that she's not absolutely, positively sure that's the truth.

"You're not coming back." My voice is getting squeaky.

"Izzy. Sweetheart." She looks down the hall at the door. It hasn't moved.

I wait for her to remember I'm alive.

"Please, Mom?" I grab her hand. I can't help it. I'm crying. "Let me go with you."

"Izzy, Izzy." She pulls me against her and I relax and let her hug me. "I can't. I would if I could." She kisses the top of my head. "It wouldn't be good for you. Haley, she's . . ."

She's what? I want to scream. A murderer? A bitch? A big meanie?

"I want to go," I say against her. I know I'm making her T-shirt wet. I'm probably slobbering on her. "Please, Mom. I need to go. Please."

"It wouldn't be fair to you, Izzy. You need to have a normal life. You need your friends and your cat and your bed."

I look up at her.

She pushes the hair that's stuck to my face back. "I'll do this with Haley and then I'll come back and when school is over, you and I will go somewhere together. All by ourselves. We could go to Oregon and see Crater Lake. You'd like that, wouldn't you?"

I think about it. I know she's trying to bribe me, but that

would be so much fun. To go somewhere by myself with Mom. I've never gone alone with her anywhere. I mean, I go to my tae kwon do lessons and to the market, but I've never gone on a vacation alone with her. I've never been in a hotel with just Mom. It would be the best trip of my life. I look up at her. I feel myself weakening. Wanting to say okay.

But I can't. I can't let her leave me here.

I pull away and duck into my room. I wipe my snotty nose on the back of my hand. I grab my purple zip-up bag off the floor that's filled with Legos that I was thinking about selling on eBay. I still kind of like to play with them, but I know I'm getting too old for them. I should be growing boobs soon; girls with boobs don't play with Legos.

Mom follows me into my room. She stands in my doorway, keeping one eye down the hall. On She Who Shall Not Be Named. "What are you doing?" she asks me as she watches me dump the Legos on my bed.

I don't say anything. I put shirts in the bag.

"You're not going with me, Izzy. Your father and I talked about it and you're staying here."

"I'm not staying here." Jeans go in next. A sweatshirt. My Little Mermaid sleep pants. My SpongeBob sleep pants. My Looney Tunes sleep pants. I love sleep pants and sleep pants are important on a road trip. You can wear them to sleep in, but you can also wear them in the car. I add a pair of sleep shorts with rubber duckies on them, just because you never know if you'll need sleep shorts.

"Izzy, I'm serious. You can't go with me."

"What'd she do?" I stick Bunny in the bag. "What'd she do that's so bad that she has to leave?" Next, I throw a book in, the first in a troll series I'm reading.

Mom leans against the doorjamb, still keeping an eye on She Who Shall Not Be Named's door. "She try to do herself in? Is that why she stole Nana's pain pills? She's trying to *end it all?*" I say it mean.

I realized I sound uglier than the murderer down the hall and I feel ashamed. I don't want to be like her. Ever. Tears roll down my cheeks and Mom leaves her post at the door.

"It's going to be all right, Izzy," she says, hugging me.

I wrap my arms around my mom like I never want to let her go. Because I don't.

Chapter 19

Julia

50 days

"I guess I'll see how it goes," I say to Laney on the phone. I'm standing in the middle of my bedroom. I'm trying to finish packing, but I can't seem to do two things at once: talk and pack. In my old, pre-Caitlin's-death life I could do ten things at once. "But I'll let you know where we are. My plan is to take about a week, maybe go see some sights on our way. I don't know. The Grand Canyon or something. I guess it depends on which way we go."

"See who throws whom off a cliff first, you or Haley?" she teases.

"I hope not," I say, feeling a moment of wavering. "Is this really a good idea? Taking my obviously troubled daughter on a cross-country trip? Once I get her in the car, then what? What if she refuses to speak to me for three thousand miles? What if she doesn't? I have no idea what to say to her. God, Laney, she's so much like I was."

"Minus the black eye pencil," Laney quips.

"Minus the black eye pencil," I agree. "If I had been in her position, at her age, I'd have been wracked with guilt too. What do I say to her? How do I help her get through this?"

"You can do this," Laney tells me softly into my ear. "I don't know what to tell you to say, but I know you'll know when the time comes. You're a good mother, Jules."

I hear footsteps and glance up to see Ben walking in the bedroom.

He goes to close the door.

"Leave it open," I tell him, moving my cell away from my mouth so I'm not shouting in Laney's ear.

He stands there looking at me.

I say into the phone, "How about if I give you a call tomorrow night?"

"Promise me. No incommunicado, Jules. You have to promise me."

"I promise. Thanks for calling back. I know it's late."

"Never too late. Never. I'm glad you're coming, Jules." She sounds emotional. "You're doing the right thing."

I don't know if that's true or not, but at least I'm doing *something*. And the fact that Laney thinks I'm doing the right thing makes me feel better. Less like a lunatic, at least. And Laney didn't have any doubt that I could manage to drive my daughter and myself across country and manage to find Maine without being raped and murdered, our bodies left alongside the road. "Thanks, Laney. I'll talk to you tomorrow." I hang up and toss my cell on the bed.

"What's with the door?" Ben gestures to it. "I wanted to talk to you."

"We'll just have to talk quietly. I don't trust her. I wouldn't put it past her to run away." I go to my nightstand and unplug my Kindle from its charger. The battery was dead. I hadn't opened it since Caitlin died, which seems odd when I think about it. I've always been an avid reader. I used to read a book a week, sometimes more. I don't know why I want to take it with me. "I sent an e-mail to Joe, resigning," I tell him.

"You didn't even call him? *Jules*."

I ignore his tone, a mix of condemnation and disappointment. "I wasn't up to it."

He watches me wind up the charger. "So you're really doing this?" he asks, still glued to the same spot, in our bedroom, but not *really* in our bedroom, hovering near the open door. Not quite fully committed. A reflection of our relationship?

"I'm doing it." I nod harder than I need to and we meet each other's gazes. He's upset with me. But I'm not sure exactly why. I don't think it's because he's certain getting Haley into counseling right away is our best course of action. I feel like my taking Haley to Maine is . . . an inconvenience. An inconvenience because he'll have to do something with Izzy. An inconvenience because he'll have to tell his mother what his crazy wife has done with his crazy daughter.

I don't like the idea that somewhere deep inside, the idea that I'm going to tick off his mother gives me a little thrill.

He rubs the bridge of his nose between his thumb and finger. "Jules . . ." He says it in a sigh. As if he's trying to get up enough energy to care.

I wish he'd yell. At least then I'd know he *did* care. I don't mind if he disagrees with me. I just want him to feel something, *anything*, strongly. I want to think that this . . . his seeming *lack of caring*, about anything, is a result of the loss of our daughter. But I know that's not true. I saw signs of it before Caitlin died. Months ago . . . years ago.

Like our sex life, I can't exactly put my finger on when things changed. Or why. I think it must have happened sometime around when Haley went to high school. I took the part-time job. Ben started putting more hours in at work and fewer hours in at home. His explanations (or excuses?) were completely reasonable; the family business took a big hit when the economy floundered and then didn't recover. He and his brothers went back to working on properties instead of managing from the front seats of their pickups. And when Ben came home, he was tired; he didn't want to hear about my boring day filled with numbers from my accounting job, or tracking down the right kind of glitter for the new skirts I was making for Caitlin's cheer team. And to be fair to

Ben, I didn't press it. He was giving more time to his business and his brothers and mother, but I didn't challenge it. If I'm painfully honest with myself, maybe I even contributed to the fractures in our relationship. We stopped going out on dates by mutual consent; we were both so busy. Dinner out was expensive; the money could be better spent on braces or a new refrigerator. Both of us were full of excuses and explanations to justify ourselves and our behavior toward each other.

Ben and I stand there facing each other and I think about all we've been through over the years, the good and the bad, and a sense of nostalgia passes over me. When we get past this, when I feel like Haley is stable, I wonder if maybe Ben and I should look into marriage counseling. Maybe we just need a little help finding our way back to each other. I know I love him. I think he loves me. But I feel as if we're so far apart right now, even standing so close.

"And you're going to just leave Izzy?" he asks.

"You say that like I'm moving to Australia. I'm not *leaving* Izzy." I throw up both my hands. "Haley and I are going to Maine. We'll be back."

"You tell Izz?"

I lower my hands to my bony hips. "She's not too happy with me. She wants to go."

"That's a bad idea." He walks over to his dresser where I've stacked a pile of his boxer briefs and socks. I actually washed some clothes today for the sake of washing, not because the cat puked on stuff.

"I explained to Izzy that Haley needed to get away from here for a few days and that she was staying here with you. I hung your polos in your closet."

"Thanks." He doesn't smile when he says it.

I stand in the middle of the room, wondering what I should have packed that I've forgotten. It feels strange to just have a small bag, but this isn't a vacation. I don't need bathing suits or ski pants. I just need clothes to cover my body. I think I have what I need. My toiletry bag is on the bathroom sink; I'll throw it in my bag in the morning. I guess anything I've forgotten, I can buy. I've got a credit card.

"You wanted to talk to me about something," I remind him.

His back is to me. He's putting away his clothes. "I wanted to discuss alternatives to driving to Maine, but I guess you've made up your mind."

"I guess I have." I run my hand through my hair, realizing how tired I am. I walk over to my bed and pick up my pillow.

"Where you going with that?" he asks.

I hug the pillow to me. "I'm sleeping with Haley. I don't want her sneaking out in the middle of the night." I drift toward the door, thinking there must be something else we should be saying to each other. After all, I'm not just leaving Izzy behind, I'm leaving him, too.

He throws socks into a drawer. "I'm surprised she didn't climb out the window already."

"Couldn't. I nailed it shut from the outside."

"You did *what?*"

In the doorway, I turn to him, hugging my pillow to my chest. He's got that look on his face again. Like I'm crazy. It didn't seem like a crazy idea when I did it. It seemed logical. Listening to Haley's muffled protests from the other side of the window was almost funny.

"I got two big nails out of the shed and drove them into the windowsills on the outside so her windows won't open."

"And now you're sleeping with her." He looks over his shoulder at me.

I think about it, considering for a split second that maybe it *was* overkill. It's not. Haley's angry. She's also scared. Not just to be in a car alone with me, but with herself. I think being scared is what will make her run if she gets the opportunity. "Yes."

He turns away from me, shaking his head.

I go in to walk down the hallway, feeling a little bit like a mother lion protecting her cub. Right now, protecting Haley from the outside world seems fairly simple. I wonder, though, how a mother lion protects her cub from herself.

51 days

Morning comes quicker than I expect.

I slept in Haley's double bed with her, ignoring her protests and the pillow she wedged between us for fear I might bump into her while she slept. I even escorted her to the bathroom in the middle of the night and this morning, when she insisted she needed a shower, stalling I'm sure; I went in with her. I looked for sharp objects she might be able to use to cut herself and confiscated cuticle scissors and two pairs of tweezers. I told her to leave the door unlocked. When she made a smart-ass comment about needing privacy to shower, I showed her the little key over the doorjamb. She slammed the bathroom door in my face, but I had gotten the upper hand and we both knew it.

With Haley in the shower, I knock on Izzy's door. "You up?" I call.

"I'm up!" she hollers. I can hear her jump out of bed. "Getting dressed."

I rest my hand on her door, considering going in and trying to talk to her again. Trying to explain why I have to do this.

Instead, I go down the hallway to Caitlin's room, hesitate, then open the door. But I don't go in. I just stand there on the threshold, like my husband, not fully committed. I want to go in, but I'm not sure I should. I'm afraid if I do, the pain that's overwhelmed me for the last fifty-one days will swallow me up. And I can't let that happen. I can't for the sake of my other teen daughter who needs me. I can't for the sake of my family.

Caitlin's room looks as it did the day she died, minus the dirty clothes on the floor that I know Ben picked up. Her bed is still unmade. There's an open calculus book on her desk and her school backpack hangs over a chair. There's even a water glass still sitting on her nightstand. It's empty. I stare at it thinking that if I bring it to my lips, I might touch where her lips had been.

I close my eyes for a second and grip the doorjamb. I need to clean out her room. It's time. It's not healthy to let her room sit like this, like she's coming back, because she's not. Haley and Izzy need to take what they want of hers and I need to pack up her things and donate them.

But not today. When we come back, I'll do it.

I back up to go, afraid that if I stand here too long, I'll climb into her bed, where the sheets still smell faintly of her, and I won't be able to climb out. As I pull the door shut, I catch a glimpse of bright pink. Caitlin's running shoes. On impulse, I grab them. I have no idea why. She and I wear . . . *wore* the same size. Holding her sneaks with two fingers, I close the door. I stuff the running shoes in my bag on the bed. I'm already dressed. I grab my phone and slip it into my jeans pocket, pick up the bag with my purse in it, and head for the kitchen.

Ben's leaning on the counter reading the newspaper. Like it's any other day. "Coffee's made," he says without looking up.

"Thanks." I drop my bag on the floor and retrieve a mug from the cabinet. I keep stealing glances his way. I feel like I should say something. Like *we* should say something to each other. I watch him. Head down, eyes on the paper, he picks up his mug, brings it to his mouth, and takes a sip, slurping a little. He's always had good table manners, good manners in general, but the slurp irritates me. Always has.

He swallows and puts the mug down again. I can't remember the last time he pressed his mouth to mine. Just before Christmas, maybe? We both got a little drunk at a neighbor's party. We had sex when we got back here. Not great sex, but when is drunk sex ever great after you get out of your teens? It was the last time we touched intimately. And that makes me sad. We had such a good sex life for so many years. I miss it.

I walk over to lay my hand on his on the counter. It takes him a second to look up. "Two weeks," I say quietly. "That's all we'll be gone. Just two weeks."

He doesn't take my hand in his or make any attempt to touch me. He just keeps his hand there on the counter. "You think you can fix her in two weeks?"

I shake my head. "No. Of course not, but . . ." I pull my hand away, feeling silly. Clearly he's angry with me. He doesn't want to touch me. He doesn't want to be touched. "But maybe if I can get her to talk—" I stop and start again. "If I can get her away from here, away from all the things that remind her of Caitlin every minute she's awake, maybe we can work through some of her feelings. Maybe . . ." The truth is that I don't know exactly what I think I'm going to accomplish. I just know I have to do this.

Ben goes back to reading his paper and for a second I'm so angry that I want to rip the paper away from him and scream at him that it's time for him to damned well wake up and pay some attention to me, to our daughters who are still living, and to our family.

Instead, I walk away, grab my mug, and fill it with coffee.

Izzy comes into the kitchen dressed in her school uniform that couldn't have gotten that wrinkled if she'd balled it up and slept on it. I consider suggesting she throw her skirt and top in the dryer and set it on dewrinkle, but I bite my tongue. I don't want our parting words to be of criticism.

"Hey, Dad," she says.

"Hey, Izz." He doesn't look up.

She meets my gaze, but she doesn't say *good morning*.

"I'm sorry," I say softly, going to her. I wrap my arm around her in sort of a side hug. Tears burn the backs of my eyelids, but I don't let myself cry.

Her lip quivers. She doesn't hug me back, but she doesn't pull away, either.

I hear Haley come out of the bathroom. "Leaving in ten minutes," I shout. I want to get this show on the road. Nothing good can come from lingering. I look down at my youngest. "How about some juice? Waffles? I can pop them in the toaster oven for you." I think about offering to make her pancakes, but she and Ben need to leave in fifteen minutes or she'll be late for school.

"Just juice." Izzy pulls away from me.

I get the OJ while she gets a glass.

I'm sipping my coffee when Haley walks into the kitchen, which totally surprises me because I was afraid I was going to have to physically drag her out of the house and into my car. The look on her face tells me she still doesn't want to go, but she looks resigned to going. I exhale with relief. "You pack a bag?"

She's standing near the breakfast table, looking out the window, bouncing that ball that I hate. She's wearing black jeans, a black long-sleeved T-shirt, and black Converse sneakers. Her backpack is on her back. She doesn't answer me.

"Haley—"

"I've got stuff in here." She sort of shrugs her shoulder, indicating the bag on her back. She couldn't possibly have more than a pair of jeans, a sweatshirt, and some panties in there.

I bite my tongue. "We should go," I say quietly, to no one in particular.

Izzy hasn't drunk any of her juice. She's just standing there.

"Walk us out," I tell Izzy. "Bring my bag?" I point to the green duffel on the floor. I bought it on one of our trips to Maine years ago. It came from the big LL Bean store in Freeport. We bought tents the same day. Ben had this idea we could all go camping. It would become our new family *togetherness* activity. We went twice. I wonder what happened to the tents. In the attic probably.

Ben is still reading his paper and slurping his coffee. I brush my hand against his arm. "Ben, we're going."

He looks up and meets my gaze. I think he's going to say, *I'll go too. We'll go together.* Instead, he glances in Izzy's direction. "You ready to go?"

Surprisingly, Haley leads the way, bouncing the ball as she walks. I realize now that she's wearing wireless headphones. Listening to music on her iPhone. Here, but not engaged. But she's not fighting me, at least. She must have concluded, at some point in the last twelve hours, that I wasn't kidding about committing her.

And I don't think I was.

We all walk out into the bright morning sun. It's already getting warm out, the way it does in the desert, even this early in the year. Looking out across the bare yards, the yucca and palm trees and how ugly it seems, I wonder why I ever agreed to move here. I wonder how I ended up spending the last twenty years of my life in a place I hate. Suddenly I yearn for the green grasses and sparkling ponds of Maine.

In the driveway, I go to Ben and put out my arms. He hugs me, but it's awkward. His hands don't go in the right place and neither do mine. I lift up on my toes to kiss him and he leans down, but he turns his head so my mouth only brushes the corner of his. "We'll be fine," I whisper. "Call you tonight."

He lets me go without reassuring me *everything really will be all right, Julia. Haley will be okay. We'll get through this. Our family will get through it.*

Haley makes her way slowly to the car. She doesn't tell Ben or Izzy good-bye. I have no idea why she's pissed at Ben. She gets in the backseat, not the front.

I turn to Izzy. She throws herself against me and I hug her tightly. "I won't be gone long." I kiss the top of her head. "I'll be back before you know it." I kiss her temple, then her head again, breathing in the scent of her. "It's going to be okay, Izzy. We're going to be okay." My last words catch in my throat and my legs feel weak for a moment. So weak that I'm afraid I might drop to my knees taking her with me. Sheer willpower keeps me upright. I have to be strong. I have to do this.

"Please don't leave me, Mom," Izzy begs. "Please. Please let me go with you. Please, Mom," she wails.

"Izz," Ben says quietly from behind us.

"I'll call you tonight." I extricate myself from the tangle of her arms. "Ben."

He takes her by the arm.

"Mom," Izzy sobs, and then she turns to her father.

Thank God he puts his arms around her.

I grab my bag that Izzy has dropped on the cement driveway. I throw it in the backseat beside Haley, who appears to have not witnessed her little sister's breakdown. I get into the driver side and start the car. Tears are running down my cheeks, but I'm okay. I'm *okay*.

I back out the drive and pull away without looking at Ben and Izzy. She'll be okay. Izzy's upset, but she'll be okay, I tell myself as I near the end of our street. Two weeks. I'll be gone two weeks. I'll be back in no time.

I stop at the stop sign and look into my rearview mirror.

Izzy has let go of her dad and walked to the end of our driveway. She's just standing there in her wrinkled uniform, her hair a mess, her arms at her sides, her hair bright red in the sunlight. I can tell she's still crying. Sobbing.

I hesitate and then lift my foot off the brake and hit the gas.

Chapter 20

Haley

50 days, 9 hours

"So, what?" I say, my tone hostile. I pull one earbud out of my ear. "Now we're *not* going?"

I stare at Mom as she starts to make a U-turn in the middle of the intersection at the end of our street. Only she does it so fast that I have to grab the back of the front seat to keep from flying around in the back. A bald guy walking his dog turns to look at us. My ball falls out of my hand and rolls under Mom's seat. I sat behind her on purpose just so I wouldn't have to look at her. I'm so angry. I can't believe she's doing this. I can't believe she's making me do it.

But maybe she's changed her mind. Maybe she finally realized how freakin' crazy a road trip with her crazy daughter would be.

I lean down to find my ball and she hits the gas, throwing me back in the seat. I try to wedge myself in with one hand while I search for the ball with the other. But it takes a minute for her to make the turn and I'm still getting thrown around. It hadn't occurred to me I'd need my seat belt before we left the neighborhood. "Mom! What the hell?" I open and close my hand, searching frantically on the floor. I can't lose the ball. I can't lose it.

We fly by neighbors' houses. Mom's driving over the speed

limit, which she never does. I wonder if she's having a breakdown. A breakdown because Izzy's having a meltdown. For a minute there I really thought Mom was going to drive to Maine with me in the backseat. I'll have to remember to thank Izzy for saving my life.

If she ever speaks to me again.

I'm half on the seat, half on the floor, and the other earbud falls out of my ear. I finally feel the little ball under my fingertips. I almost have it when Mom slams on the brakes. My face hits the back of the seat. "Mom!" I holler.

I look around the seat and up to see her glare at me in the rearview mirror. "Stay in the car."

"What?" I snatch up the ball and scramble up onto the seat to see Izzy through the windshield, still standing there in our driveway. "So we're still going?"

She doesn't answer me.

Dad is a couple of feet behind Izzy. He says something to Mom, but I don't catch what it is.

Mom is out of the car, leaning on the open door. "We're leaving in five minutes, Izzy. Get your stuff."

Izzy turns and runs faster than I've ever seen the little runt run on those chubby legs of hers. What the hell? Now Izzy's coming, too? That's even worse than riding three thousand miles with Mom. The way Izzy looks at me, it makes me just want to disappear. Or have never existed at all.

This *cannot* be happening. Maybe I should have let her commit me to the nut floor.

Dad says something else to Mom and Mom closes the door hard and walks around the front of the car and up the driveway toward him. I slide to the middle of the backseat to watch them. Mom's back is to me. I can't read Dad's lips because Mom's between him and me now.

I look at the car door, trying to think fast. I'm mad and I'm scared and I'm mad. I can't ride to Maine in this car with her. I certainly can't do it with Izzy. The way she looks at me I feel like I should be wearing a scarlet *M* for Murderer. Caitlin was reading

The Scarlet Letter in her Lit class. We were talking about it the morning before she died. We both liked the book even though none of our friends did. Remembering that makes me tear up and now I feel worse. Even more scared.

I cannot do this road-trip thing with them.

If I get out, if I run, I can cut through the Stevensons' backyard. Two blocks and I can be out on the main street. There's no way Mom would follow me on foot. She couldn't catch me if she tried. And by the time she gets in the car and gets out of the neighborhood, I'll be long gone. There are plenty of places to hide: fast-food places, a mini-mart.

If I call Todd, he'll come get me. We could head for Alaska. Today. I've already got a bag packed. But actually, there's not much in it. I wish I'd thought of this before. If I'm going to Alaska, I want to take more of my things. Too bad. So sad.

But I've got money and I've got Caitlin's ATM card. There's no way Mom or Dad thought to close her bank account yet. I'm sure she wouldn't mind if I used the money she was saving for Bonnaroo, to go to Alaska. Well, she'd probably *mind* because I'm going with Todd and she hated Todd. She used to tell me he was a loser and that I could do better. That I deserved better. She probably wouldn't say that now, after what I did to her.

I pull my cell out of my sports bra and text Todd.

Where are you?

I watch Mom and Dad through the windshield. He's pissed. I can tell by the way he's standing. Her, too. She's all stiff. But no one is yelling. My family is so civilized. No one ever yells. Except Nana and only when she's really drunk and no one will pay attention to her.

My phone dings.

At Poker's

Poker is his older brother. Another loser. He lives with his *baby mama*, but he's dating this other girl he knows from work. He washes dishes at a diner near the pawnshop all the tourists go to.

Pick me up?

He texts right back.

Thawt u wet grounded

He spells *thought* wrong. It's not a typo. He's the worst speller I've ever texted.

I hold my phone in my hand. I didn't tell Todd my mother was trying to kidnap me and take me to Maine when we were texting yesterday. I don't know why. Do I have some secret desire to ride in the car with my mom for the next week and listen to her cry? Or worse, talk to me in that quiet voice of hers that makes me feel like I'm crazier than I am?

Can you pick me up or not? I text back, hitting the keyboard hard with my thumb.

Haf hr

Now, I tell him. After I send it, I add, **Alaska, here we come.**

I stare at my phone, waiting for him to answer. If he won't come for me, I guess I'll just run. I don't know what else to do.

My phone dings.

Cool

Not my house. Will text u in a few.

I glance up at Mom and Dad; they're too busy fighting to think about me. I look at the door. I push the ball down deep in my jeans pocket and slide my hand across the seat to get my backpack. I look at them again and put my hand on the door.

Just as I'm about to open the door, Mom turns around and starts for the car. "Izzy!" she hollers. "Let's go, sweetie." She's saying *sweetie*, but her voice is high-pitched.

Shit.

Chapter 21

Julia

51 days

I stop halfway to the car, turn around, and hold my hand up to him the way he does to me sometimes. The gesture has always annoyed me. It's as if when we get into a disagreement, he suddenly wants to treat me like he's my father. "I can't do this right now, Ben."

I turn back to the car and see that Haley's slid over in the backseat. She's leaning against the door. I keep my eye on her as I walk quickly toward her. She looks like she's about to bolt. I point at her and our gazes lock. She looks down. *Caught. Busted.* The little witch was going to get out of the car.

"I'll call you tonight, Ben," I say, afraid to take my eyes off my captive in the backseat of my Toyota. "Izzy!" I holler again. There's a tightness in my chest, a sense of panic. I feel like I can't breathe. Like if I don't get out of here now . . . I don't know what will happen.

When I reach the driver side, I yank open my door and lean in. "Going somewhere?" I ask my daughter, sounding pretty un-motherlike.

She throws herself back on the seat, her cell phone clutched in her hand.

"I told you. I'll call nine-one-one," I threaten.

"You wouldn't do it." Haley says it so softly that I'm not absolutely sure I heard her say it. "You don't have the balls."

"Try me," I say just as quietly.

She raises her phone and begins to text. I stand up and look toward the house. It's been at least five minutes. It's probably been ten. Where's Izzy? I'm tempted to go into the house for her, but I'm afraid Haley will run and I doubt Ben would know to go after her.

He's still standing in the driveway, right where I left him. He still has a chance to say he'll come with us. Now that I'm taking Izzy with me, I think he just might do it. Izzy's always been his favorite. *Please, Ben. Come with us. Run away with us. Run away for us.*

I look at him, then back at Haley when her phone dings again. "Who are you texting?" I ask her, then glance at the house again.

She doesn't answer.

I look at Ben again. *Please,* I pray. Not to God. I'm not sure I even believe in God anymore. So not to Him, but to . . . the powers of the universe maybe. *Please come with us. Or please, Izzy. Get your ass in the car.*

Haley is texting like crazy.

"Who are you texting?" I repeat. She's in the middle of the backseat, clutching her phone like it's a lifeline, which for teens, I suppose it is.

Her phone dings again.

I don't know what gets into me. I reach into the back of my car and snatch the iPhone right out of her hand.

"Give me that," Haley screeches. When she can't reach it, she moves toward the door.

I slam my door shut and hit the lock button as my seventeen-year-old daughter hurls herself against the car door. I hit the child lock button on my door's console.

Haley tries to open the door several times. "Let me out! Let me out!" The door handle makes a sound every time she releases it. She's shrieking at me like a caged animal. "Give me my phone!"

I clutch it in my hand and look down at it. A text pops up.

B their in 5

At the same moment, the handle of the front passenger door rattles. Then there's a knock on the window. "Mom?"

I look up.

It's Izzy. She's standing at the passenger side door, loaded down with bags. She's got so many, I don't know how she made it down the driveway on her own. And she's got one of the pillows from her bed.

Whenever we took a road trip when our girls were younger, they all used to bring their own pillows. We haven't gone on a road trip together in years. We just got too busy once Haley hit high school.

"Mom?" Izzy's panicking now too. Her voice is muffled, but I can hear it in her high-pitched tone.

What am I doing to my children? What am I doing in this car, about to set off across the country? We're so damaged. All of us. This is insanity.

But I can't stop myself now. It's as if I'm moving forward and nothing can alter my path.

"I'm ready," Izzy hollers, banging on the door with her knee. "Let me in."

I start the car, but I'm hesitant to unlock the doors. Then I realize that as long as the child locks are engaged, Haley can't get out the back door. I lower the passenger-side front window a little and duck down so that I can see Izzy's flushed face. I'm still holding Haley's phone. I look down at the phone in my hand. The message is from Todd. Her ex. Todd is the one who doesn't know the difference between *there* and *their*. He's coming for her. He was coming here to take her away from me.

I don't know what I'm going to do with her phone, but I can't give it back to her. She really was going to run.

I lean over again and look at Izzy through the open crack in the window. "Listen carefully. Walk to the back of the car. I'm going to unlock the doors. When you hear it click, open the hatch, put your bags in, and close it. Close it fast."

"What the hell, Mom?" Haley hollers. "You think I'm going to climb over the freakin' seat?"

I ignore her. Because I think she just might. I would have, when I was her age, had I been in the position she's in right now. I once got out of the car when my stepfather stopped at a red light. I didn't go home for three days, staying with different friends so he wouldn't catch up to me.

Izzy walks to the back of the car.

"Julia? What are you doing?" Ben calls.

I turn to look through the backseat to the hatch. When I see Izzy standing there, I unlock the doors.

Haley's slumped against the back door. Her arms are crossed over her chest. Her eyes are filled with tears. She won't look at me.

"It's going to be all right, Haley," I say quietly.

She doesn't respond.

Izzy drops things into the back: two zip duffel bags, a laundry bag, a shopping bag, a canvas bag. I can't imagine what she's bringing. I can't imagine how she got it all together in ten minutes. She slams the hatch and runs around to the passenger side.

"I'm ready! I'm ready!" Izzy opens the front door and throws her purple school backpack onto the floor. She's still hugging her pillow to her chest and she's got her favorite cup in her hand. A Tervis cup with her name on it; Caitlin gave it to her for Christmas.

As Izzy drops into the passenger seat and slams the door, a can of cat food falls out of her sweatshirt pocket and rolls onto the floor. I have no idea why she's got cat food in her sweatshirt, but I'm glad she thought to bring the sweatshirt. She's still wearing her school uniform.

Izzy glances into the backseat. "What's going on with her?" she asks, pushing back in her seat and fastening her seat belt.

I glance in the rearview mirror. I still have Haley's iPhone in my hand. "Put your seat belt on," I tell Haley.

She doesn't answer, but she does as I say.

I put my own seat belt on and look up at the house one last

time. Ben's still standing there and he still looks pissed, but he looks sad, too.

But I can't be responsible for everyone's sadness.

I shift the car into gear and make a U-turn.

As I wait to pull out onto the main street, outside of our neighborhood, Haley's phone dings in my hand.

"Give me my phone." Haley's voice is low and threatening.

I look down at the screen.

Wear r u?

Todd again.

There's a break in traffic. I go.

"At least let me text him back," Haley snaps from the backseat.

I put down the window and hurl her cell phone out. It makes a satisfying sound as it hits the pavement and I imagine someone running over it as I put up my window.

"Radio on or off?" I ask no one in particular.

Chapter 22

Izzy

3 years, 8 months

Holy H. Mom just threw She Who Shall Not Be Named's iPhone out the window. It's new from Christmas. It has to be worth three or four hundred bucks.

I'm afraid to say anything. I just sit in the seat, my back pushed against the seat, staring straight ahead. I know my eyes have to be bugging out. I don't know who the one in the backseat was texting, but I guess Mom wants to make sure she doesn't do it again.

She's cussing in the backseat, but I barely hear her. She's like static on the radio to me.

I've been wanting a cell phone, but Mom keeps saying I'm not old enough. She says when I'm old enough to go places unsupervised, I can have one. Thirteen seems to be the magic number right now, but I don't think she'll make me wait that long. For now, I have an old iPod touch that I can text my friends with. I'm glad I don't have a phone because I bet She Who Shall Not Be Named would try to get me to give it to her.

I shove my pillow down on the floor between my leg and the door. There's so many things going on right this second that I can barely wrap my head around them. Mom just destroyed an iPhone. I'm pretty sure we're kidnapping the witch in the backseat and Mom . . . my mother came back for me. She told me I couldn't come with her and then she changed her mind.

I can't believe Mom came back for me.

I can't believe she came back. I'm so happy I want to cry, but I'm not going to cry because then Mom would be worried about me and I don't want her to be worried about me. She's got enough to be anxious about with the crazy one sitting behind us who isn't shouting cuss words anymore, but I think she's saying them under her breath. She hit the back of Mom's seat and then she kicked it, but Mom acted like she didn't notice so I pretended not to notice either.

I look down at the can of cat food near my left foot. I think about trying to slide it under my seat with my heel, but since Mom didn't notice it, I decide to leave it there for now. No sense drawing attention to it. Not this close to home.

I take a deep breath. I hope I brought everything I need.

When I ran into the house, I packed as fast as I could. I already had the clothes I'd packed from yesterday that I didn't unpack in case Mom changed her mind. I didn't really think she'd change her mind though. If I had thought she was going to, I'd have packed more stuff last night.

I didn't know what to grab. She said I only had five minutes and there was no way I was going to take any longer than that. But it was so hard to know what I should take. I've never been on a road trip across the country with my mom and my rotten sister. I don't even know which way we're going so I didn't know what kind of clothes to bring. Obviously if we were heading south and then east, I'd need clothes for warmer weather. North and then east and I needed stuff for cooler weather. I think I brought some for both, but I'm so excited, I'm not sure what I've got in the bags.

I'm so excited to be with Mom. It would be better if She Who Shall Not Be Named wasn't with us, but not what Liz Lemon would call a deal breaker. (Me and Caitlin and the one who sent her to her maker used to binge-watch *30 Rock* whenever Mom and Dad were out and would leave the big girls in charge of me.) Even with She Who Shall Not Be Named here, I'm still excited to be in the car. And shotgun! I love riding shotgun because you can see everything so much better. I don't get to ride in the front that much. Mom's paranoid about the airbag, but I love it up here. Riding shotgun, I feel like I'm a part of what's going on. I can hear and see everything; I'm not just watching, I'm part of the world. The backseat makes me feel like a loser.

I glance up in the rearview mirror. I don't know why. I don't care what *she's* doing. It would have been okay with me if Mom had thrown her out of the car with the iPhone, but I look anyway.

She's kind of turned sideways, her knees drawn up on the seat. She's got her eyes closed with her cheek pressed against the leather seat. She's got something clenched in her hand, but I can't see what it is. And she's got her wireless earbuds in which is proof that she belongs in a psych ward because her phone is gone. She can't be listening to music.

I look at Mom. She reaches up into the console that holds her sunglasses in the roof and gets her Ray-Bans. As she puts them on she looks at me for just a second before she looks at the road again because she's getting onto the Woodbury Beltway that goes around the city. We live on the west side of Vegas, near Red Canyon, in Summerlin.

I watch Mom as she turns the steering wheel on the car and I want to pinch myself or something to convince myself this is really happening. I still can't believe I'm in the car with her. That she came back for me. I only had one hesitation when she told me to get my things and get in the car and that was about Caitlin.

As I was throwing stuff into any bag I could find in my room, I wondered if Caitlin would still be there when I got back. I knew she wasn't enough of a reason to stay because she's dead and all, but it did make me sad to think it was possible that we couldn't talk anymore.

When I heard Mom call my name again from outside, I grabbed all the bags I'd filled on the bed and I ran for the door. Mr. Cat was meowing, but I didn't even care. In the doorway I stopped and I looked back at the posters of the rain forest and Egyptian mummy on my wall. I told Caitlin good-bye and I told her I loved her. Just in case she can't come to Maine with us.

Chapter 23

Julia

51 days

I'm shaking. I grip the steering wheel tightly and focus straight ahead as I get on the beltway that goes around the city. I'm angry and upset and strangely . . . exhilarated.

I can't believe I just threw a four hundred dollar iPhone out the window. What was I thinking?

I know exactly what I was thinking, or at least what I was reacting to. Haley can't talk to Todd if she doesn't have her phone. She can't run off with him if he has no way to contact her. So the phone went out the window.

My image of the mother lion comes to mind again.

But where was my common sense when I did it?

Do lionesses have common sense or is it all primal?

I could have just called and cancelled Haley's phone service. I could have put *my* number on hers and had a new phone instead of the old one I have that won't always connect to the Internet and sometimes drops calls.

Haley and Caitlin always got a new phone when it was released and Ben and I got the hand-me-downs. Ben and I once had a discussion about whether or not they needed the latest and greatest. I was opposed to new cell phones every year. He said he busted his ass working seven days a week so he *could* buy his teenage daughters the latest cell phones on the market. I lost the argument. Mostly because his money pays the bills. We have been using my money to save for college and to do fun things like go skiing or buy the new sixty-five-inch TV Ben had to have for Christmas.

I wonder what happened to Caitlin's phone. It's a thought that comes out of nowhere and seems so . . . alien. It's doubly weird because she's been dead almost two months and this is the first time it's occurred to me to wonder where it is. How have I not thought about it before?

In the last twenty-four hours or so I've been thinking about all sorts of things that I can't figure out why I hadn't thought about before. I feel as if I'm walking out of a dense fog after being lost for two months. I'm by no means completely free, but the murkiness is lifting and my vision is a little clearer.

I remember that someone gave us everything from the car before it was hauled away to wherever totaled cars from fatal accidents go. I wonder if Ben cancelled Caitlin's cell phone contract. Was there a disconnect fee or do you draw a bye in the case of death? It seems morbid to be thinking such a thing, but in a way it feels good. Like it's drawing me into some sort of normalcy.

But whom am I kidding? What's going on in this car is anything but normal.

I just threw a perfectly good iPhone out the window.

I basically kidnapped my teenager.

There are probably laws against holding seventeen-year-olds against their will in a Toyota RAV4. Without a cell phone to her name.

And not only did I take one daughter against her will, but I took my ten-year-old out of school without notifying anyone. You don't just take a kid out of school for two weeks without filling out the proper forms, making arrangements for homework and makeup tests and quizzes. Not nowadays you don't. I'm not even sure I'm allowed to take Izzy out of school for this long.

I know Ben thinks I've got a screw loose. Maybe he's right.

I head north, around the city. I don't even know where I'm going. I mean, I *know* where I'm going. I'm going to Maine. I'm going to Laney's house and I'm going to have a glass of wine with her on her front porch. But I don't know exactly what highways I'm taking. Yesterday I google-mapped from here to Portland, just to get an idea of which way I should go. You have to go north or south to get around the Grand Canyon from Vegas. I decided to go north for no reason other than that I like driving through Utah and I haven't in years. When we make our first stop, I'll put something into the GPS. Maybe not Laney's address, but a general direction at least, so we don't end up in Canada.

I glance at Izzy, beside me. She's looking a little wild-eyed. The cell-phone-out-the-window thing must have scared her. I don't think I've ever done anything crazy like that in front of her. It's been years since I did anything crazy at all. The impulsiveness of my teenage years ended when I married Ben and we had a family.

I glance at Izzy again. It was probably a mistake to go back for her. She shouldn't be in this car with us. Not with Haley in the state she is. My eldest daughter's so angry with me that *nothing* she could do would shock me right now. I shouldn't be subjecting Izzy to this. If I had any sense at all, I'd get off the beltway and call Ben to come get her. It would be the smart thing to do.

But then I look at Izzy again and she turns to me and beams the way she did when she was a little girl and I don't have the heart to call Ben and tell him to come get her. I just don't.

So I reach out and grab her hand and squeeze it. "You sure you want to do this?" I ask her quietly. Not because I don't want Haley to hear us, but because I need Izzy to understand the gravity of this voyage. I know she has to know Haley's a mess, but I'm not sure she understands just how big a mess her sister is. "We can meet your dad somewhere. You can go home with him," I tell her, putting my hand back on the steering wheel. I'm still feeling a little shaky.

Izzy shakes her head violently. "I don't want to go back, Mom. I want to stay with you. I don't want to go home with Dad."

She makes no mention of wanting to be with her sister in her time of need, but that's probably expecting too much.

I glance in the rearview mirror. Haley is curled up in practically a fetal position on the backseat. Her eyes are closed. She's put her earbuds in her ears even though there's no music to listen to now. She's blocking me out. Blocking the world out. Her hand is moving. I glance at the highway and then at her again in the mirror and I realize she's rolling that ball around in her hand.

"Haley and I need to talk about some serious stuff, Izzy," I try to explain. "Stuff a ten-year-old girl shouldn't have to hear."

She's quiet for a second, then, "Is it worse stuff than *my sister is dead because my other sister crashed her?*" she asks.

I feel my lower jaw quiver. I concentrate on the road in front of me. Even though I'm going the speed limit, I feel like we're moving in slow motion. It seems like everyone, the world, is flying by us, but we're standing still. "Probably not any worse than that," I hear myself say.

Izzy laces her fingers together, drops her hands to her lap, and looks out through the windshield. "I didn't think so."

I can't help but smile and for a moment I enjoy the warmth of the sunshine coming in through the windows. I wonder when my Isobel became such a wise, old soul. Maybe she was always this way and I never noticed before. "It could get ugly," I say.

Izzy cuts her eyes at me. "Uglier than the last two months?"

I press my lips together and concentrate on the road. "Probably not."

We drive for a couple of minutes in silence. Then Izzy asks, "So what did she do? She tried to off herself, didn't she?"

When I don't answer, Izzy goes on. "You might as well tell me what she did. I'm going to find out. We're going to be in this car at least five days. It's not going to be quick between you having to stop to pee every two hours and driving the speed limit all the way."

I almost laugh. My bladder isn't what it once was. I do have to stop a lot.

"So did she try to *end it all?*" Izzy's tone is not very sympathetic.

"I can hear you talking about me," Haley shouts from the backseat.

I glance in the rearview mirror at Haley. Right now, I'd prefer her mouthiness, even her swearing, to this silence. Her silence scares me. "We're going to be spending a lot of time together, girls. We need to be civil to each other."

"I can be civil." Izzy folds her hands together again. "Totally. So what did she do? She try to OD on Nana's pills? Or did she try to snuff herself by slitting her wrists? She uses a lot of gauze and stuff from the first aid kit in the bathroom. I've been seeing the wrappers for weeks."

I look at Izzy, then at the road again. I want to ask her why she didn't tell me if she was suspicious that her sister was doing something unsafe, but I don't because I wouldn't want her to think that what Haley's done is in any way her fault or her responsibility.

"Do you mind if I tell her?" I ask Haley, looking in the rearview mirror again.

"It's pretty obvious what I think doesn't matter." Haley's words drip with resentment.

I exhale, debating what to say. I wasn't planning on having this conversation today, although I have been thinking about things we need to talk about.

Last night, when I was lying in bed beside Haley, it occurred to me that we haven't talked about Caitlin's death. Not at all. We've all been floating around our house in such stupefying shock, but we haven't *said* anything to each other. Not even that we miss her.

That's one of the first things Haley needs to do, I think. She needs to acknowledge the loss. Maybe what we all need to do, me included. We need to concede, out loud, and to each other the profound loss we feel. Along those same lines, I was thinking that we need to talk about the end result. About Caitlin being gone and Haley still being here.

But I wasn't counting on Izzy being with us. And I was thinking maybe Haley and I could somehow work our way up to some of the difficult conversations we need to have. But I hadn't thought about having to talk to my ten-year-old about a complicated thing like self-mutilation. I'm not even sure where to begin.

So I just say it. "Haley's been hurting herself."

Izzy's brow crinkles. "What do you mean?"

I take a breath. "Have you ever heard of cutting?"

Izzy stares at me for a second and then recognition crosses her face. "Like cutting yourself up with a knife and making yourself bleed?" She turns around and looks at Haley and I realize this may be the first time she's looked at her sister since Caitlin died. "You gotta be S-ing me."

I look at her, putting on my "Mommy disapproves of your language" face.

"What?" Izzy asks, turning back around. "I didn't say the *word*." She rides along for a minute in silence and then asks, "Is that why she was using all the gauze?"

I nod.

Again, Izzy frowns. "Why would she do that? Doesn't it hurt?"

"I can still freakin' hear you," Haley shouts.

I don't know what gets into me. The same thing that made me throw the phone out the car window, I suppose. I signal and pull off the beltway onto an exit in a sudden movement.

Izzy's wide-eyed again.

I don't say a word until I've pulled into a mini-mart, parked the car, and shut off the engine. Then I turn around in my seat. My heart is pounding. A part of me wants to fold up into a fetal position like Haley in the front seat of my car and cry. But I don't. Instead, I speak slowly and calmly, but with a tone that makes it clear I mean what I say. "You will not speak that way to me. Do you understand me, Haley Grace? I'm your mother. You don't have to like me. You don't even have to love me, but you'll show me the respect I deserve. Do I make myself clear?"

Haley doesn't look at me, but she nods. It's a barely adequate movement to signify assent, but it's enough.

I turn back around, putting my hands on the steering wheel. I'm breathing hard. How the hell am I going to do this? I'm barely in one piece. How am I going to help my daughter pick up her pieces?

Everyone is quiet in the car. The sounds outside—the traffic, a man and his son walking past us in the parking lot—seem far away.

The first thing I need to do if I'm going to help Haley is pee, I decide. I was in such a hurry to get out this morning that I didn't think to run to the bathroom before we left. Now I really have to go.

I pull my key out of the ignition. "Can you grab my wallet out of my bag?" I ask Haley. I had thrown my handbag in my duffel bag this morning.

She makes a sound that expresses that she's clearly put out by my request, but I hear her seat belt unbuckle. I almost exhale audibly with relief. I have no clue what I would have done if she'd refused me.

I look at Izzy, who's now acting as if all of this is everyday stuff. I have no idea where I'm finding the strength to do this. I'm waiting for the bottom to fall out any second. Mine.

"Pit stop." I sound almost cheery when I speak again. "Go to the bathroom and then we'll get some snacks."

"Can I have an Icee?" Izzy asks.

I think for a second. I usually try to get her to get a bottle of juice or something a little healthier than a big bucket of frozen sugar, but I nod. Secretly, I like frozen drinks out of mini-mart machines, too, especially the Coke ones. "You can, and I think I'll have one. And while we're here, we might as well gas up. Next stop, Utah." I open my door, which unlocks Izzy's, but not Haley's, because the child safety locks are still deployed.

"I knew it!" Izzy says excitedly. "I was hoping this was the way we were going." She opens the car door and wrestles with her pillow and backpack to get out. Once she's out of the car, she pulls off her sweatshirt and throws it on the seat. She stands there like she's considering something, then asks, "Can you pop the back?"

I release the hatch, close my door, and take a breath before I open the back door. I have no idea what I'm going to do if Haley runs. I can't see myself chasing her across the parking lot, but I can't see myself just letting her go, at this point, either.

She hands me my wallet without making eye contact.

"Thank you. Now come on."

"I don't need to go."

"You're coming anyway. You don't think I'm leaving you alone in the car, do you?" I step back and hold open the door. "Go to the bathroom and get a drink. Grab a snack if you're hungry or anticipate being hungry later. I didn't pack anything." I was once one of those mothers who cut up fruit and packed a cooler of drinks when we went somewhere in the car. "It will be another three or four hours before we stop again."

She slowly gets out of the car and walks toward the convenience store door. Her body language is screaming protest, but she's going. She's doing what I say.

"Izzy," I call.

"Coming."

I watch Haley open the convenience store door and go inside. I don't want to let her get out of my sight.

"Come on, Izz," I call.

She's got her head inside the back. She sounds like she's talking to herself. Just as I'm about to holler to her again, she stands up and closes the hatch. I hit the remote in my hand to lock the car and wait for her.

"You want me to go into the bathroom with her?" she whispers to me as she walks into the store in front of me.

I eye Haley's back. "We all go together."

Chapter 24

Haley

50 days, 10 hours

I can't believe she's going to follow me into the bathroom. Does she think she's going into the stall with me too?

I go into the last stall, pull down my jeans, and sit. I pee and wipe, but I don't get up. I listen to the two of them in the other stalls. I roll the ball between my fingers because I don't want to bounce it on a public bathroom floor. That would be gross.

I can't believe she's really going through with this driving-to-Maine thing. *Unbelievable.*

I have to get out of here. I have to get away. I just don't know how, now that I don't have my phone.

I hear one toilet flush and Izzy's footsteps, then Mom flushes and walks out of the other stall. Water comes on. Izzy says something about the blue soap in the dispenser; she thinks it smells like blueberries. Mom laughs and says she thinks it does too.

I listen to the water running in the sinks and their voices. Izzy's trying to decide if she's getting a blue Icee or a red one. She's acting like she's on summer vacation. She's such a doofus. And it's so cute. I wish soap in a public bathroom that smells like blueberries could make me as happy as she sounds.

The rumble of the blow dryer echoes off the tile walls and I drop my head to my hands. Mom and Izzy are still talking.

I can't do this. I have to get away from these two, but I don't know where I can go or how I can get there. I need Todd. He'll come get me. I just have to figure out a way to call him.

A phone, a phone! My kingdom for a phone!

I did a project in the fall in English class about literary quotes still used today and how we change them. Richard III said that in a play written by Shakespeare, only he needed a horse, not a phone.

Izzy doesn't have a phone; Mom says she's not old enough to have one yet. Izzy does have an iPod touch that I might be able to text from, but I'm not sure if she brought it and even if she did, how do I get it?

I hear the bathroom door open and Izzy goes out. I can tell by the sound of the footfall that it's her. She slaps her feet as she walks, like her feet are too big for her body.

"Haley?" Mom calls.

"I'll be out in a minute."

She doesn't answer right away.

I make a loud sound so she knows how annoyed I am. "It's not like there's a back door in here. I'll be out in a sec."

She hesitates again. "Okay. I'll be in the store." She opens the door, then calls back, "Do you need anything from your bag?"

I guess she means a tampon. I wish I *did* need one. I'm starting to get a little worried. "Nope. I'll be out in a minute."

The door closes behind her and I listen, just to make sure she really left the bathroom and isn't trying to fake me out. When I'm sure she's gone, I flush and pull up my jeans. Just as I'm walking to the sink, a woman a little older than Mom comes in.

"See you soon," she says into her cell. She makes eye contact with me and smiles. I smile back. A big Caitlin smile. I have no idea why I do it. I'm not usually smiley with strangers.

Caitlin was the friendly one of the two of us. No surprise there. No one could resist her gorgeous blond hair and green eyes. I'm sure she was destined to be Homecoming Queen, Prom Queen, and Queen of the freakin' May.

In the mirror, I watch the woman go into the bathroom stall behind me. My gaze shifts to my reflection. I look like total crap. My skin is blotchy, my eyebrows need plucking, and I didn't even bother with eyeliner this morning. My eyes look little and squinty.

I squirt blue soap from the dispenser into my hand. I can't resist. I lift it to my nose and sniff.

And as shitty as my life is, it makes me smile because it *does* sort of smell like blueberries. I rub my hands together, soaping them up.

I eye the closed door of the stall behind me and it occurs to me that I don't have a cell phone but *she* has a cell phone. So how do I get it? If she sets it on the sink while she washes her hands, do I just take it and run? Then what? Run where? I don't know where we are. I'm not even sure what exit we got off on. And what if she calls the police? I'm pretty sure Todd can't pick me up from jail.

I don't want to keep her phone. I just want to borrow it for a minute.

She flushes behind me and I keep soaping up my hands. As she comes up to the sink beside me, she smiles at me again. I wonder if I remind her of someone else she knows because I don't look like the kind of girl you smile at in a public restroom, even without my eyeliner. Maybe I remind her of someone she likes. I smile back, my Caitlin smile, and wish for the one-millionth time that Caitlin were here with me. She'd know how to charm the phone off this woman. Caitlin was my little sister, but she was better at this kind of thing. Basically, she was better at life. She knew what to say to people, how to say it.

"Hi." I try not to sound like the crazy girl who cuts herself.

"Hi." The woman is soaping her hands with the blueberry soap.

I kind of half-laugh; it sounds so fakey. "Smells like blueberries."

"Blueberries?" She looks at me, confused.

"The soap." I point at the dispenser and start rinsing my hands.

She sniffs her hands and laughs. "It does, a little bit."

I nibble on the inside of my lip as I move to the hand dryer looking at her, then my wet hands, then at her again. She's some kind of Native American, but I'm not good with tribes. "Could I ask you a huge favor?"

She looks at me, her hands under the water.

"I did something really dumb," I say in my "everyone likes me and trusts me because I'm Caitlin" voice. "I locked my keys in my car and my cell phone is there. I was wondering . . . Could I use your phone to text my dad?"

"Sure, sweetie." She moves toward me. "You don't want to call him?"

I smile again and shake my head. I don't want to call Todd because I'm not sure what I would say to get him to understand that my mom has kidnapped me and that I need him to come after me because I can't just say that. This lady might tell Mom. A text to Todd is a better bet. "I better not." A half smile, half grimace. "He's in a meeting. A lawyer." I have no idea where that came from. "If I text him, he can just come for me when his meeting is over. I don't want to interrupt *and* ask him to come get me."

"Of course you can use my phone." She fishes it out of an outer pocket of her yellow handbag with two wet fingers. "But can I give you a ride somewhere?"

I shake my head, texting as fast as I can. I remember Todd's number, which is kind of weird because in the world of cell phones, who knows numbers anymore? You just start to type the recipient's name and the number comes up. But, like my mom, I have a good memory for numbers.

It's me, I text. **DO NOT call this number.**

Whose this he texts back.

I shake my head. He's such an idiot. **It's Haley. I don't have my phone, so I borrowed someone else's. I can't talk. I need you to come get me. My mom made me get in the car with her. She's making me go to Maine.**

I glance up. The woman is done drying her hands and now she's just standing there waiting.

"Sorry," I say. Another quick smile as I hit send and start texting again. **I need you to come get me. Not sure where, yet. Start driving toward Utah. Take I15.**

Drube 2 utah?

I close my eyes. Maybe this is a bad idea. Todd may not be smart enough to find Alaska. Or Utah.

Gotta go. Text you as soon as I can. Don't text to this phone again.

I send and look up and smile as I go into "edit" and delete the texts. "Thanks. I'm sure he'll be here soon. His meeting's almost over." Another smile.

"You sure you want to wait here? You don't want to sit in my car with me?"

I hand her back her phone. I hook my thumbs in my jeans' pockets. "No thanks. I'm just going to get an Icee and then, you know"—I lift my chin in the direction of the store—"wait for him." Then I open the door for her. "Thanks again. Have a good day."

"You too." She gives a little wave and walks out into the store.

I follow her, but take my time. The minute I step out of the little hall where the bathrooms are, I spot Mom and Izzy at the frozen drink machine. Mom's been waiting for me. Watching for me. I walk to the closest rack of food and reach for a bag. I check them out like I'm seriously considering getting reduced calorie Chex Mix. If Mom comes over and starts talking to me before the lady who loaned me the phone leaves, I'm not sure what I should do. What if Mom asks her if I was bothering her or something? Mom's acting so . . . not like herself that I can't honestly guess what she will or won't do. An hour ago I would have said Mom would never have gone back for Izzy. But there's Izzy standing there with her big-ass Icee.

Luckily, the woman with the phone picks up a bottle of water from a cooler near the register and pays for it and a pack of gum. She does turn and wave to me as she goes out the door. I wave back and follow up with the smile.

A second later, Mom is beside me. She has an enormous frozen Coke in her hand and a bag of pretzels. Izzy's hovering behind her.

"Who was that?" Mom asks.

I shake my head, putting the snack bag back on the rack. "Just somebody I was talking to in the bathroom." I move around the end of the aisle to get away from Mom and look at a rack of nuts.

Mom stands there for a minute and I worry that she might be suspicious. Caitlin always said Mom had a nose for when we were up to something. "You want something to eat? Something to drink?"

I almost say no, but then I realize that if Todd is going to come for me, the smartest thing for me to do right now is to play along with Mom's insane road-trip thing. I didn't tell Todd, but I'm pretty sure he's going to have to drive all the way to wherever we're staying tonight to get me. I don't want Mom getting suspicious. Maybe if I play along, she'll let me go out for ice or something and I can get away. "These." I hold up a bag of pistachios.

"I like pistachios." Izzy sucks on her straw. Her Icee is blue, which is a little gross since she just washed her hands with blue soap.

Mom reaches around me and gets another bag of the nuts. "Drink?" she asks me.

"I'll get a Coke."

She holds my gaze for just a second longer than I'm comfortable with and for some reason, a part of me, the tiniest part of me, feels guilty for telling Todd to come get me. Mom really is trying. Even if she's completely wrong about this road trip, and she is, she gets points for trying.

She nods. "Meet me at the register."

She walks away and Izzy just stands there, looking at me, sucking loudly on her straw. She's still wearing her school uniform and it's all wrinkly and she didn't brush her hair this morning. Caitlin used to brush it for her sometimes.

I walk away, kind of wishing I had a brush.

Chapter 25

Julia

51 days

We're all quiet for half an hour, after we get back in the car. I take Interstate 15 north. We'll soon cross the northwest tip of Arizona and go into Utah. There's less traffic now that we're past the Vegas Strip and I relax a little bit.

My Icee is delicious. It's been so long since I've had one. Years. In my battle against the bulge, I gave up dessert, butter on my bread, and frozen drinks, both alcoholic and nonalcoholic. Too many calories. Too much sugar. Which is why this tastes so good, I'm sure. I open my bag of pretzels and have one. "Pretzel?" I offer the bag to Izzy.

She's got Doritos and cheese puffs and red licorice. And sour gummi worms. I should have told her to put it all back. Too much saturated fat and sugar for anyone, but she was so excited back at the mini-mart to be allowed to get what she wanted that I decided *what the hell?* A few days of junk food won't hurt any of us. Haley and I could both stand to put on a couple of pounds. And if we stay with Laney, there won't be a string of sugar or triangle of trans fats to be found in her cupboards.

Izzy's holding her blue Icee with both hands. The bags of snacks are on her lap. "Sure." She wedges her drink between her legs and the cheese puffs take a nosedive to the floor. She takes the bag of pretzels, removes a handful, and offers it back to me.

"Pass them to your sister."

Izzy looks at me like I just told her to stick her head in a gas oven. Her lips are blue from the drink.

I should probably choose my words carefully; we're all so fragile. But I react to Izzy with semi-annoyance. I've had just about enough of this. "You wanted to come with us, so you're with us. But I'm warning you, this silent treatment you're giving your sister? You're going to have to let it go, Isobel. I'm not driving three thousand miles with the two of you not speaking to each other."

Haley reaches between the seats and grabs the pretzel bag from Izzy. "I never stopped talking to *her.* She stopped talking to me when I killed Caitlin." The pretzel bag rattles and I hear her bite a pretzel.

It takes me a beat to respond. I've been going over in my head different ways to open a conversation with Haley about Caitlin, about the accident. I've been trying to think about things we need to talk about that will help us get out of this hole we've dug for ourselves. All three of us are down here in this black pit; I see that now. Izzy may *seem* okay, but she's not. How can she be? I cannot imagine the willpower it's taken for her to go fifty-one days without speaking to the only sister she has left.

I put my drink into the cup holder on the console. I'm getting a brain freeze. "You can't say that, Haley."

"What?"

"You can't say that you—" My voice catches in my throat and I swallow and fight the wave of pain that threatens to wash over me. I push through. "You can't say you *killed* Caitlin." My words come out staccato and loud.

Izzy freezes, pretzels in one hand, the big cup in the other. Her blue lips are wrapped around the straw.

"But I did." Haley sounds like a little girl.

"No," I manage. "You got into an automobile accident and your sister died in that accident." I nod as I say each word, to make my point.

"But I *caused* the accident. I killed her."

I make myself look into the rearview mirror at her. "It was an *accident*, Haley. You didn't do it on purpose."

As I speak the words, they reverberate in my head. I know she didn't mean to run the stop sign. I know she didn't mean to hurt her sister. But I also know, as I say the words, that I still blame her, somewhere deep inside, where logic doesn't reign.

What kind of mother does that make me? An unfit one?

I stare straight ahead as the dry, barren, brown scenery whizzes by us at sixty-plus miles an hour. I hate Nevada. I hate the sun that beats down, baking the earth until it's cracked and lifeless. I hate the dull, monochromic landscape. I long for green forests and sparkling lakes and ponds. I ache for the scent of pine trees and grass.

I hear Haley crunching her pretzels. I glance at Izzy. She's just sitting there, drink in one hand, pretzels in the other.

"I don't know if I can do it," Izzy says softly to me. "I don't know if I can ever speak to her again. I know it's bad of me. I know I should, but I just . . ." She looks like she's going to cry. "I can't, Mom."

I reach between us and pat her knee. I can't force Izzy to speak to Haley. I know that. But this is the first time I've said a thing about it. I'm their mother. It's my place to tell Izzy it's not right to do this to her sister. It's my place to tell Haley she can't hold herself responsible for killing Caitlin. "Drink your Icee before it melts," I say kindly.

We cover thirty miles before I speak again. We're all quiet, lost in our thoughts. But it's time to dive in. I know I can't waste the precious time I have in this car with my girls. I think about some of the stuff I read yesterday about the grieving process. Lots of Web sites talk about the importance of talking about the deceased.

"You know what I miss?" I say. The question is rhetorical. I don't wait for either of them to respond. "I miss the little notes Caitlin used to leave me. The pink and purple sticky notes. Remember? She had that big cube of them. She'd leave them on the refrigerator: *Buy almond milk*. On the counter: *Home after cheer.*"

We go another five miles. Ten. No one says a word and I'm frustrated. Do I say something else? Do I ask each girl to tell me a memory she has of Caitlin? Because this isn't going to work if Izzy won't speak to Haley and Haley won't speak to me.

We cover another ten miles before Izzy speaks up. "When I had that turtle. The one that died. Caitlin used to leave me notes on the turtle bowl that said, *Feed me*." She laughs.

I smile at Izzy's sweet memory. I'm fairly certain the turtle died of starvation, or at the very least general neglect, but I keep that to myself.

A few miles later, Haley speaks from the back. "She always signed her name with hearts over the *I*'s. Like she was a fourth grader, or something."

It sounds like a dig, but the tone of Haley's voice is nostalgic.

Tears well in my eyes, but I don't let myself cry. I have a note in my jewelry box that Caitlin left me on my bathroom mirror one morning, sometime around Christmas. She was in there borrowing my good tweezers, which always made me crazy because she never put them back. The note said, *I love my mom*, with a drawing of a pair of tweezers. She signed her name with hearts over the *I*'s.

Izzy sucks loudly on her straw, getting air with the frozen drink. "Caitlin made the best grilled cheese sandwiches. With lots of butter and cheese. I miss those sandwiches."

"Rye bread from the deli and three kinds of cheese. There must have been a thousand delicious calories in one of her grilled cheese sandwiches." I sigh and reach for my drink.

I hear Haley rattling a package and look in the rearview to see her opening a pack of pistachios. "She snored," she says. "I used to lie in bed and listen to her. I could hear her all the way in my room."

"We kept talking about having her tonsils and adenoids out, but she never wanted to take the downtime," I tell them.

Haley cracks open a pistachio nut. "This is going to sound

dumb, and I know I complained all the time, but I kind of liked hearing her snore. It was like . . . everything was normal in the house. Like everything was okay."

I feel a lump rise in my throat. "Remember that time she used her phone to record *you* snoring because you kept complaining that she was keeping you awake?"

Haley laughs. Not a full-blown laugh, but more than a chuckle. "I do *not* snore. I think she faked the whole thing."

"I don't think so." Izzy shakes her head as she puts her drink in a holder. "I think it was real."

She doesn't speak directly to Haley, exactly, but I feel like it's a step in the right direction.

"I miss the way she laughed. She had the best laugh, ever. Anyone want any pistachios?" Haley holds the bag between the two front seats.

Izzy makes an event of opening her bag of Doritos and crams several chips into her mouth, crunching loudly.

I feel bad for Haley. "I'll take a couple." I hold out my hand and she drops some into it. I crack one between my teeth and the meat of the nut falls into my mouth. It's good. Salty. I didn't really want any, but it feels right to share something together, while we share our memories of Caitlin. Something about breaking bread together. I can't believe two months have passed and we've never said we missed her. "Want one?" I hold my hand out to Izzy.

"Got these."

"They're really good," I cajole.

She crunches another corn chip in response. It's kind of obnoxious, but she *is* only ten. I forget that because she acts older most of the time.

"Caitlin liked Doritos," Izzy says. "Cool Ranch. She liked the classic nacho cheese kind, but her favorite was Cool Ranch."

I notice that's the flavor she's eating.

"And she liked cheese puffs," Haley says. "And licorice and gummi worms."

The snack foods Izzy picked when she was allowed to choose for herself. I wonder if those will always be her favorites now.

I hear Haley's window go down. I look into the rearview, but I can't see what she's doing and I'm immediately apprehensive. I hear something rattle down the window and against the car and I realize she was probably just throwing out shells. I don't know why I'm concerned. The doors are locked. It's not like she's going to go out the window of the moving car. And she seems like she's resigned herself to the trip. I need to let my anxiety go and trust her until she gives me a reason not to.

"Which way are we going?" Izzy asks.

She pulls an iPad out of her backpack on the floor, only she doesn't have an iPad. Hers, a hand-me-down from Ben's office, broke just before Caitlin died. We had intended to get her a new tablet and just never thought about it again. And she never asked.

"That's not yours," Haley accuses.

It has a pink neoprene cover.

It hits me hard. It was Caitlin's.

"Is it okay, Mom?" Izzy looks up at me; she can tell I'm upset. "I took it off her desk. I wanted to look stuff up for our trip. It's still got a data plan. I checked." She hugs it against her and the bag of Doritos. "I thought it would be okay."

"It's fine." I glance in the rearview mirror. "You have your own, Haley. There's no reason why Izzy shouldn't have Caitlin's." I wait. "Is there a reason why you think she shouldn't have it?"

I hear carbonation hiss as Haley opens her Coke. "It's just weird. To see it." She points. "I got her that sticker. It came out of one of those old-school gumball machines at the bowling alley. I had to keep putting quarters in to get the one she wanted. I think that one sticker cost me like four dollars in quarters."

"Which one?" I ask. The pink iPad cover has stickers all over it. There are flowers and peace signs, the word *war* with a red circle around it and a line through it. One of the stickers says *Eat Natural*.

Caitlin was my budding hippie. I have no idea where it came from. Neither Ben nor I have ever been particularly environmentally conscious. We recycle and we have solar panels on our roof and at the office, but that's mostly a reflection of where we live. We try to eat healthy, but it was Caitlin who introduced us to organic grains and grass-fed beef. I know that children are genetically a mixture of their parents, and they're certainly affected by their environment, but I think Caitlin was a prime example of how our children grow up to be individuals.

"The sparkly pink peace sign." Haley leans forward to point at it.

Izzy flips the cover back to conceal the stickers, almost snapping Haley's finger with it. "Can we go through Bryce Canyon, Mom? It takes a little longer than just staying on this road, but there's a natural bridge there I want to see."

Haley makes a derisive sound and slides back on her seat. "We've seen that."

Izzy keeps her eyes on the iPad. "It's not actually a canyon." She brings up photos of the area on the tablet on her lap. "There are these things sticking up everywhere called hoodoos."

"Don't you remember when we went there a couple of years ago?" Haley sips her Coke. "Dad wanted us to go on this family hike and—"

"They call hoodoos fairy chimneys sometimes," Izzy goes on, talking right over Haley. "They're made of soft rock with hard rock on top and they can be as high as a hundred and fifty feet tall. It's supposed to be one of the best examples of hoodoos in the whole world. It will be cool to see them. Especially if we don't come back."

"Mom. Tell her she's been there."

"We're coming back to Vegas," I tell Izzy.

"The reason it's not actually a canyon," Izzy goes on, "is because technically a canyon is made from the erosion of a single stream. Bryce Canyon was made when—"

"Mom! Will you tell the little twit that we've been there? That she's seen the houdinis."

"Hoodoos," Izzy corrects.

I glance at Izzy. "You have been there. You were five or six. Please, no name-calling, Haley." How many times did I holler that into the back of our minivan while hauling Caitlin and Haley around? They always got along well, probably because they were so close in age, but they also teased and picked on each other unmercifully.

"Don't you remember, we saw people in the canyon riding horses and you wanted to know why we were walking. You wanted to ride and I took you to see the horses," Haley tells Izzy. "Mom had packed apple slices and we asked the guide and he let you feed them to his horse."

Izzy balances the iPad on her lap. "I thought it would be neat to see. The elevation is a lot higher than Zion National Park. Interstate Fifteen goes right past Zion. I just thought we could take the long way and go through Bryce Canyon instead."

"I didn't say I didn't want to go that way, Izzy." Haley leans forward, one hand on my seat and one on Izzy's. "I was just saying you've been there. You just don't remember."

"I think it would be cool to see it," Izzy says quietly. "You can see the natural bridge from the road. There's like a place to park your car so you can take pictures and stuff, but we don't have to do that. We could just drive by. I think the road hooks back up with the interstate." She's on Google Maps now, checking the route.

I take a sip of my Icee that's melted. It's not nearly as good as it was. "I don't know. I was hoping to make Grand Junction today. See how far we'd be going out of our way. I was just going to stay on Fifteen and then we'll be on Seventy at some point."

"We're going to *Grand Junction?*" Haley says from the backseat. "As in *Colorado?*"

I shrug. "It's a decent-size town. Five-hour drive from here, probably. I figured we'd be able to find a hotel there easily."

Haley slumps against the backseat. "I didn't think we were going that far today."

"Bryce Canyon is kind of out of the way," Izzy says. "Let me see how far."

Haley rattles the bag of nuts. "Can I see the iPad when you're done?"

Something about her tone of voice seems off and I glance in the mirror.

Her gaze meets mine. *"What?* I was going to see what hotels are in Grand Junction. Maybe find a place to eat nearby."

"Tell me how far off Fifteen Bryce Canyon is," I tell Izzy. I glance in the mirror at Haley again. She has her fingertips pressed to her forearm. I've seen her do it a couple of times since we left the house. It seems to be some sort of comfort thing. I hope she's not wanting to cut herself. "Then let Haley use the iPad for a couple of minutes."

Chapter 26

Haley

50 days, 12 hours

Izzy fiddles with the iPad for at least half an hour before she passes it to me. She's such a little twit wit. And she only gives it to me then because I ask for it three times and Mom tells her to give it to me when we get back in the car after we make a pit stop in St. George's. Mom had to pee. I told her she needed to be careful with those big gulp Icees. She kind of laughed. She used to laugh at stuff I said all the time. I can be pretty funny. At least Caitlin thought I was.

Back in the car, Mom's talking to Izzy about some project for Izzy's social studies class. Izzy wants to make an Egyptian stone tablet and Mom suggests getting wallboard from the hardware store. It's an old trick; Caitlin and I both did it. I sit back against the seat, trying to look all casual so Mom doesn't suspect why I really want the iPad. I'm relieved to find that Caitlin has iMessage. I text Todd.

You're going to have to pick me up in Grand Junction. Sorry.

Colorado, I add, just because I pretty much already know his geography skills suck.

He doesn't answer right away so while I'm waiting, I check out hotels in Grand Junction. Mom seems to have relaxed a little, now that she thinks I'm all in for her joyride and that a few days in a RAV4 will heal me.

"Ummm, there's the usuals," I say. "Days Inn, La Quinta. You get Marriott points, right, Mom?"

I see her in the rearview mirror; she nods. "See what's available for around a hundred dollars. Two double beds."

"I'm not sleeping with her," Izzy declares. She says *her* like I have the plague.

Mom sighs. "Don't make me wish I'd left you home. You can sleep with me."

I text Todd again.

You there?

"Looks like there's a couple of Marriott properties: Springfield Inn, Courtyard," I name. To myself I'm saying, *Come on, Todd, come on.*

"Can you make a reservation online?" Mom asks.

"Yup. Let me see what's available."

A message pops up. Luckily, I thought to mute the iPad.

Colorado??

Just over the Utah border. Map it, I text quickly. **On your way?**

I know he's at least an hour behind us. Farther than that, probably, but that's okay. That'll give me time to get out of the hotel room. I can just wait until Mom and Izzy are asleep and slip out and I'm free. By the time Mom realizes I'm gone, Todd and I will be headed for Canada. I figure we'll take the Alcan Highway until we hit the end of it in Alaska and then we'll just decide which direction to go, once Todd knows where his brother is. I just hope Todd remembered his passport. Mine's in my backpack with the cash I scraped together from my room and Caitlin's. Her ATM card is in there too.

"Hmmm," I say, switching screens. "A couple of places near the airport, but it looks like the prices are better if we stay a little farther out." I look up at Mom because I know she's watching, trying to judge just how nutty I am. If I'm going to get away with this, if I'm going to get away from her, I have to make her think I'm okay. But not *too* okay or she'll suspect something. That's why I've been careful not to be too nice to Izzy. Because I've always picked on her. It's what big sisters do.

"Marriott Courtyards are nice." Mom sips from a bottle of water. We all got waters when we stopped. "See if any of them have a continental breakfast."

"I like the places where they let you make your own waffles," Izzy puts in. "You spin the waffle iron." She demonstrates.

Come on, Todd. Answer me, I think. While I'm checking out the breakfast information for a Marriott Courtyard in Grand Junction, Nowhere, he finally texts back.

U want me 2 git u in Colorodo

I close my eyes for a second, wondering how he could misspell Colorado when he's got autocorrect on his freaking phone.

Only 6 or 7 hrs from Vegas, I respond. **See you tonight. Don't text me back. Will send you address where I am soon as I can.**

I wait and when he doesn't answer me, I text **OKAY???**

I wait.

K

I exhale with relief, rub my forearm, and delete the messages. I go back to the Marriott pages to find us a hotel room. As I'm going through the screens, I hear something that sounds like a cat. I glance up, thinking maybe Mom or Izzy have turned on the radio. I know. Like there's a cat station.

Neither has moved.

I check prices at the Courtyard and then go into the "Reserve a Room" page. "You have an online account, Mom?"

"My e-mail," she says.

I hear the cat sound again. Definitely a meow. I wonder if it's some kind of pop-up on the iPad. I showed Caitlin how to keep those things off her computer, but maybe she didn't know to block them on her iPad. Just as I'm checking to make sure nothing else is open, Mom says, "What was that?"

Chapter 27

Julia

51 days

"What was that sound?" I ask.

"Sound?" Izzy freezes, her hand stuffed in her Doritos bag.

I should tell her to put the chips away. Of course, if I were a better mother, we would have gotten some sort of lunch when we stopped to use the bathroom. I have no idea where we can get food between here and Grand Junction. I wonder if we go to Bryce Canyon if the museum has some sort of snack bar or something. I should have packed a cooler; I used to be that mom.

"Are you watching a video on the iPad, Haley?" I ask, glancing at her in the rearview.

I thought it would be okay for her to use it to research hotels for tonight. I want her to feel like she's still a part of this family, like we need her. But I'm not letting her watch movies in the backseat. That would defeat the purpose of locking her up in the car with me for five days so we can talk.

"No, Mom, I'm not watching cat videos."

So she heard it too.

I hear it again. It's definitely a cat. And suddenly I realize *I know that sound.* "Isobel Mae," I say sharply. There are no cars to be seen in either direction and I pull over.

A meow comes from the back of my car. Mr. Cat's plaintive meow.

"Mom tells you to pack a bag and you think that means bring the *cat?*" Haley is half-laughing, half-mocking. "You brought your cat with you in the car to drive to *Maine?*"

Izzy's still holding the chip bag. Now she's staring at me and looking exceedingly guilty. She has crumbs at the corners of her mouth. "I didn't want to leave him."

Haley unbuckles and leans over the backseat as soon as the car comes to a stop on the shoulder.

"Leave him alone," Izzy hollers, scrambling to unbuckle her seat belt.

"Where is he?" Haley gets up on her knees and begins to pull through the bags in the back. "Christ, you put him in a duffel bag?"

Last time we stopped, Haley threw my bag over the seat. I guess it's a miracle Mr. Cat wasn't hurt. I can't believe he's been quiet all this time.

The cat starts meowing again. I hear a bag being unzipped.

"You put him in a bag? *Izzy,* he could have suffocated."

Izzy starts to cry. "He couldn't suffocate. I put a tissue box on each end of the bag and there's mesh so he could breathe."

I stare at my youngest daughter. I can't believe she brought the cat. A cat!

Mr. Cat hollers and flies over the seat to land next to Haley. He's pretty agile for his age.

"And you're worried about *my* mental status?" Haley scoffs.

I watch, still not quite believing this has happened, as the cat hops from the back seat to the console between the two front seats and then sits down and looks at Izzy.

"Oh, kitty, kitty, Mr. Cat. Are you okay?" Izzy croons. "You were supposed to stay quiet. You promised me if I brought you, you'd be quiet." She strokes his back.

Mr. Cat, a tabby, isn't big. Never was, but in his old age, he seems to be shrinking. He weighs less than five pounds. Luckily, he looks no worse for wear for his ride in the duffel bag. He starts to purr.

I give my daughter my best stern-mother look. "We can't drive across the country with a cat, Izzy."

"Why not?" As she pets him, she leaves Doritos dust on his ratty fur. "He'll be good. Won't you?" she asks the cat. She peers up at me. "Please, Mom? You won't even know he's in the car."

"Except for the meowing." Haley from the backseat. "And what happens when he has to pee and poop? That's going to smell great in here."

I exhale and plant both hands on the steering wheel, closing my eyes for a second. We're two and a half hours from the house. We've got roughly forty hours of driving to go. This is a hell of a way to start out.

Maybe Ben's right. Maybe I can't do this.

But how could I have anticipated this problem? Who would check to be sure their ten-year-old hadn't packed a cat. I mean *really*. *A cat?*

Izzy reaches for Mr. Cat, knocks the bag off her lap, and spills Doritos onto the floor of my new car. Well, it's not exactly new now, but it seems like it. It's like I've lost the last two months of my life.

I grab my phone and glance up in the rearview mirror. A car flies by us. We're far enough off the road that I think we're safe, though. "Stay in the car. *Both* of you," I add sharply. "I'm going to call your father."

"Mom, please," Izzy begs. "Can't he go with us? I promise I'll take care of him. I promise he won't be a problem. You won't even know he's with us."

"What are you going to do?" Haley asks. "We should probably go home, shouldn't we?"

"We're not going home. Stay in the car." I get out, taking care the cat doesn't try to escape. I have to hold back not to slam the door. I'm not even that angry with Izzy, just with the situation. I see how it makes sense to her, bringing the cat. He means the world to her and her world is a mess. That old cat is her security blanket.

That doesn't mean I'm taking him to Maine with me.

I walk around the car and stand out of earshot. Everything is dry and stark and brown around me. As far as I can see on both sides of the highway is barren desert. I should probably keep my eye out for snakes. I stare at the baked ground and I call Ben. He doesn't pick up.

Of course he doesn't.

I leave a message. "Could you call me back? Right away?" I hesitate. I don't want him to worry that we've been in an accident or I've let Haley get away from me. "We're fine," I add. "It's just that . . . Izzy brought Mr. Cat. I didn't know he was in the car. Call me."

I disconnect. I feel like I should call someone else, but who? Not Laney. She's in class, besides being in Maine. I stand there thinking for a minute and I realize I don't have anyone to call. How pathetic is that?

I haven't had a good friend in Vegas since my dear friend Maureen died of leukemia four years ago. I just never connected with anyone else the way I connected with her. And honestly, I haven't made the effort with anyone. I've been so busy with the girls and working part-time and volunteering and . . . just life.

I guess I could call someone in Ben's family, but if I admit I need someone to come get a cat, I'll never hear the end of it. And I don't know if Ben told them I was driving to Maine with the girls. I'm not getting into it with Linda or Ben's brothers.

I can't believe I don't have anyone else to call.

Before Caitlin died, I had lots of acquaintances who weren't quite friends but their phone numbers are in my cell. People I spent time with because of the activities our children were involved with. A lot of people came to the memorial service and dropped off food at the house. I still have unidentifiable casseroles in the freezer. People called. They stopped by, but only right in the beginning. I can't remember the last time that one of those people called to see how we were. Maybe that's my fault. I didn't call anyone back. I didn't even answer the door.

I stand there, phone in my hand, staring at the car. I can see that Haley is talking, but I can't hear what she's saying. Izzy is clearly ignoring her. I don't know what I'm going to do about Izzy. I should have thought this through better. I shouldn't have brought her with me, with or without the cat.

But even in a do-over, if I'm honest with myself, I know I wouldn't leave her home with Ben. I realize now that she needs to be with me, even as broken as I am. Izzy needs her mother. And so does Haley.

I fight a lump that rises in my throat and comes out in a little sob. I turn away from the car and face the desert. "Oh, Caitlin," I murmur.

I turn back to look at the car again. Haley's given up trying to talk to Izzy. She's looking at the iPad. Izzy has Mr. Cat on her lap. She's petting him and he's rubbing against her.

I call Ben again. He still doesn't answer. I don't leave a message this time.

It's hot out here. Not hot like it will be in a month or two, but hot enough. Eighty degrees, probably. I should get back in the car. My skin is so pale and pasty that I'll burn just standing here.

But instead of getting back in the car, I pace.

What do I do now? Obviously, I can't take a cat cross-country. He has to go back. Do I just start driving toward Vegas and hope Ben calls me back and I can get him to meet me somewhere? How many hours will that put us behind?

It's not the miles I care about. It's that I don't want to lose the little bit that I've accomplished today with Haley. Just the fact that she's actually talking to me. A little. If we head back to Vegas, will that change the momentum? Will she get it in her head that we can just go home and forget this whole thing?

I don't want to turn around. I feel like I can't. Maybe that's silly. Maybe this is about Ben, and me wanting to prove something to him. Which is *certainly* ridiculous. But it's the principle of the thing.

I'm not turning around.

So, what? I sit here? Wait for Ben to drive all the way here? That doesn't make any sense, either. Maybe we could go on to Bryce Canyon. I think I recall a lodge being there. Maybe Ben could join us. Maybe a night together, the four of us, and he'll decide to go with us to Maine.

I sigh, feeling like I want to curl up in a ball and cry again. Ben's not going to come spend the night with us. He's not going to change his mind and get on board, figuratively or otherwise. I walk slowly to the car. Get in.

"Is Dad coming for the cat?" Haley asks, not looking up from the iPad.

I close my door and turn my face to the vent and let it blast cold air across my cheeks. I close my eyes, then open them, turning to Izzy. "You should have asked me about the cat."

"You would have said no," she answers quietly. There are no tears now, just stubbornness on her face and in her body language.

Her response surprises me. I expected her to argue or make excuses, but I didn't expect flat-out defiance. I can't decide if the idea pleases me or upsets me. I like the idea that she's brave enough to defy me. It's proof of her strength. It tells me she can get through this terrible tragedy that's befallen our family. It tells me Izzy will be okay. But the idea that she'd bring the cat with her, knowing it would be against my wishes, pisses me off, too.

"We're not going to Bryce Canyon." I take off my sunglasses to wipe a smudge on the right lens with the hem of my T-shirt.

Izzy wraps her arms protectively around her cat.

"So we're going home?" Haley asks from the back.

Clearly her vote.

I slip on my sunglasses, check my mirrors, put the car into drive, and pull out onto the highway. Headed north.

"What? So first her and now her cat?" Haley's loud, her tone aggressive. "I thought this was supposed to be about me."

I think for a moment before I respond. "It's about all of us. Go ahead and book the hotel room in Grand Junction. And see where there's a Walmart or a Target or something. Mr. Cat is going to need some food."

"I brought cat food," Izzy pipes up.

It's not until she says it that I remember the can of food falling out of her sweatshirt pocket back at the house. How could I be so dumb as to have not connected the dots?

Because once again, who would have suspected their daughter would smuggle a cat into the car for a cross-country road trip?

"He needs a litter box," I say.

"Unbelievable," Haley complains from the backseat. "We're really not taking the cat home?"

From beside me, Izzy, sounding quite pleased with herself, says, "Mr. Cat's been wanting to see Maine."

Laney laughs on the other end of my phone.

"It's not funny," I tell her, but I'm laughing too. What's the old saying? It's better to laugh than to cry. I've already cried enough for this lifetime.

A man comes out of the elevator and eyes me as he goes in the opposite direction, rolling a suitcase behind him. I'm sitting on the floor in the hallway, leaning against our hotel room door. When Haley got in the shower, I left Izzy and Mr. Cat (smuggled into the Marriott) watching TV and slipped out to call Laney. First I told her about going back for Izzy, then about the little bit of talking the three of us did, *then* about the cat.

"Actually it *is* funny." Laney giggles. "And I had no idea there was such a thing as a travel litter box."

"Me either. The wonders of Walmart." I sip a bottle of vitamin-water, wishing I had a glass of wine. "Found it in the pet aisle."

"And you still haven't heard from Ben?"

I sober. "Nope. He was really upset with me, Laney. About me doing this. He thinks Haley needs to be in counseling."

"She probably does," Laney agrees, "but a mother has to go with her gut instinct. Your instincts have always been good, Jules. There will be plenty of time for counseling later."

We're both quiet for a second.

"You're doing the right thing. In bringing Izzy, too. Brilliant, Jules. I don't know that I would have had the guts to do it."

"It didn't feel gutsy," I confess, fiddling with the lid to the bottle. "It felt impulsive and now it feels irresponsible."

"Izzy needs to be with you as much as Haley does. She deserves your attention too."

I lean forward, drawing up my knees, hugging myself with my free arm. "But does she really need to be exposed to . . ." I search for the right words. "Laney, this is serious. *Cutting* herself? I never knew such a thing existed when I was Izzy's age."

"She'll be okay. She's a smart, strong girl. She's like her mother."

I give a little laugh that sounds more like a stifled sob. "I don't feel strong. I sure don't feel smart. How did I miss this going on in my own home?"

"Quit beating yourself up. You *are* strong," Laney tells me. "Otherwise, you couldn't have gotten out of your bed and into your car. You couldn't have gotten Haley in that car."

"But threatening to have her committed?" I close my eyes for a second. "Tell me that's not going to be an interesting conversation later. When this is all over and we come out the other side."

"But at least you'll be able to have that conversation later," she tells me. "You'll still have your daughter to be able to have that conversation."

I press the heel of my hand to my forehead. "You're right. I know you're right."

"I am." I hear her take a sip from her glass. *She's* having wine. "You think Haley's resolved herself to doing this, now that you've made it clear it's what you guys are doing?" she asks me.

"I think so." I recall incidents from the day. "She's making it plain she's not happy with the situation, but I'm not worried she's climbing out the window anymore."

"Hotel windows don't open. You don't have a balcony, do you?"

I chuckle. "Fourth floor. No balcony." My phone beeps and I check the screen. I'm tempted not to even answer the other call when I see Ben's name. But I know that's not going to solve anything. "I gotta go. Ben's calling," I tell Laney.

"Call me back if you need to."

"I'll be okay. I'll call you tomorrow night."

"Sooner if you need me," she says.

I answer Ben's call.

"She took the cat?" he says when I say hello.

No "Hello." No "How are things going?"

I lean the back of my head against the door, resolving to buy a bottle of wine tomorrow, somewhere, so I can have a glass tomorrow night. I decided after looking at the map on Caitlin's iPad at dinner that we are going to try to make it to Lincoln, Nebraska, tomorrow. It's probably going to take us twelve hours, with stops for my teeny-tiny bladder, but with the cat in the car, I've given up the idea of taking the scenic route. At this point, I just want to get to Maine with all three of us in one piece.

"Yup. She brought the cat," I say into the phone. "By the time we heard him, it was too late to turn around. Why didn't you call me sooner, Ben? I called you hours ago."

"So this is my fault?" He's angry.

And I'm tired. Too tired to fight with him. "It's fine. It'll be fine." I sigh and brush back the hair that's fallen over my face. I actually looked at hair dye when we stopped to get the disposable cat litter box and a carrier for Mr. Cat. I didn't buy the hair dye, but I thought about it.

"You can't drive across the country with a cat in the car," Ben says.

I get to my feet. I've left the girls alone long enough. I need to get back in the room. I need to go to bed because suddenly, I'm so tired, I can barely hold my head up. "Sure I can," I say. "He was fine in the car. He rode on Izzy's lap all the way to Grand Junction. He was pretty tickled when we got the litter box, though." It's my attempt at a little humor. Ben doesn't laugh.

"What are you doing, Julia?"

"What am I *doing?* What do you mean? I told you what I'm doing. I'm trying to help Haley. I'm trying . . ." I search for the right words, words that will make my husband of almost twenty years understand how broken I've become. How close I came to doing something worse than what Haley has been doing. "I actually think I made a little progress today. We talked about Caitlin and about how much we miss her."

When Ben doesn't say anything, I go on. "You know, we

haven't talked about her. Ben, why haven't we talked about Caitlin and . . . and how much we loved her and how much we miss her and . . ." I don't finish my sentence.

He's quiet for so long on the other end of the phone that I wonder if he hung up. But he hasn't. I can hear him breathing.

His voice cracks when he speaks and tears well in my eyes when I hear the pain in his voice.

"What's the point in talking about her, Jules? She's dead. Nothing we can do or say can change that."

I take a shuddering breath. "The point is, *we're* not dead. The point is, we have to find a way to live without her, Ben. We have to find a way to help Izzy and Haley live without her. We have to find a way to help Haley forgive herself."

He's quiet again, and then he says, "Call me tomorrow night?"

I guess that means our heart-to-heart conversation is over. "It might be late."

"I'll wait up. Be careful."

I hesitate. "I love you," I say.

The phone clicks on the other end. I don't think he heard me. I consider calling him back, to say it, to make him hear me.

Instead, I let myself back into the room.

Chapter 28

Haley

51 days, The Witching Time

Hamlet is the one who first came up with the idea of the Witching Time, in a soliloquy. I remember the words from English class:

> Tis now the very witching time of night,
> When churchyards yawn and hell itself breathes out
> Contagion to this world

Thank you, Billy Shakespeare. Mary Shelley is the one who changed it to the Witching *Hour* in *Frankenstein*. Most people don't know that.

It's supposed to be midnight.

For me, it's eleven o'clock. Probably around 11:03.

At 11:03 p.m. on February 17th, hell breathed its contagion on me and my whole family. I was chewing Caitlin out about her irresponsible behavior. The party. The guys. I was trying to decide what I was going to do with her, take her home or drive around for a while until she sobered up. That's what I was thinking when I missed the stop sign.

I stare at the digital clock on the nightstand beside the bed in our hotel room. The numerals are red. It's 11:01 now. In about two minutes, Caitlin will have been dead fifty-two days. Fifty-two days since my heart was knocked out of my chest by a Ford pickup truck and splattered on the pavement.

I rub my forearm on the spot that's crusty. I got some Band-Aids at Walmart tonight when we got the crap for the cat. I got big Band-Aids. I'm hoping that covering them up will make me want to do it less. I kind of want to cut myself now, but I don't have anything to do it with. And I know I shouldn't do it. And I don't want to do it. I don't want to be crazy. Of course, does anyone?

I glance at the other bed. There's a little bit of light coming through the curtains from the security lamps in the parking lot. Mom and Izzy are sound asleep. I can see Mom lying on her back with her blond hair all around her head on her pillow. Kind of like a halo. She's so pretty.

Izzy's curled up in a ball beside her, with Mr. Cat sleeping in her arms. Her red hair is all tangled and in her face. Mom said Mr. Cat had to stay in his carrier and that he couldn't sleep in the bed. I guess Mr. Cat wasn't going for it.

Izzy looks so young when she sleeps. Like when she was a toddler and she used to fall asleep on the couch with her head on my lap while I was watching TV. Mom would say she should go to sleep in her crib, that I was spoiling her, letting her fall asleep and then carrying her to bed. But I never minded. I liked the idea that I was so trustworthy, in Izzy's eyes, that she could relax and fall asleep on me. I know Izzy doesn't remember, but when she was little, I was the one who gave her snacks and played on the floor with her with her toys. I was her favorite sister. Caitlin was never mean to her or anything. I would never have allowed that. But Caitlin was never all that interested in her. She was always too into herself.

I glance in the direction of the window.

I texted Todd earlier. He said he was on his way. I gave him the address of the hotel. I asked him when he'd be here, but he didn't answer.

I check the iPad again. Nothing.

I'm thinking I should leave the hotel room now. Wait for Todd outside. Mom and Izzy are sound asleep. I don't think they'll hear me and if they do, I'll lie and say I'm just going down the hall to get a Coke.

Mom's going to be so upset when she wakes up and realizes I'm gone. I feel bad. But . . . this whole idea of driving to Maine with her and Izzy and that stupid cat? I'm just not into it. I don't want to talk about Caitlin. I don't want to talk about the accident. I get where Mom's coming from, but I don't want to feel better. I deserve to feel this shitty. I deserve it forever.

And they'll be better off without me, won't they? I mean, this is all my fault. Mom wouldn't have spent the last two months of her life crying in her bed if it weren't for me. And Izzy wouldn't be doing weird stuff like talking to herself, hiding under her bed, and smuggling cats across state lines in a Toyota.

I slip out of bed and look quickly at the other bed. Neither of them has moved. I think about changing into my jeans. Right now I'm wearing one of Caitlin's old T-shirts I like to sleep in and a pair of Izzy's sleep pants with Little Mermaids all over them. I didn't bring anything to sleep in. Mom didn't either. Izzy brought like six pairs of sleep pants. I have no idea why. So we all went to bed wearing Izzy's sleep pants. I got Little Mermaid, Mom got SpongeBob, and Izzy, Looney Tunes. I told her that was because she *is* a Looney Tune. She didn't laugh.

I decide to just put the jeans I wore today into my backpack and wear the sleep pants. It was stupid of me not to have packed more stuff. Talk about cutting off my nose to spite my face. I didn't bring stuff to take to Maine to annoy Mom. Now I'll be driving to Alaska with nothing to wear but two T-shirts, jeans, one set of underwear, and Little Mermaid sleep pants. Serves me right.

Standing by my bed, I feel around to find my black Converse low-tops. I slip one on, then the other, keeping an eye on Mom and Izzy. I grab Izzy's sweatshirt off the chair; I didn't even bring a hoodie. As I snag my backpack off the floor, I look back at the iPad lying on my bed. I should leave it here for Izzy, but without a phone, how will I get on the Internet or text anyone or any-thing? I guess Todd has his phone, but he's always doing dumb things with it like dropping it in a toilet or leaving it on the roof of his car and driving away. I don't like the idea of relying on his ability to hang on to his phone. I pick up the iPad and close the pink cover over the screen carefully.

I think about leaving Mom a note. There's a notepad and pen next to the TV. I saw it earlier. But what would I say? I'm sorry? For what?

For everything.

I skip the note. Lame.

At the door, before I sneak out, I look back at the bed. Mom and Izzy haven't moved, but I catch a glimmer of light. Izzy's eyes. She's awake. And she's watching me.

My heart is suddenly banging in my chest. I don't know what to do. Do I just get back in bed? Pretend I was in the bathroom?

With my backpack and the iPad and wearing her sweatshirt? Izzy's a pretty bright girl. Smarter than me. She knows what's going down here.

But why doesn't she say anything? All she'd have to do is reach over and shake Mom. After that, even I can't guess what would happen. Would Mom call the cops and have me committed like she's threatened? Would we go back to Walmart and get some of those zip ties the cops use for disposable handcuffs? I wouldn't put it past Mom to handcuff me to the car, to the bed, to her.

I watch Izzy watching me and I realize she's not going to say a word. She's just going to let me go. I'm glad, obviously, because this will be better for everyone, long-term. But as I open the hotel room door and step out into the hall a profound sense of desolation comes over me and I walk to the elevator remembering what it was like to hold baby Izzy in my arms.

Chapter 29

Julia

52 days

I drift in the airy place between being asleep and awake. I know I'm not asleep anymore because I feel the warmth of Izzy's hand on my stomach and I hear the rush of air from the air vent near the window. I don't open my eyes because then I'll have to come fully awake and deal with . . . with everything going on in this room and beyond it.

My thoughts drift.

It's almost Haley's birthday. I haven't gotten her a gift. I haven't even thought about it and she hasn't mentioned it. No one in our house has. I guess we've been kind of busy. She'll be eighteen on May 11.

I remember being almost eighteen. Thinking I was an adult. Being frustrated that no one, especially my parents, would treat me that way. Of course, looking back, I certainly wasn't behaving very maturely.

I think about the day I jumped out of my stepfather's car. I could have been seriously hurt. And then I was gone three days. Eventually I realized I had to go home. I had to finish my senior year of high school. I needed food and a place to sleep and do my homework. I'd already been accepted to Cal State in Bakersfield.

If I wanted to go the following fall and have my parents at least help pay for my education, I had to make nice with my mom. That meant making nice with my stepdad. Apologizing. Saying whatever I had to say, do whatever I had to do to get back in their good graces.

When I walked back into the house after being gone those three days, I remember Mom being in the kitchen. She had been playing golf. She was still wearing a white visor. She looked up when I came in the door. She didn't run to hug me. She didn't even look all that glad to see me. Or relieved I was okay. I remember how heartbroken I was. She hadn't called a single one of my friends asking if anyone had seen me. I had told myself that she hadn't called anyone because she didn't want to be embarrassed by the idea that her seventeen-year-old had run away from her nice house on the nice lot on the golf course. That she knew I was okay and she knew I'd turn up.

But when my mom saw me when I walked into our kitchen, she looked disappointed. Like she'd been hoping I wouldn't turn up.

"You're in a lot of trouble, girly." That's what she said. That was all she said.

Growing up, I always believed my mother loved me. *In her own way,* I used to tell myself. I made excuses for her. Things were hard after my dad left. When she met Francis, it was a stroke of luck for her. But being married to him was difficult. He was a hard man to please. It was only natural that he took priority over me. I was just a little girl. And when I got older, I was difficult. I was moody and I didn't always make the best choices. It wasn't until college that I became the Goody-Two-shoes my daughters have accused me of being.

I wonder if my poor relationship with my mother is why I'm not doing a better job with Haley right now. But I've tried so hard to not be my mother. To be involved in my girls' lives. Shoot, I've devoted myself so much to my girls that I don't have a personal life. And my marriage is certainly not doing all that hot.

My mother was so strict with me . . . or rather my stepfather was and my mother always did as he said. I wonder if that made me too lenient with my girls. Is that why Haley's such a mess? Is this my fault, somehow?

Or am I just overthinking this whole thing?

And does it matter how we got here?

I lift my hand over my head and stretch. I slept surprisingly well last night, considering the weight of my woes. It was nice to have Izzy snuggled against me. And the cat.

I roll over slowly. I'm actually looking forward to today. We're going to cross Colorado through the mountains, through the Arapaho National Forest, and into Nebraska. With my merry band. I'm thinking we might delve right in today, once I'd had my coffee. We need to talk about the night Caitlin died. The details are blurry to me because I was in such shock. I wonder if they're blurry to Haley. Does she want to talk about it? Maybe not. And that's okay, but I feel like I should give her the opportunity.

I open my eyes and I see Haley's form in the bed. Then I realize her head is not on the pillow and she's not in her bed. It's just the way the blanket and bedspread are rolled up. I feel a flutter of panic in my chest and I sit up, eyeing the bathroom door. It's closed.

The clock says it's 8:15.

I throw my feet over the side of the bed and walk toward the door. I'm wearing a T-shirt I packed and a pair of Izzy's sleep pants. SpongeBob of all things. I don't know how I forgot to pack anything to sleep in. "Haley?" I whisper.

At the bathroom door, I tap lightly. I don't want to wake Izzy. "Haley?"

It's closed, but not all the way. She doesn't answer. I don't hear any water running. I hate to cross any lines of privacy. My mother used to do that and it really upset me, but—"Haley?" I hear the slightest hint of panic in my voice.

Again, no answer. I push the door open. No Haley. I open the shower curtain. No Haley.

My heart hammering, I grab the room key off the desk as I yank the front door open. I don't take the time to wake Izzy. I run out into the hall in bright yellow PJ bottoms, a bubblegum pink T-shirt, and no bra.

No Haley in the hall, either.

There's a breakfast buffet. Maybe she went down to the lobby for a cup of orange juice. I push the call button on the elevator. Then I push it a second time and a third when the elevator doesn't respond fast enough to suit me.

As the doors finally open, I hear Izzy calling me from the doorway of our room. "Mom? Where are you going?"

"Coffee. Stay in the room." The elevator doors begin to close and I step in.

"But, Mom, there's a—"

"Go back in the room, Izzy!"

The doors shut and the elevator begins to drop. On the first floor, I race out the doors before they open completely. The breakfast area is just off the lobby. There are a dozen people helping themselves to hard-boiled eggs, cold cereal, and pastries. No Haley. I force myself not to run.

Off the lobby, I check the ladies' bathroom. All three stalls. Not there, either.

Now I feel like my heart is going to burst out of my chest. Where is she? Where's my daughter? How could I have been so stupid? I should have slept on the floor in front of the door. I should have figured out a way to keep her from taking off. I should have known she was going to do this. I should have stayed home like Ben wanted me to. I should have stayed in bed with the blanket over my head.

No. I couldn't have stayed home. *We* couldn't have stayed there. We had to do this. We had to get away from the house and all the sadness there.

There's no way I could have known Haley would leave the hotel room. Where the hell would she go? We're in Colorado. She doesn't know anyone in Colorado. And yesterday, at least by the afternoon, she had seemed . . . if not enthusiastic, at least tolerant of the idea of making this trip.

The cool morning air hits me as I rush out the front doors and come to a halt under a white and green canopy. The pneumatic doors whoosh and click behind me. No Haley. No Haley on the benches near the door. No Haley in the circle drive. Someone is parked in front of the door; a man is loading suitcases into the back of his minivan. I can hear children's voices drifting from inside the van.

The car. It's the only place I can think to look. After that? I don't know what the hell I'm going to do.

I run barefoot, in my daughter's pajama pants, along the front of the hotel. The pavement is cool on my feet; there are loose stones that hurt. We parked in the side parking lot. We used that side door, with our passkey, to get in last night after we had dinner.

I fly around the corner, looking for my little SUV. There are more cars in the parking lot than there were last night and it takes me a second to orient myself. I spot my car in the third row, but it's partially obscured by a white pickup truck.

I run into the parking lot and behind the row of cars. As I come around the white truck, I stop abruptly. Haley's lying on the hood of my car reading a tattered copy of *To Kill a Mockingbird*.

"Haley," I say, coming around the car.

She looks me up and down, taking in the pajamas and bare feet I'm sure, then back at her book. She's leaning back against my windshield, legs stretched out like she's lying in a lounge chair. "School property," she says, indicating the paperback. "I guess I should return it."

I can't catch my breath. I lean forward, panting. "What—are—you—doing—out—here?" I manage.

"You thought I left?" She says it quietly, putting the book down on the hood.

I stand up and meet her gaze. My heart is still pounding in my chest. I feel light-headed. But I'm so relieved. I'm so thankful to see Haley's inky black hair that I don't even care that it looks like she dyed it with shoe polish. "*Did* you leave?" I ask her.

She holds my gaze for a long moment. "I'm here, right?"

A dark spot on her sleeve catches my eye and I stare at it. It's the arm she cuts and I'm pretty certain that splotch I see is blood.

She looks down at her arm and touches the wet shirt. Then she looks up at me.

"Oh, Haley," I breathe. "Did you—"

"Only a little bit." She speaks in a single exhalation and I see the pain in her eyes. Pain that hurts me so deeply that I feel wobbly on my legs.

I take a step toward her. I want to ask her what she used to cut herself, but it doesn't seem right to ask. What does it matter?

"It's not bad," she says. I can tell she's upset.

I'm still staring at her arm. "Let me see, Haley. Will you let me look at it?"

She hesitates and then slowly pushes up her sleeve. I immediately see a piece of bloody white gauze. Fresh blood.

Slowly she peels back the gauze and I see two wet wounds, but they're the same ones I saw Sunday and they're not actively bleeding anymore. Just oozing a little. It looks like she just dug at the old ones; there are no new cuts.

I fight my panic, trying to tell myself this is good. No *new* wounds. This is actually good. "You should clean that up and put fresh gauze over it. Maybe get some big Band-Aids next time we stop at a store, like the kind for skinned knees," I say, keeping my voice even. Then I look at her as she pushes down her sleeve to cover the bloody bandage. "You okay?"

She hangs her head. But then she nods, and looks up at me. "I think I'm okay."

I have so many questions, but I sense this isn't the time to ask them. It may even be years before I can. I need to be in the moment, though. I need to say and do the right thing at this moment. "I want you to tell me when you feel like you want to do this. Can you try and do that? Can you tell me?"

"Okay," she whispers.

And the way she says it makes me think maybe she will. She

has a long way to go, but there's something in her eyes this morning that I haven't seen since Caitlin's death. Life?

"What's going on?" Izzy appears from between two parked cars. She's in her PJ bottoms and bare feet, too. "Are we at least getting dressed before we go?"

I stand there, hands on my hips, still trying to catch my breath, and laugh out loud.

Chapter 30

Izzy

Day 2 of the best adventure of my life

Mom laughs and then She Who Shall Not Be Named starts to laugh and I start laughing too. I have no idea why. I look around. No one's in the parking lot, which is probably a good thing because if there were anyone, they'd probably think there was something wrong with us. All three of us are in a parking lot, wearing pajamas, laughing for no reason at all.

I steal a quick look in She Who Shall Not Be Named's direction. She's lying on the hood of Mom's car (probably denting it), like she does it all the time. Like she was just hanging out, waiting for us.

I wonder where she's been all night? Did she go to a bar or something? She probably has a fake ID. Of course I don't think she looks any older than me so I don't know how she'd get in. I can't believe she sat out here all night, though. She didn't have the car key, though. It's still up in the room.

Or was she planning on running away? Why else would she sneak out of the hotel room in the middle of the night like that? I know Mom was afraid she was going to go out her window again the night before last. That's why Mom slept with her.

But if she was going to run away, why didn't she? Did she realize she's totally unequipped to be on her own? Or did she not run away because she realized our family, no matter how big a mess we are, is better than no family at all?

Last night, when I woke up and saw her at the door, I don't know why I didn't squeal like a pig on her. All I would have had to do was shake Mom awake and She Who Shall Not Be Named would have been so busted. But I didn't wake up Mom. I just watched her go. I'm going to have to think on that later—when I'm dressed.

She Who Shall Not Be Named catches me looking at her and I look away really fast. Her looking at me makes me feel weird. Guilty weird.

In the house, it was easy to ignore her. Sometimes I could even pretend she didn't exist. But in the car, staying in a hotel room with her, is different. It's harder. I keep remembering things from before Caitlin bought her one-way ticket. Haley did mean things to me like tease me, but as much as I don't want to remember, she was nice to me, too. Like the time I broke this vase Mom really liked and she said she did it goofing around with Caitlin. Then she used her own money to buy a new one and said I didn't have to pay her back. She told me, "This one's on me, kiddo."

I look at Mom. "Can we at least get breakfast before we leave?"

"I don't think they have waffles at the breakfast bar. Just cold stuff." She Who Shall Not Be Named puts her book into her backpack and digs around for something. I see a flash of pink; Caitlin's iPad is in her bag. The little thief. I brought it. I should be able to carry it in *my* bag. Maybe she was going to run away and that's why she has it.

"But they have scones and blueberry muffins." She Who Shall Not Be Named looks right at me. She knows I love blueberry muffins. On Sundays, before Caitlin crossed the River Styx, somebody always used to run to the bakery and get fresh pastries. I always got a blueberry muffin, the kind with the crumbles on top.

"Saw them when I got some coffee earlier." She Who Shall Not Be Named is obviously talking to me. She takes something wrapped in a napkin out of her bag and pushes it across the hood of the car. "I got an extra one. In case they ran out."

I stare at the muffin. I really *really* like blueberry muffins and I'm hungry. I ordered a veggie burger last night. Bad choice. I stare at the muffin. It's a big one with brown sugar crumbles on the top.

"But if you don't want it," she says. She shrugs and makes a move to take it back.

I grab it and take a big bite.

Mom stands there looking at the two of us. I can't believe she's not making She Who Shall Not Be Named tell her what she's doing out here on top of our car at eight o'clock in the morning, but Mom's blind to her daughters' shortcomings. All of ours. She's always been that way. Even with me. She thinks I'm like the smartest ten-year-old in the world.

"You could say thank-you," Mom says. Instead of chewing Haley out for being out here rather than in the hotel room where we can keep an eye on her, that's what she says.

I purposely don't look at She Who Shall Not Be Named still on the hood. "Do I have to give it back if I don't?"

Mom shakes her head like she's annoyed with me and walks away, headed for the side door of the hotel. I just stand there for a minute, eating my muffin. I want to ask She Who Shall Not Be Named where she went. Why she left the room, but I can't figure out how without actually speaking to her and I'm kind of on a roll. I don't think I've spoken to her since the morning of the day Caitlin died.

She watches me stuff the muffin into my mouth. "Thanks for not ratting on me last night. That was . . . it was a nice thing to do, Izzy."

I don't say anything, but my eyes are scratchy, like I'm going to cry. I have no idea why. I'm so mad at her. Why do I care if she thinks I'm nice?

"What I can't figure out," she says, climbing down off the hood of the car, "is why you didn't tell. Did you not tell Mom because you wanted me to leave? Because you never want to see me again? Or did you not wake Mom up because you knew I didn't want you to?"

I just stand there. The muffin doesn't taste that good anymore. I wish I hadn't put so much in my mouth. I chew slowly. I don't want to cry. I should just walk away, but my feet won't move.

She's standing close to me now. "If I'd had a choice that night, I'd have been the one who died and not Caitlin. You get that, don't you?" She just keeps standing there for a minute. Then she walks away. "Come on. Let's get dressed and see if there's any more blueberry muffins."

Chapter 31

Julia

52 days

The drive from Grand Junction, Colorado to Kearney, Nebraska, makes for a long day. It takes me at least two hours, once we're on the road, to relax a little. I was so afraid Haley had taken off this morning. I was so scared I'd lost her.

But she didn't.

And I haven't.

And I have to move on.

I'm not sure exactly what Haley was doing in the hotel parking lot this morning, or when she'd gone out. (Luckily I was able to keep from falling into a self-deprecating state, blaming myself for falling asleep and *letting* her get out of the room, in the first place.) When I tried to question Haley as we were packing the car after breakfast, she made it clear she didn't want to talk about it. I let it go because I felt like we had more important things to say to each other and I didn't want to jeopardize my chances of making headway today. I just hope that really was my motivation and I wasn't just trying to avoid unpleasantness.

I made a couple of attempts at meaningful conversation, but after falling flat multiple times, I decide I can't force it. But even though I can't force Haley to talk to me and tell me how she's feeling, I can do things to keep her engaged. We spend the morning playing the license plate game, "collecting" a plate from each state. Of course Haley doesn't want to play at first, but when she spots an Alaska license plate, she gets into it. Izzy keeps track of the states they spot on the iPad and we collect thirty-eight by the time we were an hour outside of Kearney.

We play other car games too. Word games like we used to play when we traveled as a family. Of course it's a little trickier since Izzy won't speak to Haley, but we make it work. My girls' favorites were always the association game and the disassociation game. Ben and Caitlin and Izzy always liked the association game. All you have to do is say a word that's associated with the word the person before you said. But the *disassociation* game is trickier because you have to say a word that has nothing to do with what was said the last three times. Haley and I always ruled at that game.

After lunch at a burger place, Izzy decides to get into the backseat so Mr. Cat can be closer to his litter box that we've set up in the back of the car. Despite Haley's concerns, the litter box hasn't been an issue. As best I can figure, Mr. Cat uses it as a sandbox to play in, rather than for its intended use.

In the backseat, Izzy is mostly quiet although several times I see her in the rearview mirror moving her lips and looking at the empty seat beside her, as if she's having a conversation with someone. I don't say anything for fear Haley will tease her, but I make a note to myself to ask her about it later.

Haley rides for two hours in the front seat without engaging in any meaningful conversation with me. We watch the countryside go by, slowly moving from the mountains to the flat plains and occasionally one of us comments on a passing vehicle or an interestingly shaped tree. She doesn't ask if we can turn on the radio and I don't offer. All three of us seem to be lost in our thoughts today.

When we spot a bright green VW Bug from the seventies and I mention the guy who took me to my junior prom in just such a vehicle, Haley seems to return to us.

"His name was *Rudolph?*" she asks. "Like the reindeer?"

I smile, remembering Rudolph Lexington. He'd been a nice boy, despite what my parents had thought about him. "No." I laugh. "As in *Valentino.* The film actor. You know, *The Sheik, The Four Horsemen of the Apocalypse.*"

"Izzy doesn't know anything more than she did a minute ago," Haley says with a poker face.

I had forgotten how funny she could be. How could I have forgotten? Haley's humor is something I always adored about her.

Izzy ignores her sister. "Did you wear a dress?"

"Of course I wore a dress." A sense of nostalgia comes over me. "In fact, I wore two dresses."

"Two? At the same time?"

More wit from the one sitting next to me. I wish I could figure out how to bring out more this side of Haley. She's been distant all day and now suddenly she's engaged. This is the Haley I knew before Caitlin died.

I cut my eyes at Haley, trying to keep up the lighthearted banter. "Not at the *same time.* There was a cute, short, skimpy dress I really wanted, but my mother wouldn't let me buy it, even though I had my own money. Instead, she bought me this ugly navy dress with a collar that went to my knees."

"For a *formal* dance?" Izzy cackles from the backseat.

"And you wore it?" Haley asks.

"The way it worked in my house was you did exactly as you were told or you didn't go. The dress code was my stepfather's making, but my mother enforced it. No cleavage, no bare arms, nothing above the knee. No skirts or shorts."

"Was he Mormon?" Haley.

I shake my head.

"Amish?" Haley again.

Izzy laughs at her sister's joke, and I realize that even though none of my orchestrated conversations came to pass today, something is definitely happening between Haley and Izzy. It seems as if Izzy is on the verge of speaking to her sister. Of saying *some-*

thing, even if it is *F-off*, as she would have put it. I think Izzy wants to speak to Haley; she just can't quite get over the hump.

"So, I wore the blue dress my mother bought downstairs," I go on, "but I had a different dress in my bag. A friend loaned it to me. I stood for a picture in front of the fireplace in my mother's living room with Rudy in the ridiculous sailor dress. He had good enough manners not to say anything about how awful it was. Then, once we drove away in the green punch buggy, I changed into the other dress."

"Right in the car, in front of a boy?" Izzy asks.

Haley rolls her eyes in her sister's direction, but doesn't say anything.

"The dress was a pale pink. Short." I touch high on my thigh. "And sleeveless. Like a little tank dress, only it was lacy, sort of a flapper-style thing. It was pretty demure for nowadays, but daring for me." Remembering the dress and how tickled I'd been that Rudy had asked me to the prom makes me feel warm inside. "I had a great night. At least until I got caught." I watch cars zip past us, going in the opposite direction, and enjoy the memory. I'd been so infatuated with Rudy. I'd thought I was in love with him. He was my first serious crush. "After the prom, I was allowed to go out to this diner we used to go to with my friends, as long as I was home by eleven forty-five. I was going to change back into the navy getup in the car on the way home. But my stepdad came to the diner to see if I was really there and he caught me in the *hussy* dress."

Izzy leans forward. "What's a hussy?"

"It's an old-fashioned word for a girl who puts out," Haley explains.

"Mom!" Izzy exclaims.

I glance at Izzy in the rearview, amused by Haley's definition and a little concerned that my youngest knows what it means to *put out*. "I was grounded for weeks. And when my prison sentence was almost up, I got caught lying about an SAT prep class I was supposedly taking. I was actually hanging out with Rudy, and my stepdad added weeks to my punishment. I spent half the summer before my senior year in high school in my bedroom."

Haley stares at me, a bit of a smirk on her face. "I can't believe you did those things. You actually lied to your parents? Sneaked around?"

I feel my cheeks grow warm. I've never told my children much about my teenage years because I didn't want them to think what I did was okay. The lying, the sneaking around, the thinking I knew what was good for me more than my parents. Which I probably did, but that's neither here nor there.

"I was pretty disrespectful. They were doing what they thought was best."

Haley sits back in her seat and rubs her forearm, lost in her thoughts.

I glance at her several times, trying to gauge her mood. Finally, I just ask, "Are you feeling like you want to do it?"

She answers without hesitation. "A little bit." She thinks on it. "But . . . it's not too bad."

"Rubbing will irritate it," I say before I think. "You'll be bleeding again. And you used that whole box of Band-Aids. We'll have to get more."

"I'm trying not to cut," she says sharply, and looks out the window. "That's going to have to be good enough for you right now, Mom."

We ride for a half hour in silence. I've killed the mood in the car. I'm annoyed with myself. Why couldn't I just let it go? And Haley is right. She's trying. That's the first step.

It's after sunset when I take the exit off the interstate to go to the hotel where Haley made reservations for us.

Haley holds the iPad over her head to pass it back to Izzy. "Can we stop at a drugstore? I better get some more Band-Aids. And some other stuff."

"Do you want to eat first? Stop at the drugstore first?" I make my tone light. "Or should we go to the hotel and drop off *you know who*." I tilt my head toward the backseat, trying to be funny. Or at least amusing.

"Mom, you can't leave Izzy alone in a hotel room. She's too young. Somebody will call child protective services."

I laugh out loud.

Izzy looks annoyed. "I could stay alone if I wanted to." She crosses her arms over her chest. "I don't know why she has to be mean to me all the time."

The comment isn't directed exactly to Haley, but it's close. We're definitely making headway. And I'm pleased. Now, if I can just keep Haley in the hotel room tonight, I'll feel like we've had a good day. "Okay," I say. "So drugstore first, then we'll check in so we don't lose our room, and then we get dinner. You guys decide where we're going. My brain is fried."

I signal and pull into a chain drugstore parking lot. The minute the car stops, Haley opens the door and hops out. She leans back into the car. "We need anything else?"

I wonder if I should go in with her. Just to keep an eye on her. But I feel like . . . I need to give her a little space. She could have taken off this morning if she'd wanted to. She didn't and I need to have a little faith. "You need money?"

"Of course." Which sounds more like her than anything else she's said today. Or maybe more like Caitlin. Caitlin always had her hand out for money. But that's just teenagers, isn't it?

I grab my wallet out of the bag I've stashed behind her seat and pull out a twenty. "Enough?" I hold up the bill.

She grimaces. I give her a ten, too, glad I thought to get money from an ATM when we made a bathroom stop this afternoon.

"Be right back," Haley says, and closes the door before I can say anything else.

I let the interior light go out before I say anything to Izzy. I turn in my seat to look at her. She's got her bare feet up on the seat, the cat on her lap. "You okay?" I ask.

"She treats me like I'm a baby. You treat me like I'm a baby. No one gives me any credit for being as mature as I am. Did you know that Macy in my tae kwon do class still sleeps with her light on? She has bad dreams about *Monsters, Inc.* monsters coming out of her closet." She makes a face. "Which is stupid because who's afraid of those kinds of monsters? Sulley's cute and cuddly." She gestures with one hand. "That was the whole point of the movie, right?"

"I don't think you're a baby."

She doesn't say anything.

"Izz, if I thought you were less mature than you are, I wouldn't have brought you on this trip. Your sister is dealing with some serious problems. Problems girls your age aren't usually exposed to."

"Because she killed Caitlin."

"I told Haley," I say sharper than I mean to, "and I'm telling you." I check my tone and go on. "Haley didn't *kill* Caitlin." My voice cracks when I say her name and I pause a beat before I go on. "The word kill suggests premeditation. Do you know that word?"

She doesn't answer.

"Do you keep a list of words? Like Haley and Caitlin used to? If you do, you should put it on your list. To do something premeditated means you intended to do it. You made plans ahead of time to see it through. Haley didn't enter that intersection intending to run the stop sign. She didn't intend to get hit by another car. She didn't intend—"

"For Caitlin to go through the windshield," Izzy says softly.

She's staring straight ahead. I can see her face in the light coming from a sign advertising shingles shots free to all Medicare patients.

She rubs her chin across Mr. Cat's head. She won't look at me. "Did she know Caitlin didn't have her seat belt on? We always wear seat belts."

It's a good question. I never posed it to Haley. I'm not sure if I want to know the answer or not. It won't change anything. Of course if Haley didn't know Caitlin wasn't belted in, I might be able to convince her that that's a good reason not to blame herself. But what if she did know?

"It dings if you don't buckle," Izzy points out, still avoiding eye contact. "She should have heard the dinging and told Caitlin to put her seat belt on. Unless the dinger was broken. Do you think it was broken?" She looks at me hopefully. "It was a lame car. You think maybe the dinger was broken?"

The look on Izzy's face makes me want to lie to her. What if I told her the signal that alerted passengers to an unbuckled seat belt *was* broken? Would she talk to Haley then? But I can't lie to her. Of course I can't. "I don't know if Haley knew Caitlin wasn't buckled in. It could be that she unbuckled to get something." I feel a heaviness coming over me. The weight of Caitlin's death returning to sit on my shoulders and in the pit of my stomach. "I guess you could ask her."

Izzy doesn't say anything; she just keeps petting the cat.

I lean back in my seat and close my eyes for a minute. I've driven a little over six hundred miles today and I had the pants scared off me this morning. I'm tired. So tired I wonder how the girls would react to the idea of just grabbing something at a grocery store, checking into the hotel, and skipping the restaurant. We could have a picnic on one of the beds: good bread, cheese, olives, some gourmet cookies. It could be fun. And I could eat in the SpongeBob PJ bottoms Izzy loaned me. I sit here contemplating a long shower for a couple of minutes.

Then I open my eyes. "How long has Haley been inside?"

"I don't know," Izzy says.

I pick up my cell phone. Laney's texted me.

Scouts. Home by nine. Call me when you get in. Hope you had a good day.

I'll call her later. Or maybe just text her.

It's 8:43. Has Haley been in the store ten minutes? Or has it been more than ten? It doesn't take ten minutes to buy Band-Aids. And the place isn't busy. I haven't seen anyone go in since she did and only one person come out.

I set my phone back on the console. I wait another two minutes before I pull the keys out of the ignition. "Stay in the car," I say.

"You're leaving me here?"

I hear Izzy release her seat belt. "I don't want to stay here. I want to go in with you."

"Stay." I get out of the car. "And keep the doors locked until I get back."

"I don't think it's legal to leave kids locked up in—"

I close my door and lock the car with the key fob in my hand. I take one look at Izzy, watching me from the backseat, her face anxious, and I turn away. Then hurry to the sidewalk and through the automatic doors into the bright lights of the store. I glance at the checkout counter. No Haley. In fact, no customers. There's a young man in a blue smock with a nametag texting on his cell.

"Welcome to happy and healthy," he greets in a Midwestern accent, sounding entirely too cheerful.

I face the brightly lit store, trying to get my bearings. I scan signs. First aid is on the far side of the store. I walk quickly down one of the main aisles running perpendicular to the shorter ones. She's not in hair care. She's not in dental care. The makeup was up front. She wasn't there either. And the aisle of Band-Aids and topical ointments is empty. I take the other main aisle, back toward the front door. There's a man trying to figure out what diapers to get in the baby aisle. There's not another soul in the store, except for the guy up front and another clerk, an androgynous someone, who's stocking toilet paper.

The young man at the front counter looks up and slides his cell into the pocket of his smock. "Can I help you?"

"Was there a girl in here, just a minute ago? Black hair." I touch my stubby ponytail and scrutinize his face, praying he's an honest soul. "Bought Band-Aids?"

He nods. "Sure was."

I plant both hands on the counter. "Do you know where she went? She's my daughter." I feel that sense of panic coming on again. But she doesn't even have her backpack. She couldn't have left. "I was outside waiting for her. I didn't see her come out the front."

"She asked where the restroom is." He points. "Near the pharmacy."

I exhale, realizing only now that I've been holding my breath. "Restroom," I repeat. "Right. Thanks." I give him a quick smile and hurry in that direction.

At the back of the store, there's a small hallway right off the pharmacy waiting area. The pharmacy's closed. I push the heavy door labeled LADIES and it swings open. I hear the water running before I see her.

She looks up from washing her hands, surprised.

I inaudibly heave a sigh of relief. Am I being paranoid? I think I am. "Have to pee." I give my daughter the same smile I gave the guy out front. I don't want her to know I'm checking up on her.

"Again? We stopped an hour ago."

"Hour and a half." I make a beeline for the closest stall. Luckily, I really do have to pee.

Haley's waiting near the door for me when I come out of the stall. She's got a small plastic bag dangling from her wrist. She isn't wearing her usual black eyeliner today and I realize how young she looks without it. Younger than she is. Is that why she wears it?

I flip on the water and soap my hands. "Get what you need?"

"Yup."

I rinse and walk over to the paper towel dispenser. It's not the automatic kind. I pull several brown paper towels out and dry my hands. There's a small, open waste can near the door. As I drop my damp paper towels into it, I see a white and pink box on the top.

Even without reading the words, I know what it is. A pregnancy test. And I'm so naïve . . . such an idiot that the first thought that goes through my head is *aww, isn't that sweet? Whoever bought the test was so excited, she couldn't even wait to get home to find out.*

Then it hits me . . . as hard as if Haley reached out and slapped me in the face.

It's *Haley's* pregnancy test. My daughter just took a pregnancy test.

I meet her gaze and I know I'm right. And then I don't know what comes over me. She has the door halfway open and I reach out and shove it shut, practically having to wrestle it because it's on a pneumatic drive.

"You're pregnant?" I shout, loud enough for the young man in the front of the store, no doubt, to hear me. "You're fucking *pregnant?*"

Chapter 32

Haley

51 days, 22 hours

Mom startles me and I take a step back. Her voice echoes so loud in my head and in the tile bathroom that I want to cover my ears with my hands.

I don't think she's ever yelled at me like this before. She certainly never hollered the F word at me. Moms aren't supposed to say *that*. That word's for punky teenagers like me. Isn't it?

So it scares me.

She scares me.

As she pushes the door shut, trapping me inside the bathroom with her, I take another step back, without even meaning to. It's just what you do, I guess. You try to get away from the crazy person, even if she's your mother.

When Todd didn't show up last night, when he didn't even bother to text me to tell me he wasn't coming, I was weirdly okay with it. Now, I wish he'd come. I wish I could have made him come for me. I wish I were headed for Alaska right this minute. Even being in a car with loser Todd would be better than being trapped with my mother in a bathroom off an interstate.

"Are you pregnant?" she repeats through gritted teeth.

"No," I whisper. You'd think my response would be to holler

back. *I* think my response should be to holler back, but I don't. "It's negative. See." I point at the box.

I can't believe I was dumb enough to put it in the trash can. But there wasn't one of those personal hygiene receptacles in the bathroom stall and she wasn't supposed to come into the store. She was supposed to be waiting in the car for me.

"Look for yourself." I take the two steps to the trash can, grab the box, and pull the pee stick out. I hold it up so she can see. My hand is shaking. I don't know why. "Negative. See?"

She grabs it out of my hand, which is kind of gross, because I peed on it. She stares at it for a second. "Did you follow the directions?" She's still loud. And still *really* pissed. "Because if you didn't follow the directions—"

"I followed the directions," I tell her. "You just pee on the stick and wait three minutes. I probably waited four or five, just to be sure."

She stares at the pee stick again for a second and then drops it into the trash can. "Who?" she demands. "Who have you been having sex with?"

There's a knock on the bathroom door. We both look at it.

"Everything okay in there?" comes a voice. It's a woman. She sounds like she's scared of my mom too.

"Everything's fine," Mom hollers back, making it clear the woman better butt out.

I wonder what would happen if I told the lady on the other side of the door that I *did* need help. My mind races. I could tell her that a madwoman who claims to be my mother has kidnapped me and is holding me against my will.

There *is* some truth to it.

I bet someone would call the cops.

If the cops come, what will happen? They'll just talk to Mom and me and they'll find out I'm a teenager *going through a difficult time.* Once it's all cleared up, they'll let us go. Mom will be mad, but it would sure diffuse what's going on here right now.

I open my mouth to holler for help.

But then I think about Izzy, sitting in the car waiting, with that ratty cat. If the cops come, she'll freak out. What if they take Mom into custody until they talk to Dad to confirm her identity?

Then Mom will have to tell Dad about the pee stick. I don't want him to know. He won't understand. He'll think I'm a ho-bag. He's not a girl. He'll never get it.

Mom's still got her hand on the door to keep anyone from coming in.

The lady knocks again. "Ma'am?"

My mom grabs the door and pulls it open. "Could you excuse me for a second while I speak to my daughter about a pregnancy test she just took in your bathroom?"

I can't see the lady's face. The door is between us. But I can see Mom's. She's looking pretty pissy and pretty snooty.

"Sorry," the lady mumbles. "Just wanted to be sure everyone was okay."

"Thank you." Mom lets go of the door.

I hear footsteps as the employee beats feet.

Mom crosses her arms over her chest. "Who are you having sex with? That man? The one at the house where I picked you up? Do you need to be tested for STDs? AIDS?"

She's still being loud. Her voice is echoing off the bathroom walls. I know the people in the store can hear her and I'm embarrassed. Almost more for her than for me.

When I don't answer, she goes on like a crazy woman. "Are there other men other than him? What about that guy, Miguel, who was hanging around the house before Caitlin died? And Todd? I know very well you've been seeing *him*. Who else did you have sex with? Who could potentially be the father of my grandchild?"

I look down. The plastic bag is hanging off my wrist: more Band-Aids and a pack of elastics for our hair. This morning we realized we only had two to share between the three of us. Mom and Izzy got them today, but we agreed we'd buy some more.

I want to rub my arm. Hard. Or at least bounce my ball. Riding in the car all day, I haven't been getting the chance to bounce much. I miss it. I miss the feel of the ball in my hand, the smell the rubber leaves on my fingers.

"I don't know," I say quietly. I stare at my Converses.

"You don't know or you won't say?" she demands.

Tears burn my eyes. "I always use a condom. It's just that—" I wipe my eyes with the back of my hand.

I don't know why I'm crying. I was pretty sure I wasn't pregnant. I really *do* make guys use a condom. I don't want anybody's cooties. But there were a couple of times when I was drunk or high or . . . I don't know. I haven't had a period in six or seven weeks. I just figured better safe than—

"Who have you been having sex with, Haley?" Mom grabs me by both arms, just below my armpits. "Who could have gotten you pregnant?"

I choke on my tears. I don't want to cry. I don't want to be weak. I sure don't want her to see me crying. "I don't know."

"You don't know?" she hollers in my face. Then she pulls back. "Were you raped?" Her tone changes drastically. "Oh, God, Haley. Did someone rape you?"

I consider saying yes. Just for a split second.

I pull away from her and wipe my eyes with my sleeve, dragging my arm across my face so I can feel the cuts under the Band-Aids. It hurts. And it feels good. "I'm not pregnant, so why does it matter?" I tell her. But if I was—" I stop and start again. "If I was, I wouldn't know who the father is. Without, you know, a paternity test. But I'm not pregnant." I try to sound defiant, but I sound like a little girl. "It was negative, Mom. I'm *not pregnant*." Tears run down my cheeks. "I'm sorry," I whisper. "I'm sorry. But you don't have to worry. I'm not pregnant."

She just stands there for a minute looking at me. She's breathing hard. Panting. She turns away suddenly, walks away. "I'm sorry, Haley." Her voice is shaky. She starts to pace. She's shaking her head. "I shouldn't have—I shouldn't have spoken to you that way."

"It's okay." I sniff and wipe my nose on my sleeve. "If I were my kid, I might have lost my shit too. I'm a bad person." I'm shaking my head now too. I look down. "I've done all of these bad things, and now I'm having sex with random guys and—"

"It's not that, sweetie."

Mom walks over to stand in front of me. She grabs my arms again, but not hard this time. Not out of anger. "I'm upset because I see me in you."

I look up at her. That's crazy. Mom is perfect. She's beautiful and she's perfect. That's why I hate her so much. She always does the right thing. She says the right thing. People like her. "What do you mean, you see me in you?" I ask. "We're nothing alike."

"When I was seventeen . . ." She lets go of my arms and wraps one arm around herself. "When I was seventeen, Haley. That boy I told you about. Rudy." She keeps starting and stopping and starting again. "We. He and I—" She looks up at me, tears in her eyes. "I got pregnant that summer before my senior year in high school."

I know my mouth drops open. I couldn't have been any more surprised by that revelation than if she'd told me she and Dad were actually aliens, come to earth to build an alien colony. "You got pregnant?" I whisper, still pretty sure I misheard.

She nods.

"You had an abortion?"

She shakes her head no. "My mother said I had to have the baby. My stepfather, he—"

She looks down and I can tell by the look on her face that remembering this hurts her. A part of me wants to put my arms around her, but I can't do it. I just can't.

"They insisted I had to have the baby, but then I had a miscarriage at ten weeks. No one knows I was ever pregnant when I was seventeen, except my mom and stepdad, Laney and your dad and now—" Her voice catches in her throat. "Now, you."

I just stand there staring at her for a minute. I can't believe my perfect mother got knocked up by her eleventh grade prom date. I guess, technically, it wasn't a prom-knock-up. But it's sure close.

Mom sighs and walks away. She goes to one of the stalls and

pulls out a long ribbon of toilet paper. I watch her blow her nose. "Were you going to run away last night, Haley? The truth."

I try to weigh the importance of giving her what she wants— the truth—and the pain it will cause her. But who am I kidding? She knows about pain. And it hasn't killed her yet. "I thought about it," I admit, without an apology. "But then I didn't." Only a little lie. If Todd had showed up, I don't know if I would have gotten in the car with him or not.

Now she looks pale. She just stands there with the toilet paper in her hand and I think to myself that she needs to spruce herself up. She needs to get some jeans that fit. She needs to dye her hair and she needs some lipstick. She needs to start looking like she's alive again.

"We should go to the car," is what she finally says. "Izzy's outside alone."

I put my hand on the heavy door. "Are you going to tell Dad? About the pregnancy test?"

She wipes her nose with the paper and throws it in the trash can. "Your dad and I have never kept secrets from each other."

I think about that for a second. "Izzy?" I ask.

She walks toward me. She looks tired and upset and scared and I feel bad because, once again, it's all my fault.

"I don't really think this is something your ten-year-old sister needs to know, do you?"

I open the door.

"This conversation is not over," she warns, walking to the doorway. "It's just tabled. You understand me? And when we get home, you're being tested. For everything. I don't care where. Our family doctor. A clinic. But you're being tested." She holds her finger up to me. "And it's going to stop. The risky sex. I won't let you ruin your life, Haley. *Damn* it. I'm not going to do it."

Then she throws her arms around me and she hugs me so hard that it hurts.

And for some reason, I feel a little better.

Chapter 33

Julia

Illinois

The next night I stand at the bathroom door in our hotel room outside of Chicago, my cell phone in my hand. "Stay in the room, girls," I say, feeling so tired, I can barely put one foot in front of the other. "Or you're dead meat."

Izzy laughs and looks back at the TV, stuffing a French fry in her mouth.

She and Haley are sitting on the same bed, eating chicken sandwiches and fries. No vegetables; we've unanimously declared this expedition to be vegetable-free. At least until we get to Laney's where we know we'll be bombarded by big salads and plates of steamed organic vegetables.

Haley and Izzy aren't talking to each other, at least Izzy isn't talking to Haley, but Izzy *is* sitting near her sister, of her own volition. Mostly because she couldn't see the TV from our bed, but I'll take what I can get.

In the bathroom, I turn on the shower so the girls can't overhear my conversation, and I call Laney.

"Hey, sweetie," she answers the phone. "I've been waiting to hear from you." I hear her say, her voice muffled, "Boys, take it in the other room."

As we've driven east, we've crossed time zones. We're only an hour behind Laney tonight and it makes me feel closer to her. Tonight, I feel like I'm actually going to make it to Maine. This time last night, I had my doubts.

"Where are you?" Laney asks me.

"Chicago." I lean forward and look into the mirror over the sink. I look like hell. Another ten-hour day in the car. "Somewhere outside of Chicago. I'm not even sure what town. Haley made the reservation."

"So you've still got her? Excellent," she teases.

I don't laugh, but I smile. I stayed up half the night last night, talking to Laney. Crying and talking, first in the hallway outside our hotel room, then inside the room when I started to scare other guests with my crying jags. Laney was the true friend she's always been. She coddled me when I needed coddling and she told me to knock it the hell off when I started slipping into the depths of self-pity.

"How'd the day go?" she asks me.

"Good." I think about it for a second and realize it really was . . . not bad. "Pretty good," I clarify. "For some reason, telling Haley about my pregnancy has made her . . . I don't know. Less hostile. Haley's still rubbing her arm, but she hasn't cut herself since we left. If she was going to do it, I think she would have last night after I screamed at her. Don't you think?"

I'm not really looking for an answer. I take my toothbrush out of my toiletries bag on the sink and squirt toothpaste from a travel-size tube. "No, the day wasn't half bad. Haley offered to let Izzy ride up front this afternoon and she kept the cat on the backseat. We played the license plate game twice." I groan. "It's getting old, but it passes the time and it's something we can all do together without anyone getting angry or crying."

Laney laughs. "And the conversations today?"

"Meh." I stick my brush in my mouth and brush. I rinse, using my hand to cup water, before I speak again. "Sorry, brushing my teeth before I get in the shower, which I desperately need. I stink.

And Haley's waiting for her turn. And I'm making Izzy take one tonight whether she wants to or not. I have no idea when the last time was that she bathed." I shake my toothbrush. "No serious discussions today; I think Haley and I were both still over-whelmed from last night." I shut off the water. "But Haley seems, I don't know . . . okay. It makes no sense to me, but after I screamed at her like I was stark raving mad, she seemed more like herself. Like before Caitlin died. It's not like she's sprouted angel wings or anything, but today I saw several glimpses of my quirky, smart-assy . . . perceptive kid."

"She have any more contact with the boyfriend?"

"Todd?" I drop my toothbrush into my toiletries bag. "I don't think so. Apparently she'd been using the iPad to text him. I feel like an idiot. That never occurred to me. That you could iMes-sage with the iPad. But Izzy had the iPad all day today, except when Haley was looking for a hotel and making the online reser-vation. I think they're done. I said something to her about him today and she made some comment about hoping certain body parts fell off."

"Good riddance," Laney says.

"Exactly." I unbutton my baggy jeans and step out of them and add my panties to the pile. I'll have to put my SpongeBobs back on, after my shower, but I have a clean pair of jeans to wear tomorrow. I wish I'd packed more clothes. I don't know what I was thinking Sunday night when I packed. I guess I wasn't thinking anything.

"You talk to Ben?"

"Not since last night." I'd given him a quick recap of the bath-room scene at the drugstore and told him I needed him to fly to Maine. That with this new revelation, we need him. His re-sponse? He'd get back to me after he checked with the office, which honestly hadn't fazed me all that much last night. I think I was just too shell-shocked. But as I began to unthaw today, I started getting really angry with him. He didn't call me today and I'm pretty close to livid with him now. "I guess I should call him after my shower." I exhale. "But I don't think I can pull another all-nighter. I'm not going to get into it with him on the phone tonight. I need some sleep."

"He needs to man up. He needs to come here and be with his family," Laney says firmly.

"I agree." I maneuver my way out of my shirt, taking the phone away from my ear, then bringing it back when I drop the T-shirt in the dirty clothes pile. "Would it be terrible of me to just not call him tonight? To wait and see if he calls me?"

"You should at least let him know you're okay. That you're at the hotel."

I push my hair back and look at myself in the mirror again. I still don't recognize this skinnier version of myself. "Maybe I'll just text him. Leave the ball in his court."

"Jules—"

"I know. I know what you're going to say. I can't keep running away from him. Away from the mess of my marriage, but really, Laney, I can only take so much grief. And I don't know how much more I can take."

"You're going to be okay," she says, gently. "You're doing the right things. You and the girls are going to be okay."

"And Ben and me?"

She doesn't answer right away and I feel a heaviness in my chest that scares me. I've never once considered life without Ben. Tears fill my eyes. I can't go there tonight. I just can't.

"I should get into the shower," I say, not wanting to force her to say what we're both thinking, which is what if Ben won't come to Maine? What if he doesn't care enough about our girls, about me, to come and talk to me? Talk to our girls? Help me figure out what the hell we're supposed to do next for Haley?

"Get your shower," Laney says. "You'll feel better. You'll sure smell better." She laughs.

"You're funny." I look in the mirror and groan. "My roots are so bad, Laney."

"We'll take care of that when you get here. A bottle of L'Oréal and half an hour in my kitchen and you'll be the beautiful blonde I know and love."

"It's a date. I'm shooting for Rochester, New York, tomorrow."

"Yay!" Laney exclaims. "You'll be here Friday night! And we'll have the whole weekend together. Do you want me to go open up the cottage? Or do you and the girls want to stay here with us?"

"I don't know." Laney lives in a sweet little Victorian house in a town near Sebago Lake, less than an hour from Portland. I like the idea of being able to lie on her bed and talk to her after the kids have gone to bed. Maybe have a glass of wine with her. But she's only got three bedrooms, so it's going to be a little cozy. And it might be awkward for her boys, considering the circumstances of our visit.

"Let's plan for us to stay Friday night with you and we'll go from there. If Ben comes, even if it's just for the weekend, we could go to the cottage," I say hopefully.

"You'll need some space, in which case you guys should definitely take the cottage."

I smile, so thankful I have her. "I'll call you tomorrow night."

"Be safe," she tells me.

I disconnect and hold the phone in my hand, debating whether or not to hit Ben's number. The bathroom is getting steamy now. I can't see myself as well in the mirror. I hesitate and then go to texts.

Made Chicago. Safe and Sound. Sebago Lake by Friday. You coming?

I hit send, set the phone on the sink, and step into the shower. I take my time under the hot water, trying to relax and just not think about anything. For the first time in two months, I don't even cry. When I get out of the shower, I hold my towel with one hand and check my phone with the other. Ben's texted me back.

Glad you made it. Talk tomorrow.

Nothing about him coming.

I dry off, put on my SpongeBobs, and join my girls.

* * *

We turn off the light at ten thirty. All three of us are beat. Izzy falls asleep in five minutes, curled up beside me with Mr. Cat in her arms. But I can't sleep, even though I'm exhausted. I lie awake, listening to the sound of the air conditioner blowing; we all like to sleep in a chilly room.

I'm hurt that Ben didn't call. Or at least respond about coming to Maine, in his text. And I'm angry. But I don't know what to do with any of it.

I roll onto my side to face the other bed. My eyes adjust to the darkness and I see Haley, lying in the middle of the bed, her hands above her head. She isn't asleep, either.

"What are you thinking about?" I ask, keeping my voice low so I don't wake Izzy.

I see Haley shrug. "I don't know."

I watch her for a moment: my beautiful, smart, messed-up kid, and my heart aches for her. For her pain that I can't take away. "I was thinking about your dad," I tell her.

On impulse, I get up and cross the two feet between our beds. I slide under the sheet with her before she can protest. "He really hurt my feelings today."

She scoots over a little. Not too far, just far enough so we won't *accidentally* touch, I imagine. "He's not coming to Maine," she says, her voice flat. She sounds disappointed.

"I don't know. I think he *needs* to." I turn my head to look at her. "Don't you?"

She lowers her arms and I see she's holding the rubber ball. She's been wearing the same long-sleeve black T-shirt since we left; I can't see the bandages on her arm. But I know they're there and I know what's under them.

"Dad's Dad," Haley says quietly. "You can't expect anything more of him than he's ever been."

I roll onto my side, sliding my hands under my head. "What does that mean?"

"I don't know." She continues to stare at the ceiling, moving the fingers of one hand, rolling the ball. "Just that . . . you're not going to change him. *We're* not going to change him. It's not that

I think he doesn't love us, but . . ." She's quiet for a second. Thinking. "A person can only give what they have. You know?"

I don't know what she's talking about. Not exactly. But I do get that in her own way, she's trying to make me feel better, while not laying blame on her father.

I roll onto my back again and lie there beside Haley for a couple of minutes, saying nothing. I can feel her slight movement, rolling the ball in her fingers. I hear Izzy's steady breathing. Mr. Cat is purring. It's a soothing sound and I finally start to feel sleepy. "Tell me about the ball," I say.

"What do you mean?" She sounds defensive. "It's just a stupid ball."

"A stupid *pink* ball? I remember it, Haley," I say gently. "I remember Caitlin bouncing it the week she died. At the pizza place. It was Caitlin's ball."

She doesn't say anything.

"Did Caitlin give you the ball? Is that why you're carrying it around? Because if it's—"

"She didn't give it to me," she interrupts in a whisper. "I stole it out of her backpack. I did it because she was driving me crazy bouncing it and she really liked it. Then—" Her voice becomes filled with emotion.

I squeeze my eyes shut, fighting the floodgates that threaten.

"She asked me if I'd seen it, but I—" She is silent for a moment. "I didn't get the chance to give it back."

I try to think of something to say to make her feel better, something like "I'm sure Caitlin didn't mind" or "I think she would have wanted you to have it," but I don't. I get the feeling that anything I say will seem as if I'm trying to negate her feelings. And if there's one thing I've learned over the last two months, it's that you can't help how you feel. So I'm quiet with her for a while, then I say, "Do you think Izzy is okay?"

"What do you mean?" Her voice is normal again.

"I'm beginning to worry. She seems to be dealing with Caitlin's death okay, but two months is a long time to go without talking to you." I raise my hand and rest my arm across my forehead. "I wonder if it was a mistake not to take her to counseling after Caitlin died."

"She'll talk to me when she's ready."

I hesitate, not sure if I should say what I'm thinking, but I plunge ahead. "Have you told her how sorry you are?"

"What do you mean?"

"I—" I seriously consider backtracking. But I'm this far into it now and Haley's a smart cookie. There's no way she doesn't know where this is going. "Have you told her you're sorry about what happened?"

"How could I not be sorry? I think about it every day, every hour, every minute. I think about all the ways I could have changed what happened. If I'd just driven home a different way. If I'd stopped for a Gatorade. If I'd—"

Her voice catches in her throat and I reach across the bed and find her hand with mine. She's squeezing the ball, so I just close my hand over her fist. "It's just a thought," I say.

And then we drift off to sleep.

Chapter 34

Izzy

Day 4 of the best adventure of my life

When I wake up, Mom's not in bed with me. I figure she's in the bathroom, but when I push Mr. Cat off me and roll over, I see her in bed with She Who Shall Not Be Named. When I see her over there instead of here, I'm a little bit jealous. It's been really fun sleeping together, having her here in bed with me so I can just roll over and touch her, if I want. I guess it's only fair that the other one should have a turn too. But hasn't she had a lot more turns than me already? Since she's almost eighteen?

Most people think that the youngest kid in the family is the spoiled one. People talk about how parents give the youngest one whatever they want, how they fawn over them and stuff. Not been my experience. Maybe I was the favorite when I was little. I don't remember when I was a baby. But once She Who Shall Not Be Named went to high school? Everything changed. That's when I became invisible to Mom.

Three years, eight months ago.

I know. I was six; I was in the first grade. How could I remember that? I have a really good memory. Especially about this.

I remember it clearly. The oldest one went to high school and all of a sudden Mom was crazy busy with stuff going on in She

Who Shall Not Be Named's life: parents' council, homecoming float chairman, dance chaperone, you name it. And Caitlin was really getting into cheer by then, so Mom was busy on weekends with her, hauling her all over the state to competitions, doing her hair, helping make cheer outfits with other moms.

It's not like suddenly everyone was mean to me, but when my sisters hit high school and became super important, I just kind of faded into the background. Dad started disappearing around the same time. I mean, he was still here, but . . . he didn't seem as interested in me as he'd once been. I guess if I'm really fair, if I'm *objective* (I spelled it wrong on the last quiz. No *k* before the *t*), Dad didn't just start forgetting about me. He started to forget about all of us. I guess he just got tired of us.

Mr. Cat climbs back on top of me and starts to purr. What is it with him wanting to sit on my chest all the time? When I grow boobs, which should be any day now, where does he think he's going to sit?

I scratch his head and glance at Mom and She Who Shall Not Be Named. Something's going on with them. Or something *went* on. The night before last. In the drugstore, of all places. She Who Shall Not Be Named went in and didn't come out. Then Mom went in. Then they both came out looking like they'd been crying. I asked Mom yesterday what happened, but she just shook her head and told me that if I wanted to listen to the radio for a little while, I could. Mostly we haven't been able to listen to it since we left home because we're supposed to be *working through things*. Or at least the one cutting herself with sharp objects for fun is.

I hear movement from the other bed and I look over to see Mom opening her eyes. She smiles when she sees me and it makes me feel so good, the way she looks at me, that it almost makes up for her sleeping with the crazy girl instead of me.

"Morning." Her voice is soft and floaty.

She looks pretty this morning. And not sad. I've noticed the last couple of mornings that when she wakes up, she doesn't look as sad as she does later in the day. It's like, as the hours pass, the more dead Caitlin is. Which kind of makes sense because when I first wake up in the morning, I sometimes forget that she's pushing up daisies.

"Sleep okay?" Mom asks me, still only half awake.

I nod.

"Good." She stretches and then pushes her hair back and turns her head to look at me. "Why don't you hop in the shower before Haley gets up?"

I groan really dramatically. I don't like it that Mom thinks I need to be told to take a shower. I'm old enough to know if I need a shower. My hair's hardly even dirty. And when I wash it, it gets all frizzy. And the only thing worse than red hair is *frizzy* red hair.

"Go on," she says.

And because I can't just flat out say no the way Haley does, I get up to head for the bathroom.

"Put him in his kennel," she tells me, meaning Mr. Cat.

"He's fine. He's too old to run away."

A few minutes later, I'm in the shower, scrubbing my pits with a little bar of soap I got from a basket on the sink, when the bathroom door opens. The glass is pretty fogged up, but I can see that it's She Who Shall Not Be Named. She's wearing her stupid black T-shirt and my Little Mermaid pants.

I almost yell, *Do you mind?* but I catch myself. I'm not talking to her. Not ever again. She wasted my sister. In Caitlin's memory, it's the least I can do.

I turn around so if she *can* see through the steamed-up glass of the shower stall, she'll see my bare butt and get the hint.

I hear the toilet lid go up. I can't believe she's got the nerve to pee while I'm taking a shower.

"Mom says to move along. She wants to get on the road."

I hear her peeing, which is totally gross.

"You hear me, pipsqueak?" She flushes.

But she doesn't leave the bathroom and finally I can't stand it and I turn around. The warm water hits my back. *What?* I want to holler at her. *What do you want?* But I just look at her through the

Colleen Faulkner

steamy glass, one hand covering my nipples and the other my lady parts. I know she used to change my diaper and stuff, but I have a right to privacy, now that I'm almost a teenager. Don't I?

"Izzy." She's still standing there, her hands at her sides. She's staring at the floor. "Izzy, I just wanted to tell you . . ." She stops.

I look at her through the steam that makes her seem all blurry. She sounds like she's going to cry and a lump comes up in my throat.

"Never mind," she says. "It doesn't matter."

And then she leaves.

Then Mom comes in. And pees.

"Is this a train station?" I holler from inside the shower.

"The phrase is, *Is this Grand Central?*" She flushes. "I'm going to run downstairs and get coffee and talk to someone at the front desk." I hear her messing around at the sink. Then water comes on. "I don't think they gave me my discount." Her words are garbled. She's brushing her teeth. "Move along. I put the cat litter box in a bag in the trash. We'll open a new one in the car. Bring Mr. Cat down when you come. I'm not going to come back up. I want to get on the road." She shuts off the water.

I don't say anything.

"You hear me, Izzy?"

"I hear you. I left my clothes on the end of the bed. Can you bring them in here?"

"Sure."

I hear her leave and then come back. "Out of the shower, Izzy. For a girl who doesn't like to shower, you sure like the shower."

She closes the door and finally I'm alone. Next time I take a shower, I'm definitely locking the door.

I get out and wrap my hair up in one towel and I wrap the other one around my body. I take a washcloth and wipe at the steamy mirror. I look different with my hair up in the towel. Older. And a little bit like Caitlin. It makes me smile.

"See you downstairs," I hear Mom call from the other side of the door. Then I hear the door to the hall close. Great, now I'm

stuck here with She Who Shall Not Be Named, who will probably talk to me like she thinks I'm going to talk back.

I dry off and put on my clothes, which is kind of hard to do because the room is so steamy that I can't get completely dry. But
there's no way I'm dressing out in the room with *her*.

I dry my hair a little bit with the hair dryer attached to the wall
and then I brush my teeth, grab my nightclothes, and go into the
room. She Who Shall Not Be Named is sitting on her bed, watching the news. She's dressed; her backpack is sitting next to her on
the bed. I turn my back to her and stick my stuff in my bag. I get
the little kennel we bought for Mr. Cat and I put it on the bed
and then I get him and put him in it. He hates getting in it and I
don't blame him. I wouldn't want to go in a cage either.

"It's cold in Maine still," She Who Shall Not Be Named says.
"It went down to thirty-five last night. We're going to freeze our
butts off."

I close the door on the kennel kind of hard and it startles Mr.
Cat and he jumps inside. Without saying anything, I grab the
kennel and my bag and go to the door. There's no way I'm staying here alone with her if I don't have to. The hotel room door
closes behind me before I hear her holler, "I guess that means
you're ready to go."

I hear the elevator ding which means it's going to open and I
run for it. I don't want to ride in the elevator with She Who Shall
Not Be Named. By the time I get there, people have stepped off
and the door is starting to close, but I make it just in time. As I
turn to face the doors, they close and I smile.

Guess she can catch the next one.

I see Mom standing at the front desk in the lobby, but I keep
walking. No cats allowed in the hotel. I don't want to get caught
and have Mom get in trouble. There's no way they're giving her
the discount if they know Mr. Cat stayed last night.

It's not until I get to the car in the parking lot that I realize
what a dunce I am. I don't have the key to the car. I put my bag
and then the kennel down on the pavement. I see a piece of

paper stuck under the wiper on the windshield so I walk around to get it. An advertisement for two pizzas for ten dollars.

A car goes by me in the parking lot and I check out the people inside; there's a mom and a dad and a little boy and an old grandpa. I never had a grandpa. Dad's and Mom's dads are dead. Mom didn't know the first one. Her stepdad died before I was born, which I guess isn't a big deal since apparently no one liked him, not even my grandmother.

I walk around to the back of the car again. Still no Mom, but I see She Who Shall Not Be Named coming out the front door. I wonder if she has the key.

Another car goes by. Just a man in a suit. No kids. No grandpa.

I glance down at Mr. Cat's kennel.

I'm so shocked that the paper drifts out of my hand.

The door to the kennel is open and Mr. Cat is gone.

I feel like I can't breathe and my eyes fill up with tears.

I look around and I don't see him. Then I see something dart out from under a car and cut across the space between this row and the next row of cars. It's something furry. A tabby cat!

Before I can think, I turn toward the hotel and scream, "Haley!"

Chapter 35

Haley

53 days, 10 hours

I hear Izzy scream and my head snaps in the direction of her voice. She's standing at the car hollering for me and I get this weird chill that scares the shit out of me. I drop my backpack on the sidewalk and run toward her, darting in front of a car. The car toots its horn; I ignore it and keep running.

"Izzy!" I don't know what's wrong. She's standing there so she can't be hurt. "Izzy?" Is it Mom? It can't be Mom. I just saw her in the lobby.

"Haley! Help me! Mr. Cat got away!" Izzy shrieks, shaking her hand.

I cut between two rows of cars in the hotel parking lot. I'm still running toward her. It seems like it's taking forever to get to her. "Do you see him?"

"He got out." She's blubbering now. I can hardly understand her. "He got out of his kennel! I don't know how it happened. I don't know how the door opened! I put him on the ground and—"

I reach out to her and put out both of my hands to rest them on her shoulders. I look right into her eyes. "Did you see which way he went?" I ask her, calmly, even though my heart is pounding and I'm breathless from running. I was afraid she was hurt. It's just the cat. You can replace a cat. You can't replace a sister.

"I—I don't know. That way!" She points in the direction of the highway that has three lanes running in each direction.

I look, but I don't see him. I just see cars and the busy traffic beyond the parking lot, out on the highway. "You're sure he went that way?"

She rubs at her runny nose with the back of her hand. "I think he went under that white van." She points. "But I don't know! I don't know. He disappeared."

I turn to the van she's pointing to. It's in the next row, closer to the street. "Okay. You go that way." I point. "I'll go this way."

She takes off.

"Don't run! You might scare him!"

She slows down, but she's still trotting.

I move quickly, cutting between the rows, a couple of cars down from the van she pointed out. I keep dropping down to the pavement and looking under the cars. There are cars moving everywhere in the parking lot. People are checking out of their rooms, heading to their destinations. I wonder what will get Mr. Cat first, a car in the parking lot or one on the highway.

I can't believe Izzy didn't latch the kennel.

I drop to my knees and look in every direction. No cat. No damned cat. I get up and dart between two more cars.

How could she have not latched the door on the kennel? She loves that cat. Oh, God, she'll be devastated if he gets killed in this parking lot. I'm still not running, but I move faster. "Do you see him?" I holler to her. "I don't see him!"

A car goes past me way too fast for a parking lot.

"Slow the hell down," I yell at the car as it passes me.

"There he is!" Izzy screams. She's jumping up and down. She's one row behind me and eight or so spaces over. "That blue car!"

The parking lot is full of blue cars. I drop to my knees yet again and the loose gravel on the pavement hurts. "Which blue car?" I call to her, coming to my feet again. I see paper cups, I see a hair tie, I even see a sock under a car. But no cat.

Izzy's jumping up and down again. She's wearing jeans that are too short and a King Tut T-shirt; it occurs to me that I should help her dress better. Not that I'm a fashionista, but she could look way cuter than she does.

"That blue one next to the white one!" Izzy hollers.

I follow her line of vision and I see the car she's talking about. I drop flat to the ground in front of a parked car.

And I see Mr. Cat. He's next to the right rear wheel of the blue car.

I jump up and walk as fast as I can without running. And the damned cat shoots out from under the car like he's on fire.

"Kitty! Kitty! Mr. Cat." Izzy is calling his name and sobbing as she runs around another car, coming at the cat from the opposite direction as me.

The cat stops right in the middle of the lane between two rows of parked cars and I immediately slow down. "Kitty, kitty, kitty," I say softly. "That's a good boy."

His tail is twitching. He sees me.

"Good kitty. Good boy," I croon.

Then he takes off and I run after him, cutting between cars to try to head him off before he gets to the highway.

I lose sight of him.

"Haley!" Izzy screams.

As I come out from between the cars into the next row, I catch movement out of the corner of one eye, while spotting the cat out of the other. Izzy screams. The car is going to hit the cat.

I react before I think. The car is so close to me now that I can feel the heat from the engine.

I bring the palm of my hand down on the hood and the car slams on its brakes. "Slow down! Who drives fifty in a parking lot?" I holler at the driver as I cut right in front of his car.

I've read of Herculean feats in literature and that's what it feels like as I cross the last couple of feet to the cat. I know he's going to take off. I know he's going to run right for the highway and I know he won't make it all the way across. I'll be at the front desk of the hotel asking if they have a shovel so I can extricate Mr. Cat from the pavement in front of the Wendy's across the street.

But somehow I reach him. For some reason he doesn't bolt this time. Not his day to die, I guess.

I scoop him up into my arms and I pull him to my chest and I have no idea why, but all of a sudden I'm crying. I could hardly cry when I splattered my sister all over the road and now I'm crying over a stupid cat. A second later, Izzy is in front of me. She's a sobbing, snotty mess.

She puts her arms out to me and I lower the cat to her. "Hold him tight," I tell her, wiping my nose with the sleeve of my shirt. "His heart's beating a mile a minute."

"Mr. Cat, Mr. Cat, I'm so sorry," Izzy blubbers.

I hear a car tap its horn and I look up to see the car that almost took out Mr. Cat. I look at the driver really evil-like. Then I put my arm around my little sister and I move her out of the middle of the lane so the car can get by.

We walk together back to our car. I have the key in my pocket. Mom was going to the bathroom *one more time* before we hit the road, so she gave it to me when I saw her in the lobby.

I hit the unlock button. "Get in," I tell Izzy. "I'll get your stuff."

She's still crying, but not as hard. She gets into the backseat and closes the door and I open the hatch and put her bag and the cat kennel in quickly, afraid that if Mr. Cat has a death wish, he might come over the backseat and I'll be running through traffic again.

"Haley?"

I hear Mom's voice as I close the hatch. I turn around.

"Is this your backpack?" she calls from the sidewalk in front of the hotel. She's holding it up.

"Yeah," I call back to her.

I wait for her at the car.

"Why did you leave your—"

"I'll tell you in a minute," I say. I take my backpack and her bag from her.

She looks at me and I feel stupid because I know she can tell I've been crying. I wipe at my face with my sleeve, enjoying the moment when my arm hurts from the friction. "Just get in," I whisper.

She stands there looking at me for another second and I see that she looks better than she did a couple of days ago. She still needs to dye her hair and she's too skinny, but her face doesn't look so . . . haggard. It actually seems like there's some color in her cheeks. Maybe this trip is doing her some good.

"Are you okay?" she asks quietly.

I open the hatch. "I'm fine. Let's just go."

Once we're in the car, headed for the interstate, Izzy relates the whole tale of the escaping cat. We go through a doughnut drive-thru place and Mom and Izzy get breakfast sandwiches. My stomach still feels sick from the near *cat*-astrophe, but I order an iced coffee and Mom gets some of the sour cream doughnuts I like. For later.

"Poor Mr. Cat," Mom says as we pull away.

She's handed me all of the stuff from the order and I pass Izzy her sandwich and juice and I start unwrapping Mom's sandwich for her.

"You're just lucky your sister was there," she tells Izzy. "I hope you told her thank you."

There's a deafening silence from the backseat. Izzy even stops balling up the paper from her sandwich.

"Izzy Mae," Mom says. "Your sister saves your cat's life and you can't even tell her thank you?"

"Mom." I say it quietly. I don't need Izzy to tell me thank you. I'm just glad I was able to save the cat. I'm glad that for once I could do something right. Something that didn't make people cry. "It's okay."

Mom glances at me. "It's not okay. She can't keep this up. I won't have it."

I meet her gaze. "Let it go," I say. "Just give her some time."

Mom opens her mouth to say something and then closes it. Thank God.

A few minutes later we're on I-90.

"Ninety-five miles to South Bend, Indiana," I say, and I sip my iced coffee. "Association game or disassociation?"

I glance into the backseat.

Izzy's still holding the cat in her lap; I can hear him purring.

She meets my gaze and for once she doesn't look away.

Thank you, she mouths.

I smile at her and for the second time this morning, tears come to my eyes. *You're welcome*, I mouth back.

Chapter 36

Julia

Maine

"How much farther?" Izzy asks as she gets into the backseat, shoving Mr. Cat over. Since his adventure yesterday morning, he seems content to stay put and not risk shortening his life expectancy by another cat life.

I get behind the driver's wheel again. "Half an hour." I was exhausted forty-five minutes ago, but after a bathroom stop and getting something quick to eat, I feel revived. And now I'm excited. We've been in this car five days. I made it to Maine. *We* made it. "I texted Laney to let her know how close we are. She was going to hold dinner for us, but I told her we already ate."

"Maybe we could walk to Farmer's Ice Cream when we get there," Izzy says, buckling in.

"Maybe." I glance at Haley sitting next to me. She's been quiet for the last couple of hours. Not unpleasant, just not talkative. "You okay?" I ask her as I back out of the parking space in front of a little deli just outside of Portland where we stopped.

She looks out the window. I can tell she's worried about something. My first response is to start asking questions, but I bite my tongue and wait. I'm trying to learn to be a better listener.

"Are we staying with Aunt Laney?" Haley asks.

"Tonight. After that, I don't know. Her parents' cottage on the lake is empty. She says we can go there, if we want. Why?"

She shrugs. "I guess you told her—" She stops, exhales, and starts again. She continues looking out the window as she speaks. "I guess she knows all my shit."

At some point, I need to tackle Haley's bad language. I cringe every time she curses. But I haven't exactly been setting a good example over the last week. *Pick your battles.* I'm learning that. It's right up there with *one day at a time, sometimes one minute at a time.* Good parenting mottos.

"She does know what's been going on with you. I'm sorry if that upsets you, but I have to have someone to talk to, hon." I look at her, then both ways on the street, and I pull out.

It feels good to be covering these last few miles. At times, I felt as if we would never get here. Ben certainly didn't think I could do it. But I'm also a little sad to know we'll be there in half an hour. There's been a certain amount of comfort in being in the car for the last five days with Izzy and Haley. Even though things haven't always gone smoothly, or the way I imagined they might, I've felt insulated from the world in this car. Protected. Stepping out at Laney's means entering the big bad world again. I don't know if I'm ready for it. What if I fall apart again? It won't do my girls or me any good if I just take to Laney's bed.

Haley hasn't responded to the fact that Laney knows the details of her recent behavior. Choices. Whatever you want to call it.

"You know," I say, "Laney's not going to judge. She just wants what I want, what we all want and that's for you to be okay. We want you to be able to get past Caitlin's death and go on and live a happy, healthy life."

She thinks on that for a minute and then turns to me. I haven't seen the black eye pencil since we left Vegas. The black nail polish is gone too. Her hair's still that unnatural color, but it doesn't seem so shocking to me anymore. I see her face now and not the black clothes or hair. Her beautiful face that's so full of sadness most of the time. I wish I could kiss it away, the way I kissed her boo-boos when she was little.

"You really think that's possible? For me to be *happy?*" Her tone isn't antagonistic. She seems to really want to know what I think. Before I can answer, she goes on. "Do you think *you* can be happy with Caitlin dead?"

I grip the steering wheel. An interesting question for six o'clock in the evening, after driving twenty-eight hundred miles in five days.

I don't know how to answer her.

I don't think I've considered my own happiness since Caitlin died. Of course I can never be happy again. Or can I? If I think Haley can be happy, why shouldn't that apply to me?

It should, shouldn't it?

I've had happy moments over the last few days. Just seeing Haley actually smile makes me smile. That's being happy, isn't it? Even if for the briefest moment? Hearing Haley or Izzy laugh makes me happy. The pleasure I got from drinking that frozen Icee the first day in the car made me happy. If I string enough of these moments together, can I be happy?

I look at Haley again. "I didn't think I could ever be again," I answer truthfully. "I think that's at least partially why I couldn't get out of bed for those first few weeks."

"Months, if you want to get technical," Haley points out.

I lick my finger and hold it in the air. *One for Haley*. But I don't want to get bogged down in that conversation right now. We need to talk about this matter of happiness and it's only fair that if I'm asking Haley to bare her soul to me, I should be able to do the same.

"I guess what I've been thinking about, over the last few days, is that my life can never be the same. My life without Caitlin"— I touch above my left breast and my voice catches—"it can never be what it was. But I still have you and Izzy and your dad and—"

I exhale. "I think I owe it to you guys, and maybe even to myself, to find happiness. And I don't even know that I should think I'll be less happy without Caitlin. I'm just going to be . . . different happy." I can feel my forehead creasing. "Does that make sense?"

"Caitlin says I shouldn't be sad," Izzy speaks up from the backseat.

Haley cuts her eyes at me. It's her "there she goes talking crazy again" look. I glance in the rearview mirror. "I think you're right. She wouldn't want us to be sad." I look at Haley again. "Would you rather we go to the cottage than stay with Laney?"

She shrugs. "I don't know. Where are we all going to sleep at Aunt Laney's?"

"I guess I'll sleep with Laney tonight. You two will go in one of the boys' rooms and Liam and Garret will bunk together. Can the two of you sleep together without doing bodily harm to each other?"

"I can sleep out on the couch." Haley looks over the seat, in her sister's direction. "If that's what the pipsqueak wants."

"As long as we don't have to sleep in the same bed." Izzy's clearly not happy with the idea, but she's not adamantly opposed, either. "I guess it will be okay."

I smile. I might be kidding myself, but today I feel like we're actually making some progress on several fronts.

Thirty-five minutes later, we turn onto Laney's street. She lives in a sweet yellow and white Victorian house in the little town of Larkgate, only a couple of miles from Sebago Lake. The town has a main street that was revitalized ten years ago after folks from Portland began restoring the Victorian homes and businesses began to crop up. The downtown area, a block from Laney's house, now features all sorts of funky, artistic shops.

When I pull into a parking spot in front of Laney's house, she's on her front porch, leaning over the rail, waving both hands. She runs down the steps like I'm her long-lost sister. I suppose, in a way, I have been pretty lost and she's definitely the sister I never had.

I catch my foot on the edge of the floor mat and almost fall out of the car trying to get to her. We're both laughing.

Laney throws her arms around me to balance me and I hug her. "Laney." Tears well in my eyes.

"You made it," she murmurs, hugging me tightly.

"I made it."

We hold each other for a long minute, but I still don't feel like it's long enough, when I finally let go.

"Oh, don't cry," she tells me. But her eyes are teary too. Laney's the complete antithesis of me. She's tall and dark-skinned with the most beautiful inky-black hair. She takes after her father, who's Native American, the Penobscot tribe.

I laugh and wipe at my face. "I know I look horrible."

"No." She stands back to look me over. "Skinny, with gray roots, but not horrible."

I tug at my hair and bend over laughing. Seeing Laney, feeling her arms around me, is like a shot of adrenaline and love in the same syringe. I've missed her so much. Needed her so much.

Izzy gets out of the car and hangs back, suddenly seeming shy.

"Izzy!" Laney throws her arms around her and hugs her so hard that she lifts my daughter off the ground.

Haley gets out of the car, but she just stands there. I move my head, indicating she should join us.

"I'm so glad you came," Laney bubbles to Izzy. "I'm so glad you didn't let her leave you home."

Haley slowly comes around the car.

Laney lets go of Izzy and turns to Haley. She smiles, and in her smile, I see such a mix of emotions. She's sad and happy and angry with Haley, and so glad to see her still in one piece.

"What?" Laney opens her arms. "You too old now to hug me now that you're almost eighteen?"

Haley smirks and walks over and gives her a brief but genuine hug.

"I'm glad you came. I mean it," Laney tells her before letting go of her. She turns and claps her hands. "So grab your stuff."

She eyes Izzy. "Your cat, *whatever,* and come on inside. Garret and I were thinking about a walk over to Farmer's Ice Cream. Anyone else interested in ice cream?"

"Yes!" Izzy squeals, jumping up in the air and fist pumping. "I told Mom we should go to Farmer's."

Twenty minutes after dumping our bags and leaving the cat in Garret's room, we're headed for the ice cream shop, only three blocks away. Izzy and Garret, a year older than Izzy, walk ahead of us on the sidewalk. I can hear them talking about lizards and why they're the best reptile. Laney and I walk behind them and Haley brings up the rear. Liam, a freshman in high school, is at a friend's, staying the night after a track meet.

"So what's the deal with Ben?" Laney asks me quietly. "Is he coming?"

"I don't think so." Just saying it makes me so sad. I can't believe that when I asked him to come, telling him things with Haley were even worse than we first thought (if that's even possible), his response had been to say he'd have to check with work.

"Izzy!" A girl leans out the window of a car that's stopped at the traffic light ahead of us and waves.

"Megan!"

I recognize the blondie now. It's Megan, a girl Izzy's age, from down the street from Laney. The last two summers, when we've come for vacation, Izzy and Megan have hung out. She comes from a nice family. Her mother, Elaine, has always been so warm and friendly to our family. Last summer, we attended a barbecue in their backyard.

"What are you doing here?" Megan shouts.

I can hear someone in the car telling her to put her seat belt back on.

"Visiting Aunt Laney!"

"Come tomorrow!" Megan hollers as the light turns green and the car pulls away.

Izzy turns around to face me. "Can I, Mom? Can I go to Megan's?"

"I don't see why not," I answer. "We'll check with her mom tomorrow."

We all start walking again. I glance over my shoulder. Haley's still with us.

Laney loops her arm through mine. "Do you *want* Ben to come?"

I look at her and tug at the zipper of the hooded sweatshirt I borrowed from her. The sun is going down and it's getting chilly. I'm going to regret having not brought more warm clothes. "No pussyfooting around with you, is there? I've been here half an hour and you're asking life-altering, rip-out-your-heart questions."

"Who's got time for niceties? Or the energy? It seems pretty straightforward to me, Jules." She talks so matter-of-factly about things that aren't all that matter-of-fact. "Do you want him to come, meaning do you want to tackle this together, or did you leave Vegas to get away from him?"

I frown. I'm not sure I want to get into this with Laney right now. I've just driven twenty-eight hundred miles. I just want to eat a mint chocolate chip ice cream cone and talk about lizards. "I drove here with Haley because she needed to get away from Vegas," I tell her.

Laney scrutinizes me. She's got these dark, almond-shaped eyes that seem like they can see right into your soul.

"I guess when we get back—" I walk beside her in silence for a moment, trying to put my thoughts in order. I pull her closer to me, lowering my voice so my girls don't hear me. "Look, I know Ben and I have problems, but I feel like I can only handle so much. Haley's what matters right now."

"You and Ben matter too. Izzy matters."

I groan.

But Laney won't let it go. "What if he won't come?" she asks.

I shrug. Izzy and Garret have stopped at a storefront, two stores from the ice cream shop. They're peering in the window. "I guess we'll deal with it when we get back."

"Look, Mom," Izzy calls. "The fried chicken place closed." She wrinkles her nose. "Garret didn't like the chicken either." She peers in the window, cupping her hands around her face. "We should rent it for our café."

"Or we could make it a pet store," Garret suggests. He's a cute kid who looks so much like his dad that I smile every time I see his lopsided grin that was Sean's. "Izzy and Garret's House of Reptiles."

Izzy laughs and punches him in the arm. He punches her back.

Laney and I stop in front of the vacant store.

"So Southern fried chicken was a no-go in a New England town?" I ask. I can see chairs stacked on tables and a long counter that had been for orders and pickup.

Laney peers through the window. "He's right. It wasn't good chicken."

Haley catches up with us and joins us to look in the window.

"Your sister thinks we should lease it and sell lizard burgers," I tell Haley, trying to include her in the conversation.

Izzy bursts into laughter and she and Garret move down the sidewalk, headed for the ice cream shop.

"We could sell Ben burgers," Haley says, thoughtfully. "Do grass-fed beef, local cheese, homemade bread. Other kinds of cool organic sandwiches and wraps."

I look at her. "I didn't know you were interested in working in a restaurant."

"I'm not." She taps on the glass with her palm and walks away. "I'm interested in running one."

Laney and I stand side by side and watch Haley walk down the sidewalk.

"She seems pretty good," Laney says.

"You think so?" I look up at her.

She turns to me, crossing her arms over her chest. "What do you think?"

I squeeze my eyes shut. "I don't want to think. I don't want to make any life-altering decisions right now." I open them. "I just want to eat ice cream. A *lot* of ice cream."

"Fine." We start walking again. "But you're going to make one life-altering decision tonight," Laney tells me. "On the way home, we're stopping at Thompson's Drugstore and you're picking out a box of hair dye, because tomorrow morning, you and I are playing beauty parlor. I can't stand to look at all that gray hair."

I laugh. And it feels good.

Chapter 37

Haley

54 days

I'm sitting in an Adirondack chair on Laney's front porch, wrapped in a quilt, listening to her and Mom talk. It's cold out. We don't usually come for vacation until school gets out so we're never here when it's this chilly. I'm wearing a green polar fleece Laney loaned me. It's not in my noncolor scheme, but it's warm.

We each have a chair; I'm on the end with Laney next to me and Mom is closest to the door that leads into the house. Izzy and Garret have gone to bed. I'm trying to give Izzy some time to get to sleep before I go in the bedroom we're sharing and make things awkward. I haven't minded sitting out here with Mom and Laney, though. I like listening to them talk. When I was younger, I used to fantasize what it would be like to have Laney for a mom, although Liam swears she can be every bit a bitch as my mother.

Laney's telling this funny story about a kid in her third-grade class who keeps bringing her mother's underwear to school.

"So is it just the lacy stuff?" Mom asks, giggling. "Or does she bring in granny panties, too?"

"Oh, she's an equal opportunity undergarment snatcher." Laney is cracking herself up.

They've been drinking wine and I think they might both be a

little drunk. It's kind of funny to see Mom like this; I don't know that I've ever seen her tipsy before. If I have, I was too young to realize what was going on.

Laney takes a sip from her wineglass. "Sometimes it's a sports bra, sometimes a thong. One day she brought a pair of high-waisted black Spanx."

My mom is still laughing. "But *why?*"

"I had the same question. I've talked to her mom. We think it might be a security thing."

"Like Linus's blanket?" Mom asks.

"Maybe. But the thing is, she won't just leave it in her back-pack. I wouldn't care if she brought underwear to school if she just left it in her bag. No, she has to hang it on her coat hook. *Over* her coat."

Mom sniggers.

I hear a phone ding. Incoming message. Which reminds me how much I miss my phone. It's so weird to be without it. A week ago, it was my *lifeline*. But a week seems like a million years ago now. Like another lifetime. I think about the person I was last Friday, locked in Dodge's bathroom, and it's kind of disturbing because I don't feel like that person. I haven't decided yet if that's a good or a bad thing, although I'm definitely more stable. I have to give Mom credit. She was right. I needed to get out of our house, out of Vegas. For the first time since Caitlin died, I feel like I can actually take a deep breath. Maybe it's just the clean Maine air.

But I still miss my phone.

I wonder what's going on in my friends' lives. I wonder if they're wondering what the hell happened to me. Did anyone text Todd to ask him if he'd heard from me? Did he bother to text Marissa or Cassie and tell them my mom kidnapped me? And I don't just miss my iPhone because I miss being connected to my friends, but I miss being able to listen to my own music, too.

I want to ask Mom if I can use her phone just to access Spotify, but I have a feeling she's going to say "no way." Just in case I have any ideas about getting Todd to come to Maine to get me, which I don't. That loser never even texted me back. He just never showed up. I bet he never even left Vegas. I bet he never left his brother's couch. He's probably still sitting in the same place with a stupid game controller in his hand.

I hear another ding.

"Don't look at me," Laney says to Mom. They're both wrapped in quilts too. The porch lights on each side of the door are on, casting soft shadows over us. I'm almost in the dark, I'm so far from the lights. Which is fine with me. It's like I'm here, but I'm not here. Neither of them is bugging me, asking me if I'm okay or expecting me to reveal some deep dark secrets.

Mom fumbles around on her lap. "I don't know where it went," she says. "It's here somewhere."

"I'll be right back." Laney gets up. "Anyone want anything?"

I almost tell her she can get me a beer while she's up, just as a joke, but I decide against it. Laney might laugh, but I'm fairly sure Mom won't.

Mom's still looking for her phone. She knocks over her empty wineglass with her foot. "Aha!" She holds up her phone, rights the glass on the porch floor, and then holds her phone up so she can read her text.

I sit back in my chair and stare out into the dark. The street is quiet. A man walks by with a black and white dog. He waves. I wave.

We've never had a dog. Dad's not into them. I think I'd like a dog. A big one, like a lab, but not a black one. A chocolate lab. Laney used to have one, Zeus. But he got old and died.

My gaze settles on the house next door. The porch light is on there, too, but I know no one's home. An old man used to live there, but he went to live with his son in Vermont. It's for sale or rent or something. It's a cool gray and white house with a two-story porch.

I glance at Mom. She's texting an entire book.

"That Dad?" I ask.

She nods.

A second later, he texts back. She reads it, stares at the screen for a minute, and texts back just one word.

Laney comes back out onto the porch, carrying a bag of organic blue corn chips, and walks in front of Mom.

"He's coming," Mom says, pulling the quilt she's sitting on up tighter around her. She doesn't look all that happy.

"Ben?" Laney plops down in her chair and opens the bag. "That's good, right?" She offers the bag of chips to Mom.

Mom shakes her head that she doesn't want any.

Laney turns to me. "Come on," she says. "You know you want some."

I take a couple of chips because it's easier than saying no.

Laney turns to Mom again and munches on a chip. "You didn't answer my question. It's a good thing Ben is coming, isn't it?"

"Of course," Mom says so quickly that it doesn't sound like she really means it. "He needs to come."

I sit back in the chair and put my feet up on the railing. I think about going inside so I don't have to listen to this conversation. I feel bad for Mom. She thinks Dad has let her down. That he should be helping her with me—whatever that means. And I guess he has let her down, in a way. But not really. He's not been any less a part of our lives since Caitlin died than he was before she died. He started working long hours and not asking how our day was years ago. I guess Mom was too busy with us to notice. I wonder if that makes it her fault too.

"Jules?" Laney says.

Mom looks pointedly in my direction.

"Oh for Pete's sake, Julia." Laney sits back in her chair, but is still looking at Mom. "She's almost eighteen, and after what she's been through, she's probably the oldest one sitting on this porch."

"Thank you, Aunt Laney." I nod to her. "Will you be my mother?"

"I will not," she tells me firmly. "You have one, a damned good one." She turns back to my mom. "You were saying?"

Mom seems to be gathering her thoughts. "I do think Ben

should come. He should come," she repeats. "I'm just not sure I . . . I don't know. That I want to deal with him right this second. You know?"

"When's he coming?" Laney asks.

"He's not sure. Midweek."

"Good, so we'll have a few days together. And we'll have time to do something with your hair. How long's he staying?"

"I don't know that either." Mom is holding her phone, just staring at the dark screen. "I need to get Izzy home, I guess. She's missing school."

"Izzy could miss the rest of the year and still be ahead of her class next fall," Laney says. She looks at me. "How about you? You in a hurry to get back to Vegas?"

"To get in that car again? With that cat?" I shake my head. "No hurry."

Laney turns back to Mom. "You're here now. There's no need for you to turn around and go right back. You need to rest and regroup. You all do."

Mom exhales. "I should call him."

"You should," Laney agrees.

Mom slowly gets up. I guess she wasn't really drunk. All that silliness I saw a few minutes ago is gone. Nobody sobers up that fast.

"I think I'll get ready for bed." She looks in my direction. "Need anything?" she asks me.

I shake my head. I feel bad that she was having a good time and now she's sad again. *Thanks, Dad. Like you couldn't have waited until tomorrow to rain on her parade?*

Mom smiles at me, but it's her sad, tired smile. "You're going to stay here, right? You're not going to . . . go anywhere?"

I open my arms. "Where would I go, Mom?"

She picks up the quilt from her chair. "That's not an answer."

I look out over the porch rail at the streetlights. I like the way they glow and cast light in a circle that gets fainter the farther the light travels. "I'm not going anywhere, Mom."

"Good. Because if you do, it will break my heart." She smiles again. "Love you. Night."

A lump rises in my throat. I can't remember the last time that Mom said that. I mean, I know she loves me, but . . . it's nice to hear her say it.

"I'll be in in a little while," Laney says. "So don't hog the blankets. Call Ben. See what's going on in his head."

Mom's standing in the light, now. She raises her brows as if to say *who could possibly know what he's thinking,* but she doesn't say anything. I watch her go into the house.

Laney picks up her wineglass. Mom's not gone two minutes when she turns to me. "Okay, so tell me what the hell's going on with you, Haley. Your mother's worried sick and so am I. Why are you hell-bent on self-destructing and taking your family with you?"

I just sit there for a second, seriously considering getting up and going inside. Who does she think she is, bombarding me with something like this? Doesn't she realize how fragile my psyche is right now? Doesn't she realize that's why I'm here?

But I can't help admiring how ballsy she is, just blurting it out like that. Most people are too scared to ask screwed-up people why they're so screwed up. Caitlin and I used to joke about how when we grew up, we hoped we had the cojones Aunt Laney has.

"I'm not trying to ruin *everyone's* life," I say, not even bothering to try to hide my annoyance with her.

"Okay. So how about *your* life? Why do you want to ruin *yours?* Drinking, drugs, dangerous sex, cutting yourself with a razor blade." She ticks the things off like she's making a grocery list and puts another corn chip in her mouth.

I press my lips together, trying to hold on to my annoyance, trying to find some anger to go with it. It's a lot easier to feel angry than to feel the kind of sorrow that sucks you down into the kind of hole you can't climb out of.

"I killed my sister, Aunt Laney," I say. "I killed the pretty, smart one and I didn't kill myself."

"You caused an accident," she responds. "Your sister was killed in that accident. It's not the same thing."

"That's what Mom keeps telling me." I pull the quilt tighter around my shoulders. It's not just chilly out here now. It's freakin' *cold*. I expect to see snowflakes fall from the sky any second now.

We're quiet for a couple of minutes. Talking about sororicide usually puts a damper on conversations.

But then Aunt Laney folds up the chip bag and says, "Tell me about that night."

"What do you mean?" I turn my head to look at her.

"Tell me about the night Caitlin died. When I came for the funeral, we didn't talk about it."

I haven't talked about it with anyone. My friends asked, but I just couldn't talk about it with them. I wasn't sure why they wanted to know; it seemed too close to sick gossip. Mom and Dad never asked. What they know is what the cops told them.

"You both went to a party that night, right?" Laney presses.

"No. Is that what people told you?" I stare out into the darkness. "*Caitlin* went to a party; I dropped her off. I was at a friend's house. We had a project due in English class that following Monday." I think about the PowerPoint presentation about women's rights during Shakespeare's time that we never finished. It had been really good. Not just the visual look of the presentation, but the information we'd found was interesting, especially about marriage in the sixteenth century. "I told Caitlin it was a bad idea to go. Mom thought she was going to this girl's house who was on her cheer squad, but the party was actually at that girl's boyfriend's house."

Laney takes a sip of wine. I have her full attention.

"They were drinking."

"Of course," Laney says.

"Of course," I agree. "But not like just some beers. The girl's boyfriend was older. His parents were out of town. A college party." I squeeze my eyes shut. I haven't thought about this since she died. I just couldn't. It hadn't seemed like such a big deal, her going somewhere without Mom's permission, at the time. I mean, it *had*. I was really pissed at Caitlin. But she'd just broken up with her boyfriend. Mom and Dad didn't even know she had been going out with him. And she was upset.

I press my lips together. "We were supposed to be home at eleven thirty, so I texted Caitlin at ten thirty and told her I'd pick her up at eleven. She texted me back with a different address than where I dropped her off." I shake my head, remembering. I was so angry with her.

"Anyway, I get this bad feeling. I call and her voice sounds . . . strange. So I leave right then and when I get there, Caitlin's the only girl there except for this one slut." I press my lips together and wonder where my lip balm is. "Caitlin's with this whole house full of guys and—" I feel myself tearing up. "When I walk in, these two guys are—" I start feeling a little shaky. I look at Aunt Laney. "She was pretty drunk. If I hadn't gotten there when I did . . . I think they would have . . ." I meet her gaze in the semidarkness. "Let's just say it wouldn't have been consensual."

"Oh, sweetie." She reaches out and squeezes my hand. It's just a quick squeeze. Then she lets go. Like she understands I can only take so much touching before it . . . it just hurts too much.

"I grabbed Caitlin's arm and I dragged her out of that house. I really chewed her out. She was such an innocent, Aunt Laney. She had no idea what I was talking about when I told her those guys could have hurt her. I don't know how she could have been so smart and so dumb."

"So you got in the car?"

I nod. "She was pretty drunk."

"And you never told your mother any of this. Did you?" she asks.

I cut my eyes at her. "To what end?"

"Right," she says softly. She thinks for a minute. "But they didn't do a tox screen on Caitlin after the accident?"

"Why would they?" I ask. "I was the one driving. They did one on me. I was clean."

"Right," she murmurs.

"So, anyway." I lean forward. "We get in the car and we're kind of arguing. She's telling me to mind my own business." I look at Laney. "But she puts her seat belt on. I *tell* her to put her seat belt on." I look away. "And I tell her she can't be hanging with people like that. I don't care how nice her friend is. The boyfriend and his friends, they're losers and they're dangerous. But she's all sloppy drunk so she's hollering at me, telling me I'm not her mother and crap like that." I squeeze my eyes shut for a second. I'd certainly done a little bit of drinking, smoking a little pot, and going to parties, but I never *ever* let myself get in a situation like that. But Caitlin was just . . . dumb about some things.

I take a breath. Exhale. "So she's being obnoxious and she's telling me she's getting out of the car. And I'm telling her she's not. And the whole time she's running her mouth, I'm driving and the seat belt thing is dinging."

Tears well in my eyes again as I try to remember the exact second when the car stopped dinging. When it stopped telling me Caitlin didn't have her seat belt on. When I forgot she wasn't seat-belted in anymore.

"I was trying to figure out what to do. Did I call Mom and lie and tell her we were going to be late because, I don't know, some friend got wasted and we were driving her home? Or did I try to sneak Caitlin in? I might have gotten away with it. I could have hurried Caitlin down the hall to her room, then gone in to Mom and Dad's room and like sat on the edge of their bed and talked with Mom for a minute. She didn't usually wait up for us, but she always knew when we came in. We had to tell her we were home. And if we were five minutes late, she knew it."

"And then—" My voice catches in my throat and I feel Laney's warm hand on mine. And this time she doesn't pull it away. "I just . . . I missed the stop sign." I still can't believe I did it because I'm a good driver. *Was* a good driver. I didn't even have any speeding tickets. "I don't know what happened, Aunt Laney." I look at her and she has big fat tears running down her cheeks. "There was this horrible sound like you can't imagine. Glass shattering, metal bending and twisting and . . . it was so loud." I pull my hand from hers, grab the edge of the quilt, and try to pull it tighter to me. I'm so cold, I'm shivering.

"And you didn't tell your mom any of this?"

I shake my head. "Caitlin just made a mistake. It's not like she was going to start getting in trouble or anything." I sniff and rub my face on the quilt. "I wouldn't have let that happen."

We're both quiet again.

"You were a good big sister to her," Laney says.

"I wasn't. I let her unhook her seat belt and I didn't tell her to put it back on. If she'd put her seat belt back on—"

"Oh, Haley. It was a mistake." She looks into my face. "Like one of the hundreds, thousands we make in a lifetime. It was just bad luck. Bad timing. Whatever."

I stare out at the street in front of the house. I like Laney's house. I like her street with all the grass and trees, and in the summer there are flowers everywhere. I like how quiet it is here. People are friendly, but they're not like, I don't know . . . nosy.

"You have to let the guilt go, Haley," Laney says quietly.

I think about that for a minute. "Because I'm hurting Mom and Dad and Izzy?"

She stares at me, and even though I don't want to, I look at her. "Because you're hurting *yourself*."

For some reason, I don't know why, I laugh and rub my forearm that I'm still keeping bandaged. It hurts when I push on it, but I realize this is the first time I've done it in hours.

"You're so smart, Haley. And you're funny and you're a good person—"

"Don't forget *beautiful*," I quip.

She's smiling even though she still has tears in her eyes. "And beautiful. You have so much to give the world, but you're in a place right now where you have to make a choice. Are you going to give to the world, or are you going to take from it? Are you going to give the world mostly sadness, or mostly happiness? It's your choice. We each have it. I truly believe that. You know—"

She's quiet long enough that I glance over at her. Her eyes are full of tears and she's staring out over the railing. "You know, when Sean was killed in Afghanistan, I—and don't you dare repeat this, not even to your mother . . . but I considered committing suicide." She shakes her head. "I was in that much pain. But then I looked at my boys and I thought about what Sean would want and I knew that I couldn't do that to him or my boys . . . or myself. I didn't want to put more pain in the world. I want to give *good* things. I wanted to raise my boys. I wanted to teach. This probably sounds silly, but I wanted . . . I *want* to make the world a better place."

I think about that for a minute. I think about all the things Caitlin and I used to talk about doing. She wanted to be some kind of environmentalist. She wanted to make people aware of how they were messing up the planet and teach them how to take care of it instead.

"I know this is hard. I cannot imagine what it must be like for you, but . . . Haley, your mom and Izzy love you so much."

I notice she doesn't mention Dad. Which is weird because I never got the feeling she didn't like him or anything.

"Izzy's so mad at me," I say.

"She's ten years old. She'll come around. You just have to keep being there for her." She reaches out and pats my knee. "You know what?"

"What?"

"I think we should go to bed," she says, getting to her feet and taking the quilt with her.

I look out over the rail. "Is it okay if I stay out here for a little while longer?"

"Sure." She starts for the door. "Just lock the door when you come inside."

I watch her for a second. "You're not worried I'm going to try to run away?"

She catches the doorjamb with her hand as she steps inside. "Nah. Because if you run away, I'll come after you." She waggles her finger at me. "And you know it. And when I catch you, it won't be pretty." Then she smiles. "Night, sweetie."

"Good night," I say. And then I take Caitlin's pink ball out of my pocket and I hold it and just sit there in the quiet darkness.

Chapter 38

Izzy

Day 7

I walk across the back deck of Aunt Laney's cottage and lean on the rail, to look out at the lake. I guess it's really her parents' place. We stay here every summer when we come to Maine on vacation. We pay them rent, but I think they cut Mom a break because they like her. I like it here. We might stay here later in the week when Dad comes. We don't know what day he's coming. Mom's being kind of weird about the whole thing. I don't know why. I guess she's mad because he's mad we came here.

I'm waiting for everybody to come outside so we can take the canoes out. But Aunt Laney and Mom had to do something first. I guess there was a problem with the hot water heater and it had to be replaced. Garret and Liam are getting the canoes from the side of the house. Mom and Aunt Laney and She Who Shall Not Be Named are in the house.

I'm having a really good time. This really is the best adventure I've ever had. I'm so glad Mom let me come to Maine with her. I'll be glad about that forever. Yesterday, my Maine friend Megan and her mom came over to Aunt Laney's and they invited me to come over to their house and hang out and have dinner. I had so much fun with Megan because she doesn't think I'm peculiar.

She likes the Discovery Channel, too. She's supposed to go to the Cryptozoology Museum in Portland next weekend with her Girl Scout troop and her mom said I could go too. It's the coolest museum ever. They have stuff about mermaids and bigfoot and yetis. I don't know if any of them are really real, but it's a fun place to go.

Mom didn't say I could go yet though because she doesn't know when we're going back to Vegas. But there's no way we're driving back next weekend. Dad hasn't even said when he's coming here yet. I know Mom is worried about me missing school, but Aunt Laney seems to think it's no biggie and she's a teacher so I believe her more than Mom.

I see Garret come around the house, helping his brother carry one of the canoes. I pick up a pinecone off the deck and throw it down at Garret. The deck is up in the air because of the way the house is built on a little hill that leads down to the lake. I miss and hit the canoe.

"Hey!" Garret yells up at me. "Loser!"

"Bigger loser!" I yell back and we both laugh.

I turn away from the rail and walk toward the French doors that lead into the living room. Someone left them open to air out the house; nobody's stayed here all winter. Before I get to the door, I hear Mom; she's using her serious voice and I stop. I know I shouldn't listen in on conversations, but I can't help myself. *Eavesdropping.* It's becoming my new hobby.

"But I thought it would be good for us to all stay here together," Mom's saying. "Once your dad gets here."

"You asked me what I thought," She Who Shall Not Be Named says. "You can do what you want. Like you said back in Vegas, I'm not eighteen yet so I don't get to decide my fate, but if you want to know what I want, I don't want to stay here."

I hear some noises like someone's stacking stuff. I peek around the open doors that lead into the living room/kitchen of the main floor of the cottage. There are bedrooms down on the first floor and on the third floor. The house was built this way to get the most out of the view of the lake. I can see Mom and She

Who Shall Not be Named standing near the hot water tank closet. I see feet sticking out of the closet. Aunt Laney's sneakers.

Mom crosses her arms over her chest. She's wearing one of Aunt Laney's plaid flannel shirts. Yesterday, Aunt Laney dyed Mom's hair and it's all blond again. It looks good. She hasn't had a haircut since Caitlin bit the dust so her hair is longer. I like it like this. Mom turns toward me and I quickly step back so she doesn't see me.

"Okay. You're right. I'm sorry. I *did* ask." Mom's holding up one hand. "Why don't you think we should stay here?"

"If you really want to, it's fine and all," Haley says. "But *I* don't want to be here. I want to stay at Aunt Laney's. I don't want to sleep in the bed Caitlin and I shared downstairs. I don't want to lie there without her."

"You can sleep in a different room," Mom says.

I peek around the corner again. No one sees me.

She Who Shall Not Be Named has a book in her hand. She must have taken it from the shelves next to the fireplace. "I don't want to make pancakes in the frying pan she made pancakes in last summer." She makes a sound like she's upset. "It's not like I want to totally erase her, Mom, but I just—" She's quiet for a second. "I don't want to stay here, okay? Not if I don't have to. And if I do have to . . ." She shrugs. "I'll deal."

"But you've slept at Laney's with Caitlin," Mom argues. "Why is this different?"

"I don't know." Haley shakes her head. "It's just not the same thing. Maybe because we were never alone as a family at Aunt Laney's?"

"The boys and I could stay here for a couple of days while Ben's in town," Aunt Laney offers. I guess she's out of the closet now. "I need to get things ready for the summer rental season, anyway."

"I don't want to put you out," Mom tells her.

"Not a big deal. Whatever you need, Jules."

I sneak a peek. Aunt Laney is standing in front of Mom now, a broom in her hand. She's wearing a flannel shirt too. "I understand what Haley's saying. And I'm not picking sides. I'm really not, but I felt the same way. After Sean died, I tried to stay in our house; it made the most financial sense." She shakes her head. "But I couldn't do it. That's why we moved."

Mom says something, but I can't hear her.

"I loved that little house on Locust Street that Sean and I bought," Laney goes on. "But I couldn't deal with remembering every minute I spent in that house with him. I know it sounds crazy. Most people don't want to leave the places they lived with their loved ones, but for me, I don't know. I guess I needed the separation from those memories. So I could make new ones."

No one says anything for a minute, then Mom speaks. "Well, I guess we can talk about it once we know when Ben's coming. He still hasn't bought a plane ticket."

She looks my way. I think she might have seen me so I walk in like I'm just now coming in from outside. "Garret and Liam have two canoes and the life jackets on the shore. They're going back for the other canoe now. You guys ready to go?"

Haley puts the book back on the shelf. I know she doesn't want to go canoeing, but Mom said she had to. Mom told her she didn't have to have fun if she didn't want to, but she had to go.

"I'm ready," Laney says, leaning the broom against the wall. She looks like an Indian maiden today, like the ones I've seen in old photographs and on TV and stuff. She's wearing her long black hair in two braids. I wonder if she'd braid my hair for me. I know I won't look all that much like an Indian. Indians didn't have red hair, but it would be fun.

Caitlin used to French braid my hair once in a while.

It suddenly occurs to me that I haven't thought about Caitlin all morning. And now it hurts in my chest a little bit. Thinking about her. Is that bad that I haven't thought about her for hours? Does that make me a bad sister?

I'm glad I told her good-bye when we left Vegas because I haven't heard from her since we left. I tried to talk to her in the car a couple of times, then in the hotel room, but I think she must be gone. I even tried to talk to her in Garret's bedroom, but she wasn't there, either. I guess ghosts can't stay in the same place for too long. I'm sad she's gone, but I get it. It probably wasn't much fun to hang out in my room in the dark. I wonder where she went, but I think that's one of life's greatest unanswered questions, according to the Discovery Channel.

"You want us to help put the rest of that stuff in the closet?" Mom asks Laney. She points to a big pile of stuff: boxes of garbage bags, cleaning products, a fly swatter.

"Nope." Laney steps over a box of Brillo Pads. "It can wait. Let's get out on the lake while the sun is shining. It's too nice a day to be cooped up in here."

Aunt Laney leads the way out of the house and we follow her like little chickens: Mom, then Haley, then me. We go down the steps to the ground and follow a path through the woods to the sandy beach. Garret and Liam are just putting the last canoe down, half in the water, half on the beach. I like Liam. He's always nice to me and he doesn't call me names. He's a lot taller than when we saw him in August; he and Garret didn't come for Caitlin's memorial service. He's kind of cute, in a boy way.

Down at the edge of the lake, Aunt Laney starts grabbing life jackets from a pile. She throws them one at a time to each of us. "Julia and I'll take one canoe."

I catch a blue jacket. It smells musty, but it doesn't matter because we're just going to throw them in the bottom of the canoe. "Me and Garret can go out together."

"Nope." Laney throws She Who Shall Not Be Named an orange life jacket. "Garret and Liam. You and Haley. Those are the teams today."

Haley doesn't say anything. She just takes one of the paddles Liam's handing out.

I stand there for a minute. I really wanted to go canoeing, but I don't want to go with *her*. It won't be any fun. I look at Aunt Laney, then Mom. Maybe Mom will feel sorry for me. "Please? Garret and I want to practice our synchronized paddling."

"Aunt Laney's the boss, applesauce." Mom gives me a little push with her paddle. She's trying to be funny.

I don't laugh.

Aunt Laney grabs the last life jacket. Garret's already climbing into one of the canoes so Liam can push them off. I'm sure this will turn into a race. The boys always want to race.

I just stand there, holding my stupid life jacket. I was so excited about canoeing. Now I just want to go get in the car and wait for them.

"Come on, kiddo," Haley says. She walks past me carrying two paddles. "I've got your paddle."

I look at Mom again, hoping maybe she'll override Aunt Laney, but she and Aunt Laney are play-arguing over who's getting in first and who's pushing off. If you run fast when you push off, sometimes you don't even get your feet wet, but sometimes you do and we're all wearing sneakers because it's still too cold for bare feet.

I walk toward the last canoe.

"Get in. I'll push off," She Who Shall Not Be Named tells me.

I drag my feet as I walk, kicking up pine needles that are all over the sandy beach. There was no natural beach here; Aunt Laney's parents had sand hauled in. The lake is so pretty the way the sun's glistening off the water. Or it would be if I were getting to go out in the canoe with Garret.

I throw my life jacket into the canoe. Mom doesn't make me wear it anymore. Not since last summer, finally, when I proved to her I could swim fine. I just don't *like* swimming. At least not in a pool with a swim cap and goggles like I had to wear when she made me swim on swim team last year.

Haley throws her life jacket on top of mine and puts the paddles in. I get into the canoe and sit down hard in the bow, my back to her. I know I'm being a baby, but I really wanted to go out with Garret. I came here instead of staying in town with Megan just so I could go canoeing with Garret.

Even though our canoe's only partially in the water, it rocks. Since we were the last ones to take a canoe, we ended up with the old, crappy one. It's all tippy.

"Whoa, easy there, killer," Haley says.

I look at her over my shoulder. She's wearing black jeans and her black low-tops, but she's been wearing Aunt Laney's green polar fleece since she got here two days ago. It looks weird to see her *not* in all black. I grab one of the paddles.

I hear Garret and Liam push off and then I see them shoot out across the water, paddling hard. Mom and Aunt Laney are laughing. Aunt Laney says it's Mom's turn to push off. She says she distinctly remembers doing it the last time they went canoeing last summer.

"Ready, Izz?" She Who Shall Not Be Named says to me.

I glance over my shoulder as Mom and Aunt Laney launch; Aunt Laney won. Mom had to push them off and she gets one sneaker wet. One of Caitlin's sneakers. I noticed her wearing them yesterday. Caitlin ran in them; she'd never get them wet.

Haley shoves the canoe hard and I rock back and then forward under the momentum. We learned about *momentum* in science.

She jumps in and I hear her grab her paddle. "Left or right side?"

I stick my paddle into the water on the right side.

I hear and then feel her paddle go into the water. Garret and Liam are already way ahead of us. Show-offs.

I paddle the way Dad taught me, not putting too much paddle in the water, but not too little, either. We're not in sync, though, and soon Mom and Aunt Laney get ahead of us too.

I hear the sound of motorboats. We don't canoe out in the middle; we usually follow the shore, but Sebago Lake is huge. I looked it up once. It's forty-five square miles of water and a hundred miles of shoreline.

We're paddling so out of rhythm that the canoe is rocking. "Come on, Izzy. Stroke, stroke, stroke," Haley says, using the words to set the rhythm.

I ignore her.

"Jesus," Haley says after another minute. She pulls her paddle out of the water and we immediately drift right because mine is still in the water. I watch the other two canoes move farther away from us.

I move my paddle to the other side. I paddle on the left, then the right, but she won't paddle so we don't move all that much. "A little help?" I say over my shoulder, with a mean voice.

"Now you're talking to me?"

I turn around on the little bench so I can face her, bringing my paddle with me. I have no idea why I do it. I don't want to, but I can't stop myself. "No, I'm not *talking* to you! I'm never *talking* to you again."

She's just sitting there on the bench thingy watching me. She looks different without the black eye makeup. Even with the black hair, she looks a lot like Caitlin, which kind of makes me feel a little dizzy when I realize it.

"Izzy, I'm sorry. Okay?" She looks right at me. "I didn't hurt Caitlin on purpose."

I don't get mad that much. I guess I'm really upset because Garret and I were going to practice some cool moves with the canoe and now I'm stuck here with *her*. "You didn't hurt her, you *killed* her." I smack her paddle with mine.

"It was an accident," she tells me.

I see tears in her eyes.

"I'm sorry. I'm sorry. I'm sorry." She says it over and over again. "What else do you want me to say? What do you want me to *do?* If I could have died instead of her, I would have. But I didn't get that choice."

"I'm not going to talk to you," I tell her. "I don't care if you saved Mr. Cat. I mean I'm glad you did, but—" I hit her paddle with mine again.

"Izzy." She stands up and starts to come toward me. She's only half-standing up, though, using the paddle to balance with.

I hit her paddle again. Harder. The canoe rocks. Beyond her, I see Mom and Laney in the distance. When I had my paddle in the water and Haley didn't, we went right. Everyone else went left. I think I hear Mom's voice, but I'm not sure. There are several motorboats on the lake and now that we've paddled away from the shore, the boats are louder.

"Izzy, please," Haley says.

I'm crying, even though I don't want to. "Get away from me. Get away." I swing the paddle at her. I don't hit her, but I hit her paddle again and when she gets too close, I stand up and swing the paddle again. She leans back out of my way and I swing so hard that I start to fall. I let go of the paddle, but it's too late. The whole canoe starts to tip.

"Izzy!" Haley tries to grab me and I feel her fall against me. One of the paddles hits me hard in the leg as I fall.

People say things like this happen in slow motion. They don't. It happens so fast, I don't even know *what* happens.

I hit the water hard. It's so cold that it takes my breath away and for a second I can't move. The water is disorienting and it takes my brain a minute to register what's going on. I'm underwater and my clothes are dragging me down. I'm freezing my A off. My lungs start to burn. I need air.

I kick and pull with my hands, swimming up to the surface.

The first thing I see is an orange life jacket and I grab it. The stupid canoe is tipped over. I look around, pushing my sopping hair out of my eyes so I can see. I'm so cold I'm starting to feel numb.

I don't see Haley.

I hear Mom holler, but she's far away. She's asking if we're okay.

In the summer, we tip the canoes on purpose. But the water isn't cold like this in the summer. "Haley!" I holler. I can't see on the other side of the canoe. I try to jump up in the water, using the bottom of the canoe to pull up. "Haley."

I spin around in the water, looking behind me. No sister. "Haley! Haley!"

All of a sudden I'm scared and my heart is pounding even harder than it was a second ago. The water's at least a hundred feet deep here. It's three hundred feet deep in some places. What if she got hit in the head with a paddle or the canoe? What if she's sinking to the bottom at this very minute? I tread water, splashing myself in the face. I keep calling her name. Where could she be? Where could she be?

"Haley!"

I hold my breath and go under, letting go of the life jacket. I feel for her under the water.

I come up for air and dive back down. I'm so scared I can't think what to do. Not my sister. Not my sister! I need my Haley, cat defender of the world.

I go under again only I don't get enough air this time and my chest is burning and I get water in my mouth and I start flailing. It tastes bad and I'm scared and—

I feel something grab my arm and pull me. A hand.

Haley?

She pulls me up and I come out of the water under the canoe and there she is! There's my sister! I can see her even in the semidarkness under the canoe. My big sister Haley. "I'm sorry, I'm sorry, I didn't mean to tip us." I cough and choke. I swallowed water and it's yucky and I'm cold and I'm crying even though I don't want to be a crybaby.

Haley's hair is plastered to her face. "It's okay. I'm okay," she tells me. And then she pulls me against her with one hand while she holds on to the bench seat with her other hand. Even though she's wet, too, she feels warm against me.

"We're okay, Sizzy Izzy," she whispers in my ear.

Chapter 39

Julia

Wednesday morning I wake slowly in Laney's bed, drifting in the warmth and coziness of her flannel sheets and down quilt that smell like lavender. After taking two days off to spend with us, Laney went back to work this morning. We spoke briefly at six a.m., making tentative dinner plans, and then I rolled over and, miracle of miracles, I went back to sleep.

I open my eyes slowly, enjoying the quiet of the house. Laney's boys are in school and I imagine Haley and Izzy are still asleep. I turn my head and glance at the digital clock on the chintz-covered night table. It's 8:40. I reach my hands over my head and stretch. I've gotten nine hours of sleep and I actually feel rested. I can't remember the last time I felt this good, waking up. Or this relaxed.

We've had such a good time these last couple days. That's not to say every minute has been sunshine and roses. We've had some thunderclouds: the incident when Izzy tipped the canoe while trying to hit her sister with a paddle for instance. Which ended up turning out well because by the time Laney and I reached them (me about to have an apoplexy), they were climbing into the canoe, and Izzy was talking to Haley.

Yesterday morning Haley and I got into a heated argument.

She wanted to walk to the bakery and get doughnuts for every-one. Aunty Em's makes fresh doughnuts every morning, but once they're gone, they're gone for the day. It was nice of Haley to want to go get everyone doughnuts, but I didn't want her going alone. What if she tried to take off? She accused me of punishing her for the frank conversation we'd had the night before about her having sex. Sex with anyone. She insisted it was her body and it was her choice, even if she made bad choices.

I didn't let her go for the doughnuts. But I did apologize later and I promised to try to look at her more as an adult than I have. I also told her we'd revisit the subject of the sex. I warned her she would always be my daughter and I wasn't going to be able to stop being her mom, but she had a point. I can be the mom of an adult child, too, which means I need to accept that I might not al-ways agree with her choices. All I want, ultimately, is for her to be happy and healthy, and I have to keep that in mind when I make criticisms.

My gaze drifts to the double windows covered with blue and green chintz curtains. Laney's bedroom is so girly that it tickles me because she's not really a girly person. Her idea of makeup is Burt's Bees lip balm, and she can burp on cue louder than any man I've ever known.

I've always kept neutral desert tones and simple patterns in our bedroom because no man likes sleeping on flowered sheets. But I love the floral patterns and fluffy bed linens and throw pil-lows that are lying all over the floor right now. Laney even has a scarf thrown over one of the bedside lamps so that at night, it throws off pretty, subdued light. It's so bohemian.

My gaze drifts to the window again. The morning light slips through the narrow opening between the chintz curtains, falling to the honey-colored floorboards and making a bright pattern on the bed. I close my eyes and let the warmth of the sunlight bathe my face. How is it that the sun in Vegas seems like my enemy and here . . . it gives me a sense of peace? Of renewal.

Renewal. An interesting choice of words.

I get out of bed slowly, rolling the word around in my head. On the tip of my tongue. I even say it. "Renewal." The state of being fresh or new.

Is that what this place is doing for me? Is it renewing me?

I go into the bathroom and do my thing and come back to the bedroom to get dressed, thinking I'll go get doughnuts for my girls. A peace offering of sorts to Haley.

When I got in my car in Vegas and started east, I thought the change of scenery would be good for Haley. I thought she needed to get out of the house so full of Caitlin and out of town and its bad influences. But it hadn't occurred to me that maybe *I* needed to get out of the house as much as she did. And when I pulled away from the curb, the first time for sure, I thought Izzy was fine. As adjusted as any ten-year-old could be, having just lost a sibling. But spending time with Izzy, especially since we've arrived here, tells me she was just coping better than Haley and I were. Izzy needed this journey too.

In jeans and one of Laney's many plaid flannel shirts, this one in citrus colors, I sit down on the edge of the bed to put my shoes on. I keep going to the bright pink sneakers I took from Caitlin's room the night before we left. I realize they're supposed to be running shoes; I've actually toyed with the idea of taking up running. But I keep putting them on because I get some sort of comfort from them. I know it's nonsensical, but it feels good to have a part of Caitlin with me, a part that doesn't hurt so much.

I slip one sneaker on and then the other, and raise my foot to the edge of the bed to tie the laces. It's not that I'm not hurting anymore. Maine and this town, this house, aren't a magic elixir. But I really *do* feel better here. And I think my girls do too.

In the front hall, I slip on one of Laney's goose-down vests and tuck my wallet into the pocket. I'm still thinking about what making this trip has done for me when, on my way to the bakery, I reach the fried chicken restaurant that went out of business. I stop at the window and cup my hands around my face to look inside, just the way Izzy did the night we arrived.

I think about Haley joking about having a café and selling Ben burgers.

It's a crazy idea.

The chicken place couldn't make it here. What would make me think I could successfully run a business here? I don't know anything about running a restaurant.

But I know a lot about cost-effectiveness, gross and net profits and overhead. I know numbers.

I stare through the glass at the little café tables inside and then the long counter that looks like it's a repurposed saloon bar. A counter like that could mean no waitstaff costs. There's a big red, white, and blue sign behind the counter advertising what chicken meals were available, but I imagine a huge chalkboard with menu selections and information about where, locally, the ingredients came from.

I doubt it would be difficult to do well through the summer months. The town is packed during the tourist season and there's no café-type restaurant in town. Most of the restaurants are upscale. The trick would be not only to lure townies in the off-season, but to offer good enough food that people from surrounding towns would come for a Ben burger, or a grilled veggie ciabatta roll.

I take a step back, looking at the door. I imagine myself walking through it, saying good morning to staff.

It's a totally unfeasible idea. I walk away.

Ben will never agree to move. He'd have to sell his portion of the lawn business back to his family.

But he's always said he hated the lawn-care business. "Who needs lawn care in the damned desert?" he always says.

We used to dream about opening a café together, he and I.

I stare at the storefront. It really is a crazy idea. But maybe it's not. I have the money my mother left me. My stepfather's *dirty* money. Would this be a way to make it clean? I always thought one day when I did spend it, it would be for my children.

This café would be for my children. Maybe I can't put the pieces of our life back together in Las Vegas, but maybe I could do it here. Maybe I . . . we, Ben and I, could build a new life for our family here. Maybe I've been thinking about this all wrong for the last two months. My life can never be what it was going to be, with Caitlin gone, but maybe it can be something else. Something I didn't anticipate. Something good. Just not in the way I thought it would be good.

I smile to myself.

Ben's flying into Portland tomorrow afternoon. Maybe he and I can go out for dinner, and go for a walk afterward, the way we used to before he started sleeping in his recliner at night. Before our daughter died. There's a seafood restaurant around the corner from the bakery that he loves; we always go there when he comes to Maine with us. If he's open to the idea of the café, at least in discussing it, we could even come by here and I could show him the place. He might have some great ideas. We could just start with breakfasts and lunches. Ben makes an amazing cranberry buttermilk pancake that Caitlin adapted to use fresh and organic ingredients. Anything cranberry sells well in the land of cranberries.

I check out the little sign in the window with the name of the Realtor to call about renting the space. I don't have a pen with me, but I'll remember the number. I think I'll call when I get back to the house. Just to see how much the monthly rent is. Just to see if this is even realistic . . . before I bring up the idea to Ben.

As I walk the last block to the bakery, I think about our café. I go back and forth between telling myself it's the most outrageous idea I've ever come up with, and thinking it's brilliant.

At the bakery, I order a huge caramel latte for myself, and half a dozen doughnuts that are still warm when I walk back into Laney's house.

"He's never going to go for it, Mom," Haley tells me, gazing out the window.

She agreed to ride to the airport with me to pick up her father even though she really didn't want to. She's been very indifferent about her dad since we left Las Vegas. Not in an antagonistic way. More in a philosophical way, and it has me worried. It's like she's disengaged herself emotionally from him.

But as Laney has pointed out to me several times over the last couple of days, I can't expect Haley to change overnight back to the kid I knew. Or back to the kid I've got in my head that she was before Caitlin died. And how can I complain about her attitude with her father when she broke through Izzy's wall and has her little sister talking to her again?

"You think the café's a bad idea?" I ask Haley.

It's raining today and visibility is poor. I'm glad we left a little early because 95 will be heavy with after-work traffic.

"I didn't say it was a bad idea. I'm saying Dad isn't going to move to Maine and open an organic café with us."

I grip the wheel. The windshield wipers are whooshing rhythmically. "Do you think we could do it?" I glance at her, and then back at the road.

She's been wearing the same jeans and Laney's green polar fleece since we arrived. I wonder if she'd be open to going clothes shopping. She looks good in the green top. I like seeing her in a color other than black.

She has the pink ball in her hand. I haven't seen her bouncing it this week, but I do see her take it from her pocket and roll it between her fingers sometimes like a talisman.

"I could work the register," Haley tells me. "I know how to do that. But I'd like to make sandwiches, too. Maybe come up with some new things on the menu. Seasonal stuff."

"Like what?" I ask.

She actually sounds enthusiastic as she talks. It's been too long since I've heard that in her voice. Usually she sounds so . . . flat.

"Like . . . in the fall we could do a turkey wrap with fresh cranberry sauce and walnuts. Maybe make a salad with apples and pears in it. At Christmas we could do peppermint hot chocolate with fresh whole milk from the dairy and . . . and something crazy like a sandwich with goose or duck and call it the Christmas Carol special."

I smile at the idea, impressed with her off-the-cuff creativity.

"But you'd have to finish high school. And some sort of culinary classes at a local college would be smart."

She shrugs. "Maybe a business class or two? We'd have to do some research into what kind of organic food is easy to get around here. We'd be smart to start with a small menu and work our way up to a bigger one. If we wanted. Or maybe we'd offer half a dozen sandwiches and burgers, a couple of salads and just make them amazing, so amazing that people can't wait to come back and try something else."

"It would be a lot of work." I turn up the speed of the windshield wipers because it's really raining hard now. "Long days, at least to start out. And there would be no way we could open the doors before we had every step of the plan laid out."

She turns to look at me. "How much do you think it would cost? How would we pay for it?"

"Well," I say. "I've been thinking about that. We could use that money I inherited from my mother as the start-up money. Of course we'd also have to be sure we had enough money to live on until the place started becoming profitable. Something like this isn't easy to do."

"You have that much money?"

The girls know I inherited money, but I've never discussed how much there is. The amount would sound astronomical to them, but of course that's because they've never made a mortgage payment or paid an electric bill in their lives; they have no idea what things cost. "I think I'd have enough to get us started."

"Wow," Haley breathes. "It would be so cool to take an empty store like that and make it a place people lined up to get into."

I see her rest her hand on her forearm.

"How's your arm?" I ask casually, keeping an eye out for our turn.

She hesitates, then pushes up her sleeve. "I took off all the bandages. It hurt," she says, "but I just ripped them off." She touches several bumpy scabs. "I think it's looking better since I left it open to the air."

I think about our emotional wounds and the parallel. We've

sort of ripped the bandages off. It hurt, but now that they're in the open air . . .

"Have you felt like you wanted to do it again?" I ask, taking care not to allow any judgment to resound in my voice.

It's raining cats and dogs now. Traffic is getting heavier. Everyone seems like they're in a rush this afternoon, except for us. I'm not in a hurry to get to the airport. I'm not in a hurry to have the discussions Ben and I need to have.

"I've thought about it, but not enough to do it." She looks at me as she pushes down her sleeve. "I don't know how to explain it, but I never *wanted* to do it, Mom. It just . . . I just . . . did it."

I look at her and smile. I can't tell her I understand completely because I don't, but I want her to know that I empathize with her. I exit the road, following the signs to Interstate 95/Maine Turnpike South. We'll be at the airport in fifteen minutes.

I glance over my shoulder as we get to the bottom of the ramp and I start to merge. I'm just turning my head to say something to Haley when I hear someone lay on the horn behind me and brakes squeal. I jerk the wheel and a big white utility truck goes flying past me, still laying on the horn.

"Oh my God," I murmur. My heart is pounding as I ease back onto the interstate.

I look at Haley. She's pale, paler even than usual. "Are you okay?" My heart is pounding in my ears. "Haley?"

She looks at me. "That truck almost hit us." Her voice is shaky.

"I'm sorry." I feel shaky. That was *way* too close a call. "I didn't see the truck. I don't know where he came from."

Haley turns her head slowly to look out into the driving rain and I see her reflection in the window. She hasn't asked to drive since the accident. I wonder if my near-miss brought back all the memories. "Are you all right?" I ask. "Do you need me to get off the interstate and pull over?"

She shakes her head. I can't read her face. "Let's just get Dad and go home."

Chapter 40

Izzy

"I don't think it's going good," I tell Haley.

"Well, it's not going *well*," she corrects me.

I stick my tongue out at her.

We're supposed to be doing the dishes, but I keep coming up with excuses to go into Aunt Laney's dining room. If I stand on the far side of the table, I can hear Mom and Dad talking out on the front porch.

Mom and Dad were supposed to go out to dinner tonight. Like on a date. Aunt Laney and the boys were going to stay here and have spaghetti dinner with Haley and me. But Dad didn't want to go out, so Laney and the boys took some spaghetti and went to stay at the lake cottage for a couple of days. To give us some *space*, while Dad's here.

"Quit being nosy," Haley tells me, coming into the dining room to get the water glasses off the table. "Get in there and load the dishwasher."

I glance at the window. I can hear Dad talking, but I can't really hear what he's saying. His tone isn't good, though. He's talking quietly. He sounds really serious . . . and sad.

I walk back into the kitchen. Haley's rinsing dishes in the sink. "Help me load," she tells me.

I stand there chewing on my lower lip. "You don't think Dad's going to make me go back to Vegas with him, do you? Because I don't want to go back. I want to stay here with you and Mom."

She glances at me and then goes back to loading dirty dishes. "Four days ago, you didn't want to speak to me ever again," she says, putting a glass in the top rack of the dishwasher. "Now you want to stay here with me?"

"You want me to stop talking to you?" I ask. I don't really want to stop talking to her. I didn't like how I felt when I was doing it. It made me feel alone. It's bad enough having to live without Caitlin. I don't want to live without Haley, too.

Haley turns to face me, wiping her hands on a dishtowel. Tonight she's wearing a pair of Liam's gray sweatpants, Aunt Laney's green fleece, and green sock/slipper things someone made Liam, but he doesn't like them. It's the first time I've seen my sister not wearing black in I don't know how long. She took her black fingernail polish off too.

"No, I don't want you to stop talking to me," Haley tells me. "I don't want you to ever do that again. Okay? I don't care if you're mad at me. Because we're still sisters. Okay?"

When I don't answer right away, she says, "*Okay?*"

"Okay," I tell her, loud.

"Good, now come load the silverware." She points to the sink.

I slowly make my way over. I finally got my SpongeBob sleep pants back from Mom and I'm wearing them. I like them so much that I might wear them again tomorrow. "When do you think we'll have to go back?"

"I don't know. If Mom can convince Dad to move here, maybe we don't have to go back at all. You could just enroll in school here. You could go to Garret's school. Megan goes there."

I think about that as I turn on the faucet and watch water run down the drain. Aunt Laney has a cool big white kitchen sink like you see on TV in old farmhouses. "Do you want to stay here?" I ask her.

She nods.

"Why? You've lived in Las Vegas for almost eighteen years. That's where your friends are. That's where our home is."

"My friends aren't really my friends anymore. And it's where our house is," she says. "But it doesn't feel like it's home anymore. You know?"

I like the way she's talking to me, like I'm older than ten.

"Mom thinks . . . I think," Haley says, "that maybe here would be better for us because Caitlin never lived here."

"But she came on vacation here," I remind her. I'm not trying to argue with her. I'm just saying.

Haley looks down at me with her sad brown eyes. "It's not the same thing, though. I don't feel like it's the same. Do you?"

I rinse off a fork and drop it in the silverware basket. I have to reach around Haley and I bump into her, but I don't mind. I don't feel like she's an infectious disease anymore. I don't know if I've completely forgiven her for what happened, but I'm glad we're talking again because now I don't feel so lonely. "I guess not," I say. I think for a second and then I look at her. "If I tell you a secret, will you swear you won't laugh? And you can't tell Mom."

She turns to me. "I won't laugh. But is it dangerous?"

I shake my head.

"Then I won't tell Mom."

I look down at the running water. It still feels weird to be talking to her after not talking to her for months. I mean she's still Haley, but she seems different, too. Everything seems different now. "When we were home," I say softly, "I talked to her sometimes."

Haley reaches out and smoothes my hair and looks at me the way Mom does sometimes. "Me too."

"You did?" I look up at her. "Did she talk back to you?"

She shakes her head no. "She talk to you?"

I very slowly nod my head yes.

She grins. "Lucky dog."

Chapter 41

Julia

I was so full of hope when I drove to the airport this afternoon. Granted, I was apprehensive, but I was still clinging to the idea that Ben would do anything for us. If push came to shove.

It's coming to pushing and shoving, now.

We're lying in Laney's bed, me in a cute nightie I borrowed from her, him in his boxers. The girls have gone to bed. Laney and her boys are staying at the lake cottage to give us some privacy. We had a nice family dinner, spaghetti and meatballs, even wine. Then Ben and I went out on the porch to talk. That's when the family reunion started to go downhill. We picked up the conversation again, after we all turned in for the night.

I'm devastated.

My conversations with Ben this evening have gone nothing like I imagined they would go, even worst-case scenario. I actually thought we might have sex tonight. I shaved my legs.

I don't think there's going to be any sex tonight.

Not only has Ben made it clear he's not willing to move to Maine with us, but now he's telling me he's brought me information about boarding school for Izzy. He wants to send her to St. Andrews in Northern California where he and his brothers went. Now. As in next week. He wants her to fly back with him so he can *get her settled* and Haley and I can just wander back cross-country when we're ready. Apparently he and Linda cooked up this idea. With Haley turning eighteen in a couple of weeks, he realized (or *she* realized and told him) he couldn't force her to do anything, but I guess their idea is that he can still control Izzy. Still *save* her. From me.

I stare up at the ceiling of Laney's bedroom, trying to follow where he's going with this. We're lying side by side, but I feel as far from him as I've ever felt in our married life. "But Izzy hasn't even been a problem. Why would you think we should send her away?"

I'll give him credit, at least he'll look me the eye. He turns his head. "Jules, let's face it. You haven't been yourself since the accident."

"What's that supposed to mean?" I stare at him. "My *child* died."

"And so did mine. But it's not normal, to lie in bed for two months and then . . . this."

"This?"

"Driving here. Now saying we should all move to Maine and open a restaurant."

"A café," I correct.

"If Izzy went away to school, it would give you some time to get yourself together."

"Get myself *together?*" I repeat testily. "And what about Haley?"

"What about her? We'll get her counseling, like we talked about, but honestly, as I said—" He exhales. "I don't know why we have to keep rehashing stuff." He stops and starts again. "Once she turns eighteen, I don't know what we *can* do with her. Legally, she can leave our house. She can go live on Crack Street if she wants and there's nothing we can do about it."

I roll onto my side so I'm facing him and I draw up my knees, wanting to curl into a fetal positing. I'm so profoundly sad and angry and . . . sad. "You won't even *consider* moving here?" I look up into his beautiful brown eyes that I've loved for so many years. "Come on, Ben. Forget about what Linda's saying. Think for yourself. My idea for the café is a good one, and you know it. Totally feasible. I told you, the rent is dirt cheap and Laney knows someone who might be interested in being some sort of silent partner so I might be able to get some financial backing. I even talked to a couple of the restaurant owners and managers in town. There's definitely a place for the kind of café I'm talking about. Organic is big in the area and getting bigger." I reach out and lay my hand on his broad shoulder. "This was our dream, Ben. Remember?"

He shakes his head. "I can't do it, Jules."

"Why not?" I fight back tears. I'm not going to cry. I can't cry. "Why can't you? We have the money. If you sell your quarter of the business, we could easily live at least two years without having to make a profit, even pouring money into the café."

"And what if this business fails, Jules?"

His expression is earnest. I think about what Haley said about me expecting more from him than he had to give. Maybe Izzy's not my only wise daughter.

"What then?" he asks. "After I've spent my whole adult life building our lawn business at home, what do we do if this fails?"

"I don't know. We pick up the pieces and we start again." I grip his shoulder. "*Together*, you and I and Haley and Izzy."

He rolls onto his back and rests his fist on his forehead. He stares up. "My life is in Las Vegas. My life is my business. My family."

I push up with one hand, leaning over him. "*We're* your family."

His eyes fill with tears. "I can't do it, Jules." He slips his arm around me and pulls me down against him. "I just can't do it."

I rest my cheek on his bare chest and listen to his heart beating. I smell the scent of his skin that mingles with the scent of the lavender sheets. "So what does that mean?" I whisper.

"Are you set on this? Moving here with the girls?"

My voice catches in my throat. I feel like death has come to us again, only this time, it's not a child I'm losing. It's my marriage.

It's twenty years of laughter . . . and tears. And it hurts. When I spoke my vows, promising to be with him until death do us part, I always assumed that meant the death of one of us. It never occurred to me that it might mean the death of a child.

But it's the right thing to do. I know it.

And I think he does too.

Chapter 42

Haley

61 days . . . or maybe 62

I had a bit of an epiphany last night, and this morning I'm still trying to work through it. I took the pipsqueak to the bakery to get fresh doughnuts to give Mom and Dad a little bit of time alone and now we're walking back. Dad's going back to Vegas today.

We're not.

I haven't totally worked my way through this whole mess. I can only deal with so many things at once and honestly, my parents' marriage is more their problem than mine.

I looked up the word *epiphany* this morning on Caitlin's iPad. I thought I knew what it meant, but I just wanted to check. It can mean the manifestation of Christ to the Gentiles, as represented by the Magi. But it can also mean a sudden insight into a reality, initiated by a commonplace occurrence. My epiphany wasn't exactly sudden . . . but close.

Two days ago, when Mom and I went to the airport to pick up Dad, Mom almost merged us into a four-ton utility truck. If we'd collided, going at that speed, someone could have died, in our car or the other vehicle. It probably would have been one of us, considering the size of Mom's Toyota versus the size of that truck.

She didn't mean to do it.

It was raining and visibility wasn't good and there was a lot of traffic. If she *had* hit that truck, I wouldn't have blamed her. Not even if I were dead now, hanging out in my little sister's bedroom, talking to her in the dark when she's scared.

If Mom had killed me on that interstate, it would have been an accident.

And that's all it was at the intersection two months ago.

I didn't kill Caitlin on purpose. I made a mistake. A horrible, terrible mistake. But just a mistake.

So it's only logical that I stop holding it against myself. Mom and Dad never blamed me. Izzy doesn't blame me anymore. I need to let it go. The way I would want Caitlin to let it go if *she* had been the one driving that night.

I'm feeling a little shaky and I take a deep breath.

The idea of forgiving myself is overwhelming. I mean, I've spent the last two months of my life beating myself up twenty-four hours a day. *Cutting* myself up. I spent my every waking hour being angry at people at school, at Mom, at the whole world, but mostly at myself. But if I stop beating myself up over this, what am I going to do now? The Haley I was before Caitlin died is gone; there's no doubt about that. Who am I going to be now?

I have a feeling there's going to be no epiphany with that one.

"So . . . we're not going back to Las Vegas *at all?*" Izzy asks me, bringing me back to the sidewalk and the hot coffee I'm carrying for Mom. She doesn't sound upset.

I glance over at her. I can smell the warm doughnuts in the bag she's carrying. She already ate one; there's sugar on the corners of her mouth.

"I don't know. Maybe to get our stuff. Do you want to say good-bye to your friends? To Nana?"

She thinks for a minute and then shrugs. "Not really. Nana didn't like me that much. And I can FaceTime my friends."

I smile to myself.

"And Dad's really not coming back here? He'd rather stay with them than come with us?"

I exhale. "It's way more complicated than that."

When Mom and Dad sat us down last night and told us they were separating, Izzy bawled. And I got a little teary. But . . . I don't think I can go back to that house and I don't think I'm ready to be on my own, either. Hell, right now, I'm a high school dropout. I need Mom. And I need Izzy. And losing Dad . . . fall-out. There has to be some, doesn't there? And I don't think this is the end of my relationship with Dad. We'll figure things out, he and I.

I think Mom and Dad are making the right decision and I'm proud of Mom. I know this can't have been easy for her. She was only a few months older than me when she met Dad. (I can't imagine me, right now, being old enough to choose a lifelong mate. I had a hard enough time picking out doughnuts this morning.) But I think once we got to Maine, Mom realized that even though she left Vegas thinking our road trip was a way to save me, it ended up being about saving herself, too. I wouldn't say so, but even though Mom wasn't cutting herself with razor blades, I think she was as screwed up as I was.

Heavy stuff for a sunny April morning.

"You going to be okay living here with me and Mom?" I ask my little sister. "Because you can go to Vegas with Dad. Mom said so."

She frowns. "It disappoints me that you'd say that. You're my sister. You should know me better than that."

I shrug. "When a family is splitting up, it's important that children don't feel they're powerless."

"Did you read that S on the Internet?" She licks sugar off her finger. "You're an idiot."

I laugh because while it may not be a nice thing to say to your sister, I know she doesn't mean anything by it. And the fact that she's speaking to me again is worth any derogatory remarks she can throw my way.

When we get back to Laney's house, Mom and Dad are on the front porch, talking quietly. They both look sad . . . but not mad. It's clear this was a mutual agreement and there was no question that Mom would keep Izzy, which is good because I think that will make things easier for Izzy. It wouldn't be good for her to have her parents in some kind of crazy-ass custody battle like the kind some of my friends have gone through over the years.

I see Dad's duffel bag at the bottom of the steps. He didn't bring much with him; I don't think he ever had any intention of staying with us long. I wonder if it hurts him too much to be with us, with Caitlin gone now. Kind of like me not being able to be in our house. I don't get it because people are different than things, but I'm trying not to judge. I, of all people, ought to know that everyone deals with their pain in different ways. Even if I never cut myself again, I'll probably carry that reminder for the rest of my life.

When Mom sees us, she comes down the steps. "I was beginning to wonder if you got lost."

"We waited for a fresh batch. They had blueberry and the cinnamon crunch. We got a dozen." Izzy holds up the bag.

I hand Mom her caramel latte and look up at Dad, who's coming down the steps. "We're not taking you to the airport?" I ask him. I keep my tone neutral. I'm trying to be mature about this whole thing, but there's still a little part of me that's disappointed in him, that he can't be who we need him to be.

"I called a cab," he says.

He looks sad. And his eyes are red. Mom's obviously been crying, but I think maybe he has been too.

"I wish you could stay another day, Dad," Izzy says. "There's a show on Discovery tonight about how maybe aliens came from another solar system and built the pyramids."

He puts one arm around her and kisses the top of her head. "The Egyptians built the pyramids, sweetie. We have records."

"I know." She sniffs. Her eyes are getting watery too. But she's not crying. "But it's fun to watch things together."

"So maybe we can figure out how to FaceTime and watch shows together."

She frowns. "With the time zone difference?"

"Quit being a naysayer. We'll *record* the shows and watch them together." He kisses her again, like he can't get enough of her.

She looks to me. "What's a naysayer?"

"What it sounds like, but I'll explain it to you later," I tell her, seeing the cab approach.

We all watch in silence as the cab pulls up in front of Laney's house.

Dad grabs his duffel and Mom walks over to him and they say something I can't hear. Then Dad kisses her on the cheek, which makes me tear up. I have the sudden thought that maybe we're making a terrible mistake. That maybe we should just go back to Vegas with Dad and try harder. But looking at Mom's face, I know that's not an option now, at least for her. Which means it isn't for me. My first inclination when Mom and Dad told us last night that they were separating, my first impulse was to blame myself. One more way I've screwed things up. But I know I'm not responsible for this. I don't know if Caitlin hadn't died, if they could stay together, but I know that marriages often don't withstand this kind of tragedy.

Dad lets go of Mom and walks over and hugs Izzy again. Then he turns to me. I'm going to feel like an idiot if I start crying.

"Bye, Haley." He puts his arm around me.

I turn around and throw both arms around him. "I'm sorry, Dad," I whisper. "For everything."

He squeezes me, his voice breaking. "I know."

We all stand together in a huddle and watch Dad get into the cab. Izzy lifts her hand to him, the doughnuts still in her other hand.

I put my arm around her and whisper. "It's going to be okay, Sizzy Izzy. We're going to be okay."

Epilogue

Julia

9 months

"Mom?" Haley calls. I hear a tap on the office door and it swings open. I'm sitting at my desk, my pink reading glasses perched on my nose, staring at the computer screen, trying to make sense of an invoice.

Haley stands in the doorway wearing black jeans and a pale blue polar fleece with our café's embroidered logo on it. Her hair has grown; it's pulled back in a ponytail. It's still dyed, but a gentler shade of dark brown, closer to her natural color. She's still wearing too much eye pencil, in my opinion, but she looks cute. Like a normal college freshman. "Ed says we're going to need more chicken breasts before the order comes in next week."

I take my reading glasses off. They embarrass me and tickle me at the same time. They're pink with rhinestones; Izzy picked them out at a boutique in Las Vegas when we flew home for Ben's birthday last month. It was actually a fun trip; we visited the Hoover Dam for the millionth time and ate at one of the girls' favorite restaurants. A little like the old days, but not of course, because we don't have Caitlin anymore and Ben and I are in the process of divorcing. I was glad we went. There seemed to be a kind of closure in the visit. At least a quiet acceptance of the new normal.

"I'll give Cabo Farms a call," I tell Haley.

"I can call them and pick up the chicken after my accounting class tomorrow." She steps into the messy office that's piled with stuff I need to go through: clothing samples we're considering selling with our logo on them, two cases of vegan potato chips that was incorrectly delivered, and who knows what else. "I just wanted to make sure it was okay if I charged them."

"It's fine."

I can't stop staring at her; she doesn't look like the same kid she was when we got here. She's gained a little weight and she has color in her cheeks; I can't tell if it's sunburn or windburn. She bought a kayak this summer and kayaks several times a week. She says it clears her head. She's doing so well. I'm so proud of her. That's not to say she doesn't have her dark moments. We all do. But she managed to get her high school diploma through a summer program and she's attending community college with twelve credit hours, and working in the café.

"What?" Haley says, scrunching up her face. "Why are you looking at me like that?" She wipes at her mouth. "Have I got something on my face? I was trying our new lettuce wraps. The mahi with aioli is bangin'."

I shake my head. "You're fine. No reason."

"Can I have a sandwich to go?" Izzy hollers from the hallway. "Mom! Eddie says he hasn't shut the grill down yet." She walks through the doorway, dressed in her white tae kwon do dobok.

"You're going to have to hurry." I pick up my cell from the desk, check the time, and set it down again. "We have to go in ten minutes." I squint at the computer screen. "I think the green grocer's messed up our invoice again. We didn't order a case of turnips, did we?"

"I don't eat turnips," Izzy says, tightening her belt.

Izzy has shot up two inches since spring, and when I took her shopping for school clothes last month, I actually bought her a couple of bras. She might not need them yet, but soon, I think. Her body's changing too fast for me; I'm not looking forward to going through puberty with another girl.

"We didn't order a case. I ordered one bunch. To try out a couple of recipes for changes to the fall menu," Haley says. She glances at her sister and then at me. "If you want to finish up here, I can take her to tae kwon do. I'll just wait around for her and we'll meet you at home. It's Laney's turn to make dinner. We're on cleanup."

We rented the house next door to Laney and during the week, we take turns making dinner. It saves time for everyone and the communal meals are a good opportunity to make my girls, and Laney's boys, feel like they're part of a family. It's just not a conventional family.

"You don't have homework?"

Haley makes a face. "You can't ask me if I have homework, Mom. I told you that."

"I know. I know." I hold up my hand, getting up from the desk to stretch my legs. I've been sitting here for hours. I'm amazed by the amount of paperwork a twenty-four-seat café can produce. I fall into bed exhausted every night. But it's a good kind of exhaustion, the kind you experience when you've set off on an impossible journey and discovered it's not impossible. "I just didn't want you spending time running errands for me if you need to study."

"It's fine. I can do my reading in that little waiting area."

"So can I have the sandwich?" Izzy asks. She's wearing her red hair in two braids the way Laney does; Laney taught her how to do it.

"You can, but first you have to give me a kiss. I haven't seen you all day."

"Mom," Izzy groans.

I walk around my desk and cut between two boxes. "Just a little hug," I tease, opening my arms.

Haley backs up into the doorway as I wrap my arms around my youngest. "Don't look at me," Haley tells us. "I'm not getting into the middle of this hugfest."

Izzy gives me a quick squeeze and pulls away. "See you at home." She runs out the door. "Bye, Mom. Love you. Mean it."

"You sure you don't want me to take her?" I ask Haley.

"She'll be fine, Mom." She rests her hand on the doorknob. "It's ten minutes away. You know I'll be super careful."

I meet Haley's gaze. "I didn't mean it that way," I say. The first couple of times Haley drove Izzy I *did* worry myself to death, but after three months, I've relaxed. That's not to say I don't think about the accident or Caitlin. I do. Every day. Sometimes the pain is sudden and so intense that I think I'll just crumble.

But I don't.

Because I'm strong, like my daughters.

Please turn the page for a very special Q&A
with Colleen Faulkner!

What was the most difficult thing about writing *Julia's Daughters*?

I think the hardest thing about writing this kind of book is being unable to separate myself from the feelings of the characters I'm writing about. While I'm aware that the characters in books aren't real people, in order to write about their pain, Julia's in particular, because I'm also a mother, I couldn't help feeling some of that pain. The upside is that when Julia and her girls were able to laugh or feel good about themselves, if only for a moment, I felt that joy, as well.

In *Just Like Other Daughters*, *As Close As Sisters*, and now in *Julia's Daughters*, you tackle some pretty difficult life challenges. What makes you gravitate to these kinds of stories?

I come from a family of very strong women, particularly my mother, and I was fortunate enough to have known not just my grandmother, but my great-grandmother and my great-great-grandmother. They were such amazing role models and they told the best stories about their lives, stories I still carry with me even though most of them are gone now. The thing that struck me about the Faulkner women is the same thing that I see in the women in my life today, friends and family. It's in the face of adversity that ordinary women become extraordinary and I think we all have the capacity to be extraordinary women. Unfortunately, it's often only when we're faced with difficult circumstances that we find out just how strong we can be.

Tell us a little bit about how you write. Computer or longhand? Do you write every day? Do you have a special place to write where you feel most creative?

I write Monday through Friday, about nine to six, and rarely on weekends, except to make up for a missed day. I know that sounds boring and not at all creative, but I've been writing and publishing for twenty-eight years and keeping to a schedule means I make my deadlines. I have an office in my home where I've always worked, but about a year ago I started getting up in the morning and going to a local coffee shop to write. You would think that the noise and confusion around me would be a detriment to my creativity, but it isn't. Writing is such a solitary vocation; I think I like being out in the world. I write on a laptop and rely totally on the wonders of modern technology. I never print hard copies of anything, which worries my mother because she's a writer, too, and she's always worried I'll "lose" my work. The only people who read my manuscript before it goes to my editor and agent are my mom, who reads it for content, and my husband, who finds the typos.

What's up next?

The next Colleen Faulkner book will be released in November of 2016, but I'm one of those writers who never likes to share what she's working on until I absolutely have to. I consider myself more of a storyteller than a writer and the storyteller in me doesn't like to tell the same story over and over. Somehow it loses some of its magic in the retelling. By keeping my book to myself, I find I'm eager to get up every morning and get to work because each day is the first time I'm telling that story. Eventually, though, I'll be forced to share the details with my agent and editor, so you can check my Web site periodically for news on the new book: www.colleenfaulknernovels.com

JULIA'S DAUGHTERS

Colleen Faulkner

ABOUT THIS GUIDE

The suggested questions are included to
enhance your group's reading of
Colleen Faulkner's *Julia's Daughters*.

DISCUSSION QUESTIONS

1. Can you understand why Julia was unable to get out of bed for the first six weeks after Caitlin's death? How would you have responded in her circumstances?

2. Do you think the lack of communication between Julia and Ben contributed to Haley's emotional desperation? Why or why not?

3. If the family had known that Izzy was talking to her dead sister, how do you think they would have responded? Why was Izzy talking to Caitlin?

4. When Julia decided to take the road trip to Maine with Haley, do you think it was a good idea or a bad one? Did you see the logic in her reasoning?

5. Why did Julia take Izzy with them? Would it have been better for Izzy if her mother had left her home? Would it have been better for Haley if Izzy had stayed in Nevada?

6. Why do you think Ben refused to take the road trip to Maine with his family? Do you think he was justified in his reasoning?

7. How do you think events would have played out differently had Haley's pregnancy test been positive?

8. Did Caitlin's death weaken or strengthen Julia's relationship with Haley and Izzy? How did her death affect Ben and Julia's relationship?

9. Why do you think Izzy shut Haley out so completely? If Julia hadn't gone back for Izzy, would Izzy and Haley have ever been able to repair their relationship?

10. In the epilogue, Julia and her girls seem to be doing well. Do you think a family can ever recover from such a tragedy?